© 2019 Chuck Barrett ISBN 978 169 721 7735

Slugger

a novel

by Chuck Barrett

for Melody and black currant dances

Foreword

This is a work of fiction. References to real people, living or dead; to historical events; or to real establishments, organizations or locales are intended only to provide a sense of authenticity and are used fictitiously. All other characters, and all incidents and dialogue are drawn from the author's imagination and are not to be construed as real, and any resemblance to actual events or places or persons, living or dead is entirely coincidental.

The author is fully aware of the fact that the careers of Mel Allen and Red Barber brought them together for a decade in New York to call the games of the New York Yankees from 1954 to 1964, and not at the time, team and place depicted here. He is also of the belief that had they had the chance to be figures in this mystery they would have jumped at the chance.

Prologue: 1962

Smoke began to curl from the stone chimney of the cedar shake schoolhouse as the red headed man moved carefully from pine to pine down the steep slope thirty yards above it. The two room building sat on a flat bench of land jutting out from the mountainside that had been roughed-in by tectonic action then smoothed by millennia of Appalachian winds and rains. Shaped by the indifferent hand of nature into what the redhead feared was about to be a stage for the strife of humans. He just hoped it didn't go too far, didn't turn deadly.

Through the fog and drizzle Redhead could see the words, "Marie Turner, Breathitt County School Superintendant," plastered in peeling black paint on a fading white sign beneath the Coca-Cola logo on the wall facing him. His legs and knees were stiff from hiding for three hours now under the root overhang in the cold. They told his brain it was a damn fool to be ordering up this duty on them in their middle age.

The smoke meant that organizers had arrived and fired the woodstove inside, that Doc Don Rasmussen was setting up for his black lung workshop, part of the ongoing union black lung campaign. Soon the mountain folk would begin to trickle in. Men slowly dying from silicosis. Some that knew it, some that didn't, a few that would find out right there in that schoolhouse. Women who cared for them. Children who would lose their fathers at an early age yet and still go down into the mine and repeat the old, old story themselves. These and the damn precious few who fought for the rights of the rest.

Redhead wasn't looking for the workshop folks, not just then. He was looking for the men with hard faces that would come quietly through the fog, men that would be hard to see. Hidden men, men from somewhere else, maybe the next county over, maybe the next state, maybe farther off, men with unknown faces, unknown names, men with guns. He'd been waiting for three hours. He had to know how many there would be—and where. Whether they worked for the Pinkerton Agency or the Burns Agency under contract to W. E. Massey Mining or whether they were local men deputized for the day by the anti-union county Sheriff. Their job was to stop the workshop and the black lung campaign.

His job was to stop them. He would not fail.

Redhead spotted the first one off to his left and twenty feet below just as he slipped behind a thick clump of cedar, little more than a wraith in the mist, a disturbance in the atmosphere. Redhead checked the man's angle to the schoolhouse. It would be the interloper's angle of fire. Hard to say, but it looked like he had a clear line between the cedars and several tall pines whose branches didn't begin until about ten or twelve feet up.

Then an egg-sized rock rolled down out of an outcrop of boulders to Redhead's right and slightly above him by about fifty feet. Rocks don't roll on their own and forest animals don't send them rolling. Redhead couldn't see the gun thug behind the outcrop but he could see something long, black and straight between two boulder edges. Since this goon had some height on him, Redhead had to assume the man had seen Redhead's position, which complicated matters.

Down below the folks began to come up the twisted trail leading to the schoolhouse from the company housing still farther down the hill. Redhead noticed four older men, two young ones and a young woman. There was a logging road that Doc Rasmussen had used to pull up in his '57 Ford

Fairlane and just then he heard another motor come chugging up, saw Junior Jackson's Chevy unload a young black mother and baby, a black man and a white man, and a middle-aged white woman with a slight limp. Redhead eased his body out from under the root overhang and into the lee of a giant pine, cupped his hands to his mouth and gave his Eastern Wood Peewee call three times. "Peeweee-aa-weeee."

It was a signal to the folks inside the schoolhouse cabin to be still and be on the alert.

Redhead's plan was a nonviolent intervention. He stepped out into the clear, into the firing lane for the man to his left, which also opened him up to the man above him to the right. His hands were held wide and high, palms open.

"I ain't armed and I'm no threat to you boys!" he shouted. "I just want to make sure nobody gets hurt," he said. "That the workshop continues in peace. You boys got a problem with that?"

The man in front of him stepped out from behind the cedars and fired his pistol into the air — twice. It was a signal but Redhead didn't know for what.

"You're the problem, hillbilly!" he yelled back. "The damn meeting is banned and you goddamn well know it!"

This was going the hard way so far. But if Redhead could keep him talking…

"I know about the ban, that's right, I do. But they's two points about that. First, the union has grieved on it, so it ain't final yet. And second, we ain't on Massey company property, the good people of Breathitt County own the school grounds, so the ban don't apply noway. But me and the good folks inside, we're willing to talk about it, so why don't we all get down to the edge of the schoolhouse clearing and work something out. Maybe put a time limit on it, something like that."

To show he meant it, Redhead started backing down the slope towards the schoolhouse. Give ground, make the gun thugs feel they'd gained something, even though it was just visual, just symbolic.

Redhead's adversary raised his gun and fired again, just once, another signal, and suddenly, out of the corner of his eye Redhead saw a streak of orange. He wheeled, looked downslope just in time to see a man break from behind Junior's Chevy carrying a flaming torch and a small can of gas. The man slammed the torch at the first schoolhouse window he came to and broke it, tossed in the gas, then threw in the torch causing an immediate roar of flames. Then he ran straight across the front of the building, turned the corner and disappeared. Redhead had been played for a goddamn fool by the coal company gun thugs!

Redhead ran down to the schoolhouse, burst through the front door, yelling for folks to get out. He grabbed one elderly lady by the armpits and pulled her out and up the slope a good fifteen yards then went back. As he did so one of the young men was pulling a rifle out of the trunk of Junior's Chevy.

"NO! Drop it!" he screamed. "Ain't gonna do nothing but get somebody killed!"

But it was too late. As soon as the gun thugs saw the barrel come up behind the car they had their excuse and started shooting. Now they could claim self-defense. People started screaming and diving for cover. Redhead whirled back towards the schoolhouse and saw the young black mother and her baby just coming out of the door, standing in the middle of the yard looking confused and frozen in fear. He ran for her, dragged her down to the ground, pulled her over to the nearest tree and bridged over her and the baby with his torso. A sharp pain slammed like a hot poker into his shoulder. He jerked his head to look back uphill and saw a blue-suited gunman doff his hat. Then his vision went red. He kept struggling, moving his knees and feet in a lizard crawl, somehow keeping a grip on the woman's waist with his good arm. He felt his head and nose shovel into a pile of pine needles.

His vision went full dark.

A voice from very far away said, "They're backing off."

Another said, "Were you hit?"

Another voice, very close but fading said, "No…this old man…he…bleeding."

Chapter One: 1966, Ray

I was five minutes from leaving for my job at Louisville Slugger when I heard the knock. It was loud. Too loud. I cracked the door to the end of the chain bolt. Two men in dark blue suits, no badges. One wore a fancy urban Stetson while the other man had left his black flat-top bare to the air and ran the edge of one hand across it.

Both men were pushing six feet, one slender and tall, one square and bulky, both wore shiny black shoes and bulges under their ill-fitting suit jackets. Their heads were cocked sideways. Attitude, or maybe they were ducking the rays of the sun coming under the porch roof. Some folks might've judged them to be Staties or Feds, but I knew them for private. Blondie and Blackie, the gunsel twins.

"Your name Odle?" said Blondie as he rocked back and forth on his heels. His fists bumped together on the off-beat. Man had rhythm. Blackie just stood with his legs spread, knees barely bent, cop-school stance.

"Folks put a 'mister' in front of it when they're showin' me a little respect," I said. "You fellas showin' respect this mornin'?"

Blackie took the call. "We don't have to show anything, Odle. We've got questions and you'd better be showing some answers."

"Well, boys," I said, "I guess that settles it. Like I said, where I come from, you say 'mister'." I started to close the door.

"Odle. *Mr*. William Daniel Odle. That good enough, peckerwood?" Blondie. "You heard the name before?"

"You boys got some ID or are you with the Welcome Wagon?" I replied. Okay, my reply was not designed to lessen tensions, but it was better than it could have been. I tried to get hold of myself. Counted to seven. Seven usually did it. This time it took all ten.

These guys had to be a tag team of goons from the Pinkertons, better known to us as the Pinks, or the Burns agency, which outfits I knew all too well. I could still see the smoke and fire from the day the Pinks had torched the striker's tent camp back in Breathitt County during the coal wars ten years ago. The women and kids running, the men shooting, people falling down from bullets, some writhing in the fires. Again I saw the four women that had fired back, deer rifles bucking against their shoulders. One of them was upstairs right now here in Louisville's "Little Appalachia." Then there was the shootout at the schoolhouse at Doc Rasumussen's workshop, the time I'd dove over the young woman and her baby. The time I'd caught a fleeting glimpse of a shooter in the fog — a man whose features I'd missed in the blur of action and pain, but one who'd been slender and tall. That had been the Burns men at work.

Worst thing about it, these boys might just have come from the hills and hollers same as me. They were men whose families might have lived where streams were polluted from mine tailings runoff, who'd had to buy water from gouging privateers, who'd known real hunger, who'd been laughed at in school because of their ill-fitting charity clothes, who'd learned to fight and scrap for everything and had witnessed and taken beatings given by desperate fathers, mothers, brothers and others up against the walls of incalculable fear. Where you watched your sister lose the light in her eyes at 14 or 15 and get old too soon, dead-eyed, and then get pregnant just for the change of it. Some had come through the shanty towns and trailer towns, some had done their fighting with their minds and books, had been lucky in a parent or an elder who'd taken them into the shelter of some kind of concern.

Some had just been tough enough and lucky enough to stay on the Carter Family's "Sunny Side of the Street."

But these boys had likely gone to the bad side, the side where you learned to cheat, to lie, to steal, sometimes to cut, sometimes to kill—and always to do your time and nurse your grievances and resentments like you honed your blade: to a fine cutting edge. And if you were lucky on that side, the side where when you went wrong and you were caught and the offense wasn't too bad, the coal bosses or the county judge gave you a badge instead of ninety days. Some other time I might've passed the jar or hit some banjo licks or swapped a story with these boys. Northern Appalachia by the sound of their accents.

"Cut the crap, Odle," Blackie shattered my memories. "We got a contract with Louisville Slugger to investigate a suspicious death. Cops got the squeal last night, seems they found a body at the auto-lathe in the room next to yours at Slugger, guy named Frank Gorham. The word is they got a make on your fingerprints and we got questions," said Blackie.

Gorham? That hit hard. They'd found another man, Fred Durkin, in an automatic lathe machine just three weeks back, which was why Margaret and I were on the job at Louisville Slugger, and why I was working semi-undercover at the factory.

"Now boys, seems like everbody has questions," I said. "Ain't no shortage on that. One of 'em might be have I ever seen either of you two dicks-for-hire years ago back in Breathitt?"

"Choices, Odle, and you've got two." Blondie cut in. "You can answer questions here or down at the County building, 'cause the cops will take you there sure as shit. What you don't have is time, hillbilly, so what's it gonna be?"

"It's gonna be ID in the crack or goodbye to your back," I said. I was just woofing. They had no doubt been called in to investigate the murders at the bat factory. I was mildly surprised when they shoved the plastic up to the crack one at a time, Blondie first. *James Haskell*, it read. The other one read *Simon Rodgers*. They both read *H & R Security Agency, Cincinnati*, across the top, with *Special Agent* underneath. I almost laughed in their faces. "Special Agent" was the title the FBI gave to their agents.

"You're outta time, Odle," said Blackie. "Like my partner said, what's your choice, here or down at the County building?"

"You boys sure is kind," I said, "and handsome, too, but my dance card is full right about now."

"Okay Odle, have it your way!" barked Blondie. "You can duck but you can't hide."

Blackie cleared his throat and tapped the tiny windowpane on the door. "Just a little preview here. Question number one, dickhead, concerns what was found on the body. Seems your phone number was found in the deceased's pocket. You got an explanation for that, smartass?" They'd covered the scatological and the urological--somehow they just couldn't admire my beautiful face or comment on my manly chest.

"No warrant, no comment."

"No, we ain't got a warrant, dingus," said Blackie, going further down the parts list. "But we do got an appointment with Louisville Slugger's Operations Manager in about a half hour. We'll have to tell him no luck with you on the murder of Frank Gorham."

"And an hour after that," Blondie hissed, "we'll be back, only it won't be just you we'll have a warrant for, big guy, it'll be that wife of yours too. Seems her prints showed on the side of the Gorham's auto-lathe right alongside of yours."

"Looks like a Ma Barker family gang type of job, right out of the B movies, don't it hill-william?" Blackie laughed. "Picture the next scene, Odle. There's your old lady down in the sweat-room under the lights. Maybe three sweet-tongued county cops, me and my partner here, acting as unofficial advisors, of course, leaning on her. Like that, Odle? That change your mind about a little chat with us, maybe keep things from getting out of hand?"

I slammed the door. The house rattled. I shook all over. "My choice is 'goodbye'," I shouted through the door, regretting like hell that Blondie's hand hadn't been in the crack.

Damn! I felt sick to my stomach. My mind clouded over into a black rage. Not at H & R. At myself. The goons were right, they'd probably found prints — mine and Margaret's. Damn! I was about to kick the door in two, then, with a huge effort, I calmed down. "Pause when agitated or doubtful," I had learned.

Margaret and me were the lock, stock and barrel of the Odle Agency. Our business card read: "Labor Investigations," and we'd been hired by the WIA, the Woodworkers International of America, to find out about the murder of Fred Durkin, one of the guys working at Slugger in the automatic lathe room. He'd been found two weeks back with his neck sliced up in an auto-lathe. It wasn't clear if the auto-lathe was the murder weapon or if Durkin had been killed by other means and then the killer had shoved his neck into the business side of the auto-lathe. Either way it was a messy crime scene.

The union was in a contract negotiation with The Louisville Slugger Baseball Bat Company, some higher-ups of which had been pushing to blame the murder on union in-fighting, saying Durkin had been a divisive figure, agitating against the union leadership in general and against the idea, now gaining steam, that a strike might be necessary.

You might say that Margaret and I were in a highly specialized branch of the detecting business. I'd been a labor organizer for more than 30 years before deciding to go into the detective business on behalf of unions. I was undercover on this assignment in more ways than one. The Odle Agency wasn't hired by the local, which was headed by a guy named Billy Jenkins. We'd been hired by the national offices of WIA, which had cut a deal with the Slugger's management to tolerate us on the grounds that even though we worked the union side of the street, we let the chips fall where they may, and if the union was involved, we wouldn't cover it up, but if neither the company nor the union was responsible, it was best to get the case solved, the sooner the better. Management had no more confidence in the local police department than did the WIA. Since Durkin had been killed in the lathe unit, the company put me on the manual re-sand job in the factory room next door to the auto-lathe room, the next best thing to actually being in the room where they'd found Durkin. They couldn't put me in the lathe room due to my inexperience and lack of seniority. Those jobs paid higher and were higher on the union seniority scale. New guys had to work re-sand, lacquer dip and other lesser assignments during their probationary period.

The WIA also had reasons for hiring Margaret and me to work the Louisville Slugger case that had nothing to do with murder investigations. They'd contracted with Odle Agency to go to Louisville two weeks ago on the murder, all right, but not quite incidentally, to put some steel, or in this case, some good hard hickory, into the local at Slugger. On top of the weakness of the local, there was a rumor of some kind of corruption or illegal gambling involving the union or at least its key leaders. So we'd also been hired to investigate the union itself, see what could be done about the situation. The word was that the local had gone soft, and some said they'd gone sweetheart, corrupted by the company.

Not that the national union bosses would lift a finger to save us if we got too deep in cow pies. They wouldn't. We were on our own, more or less.

And these H & R guys would be back. Their kind never let go.

Of course I knew a little about Frank Gorham too, a man who worked in the billet room selecting choice grained blanks, called billets, for the professional bat unit. I just didn't know he'd been killed until Blackie and Blondie gave me the news. Worst of it was that I'd taken Margaret into the plant last night to see where Durkin had got his. I'd showed her the way the lathe normally worked, which required touching it. Making prints. Then she'd stepped up next to it and put her hand on the side to steady herself, making prints of her own. It didn't take a weatherman to see that the wind blew right at me. We hadn't violated any laws, of course. There was no crime scene tape to keep us out, the tape had come down the day after Durkin had been murdered. But how could I know somebody was going to kill Gorham and drape his body over the auto-lathe next to Durkin's later that same night? Then again, could somebody else have known Margaret and I had been there? Seen us? Then decided it was the perfect time to kill Gorham? Too strange to be real—or was it?

I had no idea why Gorham had been killed and still less of who had killed him. And as with Durkin, we didn't know if it was the machine that was murder weapon or was it just made to look that way after the fact. But the threat to Margaret from the H&R boys scared the hell out of me.

"Will? Oh, Will? Who's that at the door, sweetheart?"

"Couple of gunsels, Margaret. Call themselves the H & R Security Agency, out of Cincinnati, or so their cards say. Never heard of 'em, but Burns Agency is breaking up, so they could be jumping off from that outfit. Said they was "advisers" to the local cops. Bullshit, I say.

"But they also said a man named Frank Gorham was killed last night, they found his body on the same lathe as Durkin. Must've happened right after we was in there checking out the scene. And the hell of it is, Slugger hired these two gun thugs to work the case, and what's worse'n that is that them goons say the po-lice has found your fingerprints on the lathe from our being there last night! Them fools is threatenin' to have you downtown goin' through the third degree or some such crap! Well it ain't gonna happen, no way, no how, by God! If'n those assholes think they can…"

Margaret was standing at the top of the stairs with her hands on her hips, her mouth clamped tight like I'd seen her so many times before, tryin' not to knock some sense into my head so's I'd do it myself. I stopped and shook my head. No point in aggravating things until we knew more about what was really going on. I trudged up the stairs then.

"They may just be blowin' smoke for all we know," I said, "far as the po-lice having any actual fingerprints. Or maybe not. We sure didn't know it was gonna be another damn crime scene when we was there last night." I paused, sighed, imagining the grisly scene all over again, then shook my head and the grim thoughts out of my mind.

"Gotta get on down to Slugger, hon. Don't want to get docked for bein' late and mainly I don't want to draw no attention to myself, 'specially not this mornin.' I'll try an' brace the big boss and see what the hell he's up to, hiring the H & R thugs into the plant. I'll try and slip back here on my lunch break, let you know what's up."

"One thing is sure, Ray," Margaret said as I got up to go, "those thugs didn't come all the way from Cincinnati and contract with a penny-ante outfit like the Louisville Slugger bat factory just on account of the murders of some run-of-the-mill floor workers."

"Yep, you're right," I said, "which may be a sad comment on how we is seen by the world at large, but it tells me that WIA was right in hiring us for this job, sure enough."

"Tell you what I'll do," Margaret said as I got my cap, ready to go, "I'll go down to the Louisville library and do some research on labor fights, look for signs that there's been provocateurs or other reasons for H & R or the Pinks or Burns or any other gun thugs to be here outside of the Slugger situation. And Ray," she said, taking my arm and leaning up to peck me as I made to step through the door, "you'd best be on the lookout double hard, love one."

Chapter Two: Ray

I jogged down the three steps of our front stoop to Jacob Street, turned right and walked down the two blocks to where Jacob did a dogleg into 2nd Street and then continued on to dead end into Preston Street and the front entrance of Louisville Slugger. I walked through alternations of sunlight and shadow that slanted through silver maples and black walnuts, light that shot down onto puffs of forsythia that were just beginning to drop their yellow petals as the green leaf-buds came out. Near about every house had its share of jonquils busting into bloom. I drew some good Kentucky spring air down deep even as I kept my baby blues peeled for Blackie 'n Blondie. Just as I got beside the last living American Dutch elm, or one of them, I caught a dark figure's motion out the corner of my eye. Quick as a flash I kicked a pebble at the tree, like I was just goofing, and followed it on over. That's when Blondie stepped out from behind the trunk.

"Mornin' stranger," I said, and doffed an imaginary hat. "Best I should give you a caution, son, that it is flat illegal to pee on an American Elm, 'specially here in this neighborhood. Not to mention, it's downright tacky."

"Shut the hell up, Odle," said Blondie, who by now was a sure enough strawberry blond on account of his face had gone red.

"Ain't you boys scared to be apart like this, Tweedle-dee?" I said. "Tweedle-dum just might stick his foot in something that come outta the ass end of some animal if'n you ain't around, won't he?"

Blondie stepped closer. "Your shoulder hurt when you woke up this morning, Odle? A little stiff maybe? You sleep on you left side anymore?"

I laughed. "Well, well, you're dredging up ancient history now. You saying you shot at me, Blondie? You confessin' to a felony here?"

"Yours to find out, if you got any memory left, old man. But rest assured I sure won't forget that warrant for your bitch, hot-dog," he growled.

I jumped at him but caught myself in mid-stride. Pulled up like a mule on a plow line. No. I wasn't going to let this damn fool mess my mind. I turned away, reached the middle of the street, then stopped, doffed my imaginary hat again. "I'll forget that one," I said, "as a favor to myself. Bottom of the mornin' to y'all." I walked on down the street.

But I wondered. Was he really there at the Breathitt County schoolhouse incident? And worse, was he at the tent camp shootout? I worried those possibilities for about a hundred yards, then I decided to let it go. No doubt H & R had a thick dossier on me from which he could get the information. They could have glommed it from Burns or the Pinkertons or some government agency for all I knew. Blondie was trying to screw around with my brain. And I was letting him into my head. Worse thing a man like me can do is let the rats run in the attic — worrying about something I have zero control over and no facts to go on. First things first — and right now it was getting to Slugger and checking out the lathe where Frank Gorham's body had turned up.

I made a mental note of how Blondie had gotten me to react and how I'd come close to doing something I'd have had to make amends for under the principles of Alcoholics Anonymous. I had nearly five years of sobriety thanks to AA and had learned to take my inventory every night — and to look for my part in disputes where I'd let a resentment or fear build up and blow up into acting out against someone — even when that someone might be a sumabitch that deserved it.

20

We alcoholics just can't afford resentments. We have to look for where we put ourselves in a position for whatever we resented to happen, or where we were at fault (if that was the case), or had some part in it, then let it go. We aren't required to be doormats for bullying or repression — far from it — but we have to abide by certain principles or we'll lose our protection against drink. I decided I'd call my sponsor, Jimmy G., that night and run it past him. If Blondie was the guy that had shot me and if he was going to be on my tail on this case, I was going to need all the spiritual help I could get, and that meant letting my AA mentor, my sponsor as we called him, in on the deal from the very start.

The plant didn't look like much that morning, it never did. Two hundred feet of drab two-story brick frontage masked three identical buildings going back a full block to 1st Street. The front of the plant needed paint and the window fans on the second floor, like always, were barely turning, not moving a damn bit of that contaminated air from the lacquer vats up there. Dust clung in big brown globs to the window corners like mud-dauber hornet nests.

But today it was worse. The Kentucky spring of Jacob Street seemed to have missed Preston Street and Slugger. The sun was out but the windows ate the light, staring opaquely out of the walls like they were eyes in Lil' Orphan Annie comics. The boys just milled around out front or jammed into the Starlight Bar and Grill that sat smack dab on the corner of 2nd Street and Preston, across from the plant entrance. I stuck my head in, looking for Danny B, an AA buddy, who worked in the pro-bat section. We don't have to shy away from bars, the program tells us, long as we've got some legit reason to be there. Danny usually went in there of a morning to check the pulse of the union campaign, being as how he was a steward.

I looked around for Danny but didn't see him. Light fell on the bar in dim pools from the three small widely spaced windows, nearly gray from grime, high on the wall behind the bar. The bar itself was badly scarred, dug out in lines from knives and broken bottle edges, the etchings of petty wars, old grievances or just idle artistry. I could barely see the baseball club pennants heavy with dust on the back wall. Photos of the great major league sluggers of all time tried to look fierce on one of the side walls with their bats held menacingly off their shoulders as they waited for the pitch they would smash for extra bases. Merle, the Starlight owner had always gotten the word when one of the stars was visiting the bat factory for his own personal bat "fitting," and he never missed a chance to get in line for a photo handout.

The joint was packed and the voices were loud and jumpy. There would have been a dozen or so drinking their breakfast on a regulation day, but today the jitters of murder in the air had spiked the jitters of the alcoholics and the normies alike.

A hand tapped me hard on the shoulder and I turned. It was Arthur Benson, the Slugger Chief of Security.

"Boss wants ya," he said. The boss was, of course, Alan Worthington, Operations Manager of Louisville Slugger.

The background noise dropped a good 10 decibels right there as everybody nearby in the bar turned to look, like when somebody tries to mention a hot betting tip on the horse races.

"What the hell for?" I snarled, making sure the room got the defiant tone. By then the non-sound wave had spread and the room was nearly quiet except for the soap opera blathering out of the TV on the wall and a couple of old codgers in the rear who hadn't heard Benson or noticed the drop in sound.

"He just wants ya," said Benson, and walked out of the bar. "I ain't got time for this shit," I said with a shrug at the room, and eased towards the door and meandered slowly through the edge of the crowd then faded right on out of it. I saw Benson standing at the entrance into the south side alley that ran parallel to Broadway, the main drag of Louisville just two blocks down. I followed Benson on up the alley fifty feet to a little steel side door. A bare bulb fixture stuck out of the bricks above a little two-step stoop. Paint peeled off the solid steel door. The bricks lined around the doorframe were in need of pointing up. A couple of go-getter weeds had stuck their heads up to the blows of whatever feet tramped the cobbles of the alley. Some executive entrance, I thought.

Benson opened the door with a key. He nodded, I nodded, and without a word he led me back down a narrow dark hallway to another steel door, no name, no brass plaque. Benson didn't knock, he just slapped a key into the Babson lock and shoved. The door actually creaked when it eased open. I half-expected to see Bela Lugosi stick his head up out of a coffin.

First thing I did see was the head of Billy Jenkins just sticking over a stuffed green leather chair. Knew it had to be him because, even though the man was just 40, nobody else on God's green earth had hair as plumb-white as his or ears so much like handles on a jug. The hair was wavy, like Billy had decided that if a little dab of Brylcreem would do you, he needed double. On my left the wall sported a three by five foot painting of a deep mountain gorge in the eastern mountains above a long shelf holding a Kentucky Long Rifle. Next to it sat a powder horn and a tin ammunition cup. Must have been a piece that old Worthington had inherited from some ruthless merchant ancestor who'd fought for the Brits back east against the upstart patriots. It was a weapon to be admired in the right hands, however. I'd seen folks back in eastern Kentucky compete in shooting contests with the Long Rifle.

On my right a couple of leather chairs, now empty, were grouped each side of a coffee table next to a door into the company's administrative office complex. The door had a window and the window had a shade. Pulled down.

The centerpiece of the room was Alan Sims Worthington himself, sitting upright behind his mahogany executive desk, another antique with Federalist stiffness in the design. Some people might be surprised I'd know about Federalist furniture

23

and that, but my mother had studied antiques for a half-century or more, getting to the cities like Ashland and Huntington and even Lexington from time to time and hitting the antique stores. But she didn't stop there, she got books out of the libraries—best library card collector in the world—and did her homework. And yeah, she could read right well, thank you, and got me to reading when I was four, something I haven't stopped since. Got me through four years of Berea College on a scholarship, the school that educated more Appalachians than any. Well, reading I got from her, and a natural gift for the gab I'd got from my Irish Daddy.

The chair Worthington sat on was a green leather wingback on executive rollers. His hair was razor-cut, grey with hints of dark brown. His face was horse-country tan, the nose long, the mouth narrow and lips thin. The eyes that contemplated me were blue ice. We locked gazes for a solid minute.

It didn't take a detective to see that the empty chair right beside Billy's was for me so I gave Worthington a sassy grin, took one good stride and a short sidle in front of the chair, and sat.

"That's good, like Nero Wolfe, I like eyes at a level," growled Worthington, hoarse of voice, maybe from years of Maker's Mark, what the boys on the line said he favored the few times anybody had ever seen him hoist a glass of bourbon. "Wolfe is a famous detective in fiction, in case you've not heard of him." I filed the voice quality away as something we had in common—different ends of the booze spectrum, no doubt, but I'd been taught to look for the similarities.

"I like eyes at a level all right," I said, ignoring the implication that maybe, being an ignorant hillbilly, I hadn't read Rex Stout, "specially if the head behind 'em is on the level too." I couldn't help it. Happened every damn time I come up against the bosses. I caught Billy out the corner of my eye. He cringed so deep he nearly ducked.

"What's in my head is my business, Odle, and I'll thank you to keep that in mind."

He hadn't changed tone towards the hostile, so I kept mine mild too. "That I will," I said. "Now that you got me in here and roused the curiosity of my brothers outside the plant, now that they're taking bets on whether I'm a snitch, perhaps you'd just explain what you want with me?"

Billy looked at me like I was crazy, wrung his hands, then felt moved to stick his nose in by way of his mouth. Couldn't stand a little cracker/Anglican dialog, I guess.

"Now boys," he said through a phony grin, making it Worthington's turn to grimace in disbelief, "we all have some legitimate concerns and business here, so why don't..."

"You shut up," barked Worthington, the whisky gone and the voice clear and cold as December. That was enough for Billy. He folded, sunk down into the leather chair, grabbed one hand with the other, and placed them on his lap like a kid just rebuked by the school principal.

I noticed one thing though: Billy's slunk down body may have said obedience, but the slits of his green eyes blazed with hate.

I said nothing. I knew a bit about Billy, and I had my doubts. Seems he showed up about a month after the last contract was signed with a new car--not a Caddy, mind, but a Buick. Maybe it was from a raise he negotiated with the union board, maybe something worse, but the AA old timers taught me to keep on my side of the street. So doubts had a place, and doubts would fire my keenest curiosity about old Billy, but they didn't have to turn into judgment or condemnation, not automatically, not without evidence of fact.

"Look, Odle, I don't have any reason to like you," Worthington said, sitting back in his exec chair, joining his hands behind his head. "And they tell me you're quite a long-time union man, so I have to factor that in as I define this transaction. So be it. From where I sit, these murders have a potential to slow or shut production down, either short term for investigative purposes, or for longer, depending on who the perpetrator turns out to be, and I can't tolerate that. The Jefferson County police, the City of Louisville police, and just this morning, the Kentucky State Police, have all decided to investigate. If it had been one murder, we wouldn't have this goddamn swarm of cops around here like drones in a hive. But with two, they now see it differently. One killing could be explained away as the usual stuff. You know, hostilities over somebody's wife, somebody's sweetheart found with somebody else, or a conflict over a debt or a promotion, some liquor thrown in, whatever. A typical someone has treated someone else wrongly category of thing. You with me?"

I stifled hard. I squeezed my cheeks and sucked the insides. I was on the job and I just couldn't let myself laugh out loud. Only an Episcopalian julep drinker could screw ol' Hank's "Somebody done somebody wrong" song into that. So I squeezed and sucked and kept my mouth from braying and then, serious as I could get, I nodded.

Worthington rocked forward in his exec chair and made a tent again on the desktop with his elbows and hands. "I've been informed, never mind how, that you have a history not only of union and red agitation, but also one of snooping to either protect a union or help bring one in. Distasteful in the extreme in my view, but though that's as may be, you may have your uses if you can get to the bottom of this disturbance before the police decide it's a company problem and want to close the operations while they investigate." He was on a roll, so I let him go on.

"We ship 16,000 bats out that back door every day. Louisville Slugger is not just the best baseball bat in the world, in most places and in most leagues it's the only bat. And what doesn't bear our label is still made by us, and I want to keep it that way. I can't afford a shut down of a couple of days, let alone a week or more. So this thing has got to be solved and an end put to it. That's your writ here, as far as I'm concerned. You with me?"

"With you?" I said as I mentally filed his vulnerability to shut-downs away. Once an organizer, always an organizer. I also stuffed the heat coming up inside of me on account of his failure to mention that he'd hired H & R to do the same thing. But for Worthington's benefit I straightened in my chair and leaned over to the desk, pushing aside the gold and onyx pen set that stood between me and him.

"No, Worthington, I'm not with you. I'm with Odle Agency, private consultants, and I'm a union man, as you said. But I'm not with this here local, either. WIA national office is cutting my checks. But you need to know only one damn thing: Odle Agency is me in the work place and my wife in the office, and what we go after is the gut-level, bottom-line truth. Maybe that's right smart old-fashioned to you. Maybe it sounds corny to you. But I don't give a damn what you think. I'll give you respect just like I do everybody else in God's hurtin' world. Though I favor the union, I won't cook my investigation. If they're wrong, or one of the brothers is wrong, they'll take their weight. Not fear nor favor, that's my way."

Worthington scooted forward in his chair and hit the desk with elbows flared and hands clasped just in front of mine. He had a half-sarcastic sneer, but his eyes were deadly serious, no anger, just changing from blue to gray and deep as a well. He stayed quiet, though, and as Billy sunk another two inches of himself into the chair, I went on.

"As to the murders, fear nor favor means I might lay it on your doorstep, I might tag Billy here, or I might lay it on anybody or anybodies here in Slugger or anywhere else the facts and the truth leads to. And if I cain't solve it, I won't. No frame-ups here. And one more thing…"

"Hold it, Odle, I don't need your self-righteous self-promotions or Boy Scout bullshit," Worthington cut in. "I want this thing solved just as much as you do. But if this company is involved, I want it handled with discretion. Do you know what that means, Mr. Odle?"

"Well now, things is looking up. Seems I just got promoted to a 'mister.' And gee whiz and by God, Mr. Worthington, it's right hard for me to catch on to, but yeah, if'n you check the record, you'll see where I managed to solve a couple of these killings in the middle of union job actions and not smear the stink on anybody but the one what done it. No press either—that what you mean?"

"That will do," said Worthington, not a trace of reaction in his voice to his being sassed.

"Now for my last point," I started up again. "There ain't no doubt in my mind that there'll come a time in this investigation where I can use your help. Them foremen of your'n is gonna come to you and want my ass fired. Happens ever time. I'm sticking my nose in their business or in their buddies' business, and some of the strawbosses on the line decide to skip the union rules and bitch straight to the big boss. One way or the other it's gonna happen. What I want from you, sir, is a word or two here and there to turn down the wick and make those foremen ease up on me. Maybe you can back my play as far as me keepin' this job till I get to the bottom of the killings. What do you say to that?"

"I say this," Worthington replied, his eyes still aimed dead at mine, "I say that if your 'play,' as you put it, is as straight as your lofty pronouncements claim it is, then I'll make sure you don't get fired on the whim of anyone, regardless of company rank. But if you double-cross me or this company, Mr. Odle, you'll be out of here the same day. Now, what do you say to *that*?"

I sat still for the required seven seconds, then rose as I spoke, raising my voice as I did. "I say how come you sat here faking all this 'you could have your uses' cooperation shit and ain't told me about the H & R Blockheads you hired? I say you better call those birds off me and my wife or I'll lead a goddamn revolt right here into this office. I say all this high-falutin' talk you just laid down is a bunch of blue shit to go with the blue words, blue eyes and blue blood."

Worthington jumped up. "Wait just a fucking minute here…"

"Got down to the street right quick didn't you!"

"I'm not going to let any man come in here and…"

"What's it gonna be, boss-man? You gonna call 'em off?" I ended the verbal volleyball. "Or would you rather tell the press why the company is so scared of a murder investigation that they called in the gun-thugs to protect it?"

Worthington flinched. Jerked his head back a half-inch. Bingo. I'd hit the bulls-eye. Worthington paused, pulled his shoulders up, forced his hands down to the chair arms, took a deep breath.

"Okay, Odle, I'm not going to continue this pissing contest with the likes of you. Your threat is about as scary to me as a wisp of breeze to an eagle. The agents you mentioned, Haskell and Rodgers, can be explained as collaborating investigators. As I said before, you could be useful despite your attitudes and bad manners." Worthington paused after this, looked at the desk, then up at me, sighed, and went on. "I take it that Haskell or Rodgers made some threat against you or your wife?"

"You take it right." I'd cooled down too, and since Margaret was involved, I played it straight. "Me and her was in here last night looking at the lathe where Durkin got it, trying to get a feel for why the killer either killed him there or made it look like he was killed there. It won't a crime scene by that point, so we didn't cross no lines about preserving the scene. Must've left some prints. We weren't trying to hide the fact that we were there from anybody but the workers and your foremen. But the H & Rs must've got the nod from you to go and do the same thing after they discovered Gorham's body early this morning. They found the prints, got the cops to make a run on 'em, and since we're licensed and printed detectives, our prints are on file, so naturally our names showed up. So they're over to my place this mornin' doing their gun-thug imitation and threatening to take Margaret downtown and sweat her."

"Then they went beyond their authorization, and they'll be reined in. Forget about the threats."

"I cain't do that," I said, even-steven. "But since you're going to chain those dogs, I'm ready to go back to the deal we laid out a few minutes ago."

"I'll do that. Right away. You investigate, they investigate, and no one threatens or harms anyone else. At least as long as both sides maintain the goal of getting at the facts and not needlessly embarrassing this company. You don't have to share information, but you have to keep out of each other's way. Right?"

"Okay to that," I said to Worthington. Time to quit taxing the grace of the Almighty and get gone. I turned to Billy, who by now could have been a cartoon drawing, he was so flat against the seat. "Come on chief, let's get outta here afore the boys outside think we're selling 'em out," I said.

"Thank you, Mr. Worthington," said Billy as he stood up, his Cincinnati Reds cap in his two hands at his waist, the eyes still smoldering.

I nodded, Worthington did the same. Billy and I went out the door past the waiting Arthur Benson and on down the narrow hall. I stopped just inside the alleyway door.

"Remember," I whispered to Billy. "I don't expect no less from you, brother, than from him, which means you keep your mouth shut about this meeting," I said. "You with me?" I figured Billy was used to keeping quiet about his secret dealings with Worthington.

"Sure thing, Ray. I'm with you," he said, bobbing his head up and down in a smarmy voice, then, as we walked on down the hall, I barely heard him hiss, "long as you remember who's chief of this local," behind my back.

I turned, "You got something more to say, Billy?" I said.

"No problem, Ray. Just that we got a good thing goin' here, ya know. We got three percent in the last contract, man.

That ain't nothin' to sneeze at, so don't go throwin' it all away tryin' to be Mr. Tough Guy. We got an understanding, me and the Boss, and it works out okay for both sides."

"You don't say, Billy. Well where I come from that sounds like a sweetheart deal. And that don't fly, nossir. That's a scab union, pure and simple. You runnin' a scab union, Billy?"

All the sudden Billy lost his Pillsbury Dough-boy lookalike face and manner. His lip curled, his eyes sparked fire, but his words didn't match. "You got it wrong, Ray. It's just a way of doin' business that's best for the boys. It gets 'em the most good in wages an' benefits. That's what it's about, ain't it? I don't need no big ego for myself, Ray, an' I don't need you having one neither. An' the sooner you learn how things work the healthier it'll be for you."

By then we'd reached the door back onto the alley. It was a threat, all right, but I figured it was no use arguing with Billy any more right then. "I'll take you up on that learnin' how things work, Billy. But I mean how they really work. It ain't mainly about wages and benefits. It's about workers' power and shop floor control. No holds barred when it comes to the workers. So we'll see about your 'way of doin' business.'"

With that I opened the door and found myself staring smack into the set of baby blues owned by Blondie.

"Howdy, Blondie," I said, moving on past the H & R agent right on off the stoop and down the alley.

I didn't look back, but I could feel the heat on the back of my neck.

I didn't hear Billy's footsteps coming behind me either — and wondered why.

Chapter Three: Margaret

After Ray left, Margaret Odle took care of some WIA paperwork then set off for the library. It didn't take long for her to spot the tail. Not a very good one, maybe he was being deliberate, an open tail, just trying to intimidate her, but she knew she had a tail nonetheless. She walked down Floyd Street one block from Jacob Street to the bus stop on Broadway and heard the soft slap of leather matching her footsteps on the concrete of the sidewalk. No, almost matching. Just a little harder due to his extra weight, but he was trying to make his footfalls hit on the same rhythm as hers so as to disguise the sound. There were lots of elm and oak trees lining the sidewalks so Margaret figured if she turned he'd just duck behind one of them or else he'd duck into the little park behind the radio station, so she didn't give him the satisfaction of knowing she'd detected him.

Margaret caught the number 23 bus for the seven-block ride down Broadway to the turn on Third Street where she'd get off just after the turn. She sat near the front next to an elderly lady with her shopping bag in her lap. The man got on after her and Margaret got a good look at him as he passed her seat. He had all the signs of a security agent and fit the description Ray had given her of Simon Rogers, the one he called Blackie.

When the bus turned on Third Margaret stepped back to the rear exit and as she passed Blackie's seat on the way she said, "Good morning, Agent Rogers, I'm going to the Louisville Public Library, Main Branch. See you there." As she stepped off the bus Margaret chuckled right out loud. She'd hadn't seen a face quite so flushed in many a year.

Margaret walked up Third, crossed Broadway, then on up another block to York, turned and walked into the Main Branch of the library half a block later, Blackie in tow. The library's front façade was a tall imposing structure built in 1906 with funds from that old robber baron Andrew Carnegie in his do-good phase and was quite impressive. Blackie tagged along to the front revolving door, where Margaret stopped in mid-turn and wheeled on him for a little chat through the glass section where he'd come in behind her.

"You threatened me this morning, Mr. Rogers," she said, putting her face close to the glass. "I don't cotton to that one bit. Ray and I will see to it that you stop, you can bet on that. And since you work for H & R you know by now that neither of us can be intimidated by this Mickey-Mouse stuff you and Haskell pulled this morning. We've survived a lot worse than anything you can throw at us. You don't work for the police and have no authority in the murder investigation, none at all. Your writ is worthless with me. Do I make myself clear?"

Margaret didn't wait for a reply but turned her back on him and pushed on into the reception area on the main floor, walked over to the front desk and asked the librarian for the newspaper microfiche section. She didn't hear footsteps behind her when she followed the librarian through the card catalogue room and down a short hallway into the microfiche room. Blackie was gone — but not forgotten. She figured he'd be waiting outside when she left the library.

Five hours later when Margaret left she had some goodies. She'd found a few items that might prove to be useful later on.

Item One — there had been a brutal repression of a strike at the Olin-Matheson munitions factory across the Ohio River in Charleston, Indiana, last year. The workers had tried to negotiate a better deal for themselves in view of the enormous profits being brought in by the company's massive Vietnam War contract but they'd been totally stonewalled. In desperation they'd gone out on a wildcat strike with no organized backing. The company had gone to court, obtained an injunction declaring the strike to be illegal, and mobilized the local police and state police to come in and bust up the picket lines and arrest the strikers. The workers had been demonized in the press as practically working for the Vietcong, and it was sad to say, they'd done almost no work in the community to prepare support for the strike. But the worst was that the company had infiltrated the union with provocateurs who'd brought on the strike before preparations were completed.

Item Two: Virtually the same scenario had taken place at General Electric's Louisville Appliance Park plant two months ago when punch press workers in the air conditioning building, one of six major buildings at the plant, had gone out on a wildcat. Their issue was safety and wages conjoined. The base rate was low so the men had to rely on piece rate bonuses to make a living, and the piece rate was low too, so working under the pressure of time, the punch press men had often bypassed pliers and other slow-making safety aids and kept losing fingers, hands, and worse in the punches when they got tired and lost their coordination. All it took was a split second, lagging behind, leaving a trailing body part under the punch when it came blasting down.

They'd managed to get about half of the plant's 14,000 workers from buildings six, five and four to go out with them but couldn't convince the rest to take the admittedly serious risks, again with insufficient preparation. Once again the company had gotten a court injunction and the local and state police had broken the strike with massive arrests, beatings and intimidation on the picket lines. And once again the union had failed to organize community support.

Item Three: the story about the GE strike went with a picture of three of the strikers on the picket line brandishing ax handles. One of them looked very familiar to Margaret. She couldn't quite place him at the time. But she resolved to study on that picture again until she could identify the man. Margaret was just quite sure she'd seen him before —

34

somewhere back in the mountains in her organizing past with Ray. Like with any snake, he was bound to rear his head, and when he did, she wanted to be ready to spot him.

Item Four: There was a small paragraph that said that the Kentucky Bureau of Investigation had formed a special unit to investigate "outside agitators" it said were involved in labor unrest in Louisville.

Of course Margaret went out the back way when she left the library and wondered all the way home if Blackie was still standing around trying to look inconspicuous in front of that revolving door. Some men were quite silly that way.

Chapter Four: Ray

After the set-to with Worthington and Billy I milled around with the rest of the men in front of the Slugger plant until the whistle blew for the shift. Then the big ten foot high wood and iron door rolled sideways on its steel tracks and eight inch wheels, throwing thunder off the walls of buildings all up and down the 200 block of Preston Street. Scores of men formed a drab ragged line, sucked deep on the last of their Pall Malls, Lucky Strikes and Camels, puffed like locomotives into the air, flipped arcs of glowing butts out from the line onto the pavement and shuffled into the cavernous gloom of Slugger. Danny B caught me just as we squeezed in to pick up and punch our time cards at the company checkpoint.

"Hey Ray," he said and grabbed my shoulder in a friendly shaking, "you gonna work your station today? The word is out about Gorham. I hear some of the boys are sittin' down until Worthington meets with 'em and gives 'em some answers to how come two of 'em come up dead so quick. They're gettin' kinda nuts thinkin' they're all on some hit list or something."

His eyes were steady, but his face went a bit twitchy. Tension. It was in the air. In the barked-out small talk among men huddled in little knots on the way into Slugger. In drawn faces and grimaces through tight lips and thin streaks of bared teeth. These were men who had no margin. Guys who had kids and wives to feed and house and clothe. They didn't have stocks or bonds or real estate. All they had was a paycheck. They were next-to-the-bottom on the ladder. The last people to get ahead and the first ones that got ridiculed—

most people had quit using the word nigger but peckerwood, hillbilly and mountain-monkey were still okay.

They remembered times and relatives back in the eastern hills populated by broken trailers, gnawing stomachs, competition for crumbs, alcohol and enmity. Times, people and places not so far away.

So when they had a union fight or an incident on the job that caused a day off or a longer shutdown, it hurt. Might make the difference between nothing but beans and cornbread or maybe a little chicken or beef thrown in the pot.

"I'm here for what's going on with the men on the line, Danny. Why not?" I said. "It's either sand bats or put my butt down on the break bench, whatever the majority of the boys decide. But I don't expect no good'll come of hunkering down on that bench if'n we ain't prepared for a fight."

"Okay, what the hell, let's just go on in and get to work on our case of brown lung, why don't we?" Danny said, and shoved me towards the worker's punch card rack.

I laughed. We went through the tiny hallway to the punch-clock, punched, then parted, heading for our separate areas of the plant. Danny had been around the block a few times, just like me, and I figured he'd done the Twelve Steps, so he was not just sober, but tried and steady. He wasn't a mountain man like me, he'd grown up as part of the Bunce family clan in the German Butchertown neighborhood of Louisville during some of its darkest days, when drunks outnumbered near about everybody else on the streets, especially after dark. Danny hadn't joined the Scouts but he'd gotten his merit badge in booze from the age of 13 on and grown up tough until the bottle, jailhouse weekends, workhouse stints and hospital emergency rooms finally beat him into submission.

He worked the hand-turn lathe in the P.R.O. section at Slugger, turned bats inch-by-inch according to the specifications of each Major League player on his list, about twenty-five ball players. Those guys were the gold-plated Cadillacs of Slugger, all right. No expense was spared. It

37

wasn't going be a problem for Danny that morning, working his job, because the auto-lathe rooms were three rooms away from the P.R.O. section and there wouldn't be any crime scene tape blocking him off. But my job was in the sanding room right next to where Durkin and Gorham had got it, or at least where their bodies had ended up, and like Danny had said, rumors were flying. I had no idea what to expect but I wanted to get there before anybody else did and see what I could see.

As it turned out I needn't have worried. The rest of the boys on the auto-lathe jobs decided to confront Worthington about the idled machines. They held a quick election for mouthpieces, elected a brash guy named Jack Duvall and a smooth talker named Sam Campbell and within ten minutes of their hitting the lathe room they went "down front" to the main office. The rest of the boys took off for the lunchroom. I held back and surveyed the scene, wanting to make sure I missed nothing before I got close to the auto-lathes themselves.

The room was a cube about 25 feet square. Like all the workrooms at Slugger, the ceiling was low and the ducts that served the dust exhaust system were small to the point of just plain useless. When the joint was jumping, we worked in the middle of clouds—brown clouds, wood dust clouds, clouds that over the years gave you a lung disease known to the docs as eosinophilic granuloma, clouds that could disable and kill just like coal dust gave you silicosis and cotton dust gave you byssinosis.

The crime scene tape stretched between two of the big auto-lathe machines. The auto-lathes turned billets, straight wooden cylinders 37 inches long by 2.75 inches thick, into an actual bat according to a formula for the bat being made on the production run of the day: Little League 24", College level 32", general merchandise bat at whatever length and size. Into the holding spikes of the auto-lathe went the billet, out came a bat ready for sanding, branding, lacquering and finishing.

The machines were monsters, all right: huge four-foot wide maws like a T-Rex at lunch time. The jaws and cheeks on each side were spiked rollers of solid steel. The teeth were formed by a huge set of spikes that jabbed out of a wheel running on each side of the mouth, eight pairs of teeth to the wheel. You slapped a billet's stub onto the right-side tooth then stuck the left tooth into the billet's other end using a lever to extend the tooth, all while the cylinder of teeth moved up and into the maw. It never stopped turning, the spikes kept coming, and you had about four seconds to slap the bat in before it would roll out of sight into the back.

I didn't want to seem too obvious, but I turned to my left and looked at the T-Rex behind the tape that had eaten Frank Gorham, then wished I hadn't. Blood stains splattered all over the inside jaws, and peeling back from the spikes, the teeth, some discolorations that looked like tiny stains from what might be yesterday's jerky, or might have been bits of skin that had formerly covered Frank's bones that the crime scene cops had just left behind for no reason. The maw had gorged last night. The colors of mayhem had blended with the grays of police crime lab fingerprint dust to make the lathe darker, more sinister, like something on the set of an old horror movie. The monster just sat there now, dead and still under the weak overhead fluorescent tube. Cold, remorseless.

And why not? I reminded myself. The real monster was a man. The lathe hadn't killed Frank. Or Durkin. A man had. A madman? A ruthless man? Or a man with a mission? Whatever, I needed to get the bastard.

I felt sick and I put my hand over my eyes, pretending to wipe off the sweat. It was hot enough, all right, but I needed cover, didn't want to look weak, and I didn't want to look like a private eye, either. So sweat would do for an excuse to stand there a minute longer, look see if anything stood out, meanwhile trying to ignore the roiling in my stomach.

I kept reminding myself, too, that there was no evidence as yet that the lathes were implicated as murder weapons in either of the two killings. Each man could have been dead before his head was stuck into the lathe's spikes and the machine turned on.

My brain beat a retreat, ordering up a moving picture of myself working the auto-lathe job. I saw myself as I might have stood in front of the machine and slammed billets one at a time onto the spikes, right side first, then the left, then pushed the button and watched the knives glide down the length of the spinning billet, shaping it into a bat, jerking the lever that released the bat from the holding spike at each end, then slapping it onto the cart to my right and reaching for the next one on the cart to my left.

That was the dance. Lean left, pull, straighten to center, spike billet right, spike billet left, grab newly formed bat, drop on cart…lean left, pull bat, straighten …on and on and on, a full eight hours with two five minute smoke breaks and a half-hour lunch. That didn't count having to roll your cart full of finished bats into the next room where they would be checked before another guy grabbed the cart and took it to the sanding room. The Manuit rate for the job was 1,600 bats per shift.

Normally the room was so thick with dust you couldn't see the machine across the way, but today all four auto-lathes stood empty, spikes still, each one gaping open at the front. The clouds of yesterday's dust had settled thick on every surface in the place.

Now, looking at it, the location of the break bench had always hit me as comical as hell. Here you got this room which was normally so thick with dust you could barely see the details of one machine from the next one ten feet away, yet and still these boys would get their five minute break on the bench and set there and smoke like chimneys the whole damn time. A little voluntary insult by way of Mr. Camel added to the general assault and injury of Mr. Slugger.

Satisfied that I'd seen enough, I beat it, went out of the lathe room to the rear of the plant to take the temperature of the workers, deciding to follow the route of a log as it became a bat and check on some of the key guys that way.

I had to admit that Slugger had a helluva operation, taking the wood from log to bat in quick time despite a ridiculously cramped factory floor space. The plant had been constructed out of an abandoned warehouse in the late 1890s. The ceilings were low, rooms small, passages between rooms narrow. The logs got rolling, literally, by six guys out in the lumber yard shoving them onto a ramp one log wide that ran on steel rollers. Two other guys stood near the end of the roller ramp with paint brushes to slap stripes on the bark every four feet, classifying them as to straightness and quality of wood even as they marked off the cuts that would be the first step in turning logs into bats. Then they went by conveyor into the plant proper.

You stepped inside and your brain got blasted by a hell's symphony of screaming saws, banshee sanders, and a thousand hard slaps of wood on wood as the sounds caromed endlessly off the eight foot ceilings and slammed against the bare concrete walls. The only sound-absorbing stuff in the whole of the place was the workers' heads. The wood plank floors were dutifully swept each day and oiled once a month. Oiled? Yeah, I suspected just so the dust would stick better to a man's shoes.

But I didn't give it no mind, at least not nowadays, so I inhaled the first clouds of wood dust, and soldiered on back. The route you had to take between saws, sanders, rooms and work stations was marked by a bright yellow stripe we called the "yellow brick road." Only at the end of it you didn't get brains or courage or a heart, you just got a paycheck—and for almost everybody, a lousy one at that. I stepped on the first foot of it and commenced to lose myself in Slugger.

At the first stop four guys were gunning chain saws cutting the logs into four-footers. Next to them the ramp became a conveyor, with one guy on each side of it shuttling the four-footers onto it and into a saw tube, out of which the logs emerged as "rounders" without the bark, nude as babies, clean, no knots, and straight as a Willie Mays line drive. The next crew stacked the clean rounders eight high on rolling carts and shoved the carts down a short ramp into the next room, where, straight away, they went into the billet saws.

Mike the Bow, a black man with huge arms, a great big laugh and more brains than half the boys in Slugger, ran the operations in the room like a Marine drill sergeant. Nobody messed with him and everybody respected him. Mike was one of the best bow hunters in the state of Kentucky.

"Hey Ray, I don't like this shit about Gorham, man," Mike yelled when I passed by just six inches away. "I got a bad feeling down my gut behind this."

"Reckon so," I said, "just like ever-body else in Slugger, doncha think?"

"Now Ray, you too cool to hand me that old boogie-joogie," Mike said, a big frown crossing his normally wide-open look. "I figure the heat gonna get downright intense, okay, and the company ain't gonna want no deep long investigation, right? So way I'm looking at it, somebody in the union gonna get nailed for this shit, and soon, and I don't want it to be me, and you know damn well why."

"Because you're black and the union won't protect you?" I said.

"Well give the dude a gold star."

I leaned over, laid a hand firm and tight on his shoulder, and put my mouth next to Mike's ear. He jerked away, but then I felt his shoulder relax, so I spoke. "Mike, I gotta tell you, and I hate to cross your line, but you're full of shit your own self," I said. "You're too smart for that. The rank and file in this union has been working on making it a solid union for two months now. Yeah, it was a sweetheart for a long time, but she's coming to be a decent one now, and you damn well know it, Mike, 'cause you've been one of the best men what's been making it thataway." I looked him square in the eye,

42

then gave him a quick little nod, raised my eyebrows and one palm as if to say, "Am I right?"

Mike looked me a hard one, then let his shoulder drop, shrugged, and finally gave me a half-hearted nod of assent. "We'll see," he shouted. "You gonna watch my back?"

"Damn straight, brother," I shouted back, and walked off into the next room, hitting another wall of sound.

The next saw job cut the rounders into billets and left a knob on each end. The knob was a circular stub of wood that would be used through the rest of the bat-making process to slam the bat into a whirling mechanism that would turn it for sawing, shaping, sanding, dipping, burning and buffing operations. The billet was a pre-formed semi-bat, a shape similar to a bat but without the specifics of length, taper and rounding that would form the final dimensions of the model of bat it would become when finished off.

From the billet room the bat went to the auto-lathe if it was a standard commercial bat, where it was turned into one of literally scores of bat models that bore the Louisville Slugger label—bats for recreational use, Little League official bats, softball bats, college ball, bats for foreign countries, souvenir bats—you name it, even bats with other sporting goods company labels.

The last guy in the billet room, George Salvatore, would stack the finished billets into his cart, this time with about 140 per cart. George had just dumped a billet when I started past him and he motioned me over to the cart. He was a skinny-ass white boy with a red drinker's nose, a bald head and four blackened teeth, two up, two down.

"Hey, Ray," George shouted above the din. "Three guesses who, or mebbe I should say what, is behind these killings? And you know…" he paused.

"The first two don't count," I dutifully replied. "But I really don't know, George," I quickly added, "and you don't know shit from Shinola." I didn't want to give George any slack. He had a rep of being a bit of a whiner. Always blaming the company for this or the union for that and trying to draw the men out one way or the other. Line guys, foremen, bosses, it didn't matter to George, he'd just blurt out his complaints then lean back and listen. Made me wonder about George, but I kept my judgment in reserve. I waved George off and kept on walking the yellow brick road.

One set of billets didn't go the auto-lathe route, and that was the set destined to be professional baseball bats. A designated man from P.R.O., or the professional bat section of the plant, came back and made selections from the round billets based on the grain of the wood, and put a big "P" in red crayon down the length of the round billet. The turning of the billet into a bat would be done by hand in the P.R.O. section to the specifications of the individual Major League ball player.

Frank Gorham had been the P.R.O. man in the billet room, pulling the best billets based on the grain. It had to be straight and the grain had to have narrow V angles as it veered off the center line to make the bat strong and less likely to break. Frank had put a blue crayon mark on his selections and the blue-bloods, as we called them, went to P.R.O., where they got the royal treatment to become bats for the major leagues.

"Hey Harvey, what's up old man?" I hollered at the black worker standing at the doorway out of the billet section. He had a clipboard in his hand and checked the different models coming off the rounder lathes, making sure the right model runs were matched up with the right auto-lathes.

"Nothing a cracker like you'd understand," Harvey Sampson yelled back over the horrific din of the machines, grinning. Sampson was known as a hard worker and a strong union man who played things straight and didn't take a lot of crap off of anybody. Yet he was a man with an open mind. I'd liked him since my first day on the job at Slugger.

"Okay, just so long as we understand each other," I shouted, giving him a fist on the shoulder. Then Harvey pulled me over for a quick chat.

"Benson tells me I'm gonna take Gorham's place pickin' out the P.R.O. bats, Ray. Ain't that a kick? Never figured they'd put a black man on that job!"

"They givin' you a raise?" I came back.

"Yeah, only a few cents, but hey! I can use it like the devil, man, times is hard at the Sampson house, you gotta believe that!"

"I know what you mean, Harvey. Well, congratulations, that's good all around," I said and stuck out my hand for a shake.

He gave me a shake all right, then a fist bump too.

Just as I got back to the sanding room I ran into Danny B. "Hey Ray, gimme a hand, will ya?"

We walked further up the yellow brick road and into the short lateral hallway that led to the first room in P.R.O..

"You know that boy on the second billet saw? The one always wears the red bandana over his hair?"

"Yeah," I hollered, just so he'd know I could hear him above the general scream.

"He's talking strike. Throwing out a whole lotta horse pucky about the company letting Fred Durkin's murder go, not to mention Frank Gorham's too, saying Slugger's road-blocking the cops and the investigation so's it'll take a long time. Since Slugger won't talk with the union till the murder investigations are over, it'll delay the contract negotiations."

"And you don't believe it?" I said, checking on Danny's degree of indignation.

"Hell no, I don't believe it, Ray. That's the kind of junk that gets the rumor mill so fired up that nobody's got a clear head when the deal goes down. I've seen that shit before and so have you. Half the goddamn time it's the company that's putting out the sorry junk just to provoke a bunch of hot-heads to go out on wildcat. Since the sensible men won't go for that, it'll divide us and the company will conquer. You know, get the boys fightin' amongst ourselves. Some for it, some against it."

"Yeah, I've seen it too," I said. "You think many guys are buying it?"

"Not hardly. Shit, this dork is so full of fifty-cent words that the boys don't know what the hell he's going on about 'cept he's gotta be a college kid and they don't trust that no farther than they can throw it."

"What kinda words?"

"Oh, words from some movie about the '30's. Like 'working class,' 'proletariat,' 'bosses,' 'capitalist class,' stuff like that."

Now Danny really had my attention. I had damn well seen this before, but not the way he thought. "How long he been here?" I wanted to know.

"A month."

I pulled back from Danny and looked him square in the eye. "Okay Danny," I said. "They's a contract we gotta bring in for this here union, weak as it is. And I know I'm no official nobody in the local, but one thing those coal wars taught me back east is that us working guys got to take charge of each other and keep it together. So in the interest of that, I'll check him out. Meanwhile don't you go trashing the boy, Okay? I'd just as soon keep as many twists out of the sheets as possible right now."

Danny nodded his okay, slapped his palm on my shoulder, jumped up to head back towards his unit. I grabbed him so that he'd stop and pulled myself up to his ear.

"Whoa, hoss. What's the kid's name?"

"Ted somebody or other," said Danny.

"Well it ain't Ted Williams, that's for sure," I said, looking across at the kid's skinny arms.

"An' I gotta go to bat, or at least make one," shouted Danny as he walked off.

I watched Danny walk past the kid he'd been talking about. The boy stood six feet. His glasses were already covered with dust and it wasn't nine in the morning yet. He wore a V-neck Tee and baggy green khaki pants. His red sweatband pushed

46

up brown hair and made it wave, otherwise I figured it'd be straight and lanky. The boy was slim, but I could tell his arms were strong because they didn't dip when he lifted the finished billet off the conveyor as it came out of the end of the saw. The guy didn't seem to notice anything but the job. He was new, after all.

"Right on," I thought to myself, grinning like a fool. It had been a few years, but man-oh-man this kid's description brought back a few memories. My face turned red at the thought of some of the dumb-ass things I'd done. But hey, we all got to start somewhere. Couldn't judge the boy too harsh. Some of the stuff on my AA fourth step inventory made me cringe to this day—cheating on my first wife, lying all over the place, stealing stuff when I could've paid. And lying my ass off to impress the boys on my first few organizing jobs. Trying to look like somebody I wasn't. Joe Hill the second.

I spent the rest of the morning till the 11:30 lunch break sweeping sawdust and chips off the floor in the auto-lathe room, close as I could to the crime scene tape the cops had left around the auto-lathe. As soon as the green light went to flashing on the wall, signaling lunch, I maneuvered the broom right up to the crime scene lathe. The boys on the bench cleared out likity-split, so I took a chance. I stepped over the tape and took a quick look at the machine that had held what was left of Gorham. What I wanted to know, and damn bad, was if it had also killed him.

Chapter Five: Radio One

Mel Allen: This is Mel Allen for Mutual Radio, baseball fans, right here with that old Southern smooth talker, aka Red Barber, and I gotta keep saying it – what a day for a ball game! Wish you folks out there in Cincinnati could be joining us here at Connie Mack stadium in way off Philadelphia in this the first day of Redlegs baseball. We hear it's raining cats and dogs out there in Cincy, sad to say, but it's dry and balmy here in Philly.

Red Barber: Yessir, Mel, it's no baloney, we're standin' in tall cotton with the sun shining through a cloudless 68 degrees. You'd think Mayor Tate had some pull with the Man upstairs and ordered up the Opening Day Weather Special all right.

MA:…Yep, Red, and it seemed to suit the District Attorney, Arlen Specter, right well, too, when he threw out the opening ball…well, back to the ball game here in the top of the second inning, folks, 'cause here comes Vada Pinson striding over from the on-deck circle to toe the base at home plate…

RB: … Jim Bunning goes into his windup, uncorks the pitch from that rangy six-two frame of his…

MA:…and it's strike one on Pinson, Red, zipped it right past the Cincy batter who's still standing up relaxing like he's waitin' for the six-oh-five to Hoboken…you'd think he didn't have his team mate, Pete Rose, dancing down the base path at first…

RB:…that's right, Mel, courtesy of a Dick Allen bobble at third base on the first play of the inning..

MA:…something you almost never see – guess it's opening day jitters, ehhh Red?

RB:…yep, and ol Vada is a crafty batter but that time he looked a little sleepy at the switch, Mel…

MA:…well, whatever's goin' on with Vada, Red, we're having the time of our lives bringing these special Game of the Week broadcasts to you folks courtesy of the Mutual Broadcasting Network and those fine smokes put out by Lucky Strike…

RB:…Yep, Mel, like the jingle says, L.S. does indeed mean M.F.T. — Luckies do mean fine tobacco! Smooooooth, man!

MA:…and here I thought you inclined to a little chaw on the sly, Red…

RB:…not when I'm broadcasting for Lucky Strike, Mel…you don't wanna start a rhubarb with the sponsor on the first day, do ya?

MA:…well, while we've been jawing up the sponsorship Bunning has even'd up the count at two and two…

RB:…that's right Mel, and here comes the 2-2 pitch…

MA:…swung on…crack!…it's a hard hit ball, Red, going, going, it's off the right field wall…

RB:…Rose is tearing up the pea patch now, rounding third for home, Mel!

MA:…Safe!…and Pinson's into second standing up!

RB: That makes it one to nothing for the Redlegs, Mel. They're off to a good start for the fans back home in Cincinnati.

MA: That's right, Red. Maybe that'll bring a little sunshine into the hearts of the fans if not into the skies above their heads.

RB: You bet, Mel. Now if you've been drawing a little rough when you light up lately, why don't you listen to this little message from the fine folks at American Tobacco and Lucky Strike…

MA: …and if you listen up, folks, you just might recognize the voice of this notorious penny pinching guy…why, they say he's even tighter than Mr. Barber here…

JACK BENNY:…Hello folks, I'm Jack Benny, and I'm here to talk about…

Chapter Six: Ray

After lunch, the boys from the lathe room decided to up the ante with management and so the whole crew had gone down to the front office this time to have it out with Worthington and Benson, still trying to get their auto-lathes released to do some work and make some piece-rate pay.

I knew my working brothers, and I knew Worthington was tight as a bull's ass in fly time, so I figured they'd have to be in there with him a while. So with security, management and labor all twisted up in a knot in the bosses' office, I eased myself into the room and creaked under the tape. I say 'creaked' because even though I'm right smart fit for a 58 year-old, my knees always pop and my back creaks when I bend down and straighten her up again. I had brought a clean painter's glove we had laying around in the tool shed at Jacob Street. After I'd sidled a few feet from the tape to the auto-lathe, I put my gloved hand in an angled steel upright of the frame that held the auto-lathe at just above waist height. The frame was clothed in a steel casing for the most part, putting the interior of the machine out of reach, but I could see that there was a shelf about halfway down to the floor, mostly hidden from view and touch. But the casing stopped about two inches above the shelf so you could stick your hand or some small object back partway along the shelf out of sight in the dark of the casing.

I reached for the shelf and ran my fingers into it. My glove came back with nothing but a streak of fingerprint dust, black, not bat dust-bunny brown. So the police must have found the shelf and cleaned it off. Well, what did I expect? They weren't all bozos like the H&R Blockheads. Yet and still, the shelf should have been dirty, it should have been chock full of bat-bunnies, sawdust balls glued together by the humidity of the place. That gave me pause. Gorham had to have been using it for more than a stash spot if it was that clean.

I looked at the glove, humphed to myself, and stuck my hand back into the shelf as deep as I could, this time bending over as far as I could and extending my arm deeper into the shelf until it got too thick to go any farther. I hit pay dirt. Well, it was paper, not gold, but as it turned out, it paid big.

Just then I heard the garble of voices, the grumbled curses of the boys coming back from the front office. No time to play blind man's bluff, I just grabbed. My fingers closed around a stack of papers, maybe an inch thick, and I yanked. I saw it was a packet of small postcard sized envelopes bound in a rubber band. I whirled and got the packet up under my shirt, bent myself near about double, slid under the tape. Just then I heard shoe leather slapping concrete.

"Asshole blue-blood." The words came through the archway of the room, pushed ahead of the speaker. I saw a flash of white Tee shirt in the corner of my eye. I sprinted out the archway on the opposite side of the auto-lathe room and down the yellow brick road. I wasn't skipping like Dorothy and Toto either.

Just about quitting time Benson came around and told us the plant would be shut down the next morning to give the cops a second go-over of the whole place. Benson wouldn't say why even though I asked him if they'd found evidence someplace outside the sanding room. "No comment, Odle, just keep your big nose out of this, y'hear?" he said, obviously trying to do his bit to make sure nobody could suspicion that my questions had come out of my investigator role. On the way out the door I caught up to George Salvatore and asked him if I could drop over the next afternoon, it being Saturday and the plant closed, said I had some things on my mind about the way things were going at the plant. He stopped smack in the stream of sweaty bodies pushing out the door, gave me a funny look, then shrugged like he didn't have a care in the world and said "sure."

Margaret looked up when I got home from the shift and crossed the threshold of the apartment. She'd had one of those intuitions that was strong as hell and damn near certain and naturally she'd been right. So she wasn't asking an open question, she wanted to be proved right.

"What did you find in the lathe?" she asked with a big twinkle in her eye.

I lifted my shirttail and pulled out the packet of envelopes. "The bacon," I said, giving her the grin she was looking for. Margaret did an about face and walked the length of the hallway behind her and into the Odle Agency office. She eased down into the old oak teacher's desk we'd hauled all the way from Breathitt County. I popped the rubber band and spread the envelopes like a fan out across the doodle-covered blotter.

Each envelope had a date range printed on it in block letters. There were six envelopes. The first read "Ap 6 – 13." The last read "May 21 – 27." No, one was out of place. The last one by date was in the middle. It read, "May 28 – Jn 3."

Margaret reached over and tapped each envelope. Then did it again. She looked up at me, eyes wide. "You see it, Ray?" she said.

I didn't.

"There's one missing. A week. April 22 – 27."

"Yeah, I see it now. It's the one next to the June one, the one that was out of place."

Margaret started opening envelopes. Soon as each one was open, quick as a flash she riffed the envelope with her fingers and popped out a slip of paper. There was no identifying name or logo. The one for April 22 – 27 had a hand printed number running at the top: "206-4477." Below that were three columns. The first was labeled "ID," the next two were labeled, also in block letters: "C -120, A +130 and B-110, Y+120." Below the first column were first names. Names of Slugger workers I recognized: Harvey, Ted, George, Danny, Larry, Arthur. Other names I didn't. Beside each name, under the second and third column, was a letter and number combination. The first one read: George C-25; the second said B-20.

"What the…" I said, scratching my nose. "All I can say is some of them names look like names of boys down at

	206-4477—A=10		
ID	C -120, A +130	B-110, Y+120	P-C
	A3, C1	B7, Y3	
George	C-25	B-20	c62.50,p42
Danny	A-20	Y-20	p20,c44
Ted	C-15	B-10	p33,p21

Slugger."

Margaret didn't speak, just studied, her head bent only a little bit, looking on from a distance like a sharp-eyed blue jay studying the lay of the sparrows on the feeder before he makes his swoop.

"Well, I'll be…I'll just sit right here and *be*," she finally said. Then she looked across the desk at me. "Who did the Yankees play the third week in April, Ray, you 'member?"

I went at my nose a bit more on that one. Then I had it. "Got it! It was Boston. The Red Sox. I remember 'cause Mantle got scotched at the plate and that new guy, Yastremski, knocked a grand slam in the bottom of the eighth to win it for the Red Sox against the odds."

"Funny you should say that last word," said Margaret.
"What?"

"That about 'odds', that's what. Think about it. Look at the paper with the numbers and…"

"Damn, damn, and double-damn!" I said. "That was the score, Boston 7, Yankees 3. B7-Y3, just like on that slip."

53

"And under the score are names, and with the names, letters for one of the two teams for that game, with these pluses or minuses and another low number. Odds is right."

"But what I don't get," I said, "is who's winning and who's losing here, and by how much? All them numbers don't add up to nothin' for me. But I bet you get it, right?"

"No. I'm just a sweet little country gal, Ray. You'll have to talk to somebody, maybe one of the guys on the list, and maybe hint around about baseball and betting or some such."

"With all respect, Margaret, that's a wee bit too risky, way I look at it. But I can talk to Danny B about it. I can talk to him about damn near anything, him bein' my buddy in the program an' all. Besides, that man knows more dirt about what and who's goin' on at Slugger than anybody."

"Good," said Margaret. "There's one thing sure, though."

"What's that?"

"Our man Gorham is more than a snitch, Ray, if he's even that. This is some well-oiled kind of betting scheme. Game dates, team initials, code numbers of some kind. Bunch of pluses and minuses. I don't know exactly what's going on here or how this particular scheme works, but it's clear this is a runner's sheet and it's part of a system. I mean, pre-set odds on slips? There's only one organization I know of that does it that way. If a man wants to go that way, he's got to cozy up to…"

"…the Outfit," I broke in.

"You think Gorham doubled-crossed them?" Margaret said.

"Dunno," I said. "Could be he skimmed some of the winnings that should have gone to the organization."

"Or he was free-lancing, signing up some private bettors, off the books and got caught," Margaret added.

"Right, or it could be he was doing a little blackmail number on one or more of the boys he had on the hook— threatening to tell their wives or some such," I said.

"Yes, or even a little off the books unauthorized extortion, threatening one or more of the boys who'd gone into debt over their losses," Margaret said.

"Like, knee-capping, or worse," I threw in.

"And the last two possibilities could be true whether Gorham was a runner or not," Margaret said. "He could have come by the betting slips another way—found them or cadged them somehow and figured out what they were just like we did."

"Yeah, you're right," I said. "I didn't see that last bit. Either way it gives us one of the elements of the crime, all right. Motive. But if it was the Outfit, how'd they get a hit man inside the plant to make the kill and stash Gorham on the auto-lathe?" I went on. "Unless the mob is already…"

"…inside the plant," Margaret finished the thought. "An individual getting revenge on Gorham, the mob, take your pick."

Margaret rolled her desk chair back from the desk and over to the window. "Then there's H & R," she said, staring out.

That made my mouth come to a complete stop. It didn't have to be the Mob. It could be the gunsel thugs. They could have come across the same kind of information and used it against Gorham to turn him against the union. He might have resisted—and things could have got out of hand.

And even though Margaret had put them on the list, it didn't have to be H & R either. We could be stumbling into something dark, something rotten we knew nothing about, something we'd stirred up almost by accident that had brought out a killer—a killer that could come right back on us. No, forget "us,"—on Margaret. I started working my jaw, grinding my teeth like I always did when my head was spinning but my gut was frozen tight.

"I gotta admit, Margaret, I'm feeling kinda lost right now. Don't know where to go next." I'd learned not to bluff Margaret. I didn't have to be the hero or have all the answers all the time.

"Right, Ray," she said, real business-like. "I don't know either. So we're right where we want to be—together, Okay? Nobody's a hero, nobody's alone. We just have to keep at it and do the next right thing," said Margaret.

"Which is?" I said.

"Detect. We're the Odle Detective Agency," said Margaret, shrugging her shoulders. "We've got to do some detective agenting, I suppose."

"I reckon," I said. "Maybe that number at the top of these slips is a phone number. Maybe you should dial it."

She did, and held the receiver out so I could lean down and hear it too. The phone picked up on the third ring. A distorted nasal voice said: "State your code."

Margaret put the phone down and we looked at each other. She nodded. "Organized, and how!" she said.

"Yeah, they must have a guy going around signing people up and giving them an ID code."

"That's the letter and number on the top of the slip," said Margaret.

"Maybe before every game he takes the guy's bet and collects his money," I said. "After the game he comes around again and gives him his winnings, if any."

"One dumb thing he did, and thank our lucky stars for it," Margaret said. I looked my question. "Seems like the whole thing might've been a little too complicated for our boy Gorham. Seems like he couldn't just keep the letter-number for the names of the customers. Seems he…"

"Penciled in the names too," I said.

"That's it," she said.

"How's it lucky for us?" I asked.

"Gives us some folks to talk to, do some detecting, now doesn't it," she said. "Being as it's Saturday tomorrow and Slugger is closed after the morning shift, you can get busy calling on folks.

"First is Mrs. Durkin," Margaret went on, "because she might have some idea of why somebody would want to kill her husband, or if she doesn't, then that might at least eliminate a personal or family angle. Of course if it's something like that, the cops are likely to find it, and that's all to the good, because it means we don't have to worry about the union getting blamed. But somehow I don't get that feeling. On second thought, I'll call on Mrs. Durkin. Might be best for a woman-to-woman kind of talk, especially seeing as how she's still no doubt grieving and all.

"But for you, digging in that Slugger patch is what you have to do, and the first name of the three Frank Gorham left us is George Salvatore, so you might as well start with him tomorrow, then whatever time is left, start down the rest of the list of those boys."

"Matter of fact, I already made a date with him anyway when I was on the way out of the plant today, even before I seen these betting forms," I said.

"Perfect," said Margaret.

Margaret looked out the window while I just shifted my weight from one foot to the other. After a few minutes of that, I started pacing. Stymied, nothing to do just then, so my pacing got longer, from the office through the bedroom to the staircase and back.

"Seems like you have a meeting tonight, don't you, sweetheart?" Margaret broke into my pacing and mental gymnastics. "And why don't I just step on down to the library, it's open 'til six, and I can look up all those weeks in the sports pages. Make a list of the games with teams whose names…"

"Okay. I get it," I said, damn glad for the reminder that in just a bus ride and a little wait I'd get some relief from what we AAs called the "kids playing in the attic."

Margaret smiled, put her arms up. We hugged. I felt her firm breasts lifting up to me under the blouse. I put my hand behind the small of her neck like she loved me to do. Kissed her cheek, gave a final squeeze to her shoulders and neck. She pecked my cheek like a butterfly.

I beat it. The evening sun flooded my bones and brain the minute I stepped off the porch. I whistled all the way. Going to a meeting. Taking action, nothing like it.

Jimmy G. and I stood around under the single wan light on the little porch stoop over the door of the Louisville Central Office of AA where the Last Ditch Sobriety Group meeting had been held. Everybody else had either bolted for home (or the nearest bar) or jawed for a while after the meeting and left. Like Jimmy and my previous sponsor back in Breathitt always said, there's the meeting before the meeting, the meeting, and the meeting after the meeting — and you never know which one will give you what you most need.

Jimmy was about my height, a little chunky, had a resonant baritone with which he could joke and pun with the best of them. In fact he'd once worked the club circuit as a standup comic until he stepped off the stage one night and broke his leg when he was so drunk he confused the stage lights with the spotlight.

"Now let's see, Red," he said as he slouched against the wall and ticked it off on his fingers. "You're tellin' me you worked as an organizer for the Black Lung Campaign, knowing that the coal companies had hired the gun thugs to put it down, right?"

"Check," I said.

"And you got a bunch of other guys with you and tried to entice the gun thugs at this particular meeting to come out in the open."

"Check."

"And you knew some of your folks had brought guns."

"Check."

"And you knew that the gun thugs had a track record of starting trouble, shooting up meetings of the Campaign and torching and such."

"Check."

"So when the balloon went up you ran into the middle of it instead of seeking protection behind a tree or something."

"But if I hadn't…yeah, okay, check."

"And you took on this case at Slugger knowing that often companies hire private cops—gun thugs as you call them, sometimes accurately, to protect their interests in murder cases, and that these guys have a way of becoming kind of rough."

"Check."

"Does that suggest anything to you?"

I stared at the ground for a while, then cleared my throat, scuffed my heels, and finally coughed it up. "Yeah. I ain't no victim. By doing what I do for a living I sort of asked for it then and I'm letting myself in for it now. So I just gotta do the next right thing in front of me."

Jimmy let out a long sigh. "Good," he said. "That pop I just heard was your head coming out of your ass. Have a good evening, Red—unless you have other plans."

With that he walked off into the dark.

Unless you have other plans? he was always saying shit like that.

Drove me crazy. But I was just beginning to catch on to what he meant.

Chapter Seven: Margaret

The Louisville Courier-Journal loved baseball. The editor had a son who played for the AAA Cincinnati farm club, the Louisville Bats. Whatever the reason, the paper gave good coverage on the national pastime, especially on the exploits of their almost home-town major league team, the Cincinnati Reds. Going back to her rebellious teenage tom-girl days, Margaret liked baseball, and so for a while doing her research she got kind of lost in all the sports pages for the six weeks scratched onto Gorham's envelopes. She looked extra hard at the stories for the missing week, too, but nothing stood out. Well, almost nothing.

The stories from the other weeks just covered the games. Cut and dried stuff, a story on each major league game that took place the night before, or if it was west coast, the day before, or if it was the Cubs, the afternoon before, because Wrigley Field was the only major league stadium that didn't have lights and couldn't play at night. Damn stubborn of those Chicago folks, but they were entitled, Margaret figured. The stories were right interesting to Margaret, but maybe if you didn't care so much about the game, they wouldn't be. Who won, who lost, pitchers, hits, walks, strikeouts, double plays, deeds of the mighty hitters, that was the gist.

But an item in the week of April 22-27 made her do a double-take. There were the usual routine stories. The Yankees lost, what else was new? The 1966 Yankees were beginning to look like their cross-town National League upstart rivals, the Mets. The Dodgers lost by a thread, yes indeed. The Cubbies blew another one, lost to the Reds in the top of the ninth, ho-hum. But it was a sidebar to that story which grabbed Margaret in the gut.

Seems Jersey Jack Danielson got into a ruckus with the Reds' owner, Bill "Billy the Ace" DeWitt, known as "the Ace" because of a murky reputation for major league card games as well as his having been an ace pitcher in the early days of the present era of baseball. The story said Jack went roaring into Bill's office after the April 24th win over the Cubs. He was sore over a broken bat and demanded that Bill cancel the deal with Louisville Slugger for his ball bats. Bill never let anybody forget he was the Ace of the Cincinnati Reds, though, and threw Jack out of the office, but not before ordering him benched for two days. The Reds' PR man, Harry Anderson, came out and tried to smooth it all over with the press boys, but the Courier's man in Cincinnati ended his story with a quote from Jersey Jack that must've snuck past the editor's pencil.

"That's my third busted bat since the opener. It stinks all the way to Louisville," Jack was quoted as saying, "and I don't give a damn who hears me say it!"

There were a few other baseball stories that week about the early going in the season, and of course a bunch of hype towards the end of the week about the Kentucky Derby that was two weeks off. Margaret gave up on April 22 − 27 and picked up that day's Journal, June 7th.

She moved on from the sports pages to the national news.

Damn! They shot James Meredith down in racist Mississippi! The story said he'd been on a walk against fear and got ambushed out on a main highway. He wasn't killed, but they got him in the leg, the state cops had taken him to the hospital and he would recover, it said. It's a wonder the Staties didn't finish the job in the van, Margaret thought. That's what the Ku Kluxers had done when the Neshoba County Sheriff's officers had turned Mickey Schwerner, James Cheney and Michael Goodman over to them after they'd been taken into custody two years back during Mississippi Freedom Summer in 1964.

The system down in Mississippi was a lot like the one in eastern Kentucky, where mountain folk had to stomach the county court-house's ring dictating things, like the machine in Breathitt County, where the sheriff, the judges, and the vigilantes were all in cahoots with the coal company's goons. In Mississippi and the rest of the South, it was the White Citizens' Councils, composed of the blue-bloods with the silk stockings and plantations and banks, that called the shots with the local sheriffs, the county judges, and the state cops. And should that not be enough to keep black folks and uppity working class white folks in line, the White Citizens' Councils had a pipeline right into the KKK through the local sheriff.

The whole of the system was designed to keep you in your place, white or black, especially black. But Margaret had seen it work against her fellow whites too.

If a man stood up against the bosses, the word would go out and the first thing would be that he'd be shunned, people would walk on the other side of the street when they met him in town, move away from him at church, or quietly turn their eyes away, shrug their shoulders, reply in monosyllables to his attempts to strike up a conversation. Suddenly even the weather was uninteresting as a topic of talk around him. The daylight was in permanent shadow over his head. But if a man kept on challenging the bosses he'd just as likely as not find himself out of a job, or if he was a sharecropper, he'd find himself out of a house, his bill at the plantation store due immediately payable, or he'd not only lose his house, he could be fined, and if he didn't pay the fine, he'd be put in jail and forced to work for the same landowner as a means of paying off his court fine and "costs." The whole thing was nothing but a return to slavery by a different name.

In the case of the Eastern mountains, the gun thugs would evict him from company housing, which is where most miners lived, call his bill due at the company store, which meant he and his family had no more credit and his pay would be docked at 90 percent or more, which meant he'd be forced to leave the job even if they didn't fire him outright. If somehow he or his family managed to live in a tent, which sometimes happened, or scrabble and scuffle up enough to eat, and still fought against the company or stuck with the Black Lung campaign, then he'd get assaulted one night, his knees broken, or just plain shot, or wounded in an unequal knife fight, or he'd be missing for days or weeks until his corpse turned up in some godforsaken hole.

Margaret's ruminations were suddenly disturbed by the sounds of more than a dozen tiny feet as a grammar school class came marching by. They held hands, two-by-two, following their teacher and the librarian, evidently on a tour of the library and equally evidently silenced for this part of tour through the reading room. Margaret sighed, remembering similar tours in the Charleston city library and the incident in which she'd broken ranks and run in and out of the stacks playing hide-and-seek with an equally rascally boy. Another late afternoon in the Principal's office had been the result. She couldn't help grinning as she turned back to the newspaper.

The grin didn't last long. Her eyes landed on an article that told of Muhummad Ali's press conference where he stated that he wouldn't go "10,000 miles to help murder, kill and burn other people simply to help continue the domination of white slave masters over dark people the world over." Ali was refusing to fight in the Vietnam War and had addressed a march put on by SANE and Women's Strike for Peace where he spoke to more than 10,000 marchers in New York City. "No Viet Cong ever called me nigger," he said.

Indeed, Margaret thought. She recalled the history of the war in which her country had pledged to support the Geneva Accords of 1954 which had settled the first Vietnam War, the war of independence for Vietnam where Vietnamese had won their it from the French, supported by the U.S. The Accords had set up a temporary division between north and south but had promised the Vietnamese people free elections in 1956 to elect a government for the whole country. But the South Vietnamese temporary government had refused to hold the elections and, supported by the U.S., had broken the Accords, plunging the country back into civil war and insurgency. Even though the north was communist and the southern insurgency had communist elements in it, the U.S. was on the wrong side of history once again, Margaret thought, as she read about the demonstrations against the war, which by now had caused the drafting of 170,000 American men into the military, killed more than 7,500 of them so far, not to mention tens of thousands of Vietnamese.

And who bore the brunt of the dying in America? Black folk and poor working people of whatever race. The ones who couldn't get college deferments or other wiggly ways out of the draft. And they died. And they killed. And they came back maimed and wounded in body and in mind. Before Ray and Margaret had moved to Louisville they'd seen them coming back to Breathitt County and had been shocked at their condition. Then more shocked at the lack of support they received from the government. The support, both medical and psychological, was abysmal — it included suspicion where there should have been acceptance, bureaucratic obstruction and delay where there should have been expedition and service, and incompetence where there should have been expertise. It was almost as if these men, and some women too, were being shunned.

Margaret heard feet quietly moving behind her, this time solitary ones, and looked up to see the Librarian making her final rounds, looking at her watch. She was the old-fashioned type, literally with her hair in a bun, her ankle-length dress swishing as she walked. Rather than speak, this was her way of saying it was time to close up.

Margaret smiled at her and left, walking the five blocks home on a lovely soft evening, reveling in the sweet southern air.

But she also pondered about the very long-odds possibility that Jersey Jack's display of anger was more than sour grapes and extreme disappointment. After all, he was a seasoned professional baseball player at the top of his game in the Major Leagues. Broken bats were an unfortunate but not unheard of factor in the game. Louisville Sluggers were perhaps the least likely bats to break of all—no, correct that, were definitely the least likely bats to break—so why didn't Jack just cool his anger after stalking off the field like every other major leaguer did? Why risk his contract? For that was what he did by storming into the general manager's office and demanding something he knew perfectly well was totally impossible. And if he knew it was totally impossible for Billy DeWitt to comply, was Jersey Jack trying to send a message to someone? DeWitt? Or somebody else by means of giving the story to the press?

And if the whole thing was some kind of theatrical performance, who was the intended audience? Was this a smokescreen or a deliberate miscue of some kind? If so, what kind? Or was it a miscue of the pyrrhic kind? Was Jersey Jack upset—or was he doing exactly what he intended on doing, and if so, for what reason? As the old detective slogan went, *qui bono*? Who benefits?

There would be a lot for Ray and Margaret to talk about before their heads hit the pillows that night.

On the way home Margaret also thought about Ray and their little detective enterprise. Ray was one of the rare ones, a man with a drinking problem that had owned up to it, and in the process had owned up to a whole lot of what he'd done in his life to cause some of his worst troubles. He'd quit blaming the world, picked up that sack of responsibility and slung it over his own shoulder just like a man down in the South Carolina cotton fields where she'd grown up takes the weight of his cotton sack and pulls it down the row, never mind that he could complain about the injustice of the overseer, the pay, the boll weevils or the stifling heat.

Ray Odle was a fair-on-to-big man who knew how to dance and do dishes as well as cook. "Now I say you can't beat that in a man these days," Margaret thought, then realized she'd said it out loud and looked around sheepishly to see if she'd been overheard.

Ray stood a good six feet, two inches, trim with a rugged face, a big nose he always joked about because it couldn't smell worth a hoot, and a head of wavy red hair — well, it used to be dark red but now was shot through with streaks of gray. Made him more handsome than ever, far as Margaret was concerned. That and the fascinating hazel green and gray eyes that kept changing color with his moods.

And Ray Odle was known all over the coalfields in the eastern mountains of Kentucky as a straight shooter — not with a gun but with his word. He stood by it and you could count on it being the truth and on his keeping it come hell or high water.

It was a gunshot wound that first made Margaret take him into her life. He'd gotten hit in the shoulder when the gun thugs shot up a Black Lung Campaign meeting. It was his honesty that caused her to keep him in her life. She'd nursed Ray through his convalescence and got to know the man. Margaret had spent some twenty years in the eastern Kentucky mountains by then, having started as a Packhorse Librarian with the WPA in the Thirties, but she was still somewhat of an outsider, a runaway from a North Carolina tidewater Baptist women's college, and Ray was pure mountain man. Though they'd met as organizers in the Black Lung Campaign, most folks figured they'd split up as soon as he got healed enough to make it on his own. It didn't turn out that way. Somewhere in the middle of his convalescence Margaret made the decision to make being there for Ray the center of her life, whether he loved her as a help-meet or

66

husband or not. He did the same thing. They fell in love, of course, but that came later. The commitment came first. It still did.

They'd spent the first year of the Odle Agency's life putting out brush fires in the coal fields — solving a couple of cases where old feuds had led to murder. One where a coal foreman had shot and killed the UMW organizer in his district and nearly started a union-company war over it. But they found out that the real motive had been that the junior coal boss had been cheating with the union man's wife, it had nothing to do with union organizing or repression, just another Hank Williams song come to life.

Margaret and Red got called out of the hills to several other jobs in the next year, worked in St. Louis on a machine shop job connected with the auto industry and the UAW, a job in New Jersey involving GE's defense contract and a dead body in the machine shop, and a job down at Dan River Mills cotton where civil rights organizers were trying to bring black and white workers together, nearly causing a KKK lynching.

It was the travel that showed the two middle-aged lovers that as much as they considered the hollows and hills of the eastern mountains of Appalachia their home, they had to admit that getting to and from a little cabin on the hill, as Mack Wiseman's song had it, wasn't very practical on the old Chevy pickup or on the Odle Agency travel budget. So they decided to move to a town where travel to and from was easier and where Kentucky's Appalachia had created a haven for its kinfolk — and Louisville had won, hands down. It was a place with a robust mountain folk community and was close to Breathitt County, Margaret's old stomping grounds, and Lawrence County, where Ray was born and raised, yet contained all the road, train and bus connections they would need for getting to and from jobs elsewhere in the country. Yes, the world had airplanes but they flew too high on the hog for the Odle Agency.

Margaret still felt a jolt of anticipation and joy as she walked up to their flat, hoping that Ray's craggy face would greet her when she came through the door. That was a good sign for a middle-aged lady indeed.

Chapter Eight: Ray

After leaving the apartment, I had just enough time to walk the eight blocks to Brown's restaurant for my weekly Wednesday pre-meeting supper with some of the guys in the program. After eating we'd hit the men's stag meeting.

When I got there I felt a little nervous and out of place, like I always did. Brown's was a legendary institution in Louisville. All kinds went there, of course, but the majority were middle class, and here and there a few horse-country types, the kind of folks with tweeds and leather collars and elbow patches, and little felt hats. You didn't see a lot of mountain folk in there — at least not the ones that still claimed that heritage. The signature dish, Hot Brown, was turkey and bacon under a special sauce they made. I always got that.

Danny B was the only other Slugger guy there. I was a few minutes late, which also made me nervous, but they'd saved me a seat at the circular banquette table, right next to Cash Cow Conrad. Conrad was a muscular, gray-haired, chain-smoking ex-bond trader who'd made and lost two or three fortunes only to end up broke and ten thousand bucks in debt to his best friend's estate, a man who'd been his sponsoring Masonic Deacon. He'd been very close to the Deacon, who'd spoken for him as a Masonic candidate, but then repaid the man by conning him on the intrinsic value of the worthless bonds he'd offered as collateral for the loan he'd obtained from his Deacon friend. He'd quit bond trading and been working as an actuary at Metropolitan Life for some 21 years in his sobriety and had paid off the debt just last year. His biggest regret was that he hadn't finished paying the debt while his Deacon friend still lived.

"Got your Hot Brown on order," Danny said as I sat, mumbling apologies for being late. Next to Conrad sat Shirtless Henry, a 240 pounder on a five-five frame who'd come down from Wisconsin where he'd gotten sober. The old-timers called him Shirtless because he was heavy into crap shooting and always lost his shirt when he gave in to the lure of the bones. Henry reached across the table to shake my hand with a hearty "Hey Big Ray how's the batting in the belfry?" He didn't sell used cars, he sold used RVs.

Around the table from Henry were Andrew the CPA for Shelby County, Stephen the Assistant Bank Manager at a Bank of Kentucky branch, and Radio Ralph, who'd been a sports announcer at 84 WHAS until he'd blurted out a frank description of the chest endowments of the Mayor's wife on opening day two years back when she'd walked out in a tight-topped Louisville Bats jersey to throw the ceremonial first pitch. The station fired him on the spot and he decked the soundman on his way out for laughing at him.

He'd been drunk then but was dry now and it worried me. I mean, being sober means working the steps in AA and getting hold of a piece of serenity, being kind of in the middle and not swinging way up or way down all the time. Radio Ralph looked like a guy who was white-knuckling it to me. Not drinking, but not easy inside his own skin either. Not that I had all that much more time sober than he did. But mine was good time, and I had worked at it, and the obsession to drink had been lifted. It just didn't pull at me any more. Ralph though, there was nothing easy about him. But I figured I'd better stay on my side of the street, let Ralph be Ralph. After all, he had a Higher Power and it wasn't me.

The guys tossed the small talk around for a while until the food came then everybody dug in like guys do. Eating was serious business. The tradition of our little group was you had coffee and pie with ice cream for dessert, and this night

Brown's had their usual killer apple and pecan pies, plus a rhubarb on special. The rhubarb tempted me for about five seconds but I went for the pecan like I always do.

While I was letting each bite melt in my mouth and not paying too much attention to the talk between bites, Henry flipped Ralph something across the table.

"Hey, Ralphie boy!" he boomed out in a bad Art Carney-Ed Norton imitation. "Take a look-see at this one, willya? Got it from a guy over in Franklin, Indiana. 1948 Willie Mays. Whatcha think? Worth something?"

I gave it my own look-see.

"Wait a minute!" said Ralph. "That's Mays' first year with the Black Barons in the Negro League. A new one on me, I'll say."

"Then I must really have a winner," said Henry. "Nobody knows baseball like you, Ralph—if you say it's a rare one, then that sure as shit must be the case."

Ralph handed the card back. "Why don't you let me borrow this for a couple of days, let me catalogue this, Henry," he said. "Put it in my record books, maybe do a little research on its value?"

Henry shook his head from side to side. I couldn't hear much of what he said beneath the clatter of plates and general chatter which unfortunately for the detecting trade rose to a high pitch just then, but the words "I don't think so" came through the din just fine.

Then Henry's voice boomed, this time more like Jackie Gleason on a tear than Art Carney. "Look, Ralph, don't be so goddamn paranoid. I'll just come over to your place with you after the meeting and you can do whatever you do and that'll be it. Over and done, then we go our separate ways. Nothing could be easier. What say?"

"Well, if that's the way it's gotta be," grumbled Ralph. "I 'spec we gotta go now or we'll be late."

We'd all paid our checks while this was going on. There was a general shuffling and scraping of chairs as we got up to leave.

On the way out of the crowded entrance I pulled Ralph's elbow to get his attention.

"I'd like to talk with you sometime, Ralph, 'bout this hobby of yours. Didn't know you was an expert on baseball cards."

Ralph's eyes grew wide and his shoulders went into a shrug. Henry was right in front and turned his head to reply before Ralph could speak.

"Ain't just baseball cards," he said. "Ralph's been keeping stats on the majors and minors for twenty years, drunk or sober — ain'tcha Ralph?"

Ralph shot a look like daggers at Henry.

"Somethin' to do," he mumbled and hustled on out the door.

I didn't get to speak to him again. He rode to the meeting in Andrew's car and I rode with Danny.

"What's with Ralph?" I asked Danny.

Danny looked out the drivers' side window and gave an exaggerated shrug. "Just touchy about his baseball records and cards I guess. Works down in the basement of his house with piles of bound register books he's filled out every year since he was a kid. Green shaded lamp hanging from the ceiling, sits under it on a stool in front of a high antique desk. About a year ago, just after he came into the program, I visited him, friendly call, you know, for support, being as how he didn't have a sponsor yet. Didn't answer the door so I stuck my head in and hollered his name. Heard his footsteps slamming up the basement stairs faster than jack-be-nimble. Heard the basement door shut, then a click from a lock of some kind. He came to the door stuffing a padlock key in his pants. Figured it was kinda weird, didn't say nothin' though. His business, best left as it lies." Then he switched the subject. "Damn traffic's bad for a Wednesday," he said.

I took the hint. We talked about the weather, traffic and the Derby the rest of the way. I kept wondering about that phony shrug and how come he changed the subject.

The meeting was in a church basement, this one being the Oak Street Baptist Church about a mile from Jacob, and like Jacob Street, stuck in a changing neighborhood, one going down not up on the class scale. I hated to go to meetings in Southern Baptist churches, being as how most of them hated unions and Black folk and strong-minded women, but I hated the idea of drinking again even more, so I went.

Down in the basement it was poorly lit with sparse fluorescent strips that gave everybody a greenish cast. There were about twenty men sitting in rows, none of that circular seating touchy-feely crap for us men. The book says AA is a fellowship of "men who would not ordinarily mix," and it was too true. Here were bankers and lawyers fresh from work at oppressing the working class, most of which had taken their ties off and hung their suit jackets on the backs of the folding metal chairs. Then there were assorted ditch-diggers, welders, a couple of farm workers, factory workers from GE's Appliance Park, and three of us Slugger workers: me, Danny B. and Harvey S., the billet room guy. Nobody was sitting next to him when I came in so I dropped my hillbilly ass next to his black one. In between the banker-lawyer bunch and us blue collars were several guys that did craft work: a furniture maker, one guy that built custom bluegrass instruments like mandolins and dobros, and a guy that claimed to be an artist—a Shoshone Indian who'd gone into wood carving and made sculptures.

The meeting leader called on people to speak on the topic of "what's going on with you today or something addressed to the newcomer." The topic became anonymity, but I got to admit I drifted off. The old timers had taught me to look at each person when they shared and try to get something out of it. Said that your Higher Power spoke through other alcoholics in meetings. Well, I reckon I tuned the ole Higher Power out, and I was indeed meditating on anonymity. But my take on it that night was wondering where anonymity left off and secrecy began. Locked basement full of self-wrote baseball statistics? Guy who would know that Willie Mays had his first shot at pro ball with the Black Barons? And remember it that damn quick? Guy like that, working in complete anonymity, could be some kind of closet Jimmy-the-Greek. Was Ralph just a fanatical but secretive and quirky student of the game? Or something else? How did those slips get made and printed up? Who decided the spread odds anyway? What were they based on? I did have the presence of AA mind to realize that all of this may have hinted at the fact that I just might be a suspicious bastard.

All the sudden the leader was saying "Will all who care to…" and only then did I realize he hadn't called on me. Next thing I knew I found myself standing up for the Lord's Prayer.

Danny drove me home. He was silent, kept looking over at me, hesitating. I figured if he wanted to talk, he would. Finally he opened up.

"You know, Ray, we talk about what works in the program is one alcoholic talking to another. And sometimes it don't matter which one has the most time sober, it's just necessary to get something off your chest. Well, what you see here in the seat beside you is a hurtin' man that needs to talk about it."

I nodded. "What's on your mind, Danny?"

"In a word—gambling. I put the plug in the jug a long time ago, as you know, been nigh onto 25 years. But just because a man has licked the drink problem don't mean he's a saint. And in my case growin' up poor in Butchertown left it's mark on me in more ways than booze—so, here goes. I got no sense when it comes to games of chance. I lose it faster than I can make it and I can't stop—or at least I can't stay stopped. So

I'm in a huge hole, Ray. Now don't think for a minute I'm trying to hit you up for some dough. That ain't it. I'd never do that to an AA pal of mine, nossir."

All the while he was talking Danny was working his hands around the steering wheel, sliding them one at a time up and down and sideways, slipping them all the way down then all the way up till they met at the bottom then at the top. Didn't move the wheel, they were loose against it, but it made me nervous just watching and hearing the squeaky noise it made as his hands slid around.

"Didn't think you would, Danny." I said to relieve some of the tension.

"Well, Suzanne, my wife, you know, and the kids are hurtin' even worse than me because of all of this. It's just like I was still on the booze in some ways, Ray. There's no money for schoolbooks, clothes, extras of any kind. Hell, I even blew the rent money several months this winter. Damn near got put out into the street — wife, four kids, furniture and all."

Danny pounded on the top of the steering wheel and damn near sobbed. "It's shit, man! I hate myself for it! I don't look in mirrors anymore. Not ever. I'd smash the face of the sonofabitch that was looking back at me. That's how shitty I feel."

"Sounds like me near the time I hit bottom on the drink problem," I said.

"I get the shakes sometimes, Ray. Ain't had a drop to drink, yet and still I get the shakes from seeing a bill or a notice cross my doorway. I'm always lookin' over my shoulder for the tin star of some Sheriff or some suit with an eviction notice or some bailiff with a summons. I'm a wreck some days."

Danny's eyes were big as silver dollars and he'd started to sweat.

"I come to work just to hide out — yet I'm plumb terrified one of those process servers is gonna come bustin' through the door at Slugger, or that Benson or Bob Stills is gonna pull me off the lathe and tell me I'm wanted in the front office and it's gonna be one of those guys. I have nightmares all the time. I'm dead certain that one night I'm gonna have to pack it all up in a hurry and move the family in the dead of night. Do a geographic just to try to duck 'em. Here I am, 24 plus years of sobriety reduced to fear and loathing and slinking around in my hometown like a common criminal on the lam. Me, the great Danny Bunce, the man who sits with the gurus at the Friday night meeting! Sponsor of dozens, spiritual he-man!"

Then he went silent, his expression dark as the night outside the car. I waited.

"You ever ask for help?" Finally I took a risk, unsure whether to speak at all, but it was heartbreaking to see him like he was just then. "I don't mean to sound stupid, Danny, but you know if the shoe was on the other foot, that's what you'd be askin' me."

"What help? You mean see a shrink? I can't afford that—I'm broke, remember?" Danny's tone was going from remorseful to hostile at this point. Time to cut to the chase then back off.

"I mean Gambler's Anonymous. You do what you know best. What you taught me. You ask your Higher Power for help. You go to a meeting. You get a sponsor. You work the steps."

"They got a program for gambling?"

"Yep. Just like AA."

"Damn! Never knew that."

"No surprise there, I ducked AA for nearly 30 years myself. Didn't want to know about it," was what I said. But not what I believed. How could that be—him not knowing about G.A.? Most guys who got into AA or any of the twelve step programs sooner or later heard about the other twelve step programs. And Danny had been around for nearly a quarter of a century. It just didn't add up. For the first time since I'd known him I grew both suspicious and, I had to face it, a bit angry with my AA pal.

Then Danny's head seemed to recede into his shoulders just a little bit. His neck got tight, the muscles stood out. I could see his shoulders rise and tense. Uh-oh.

"Look here, Ray. Just cause I let down my hair a bit with you and talk about some of the shit that's worryin' me don't mean I can't manage my life in the end. I'm a man to reckon with and don't you forget it. Some guys around here seem to forget that little fact, some guys are gonna regret it. You'd be wise to remember it yourself — and if you want to be helpful, you might just spread the word that Danny Bunce has had it up to here with punks and snitches and self-righteous goody-two shoes. Tell 'em it's bad for their health to corner the tiger."

I gave Danny a mild look and a soft voice. "Ain't makin' no accusations, Danny. If the shoe don't fit, don't wear it — don't even try it on."

We rode the rest of the way in silence. Danny's was resentful, mine was thoughtful, filled with questions about Danny's disclosures and non-disclosures. He was genuine in his remorse about the effect of the debt on his family, of that I had no doubt. But why did he bring it up to me at all? Was it a temporary slip in his internal control? Was he holding back a pressure so strong he couldn't hold it down? In the end the whole evening left me with a welter of confusing feelings: suspicion, anger, sadness. Ralph, the meeting, and Danny. I let it all rumble around in my head as we pulled up to the Jacob Street address that I called home. I thanked Danny for the ride, got no response, and watched his car pull away into the Louisville night.

And then I filed it all away, eager to tell Margaret about the '48 Black Barons Willie Mays card.

Chapter Nine: Radio Two

MA: Mel Allen back again live, radio fans. Sorry about that break, but Lucky Strike pays the bills so you can hear the best of baseball right in your own living room. I've got Red Barber right here with me giving us the inside dope on the game. Looks like they're getting ready to resume play here in the bottom of the eighth, eh Red?

RB: That's right Mel, and at 5 to 1 Braves, the Redlegs have their work cut out for them.

MA: And the Reds have managed to load the bases, just like in the game book with the first three men in the rotation, which brings up the cleanup man, Jersey Jack Danielson, that young slugger they brought up last year from the Triple A league.

RB: Yep, and what a difference a year makes. Jersey Jack did okay in '65, but this year he has been knocking that apple out of one park after another.

MA: And if he's got one of those in him, this'd be the time to do it, Red, with the bases loaded and two away.

RB: Well here he is, Mel, Jersey Jack, swinging practice cuts like that 36-inch Louisville Slugger bat weighed no more'n a popsicle stick.

MA: Okay folks, heeeere's the windup--fastball low and outside--Jersey goes for it! Crack! uh-oh, don't like the sound of that, it's a hopper down to the shortstop from a cracked bat!

RB: Yep, Mel, there's gonna be a rhubarb now, 'cause Jersey Jack's out at first and doubling back...

MA: ...he's picked up that bat, Red. He's looking awful hard at that Slugger label...

RB: You're right, Mel, oh my, what a look... well, for the love of Mike, Jersey's stomping back to the dugout waving that bat like he's conducting the band with it!

MA: *Yeah, Red, and the tune wouldn't be Louisville Lou I'd bet!*

RB: *Now where did that come from, Mel?*

MA: *You mean you ain't heard of that vampin' lady Louisville Lou? Well sometime after we're off the air I'll sit you down and tell you all about her, Red.*

RB: *You do that, Mel, meanwhile the Braves have come to bat and Matty Alou is on deck and we've got a game to call…*

Chapter Ten: Margaret

Fred Durkin had lived in Shively, a one-time sundown town on Louisville's southwest side, the infamous scene where a black family had been dynamited by white racists in the 1950s. A civil and labor rights activist couple, Carl and Anne Braden, had been prosecuted for sedition against the state of Kentucky for having sold the house to the black family, allegedly to instigate the racist violence as a way of furthering the civil rights cause. The case was too absurd and convoluted even for so-called southern justice and was eventually thrown out, but not before Carl Braden had served eight months in prison. For folks who aren't acquainted with the delicacies of southern race practice vocabulary, a sundown town is a place where they put up signs that one way or another tell black folks they better not be caught there after the sun goes down.

Shively should have been a mere suburb of Louisville, in fact the city had been about to annex it, but the eight whiskey distilleries in the immediate area pushed the ward heelers of Jefferson County to incorporate it as a separate town so as to avoid higher city tax rates, promising to keep a goodly flow of tax money coming into the relatively small stick-built town, and from what Ray picked up from the Slugger rumor mill, the flow kicked back into quite a few private political pockets too. Things were cozy and white and the powers that be had kept it that way.

It took Margaret two bus transfers to get out to Shively and find Fred's neat, modest one-storey blue-gray German siding ranch house. The grass had grown up a little tall, so she guessed that Irma, his wife, hadn't found anybody to take Fred's place behind the mower yet. The house looked well kept, maybe had been painted just a few years back, and Margaret could see a few newer asphalt tiles on the roof. There was no garage, just a carport with a '62 Chevy four-door parked in it. The mailbox flag was down and the curtains were drawn across the front room picture window. There were a few kids playing cops and robbers a couple of blocks up the street in front of similar one-storey wood-sided houses, but whether out of consideration for the widow or simple coincidence, the block where Durkin had lived was filled with only the rush of a strong west wind pushing through the mix of poplar and pine trees that looked to have been planted about a dozen years ago when the development had gone in. Margaret felt an eerie stillness that wasn't quite accounted for by kindness to the widow. The block just seemed to be holding its breath — or at least the humans seemed to be. The trees made sighing sounds, and Margaret caught the scent of fear on those exhalations — human fear.

It all fit with what Danny B. had told Ray about Durkin. A fearful man, but a hard worker, a family man, kept his head down, his nose clean, paid his bills, kept his mouth shut when disputes arose at Slugger. Went out of his way to avoid black workers, so it didn't surprise Margaret that he lived in Shively, a place that loudly voted "law and order," yet broke the law with dynamite and could have killed had circumstances been just slightly different--had the child of the black family been in the bedroom that had been dynamited, where a fire took hold, and not in her parents' bedroom that night.

But Margaret was not here to condemn Durkin or his wife, whom she didn't know. Maybe Irma Durkin had opposed her husband's attitudes on race. Or maybe not. Margaret had a job to do and Irma might have information that would help her do it. And racist or not Irma had lost her husband, and that was a tragedy and a hurt that Margaret had to respect.

There was a doorbell to the left of her door, white with dark blue trim. Margaret pushed it but heard nothing. She stepped back away from the door so as not to press close in a threatening way at the entrance if Irma came and cracked it open.

Which, after Margaret waited a couple minutes under the rushing sound of the breeze, Irma did. Margaret looked into the dark slot, open about five inches on a chain latch, saw nothing, and spoke into it.

"Good morning, Missus Durkin, if that's who I'm talking to. I'm Margaret Odle, from the Odle Detective Agency. My husband, Ray, works down at the Slugger plant, and I wonder if I could have a few minutes of your time just to talk?"

A surprisingly clear but soft voice came out of the crack in reply, "You with the company or the union?"

"Well, not exactly either one, Missus Durkin. I'm not going to try and kid you or play games. I didn't know Fred, but I can truly say I am sorry for your loss. When any working man dies it is hard on the family left behind and I'm sure you have been hard hit. So I'm sorry for that and I know this is a very tough time for you." Margaret waited a long minute out of respect and to see if Irma had anything to say. She didn't, so Margaret went on.

"As for me, Ray and I are working on a contract with the national office of the WIA, which is a national union that Fred's local is affiliated with. The national office sent us to investigate his death, to find out what really happened, and in the process, make sure that the union doesn't get blamed unless it was the union, or some member, that was actually responsible for it. We won't lie for the union, but we won't let the company get away with lying about the union, either. Of course your husband's death might have nothing to do with either the company or the union. But it would help us do our job if I could talk a few minutes with you about Fred and what he thought about Slugger and his job and the union, things like that. Would that be all right with you?"

"You from the eastern mountains, Mizz Odle?" came the reply, still out of the darkness.

"Well, not exactly. But I had the privilege of living the last 32 years in Breathitt County."

The door closed, then opened, chain off, and Irma Durkin stepped out onto the front door stoop. She stood five foot two or so, had graying hair pulled straight back from either side into a pony tail, no makeup, a slim figure and a flowered house dress over navy blue slippers.

"Pikeville," she said, "come on in. Would you take a cup of coffee?"

"I surely would," Margaret said, "black," anticipating her next question.

"Come on back to the kitchen," Irma said and walked through the small living room furnished with a settee and an easy chair, around an open dining area, and into the kitchen. Margaret slipped onto a stool at the counter and soon had her hands folded around a chipped L&N railroad mug of black coffee. Irma preferred to stand leaning against the other side of the counter with a souvenir Louisville Slugger mug, her coffee heavily laced with milk and sugar. Margaret noticed the knobs right away as she watched this mountain woman standing, sometimes talking, opposite her. Knobs of arthritis in her knuckles as she gripped her mug of coffee, knobs on her elbows, knobs raising the thin cotton of her house dress at her shoulders. She wasn't that old, or at least didn't seem so by the look of her hair, her eyes, but she seemed to be tightly bound, knobby from tension held fiercely, so fiercely, and for so long, that it had brought on the accretions and distortions of a disease of joints.

Margaret started out with small talk about Irma's house, found out that it was one of the oldest in Rone Court, the original development of fifteen houses that had formed Shively some twenty-five years earlier, back when they still used wood siding and brick chimneys and car ports instead of garages. Irma was proud of their having made it to Shively,

83

having come from little Appalachia in Louisville, the section where Margaret was now living. Irma was from Pikeville, Kentucky, in Pike County, had come with her Ma and Pa as a little girl when the coal tipple had shut down up the creek where they'd worked back in the late 40s, but Fred had been born right here in Louisville.

Irma said that the forced move had crushed her Pa down into the bottle and he'd disappeared. Her Ma had gone to work two shifts as a hotel maid to try and feed Irma and her three younger sisters and one little brother. Irma had grown up having to take care of her little sisters and brother, then when they were old enough to be in school, she'd gone truant from high school and gone to work herself, dodging men pawing at her behind and breasts as well as the prying eyes of truant officers while flipping burgers at a diner down by the Oak Street yard of the L&N railroad.

"I met Fred Durkin there one night when he was working the extra board, on-call for shifts at night at the yard. He was cute as a button back then, sure was. I don't know what in the dickens got into me, but I just up and went all bold on him for some reason I ain't yet to figure out, and asked him to a church ice cream social, and the rest was history, as they say." She stopped to stare out the window, remembering.

"That man worked some pretty awful jobs after that, too, trying to keep us goin' — I mean digging ditches, painting houses part-time, then working the night shift at G.E., before he got on at Slugger back in 1952. He was damn grateful for that job, grateful for the job and grateful to a certain neighbor out here in Shively who'd helped him to get it. At least at first, but that ain't the half of the story."

Margaret decided to wait, let the proud woman tell the other half of the story in her own good time. As Irma talked Margaret studied her face, which was a picture book of her life as a mountain woman trying to live in the city. There was a hardness in it, in the lines above her cheeks, around her eyes, down the sides of her mouth. But her smile erased them all, or not so much erased them, but turned them into lines that made you want to smile with her, made them have a beauty, a sense of goodness coming from somewhere deep down in her, a place hard won and well protected, not easy to reach, but real.

Margaret asked about her family, discovered that she and Fred had the one son, Billy, who was off in Lexington at the University of Kentucky in his senior year. She seemed proud of Billy's ability in science, seemed he was a chemist and headed for a job with Procter and Gamble. Margaret asked if he was named after a grandfather or some other relative, just kind of warming her up in the general course of the conversation. And got a surprise.

"Not hardly," she said. "Back twenty years ago my husband was besotted with a man, his best friend and old-fashion bosom companion, a man he badly misjudged, as it turned out, but one he did ever' thing a brother might do with a brother—fishing the creeks and farm ponds and lakes around here on Sunday mornings—so much so I had to get after 'im about missing church an' settin' a bad example for young Billy. Then there was him working on that man's jalopy trying to turn it into a race car, a sure 'nuff sow's ear to a silk purse project if ever there was one, not to mention going to ever' Colonels baseball game they played at home till they folded after the '63 season. Well, Freddy named our son after that man, and now poor Billy is stuck with the name and Fred is stuck with the shame."

Margaret waited, didn't ask the obvious question. Irma had opened the door, and either she was going to walk through it and tell Margaret or she wasn't. Margaret just looked at her with as open and harmless a look as she could give, which was easy because Margaret felt no judgment of this woman.

"Well, you might as well hear it from me as from somebody bad mouthin' my Fred, or from some stranger as has no interest in his good name," she finally continued, after a long

85

look up and down Margaret's face and what of her body Irma could see above the counter, a look of final assessment if there ever was one.

"You look an honest woman, and I've had enough years to be pretty good at tellin' the honest ones from the sneaks, the ones with backbone from the yeller ones, an' the traitors from the friends. An' I knew that Fred had got hisself close up to a wrongun' from the minute I laid eyes on that Billy Jenkins, sure did."

"You mean the Billy Jenkins that works at the Slugger plant and heads up the union chapter?" Margaret was stunned.

"The very same," she said, "but what happened down at the plant ain't the betrayal I'm talking about. It happened right here in Shively. Right here just a couple years after we made our down payment on this place and moved in. See, Billy's dad was connected to the developer out here, worked for the developer's bank, kind of a salesman, and he sold a house to them Braden people, these Civil Rights agitators, who then sold it to this family of colored folks, the Wades. Well, all hell broke loose when us white folks found out about it. Far as we was concerned, it was downright underhanded.

"That was in 1954, like I said, two years after Fred and I bought and moved in. Only we didn't buy from no bank, we couldn't afford it. Fred had just started at Slugger and I had to quit at the diner since it was too far to go from here and we only had the one car. So we bought it on terms through the builder, or really his finance man, who was Billy Jenkins' daddy's boss, no money down. There was some paperwork, of course, and Freddy, he signed it happy as a jaybird. Well, I have to say I didn't give it no mind either. You'd think that after so many of us mountain people had been rooked by the Broad Form Deed we'd be a might more suspicious of bankers and developers and the owners of things we're borrowing from, but we ain't and we get taken ever' blasted time."

"Amen to that!" Margaret said and thumped the table with her fist.

86

"Right soon as they could the folks around here got up a secret committee to drive the Wades out and demand that the county prosecute the Bradens on some type of charge, put 'em in jail. Well, I didn't hold with that. I didn't like the idea of the Wades in here, property values goin' down and all, but I figured they had a right to be here an' won't nothin' I could do about it. That was how I felt at first. I wasn't exactly with the sundown community idea but I sure didn't like the idea of no coloreds in my neighborhood neither.

"Then, one day, this Baptist church lady come knockin' on my door and asked to speak to me about it. I didn't rightly want to have nothing to do with her, but I was taught to give people a chance, to be polite, and that sometimes the Lord comes to you when you least expect Him and in the form you don't recognize, like it says in the Bible, the least of these. So I let her in and we talked. Well, the short of it is that she made me see that hate don't do no good, and lo and behold she took me down the street and introduced me to Mrs. Wade, and we had a cup of coffee, and I realized that she was a fine Christian lady too."

"So you got up close and personal," Margaret said. "Happened to me in the fights we had in the coal wars back about that same time. Some of the best brothers and sisters in the fight were black, and you know, I realized that the color of the foot standing on my neck was white, not black. Changes the way you see things, doesn't it!"

"Don't know about all that, but she was nice. And it was that very night they blew up half that poor family's house, just like that committee said they would. I got after my Freddy and we talked and talked and prayed about it, and we went to some meetings a few of the people had out here, friends of the Bradens and one or two from Shively who was trying to help the Wades, and, well, we decided we couldn't go along with it no more. So when the committee asked us to sign a petition agin' the Wades, we said 'no'. That brought Billy Jenkins around to our door.

"Uh-oh, I was afraid that's where you were going," Margaret said.

"He threatened to move Fred to second shift at Slugger. But my Freddy, he don't scare that easy. He might not be a leader or out front type of man, he's quiet and he won't take a stand in public if he can help it, but once he makes up his mind, it's made up. So he told Billy no, go on and do what you got to do."

Margaret admired folks like that. They are the backbone of every movement and organizing campaign she'd ever been a part of. She knew you have to have a few out-front types, sure, but mostly you need the Fred and Irma Durkins. And she told Irma that.

"That's as may be," she said. "But for all the good it does the cause, it didn't do us no good 'cause Billy went right ahead and put Freddy on second shift. Then a couple weeks later the committee and old man Jenkins, Harrison Jenkins, Billy's daddy, the builder's agent, started a case in court saying the Wades had violated nuisance laws by making noise and having too many people in the house and trashing up the neighborhood. Well, the Wades said they needed character witnesses, people who'd go into court and just say that the Wades was decent and didn't make a lot of noise or trash the neighborhood, stuff like that. Well it won't nothing more than the truth, so I agreed. And my name came out on a list that was sent to the lawyers for the committee and old man Jenkins. So I got visited by the committee and told if I knew what was good for me and Freddy I'd take my name off that list. I told them I won't afraid and to get off my property."

Then Irma's voice got real soft. She put her cup down and her hands on the counter and looked at me, her eyes growing wet around the edges.

"That's the night they burned a cross on our front yard," she said. "My neighbors, my friends, my fellow Christians who'd sung hymns to the Lord with me for two years on Sunday mornings and evenings and on Wednesday night

88

prayer meetings. The next morning old man Jenkins come by and caught Freddy before work and told both of us that if I testified in court he'd have to call in our loan and we'd have to pay up within 30 days or lose the house."

"Now that's what I call real hard ball," Margaret said, low but with an edge of anger in her voice. She'd had about all she could take of Christian hypocrisy and betrayal in her own life after seeing it happen over and over again in the coal wars.

"Well, we had no choice but to turn to the folks that was helping the Wades and ask if they could now help us. We won't goin' to back down if we could find any way a'tall to help it. We met with Anne Braden and got the surprise of our life. Turned out she won't no Communist like ever'body said, she was a Christian too, a church going lady, and when it come down to it, a real kind woman. She fixed us up with a lawyer who filed some papers in the same case quick, fast and in a hurry, which said it was witness intimidation, which is against the law. We told what happened under oath in what they called a deposition and that was the end of that. Old man Jenkins went away.

"So we give our testimony for the Wades in court, and so did a few other folks, although only one other from Rone Court, and the case against them was thrown out and that was that. Except there was more an' more incidents, a firebombing of the Bradens' house, and then the Bradens was arrested and charged with trying to overthrow the government of Kentucky. They called it 'sedition' or some such, and all hell broke loose in the press. Then Anne Braden's husband, Carl, got convicted and did eight months in prison before the appeals court finally threw the whole thing out. Turns out you can't be convicted of what that 'sedition' thing is against a state government, only the federal government.

"But the pressure on the Wades was something terrible and it kept on and on. So the Wades moved out. And Shively is still lily white and proud of it."

Irma looked out the kitchen window for several minutes. Margaret just waited. "That's some story," she finally said. "You have good reason to be proud of yourself and Fred too. Are you?"

She turned her head and eyes down for a bit, then chuckled softly and raised them, looking clear and straight into mine. "I don't believe in praying on the street corner, but I guess I am. It changed my life in some ways, and I think for the better. So yes. And I believe Freddy would have said the same."

Then her eyes clouded over. It was like when a storm cloud comes over the nearest hilltop and sends its shadow ahead and darkens the whole world in an instant. She drew in a great bellows-full of air and heaved it out forcefully. She was calm, the calm before the storm, holding everything in check. Yet Margaret knew the storm would not come, would never come, of its own accord. For Irma Durkin had not let it burst yet, was not the kind of person who would do so easily, if ever. That was the testimony of the knobs.

"But there's more," Margaret said, not a question.

"Yes. I guess there is. Billy kept after Freddy at Slugger. Oh, he tried to get him fired. Kept taking bats—piece rate, you know—off his ticket and giving them to other men, saying Freddy hadn't made his day rate, sometimes cutting his level of piece rate so we'd have less and less money. He'd do it every few months, not so much as to make it real obvious, you know, so that the bosses wouldn't know he had it in for Freddy, but just to try and mess with Freddy, mostly to keep Freddy from getting promoted. But Freddy kept his own count in a notebook after the first few times, and he'd go to Benson, sometimes all the way to Mr. Worthington and show them his notebook. And since Billy wasn't a supervisor or anything, they finally told him to butt out and leave Freddy alone. But there was bad blood, no doubt about it. And to some extent it worked for Billy, because since there was a question about my husband, Freddy got passed over for promotion into the P.R.O. section at least twice since the Wade case."

She paused quite a long while at that point. Then Irma Durkin gave me a long look. A look of concern. "I'm going to tell you this, Mizz Odle, one woman to another. I know you're different than me and maybe you're a whole lot stronger. But I'm giving you a warning. That Billy Jenkins is like a cur dog. A mean sly cowardly cur dog. He won't bark at you, he won't run at you in the front and attack. But he'll be silent as the fall of night and run up behind you and slash your legs from behind and cripple you if he can. Better watch that man."

"Thank you, I'll take your warning seriously," Margaret said. "But back to your story. The passing over for promotions at Slugger was not the worst of it, right? That's not what caused that huge whoosh of breath back a minute or so, is it?"

Irma looked out the kitchen window again. Then came back to Margaret.

"No. It was something to do with the union. I...I don't know what it was exactly. I just don't...Oh God, I wish I did! We argued, Mizz Odle. We argued about it and we almost never fought about anything. Freddy had been moping about the house after work for weeks and I'd been after him about it. He kept going down to Slugger on Sunday afternoons, saying he had to check on some records, which I'd never seen him do before. Records? What records? I'd never had any reason not to believe him before, but this time I just couldn't. I told him so. He got really mad, and so did I.

"Then that blond-headed man, that Haskell fellow, Worthington's attack dog, showed up out here one night banging on the door demanding that Freddy come out. Fred refused, told him to go to hell. The man kicked on our door and threatened to shoot the lock off. I was downright terrified and ran for the phone to call the police but Freddy grabbed me by the shoulders so rough it nearly jerked my arm out of the socket. He never done nothing like that to me before, never. Finally Haskell went away, yelling that he'd see Freddy at Slugger and Freddy had better have some answers. But Mizz Odle, I never knew what the questions were, much less the answers!

"And no matter what I said, no matter how many times I begged, Freddy refused to tell me anything other than he'd found out something about the union gone wrong and he was going to fix it. He said it was just like the Wade thing in a way, and that if I'd just leave him alone and let him take care of it, I'd be proud of him some day, so let it be. So I did, I did let it be, and oh God, Mizz Odle, look what happened!"

She wrung her hands and Margaret reached across the counter and held them.

"I don't know what was going on, Mizz Odle, but whatever it was, I fear it involved Billy Jenkins and the union election and I think it got my Freddy killed!"

When I let go of her, she put her head down into her hands and let the sobs come, stifled, silent, held back as much as possible, only letting them out to the degree absolutely necessitated by the force of emotion and biology.

Margaret waited, her own eyes filling with tears. While she waited, she thought over what she knew, what she'd heard. Jenkins was a weak union president, no doubt about that. Ray had seen it with his own eyes and told her so. And Margaret believed Irma about the Wade case and Billy Jenkins' betrayal of her husband. The bad blood from that had been compounded by Jenkins' attempts to hurt Durkin's status at Slugger, and finally whatever Fred had found out that was "wrong" about the union. But all of that pointed to Fred having a motive against Jenkins—but it was Fred Durkin's head on the auto-lathe, not Billy Jenkins's.

Finally Irma's storm passed. She pulled herself up onto the other stool by the counter, no longer able to stand, and sat quietly, leaning with her elbows on the counter, head slumped forward, her knotty hands folded flat on the counter top in the repose left to her in the storm's aftermath. Margaret decided that more talk would be a burden, that Irma Durkin needed time alone and rest. Margaret spoke quietly into the stillness.

"I just want to say I've spent my share of time at the front lines in the fights for working folks, Mrs. Durkin," she said, "and it's always been an honor to meet someone with the courage you have. I need to take my leave now, but I thank you for this time and what you've given of yourself this morning, I do. I know it hasn't been easy."

Irma lifted her head and let her now red-rimmed eyes fall on Margaret's. "It's been necessary, and somehow telling it to you has made it better, Mizz Odle." She paused, looked out the kitchen window for a long minute at the madly whirling poplar leaves, the successive bending waves of the evergreens. Then turned back and resumed in an even voice, a voice coming from the calm the storm had left in her.

"I'm not one to be out there in them fights you talk about. The one I told about came to me, not the other way around. But I'm glad you're out there doing what you do, and I hope I've helped you just a little bit. Come back to see me if I can be of further help."

Irma Durkin reached her bent hands across the counter, lowered them, and placed them gently upon Margaret's.

"A good morning to you," she said, looking straight at Margaret with brightening eyes. "A very good morning."

They held the gaze and the hands for a good while.

"Then I'll say goodbye," Margaret finally said, "and let myself out."

Margaret stepped through the door of that ordinary house and looked back to see the aluminum storm door automatically close on the storm, now contained, not entirely passed, that resided inside Irma Durkin. And as she walked down that street in Shively, Margaret noticed more than a few window shades slip closed as she passed. Margaret wondered what kinds of storms were contained inside those structures, and what kind of violence would be unleashed, and against what kind of people, if they were to break open on the outside.

And then on the two buses she had to take to get home, Margaret thought about the two ordinary, hard working people who'd been Irma and Fred Durkin. White people who'd come up fairly rough, and much like millions of their fellows, had followed the Christian road, had taken their knocks, but had come out kind to their own kind, had kept to their own kind and kept away from other kinds. But then the other kind had come to their neighborhood, into their lives, their consciousness, to their direct attention—and they'd been forced to pay attention and to choose. To choose enmity or kindness, hostility or friendship, war or welcome.

And sadly, between church and charity. The preachers and Bible pushers and false prophets and Pharisees of their neighborhood, prideful in their explicit religiosity, had loudly proclaimed themselves for Christ and against the "communists" who'd tried to introduce them to a black family. But they'd burned the welcome wagon and bombed the home of the family and its child, then tried to throw Irma and Fred into the street for merely abstaining from blind hatred and violence.

Between church and charity. "And there abideth faith, hope and charity. But the greatest of these is charity." That's what the Apostle Paul had said, and by charity he meant love. The Durkins had chosen charity.

Now what has to be figured out, she thought, as her bus window view slipped block by block from the Southside suburbs into the streets of inner city Little Appalachia, was whether Fred Durkin had died for his quiet, simple stand for charity—or for something else.

Chapter Eleven: Ray

"Willya have another cup of this chicory coffee, Ray?" George asked, pulling a thermos of the nutty smelling brew from the table and tipping it over my mug. "Sure," I said with a grin, "you make it strong as yesterday's socks, just like I do at home."

We were sitting on his back porch about nine that Saturday morning watching his oldest son shooting hoops on bare dirt at a somewhat tilting backboard George had nailed to an old oak tree. " George tipped the thermos higher and higher. A couple of drips came out, then nothing.

"Ellie why don't ya brew up some more coffee?"

I heard a muffled voice say something my ears couldn't make out and feet began to scrape behind the screen door that led into the kitchen. About a fourth of the screen had ripped away from its frame so the flies came and went as they pleased.

George Salvatore lived in a one-story shingle-sided house on a weed-punctuated side street right on the no-man's land between the far, poor, black West End of Louisville and the white East Side. I'd taken the Broadway bus and noticed the storefronts getting shabbier and shabbier as I went west. There was an oil refinery smack in the middle of the West End and the haze and stench floated down and seemed to coat the streets in gray film for many blocks around it. When I walked up from Broadway I'd noticed a "For Rent" sign leaning up from a patch of intermittent crabgrass by the front walk.

We yakked about the plant being closed that morning, then about whether or not the union would get the blame for

Gorham's murder. George just repeated the generalities that went round and round the smoke break benches at the plant. He ventured nothing original.

Ellie came out with coffee wearing Bermuda shorts and a haltertop that showed her fulsome breasts in obvious good shape, despite her years. She poured me a cup, then leaned across the old telephone wire spool serving as an outdoor table to fill George's cup. He took a good look down her haltertop and wiggled his eyebrows. Ellie snorted at him, flapped her free hand dismissively and said her mother was needing her help inside, and left.

"You fixin' to leave this place, George?" I said, sipping on the hot savory coffee. He waited till he'd got his cigarette lit before he made to answer me.

"'Fraid I have to. Can't make the rent. Her Momma's got to have a gall bladder operation and that'll take what little savings I been squirreling away from the piece-rate down at Slugger. Damn sure seems like a man just can't make a nickel these days no way."

"Ain't easy, won't get no easier, the way things are goin'," I said. "Makes you dream about that man on the TV walkin' up to your door with that million dollar check, don't it?" The coffee was good and welcome. It had some chicory in it, took my mind back to the chicory coffee my Momma's people made over to eastern North Carolina, little place outside Goldsboro where her mother, six aunts and an uncle had been raised. She and Daddy had met at a Southern Baptist church camp called Ridgecrest in the western mountains of North Carolina back when Daddy was a teenager and still religion-minded. They walked the aisle of the church to rededicate themselves to Jesus and I guess they liked the experience so much that just eighteen months later they did it again to get married. But Daddy made it clear that his home was in Lawrence County, Kentucky, so Momma was the one who moved, not him. But she longed for that piney woods country of eastern North Carolina all of her days, right up till the day

96

she died of a heart attack at sixty-one. Her old home was a place of hard-scrabble four and five acre tobacco farms with maybe a few dairy cows, maybe some corn for feed and garden, and here and there a whiskey still back in the pines for hard times and low tobacco prices.

In my head I drifted back to her family's reunions that happened every fourth of July. Once in a while my Daddy took us down out of the hills of eastern Kentucky to join them, when he had time off owed to him from his job and couldn't find an excuse not to go. Seemed he didn't like that bunch, always said they put on airs like they were Old South or some such, instead of the farming and merchant class rednecks they really were. He hated the uncle, especially, because the man was a prison-gang shotgun Captain who always showed up with his blood-hounds and guns talkin' about nigger this and nigger that. Daddy figured him for Klan, and 'cause of that, he always told me never to listen to the bastard. Which for Daddy was a break from his usual refusal to use curse words.

"That'll be the day," George snorted, yanking me back to his patio and the Millionaire TV show I'd just mentioned. "If it weren't for bad luck I'd have no luck at all!"

"Me too," I said. Then I tried to turn the conversation in the direction I wanted to go. "Had to learn the hard way to stay away from cards and dice, just cain't take no chances on chance. Do an' I'll be busted quicker'n Jack be Nimble."

"Yeah. Prob'ly I should take that advice too," he said. "But somehow I keep thinkin' I can get a little extra, you know, to make ends meet, maybe keep this place. But it don't seem to be workin' out thataway."

Just then his kid whooped and came running up to us and bounced the basketball off the wall of the house.

"Jason, I done told you..." barked George.

"But Dad, I just hit ten jumpers in a row from beyond the foul line!" Jason crowed.

"You tear them shingles off the wall here, son, and it's gonna be me and you goin' round and round an' you know who wins at that!" George looked hard, then relaxed his face a little. "Jason here," he said, turning to me, "made the first string on his JV team last year. Had a sixteen-point average. Them boys just missed going to the state tournament. Done right good."

Jason stood a bit taller at this, then grabbed the ball and headed back to the hoop.

I picked up the thread from where we'd been, taking it closer to my goal. "So…you do a little poker or something like that on the side?"

"Well, no, not poker. But I do a little betting here and there."

"Horses, ehh. Seems to go with the territory around here," I said.

"Nope. I guess it don't hurt none to tell you. You seem like a stand-up guy to me. Not horses, baseball. Kind of a busman's holiday type wager, seein' as how we're sort of in the business."

"Well now, that's interesting, George," I said, acting ignorant and leaning over towards him. "You mean the boys at the plant got some type of pool goin'?"

"Nope, not like that. Some of us are in it, but it's a city-wide thing or maybe bigger, I don't rightly know. There's a guy at the plant that comes around and takes bets for the games for the coming week, then after the week is over, he comes around to collect if you lose or give you the winnings if you win."

"Don't say? Sounds right smart organized to me."

"Boy, you said it," said George, his face showing the extra blush of excitement.

"Okay, but how exactly does it work, you don't mind my askin'," I said.

"Well, there's some outfit somewhere that makes up the odds on who's gonna win and who's gonna lose, see. I don't know where they are at or nothin', but the man that comes around to the boys has these slips with the games and odds wrote up in letters and numbers, sort of a code. We give him our bet, how much for which team to win or lose, on each game. He puts it on our slip an' he's got a master slip himself where he writes it down. And you wait an' see how she comes out."

"Now, what do you mean by 'the odds' on this stuff?" I asked.

"Well, what it come down to is you're betting against what they call the moneyline," said George. "Hold on," he jumped up and ran into the kitchen. I watched Jason at the hoops raising dust in the breezeless air, grabbing a rebound, dribbling back to about twenty feet, wheeling and shooting a jump shot, over and over. He only missed about two in ten.

George came back with a piece of lined school notebook paper and a fat black pencil, the kind where you unravel the outer wrapping with a string to keep the point sticking out. "Okay," he said scribbling on the paper, "a moneyline odds figure might look like this:
WHITE SOX -120; YANKEES +110." He showed me his paper.

"See, they leave the decimal point out, so 120 is the same as 1.20. If you want to bet on the favored team, the White Sox, you have to bet $1.20 for every $1 you want to win. If you want to bet on the underdog Yankees, you only have to bet $1 for every $1.10 you want to win. The betting man calls this here the dime line, because ten cents separate the top dog from the underdog. Got it?"

"So far. But I'm still kind of fuzzy on it." I scratched my head for emphasis. I wanted to keep him talking.

"Okay, here's an example: figure that using the moneyline with the White Sox and the Yankees, you want to win about $100. If you place your bet on the favored White Sox, you will pay the betting man $120. If you win, you get your $120 back, plus $100 in winnings. If you lose, the bookie keeps your $120. If you bet $100 on the Yankees, you'll get your hundred dollar bet back plus $110 in winnings if they win, and only lose $100 if they lose."

"So the organization, or whoever," I said, "is betting that the moneyline odds are right, and they're also betting that more of you guys guess wrong than guess right?"

"Yep. And of course it costs ten bucks to play, and they keep that, win or lose."

George fidgeted with the pencil, doodling some stars and Xs on the page. I sat back and studied him a minute, nodding my head, then scratching it, acting like I was working hard to take it all in. Just then Ellie popped open the screen door and asked if I wanted more coffee. George crumpled up the paper in a flash. I said no and Ellie threw a hard look at George, then went back inside. He stuffed the wad of paper in his pocket. "Good shot!" he shouted over to Jason, not seeing that Jason had missed.

"So," I said, "who's the betting man what comes around at Slugger? I mean, can a new guy like me get in on this deal?"

George looked surprised, then stuck his thumb on his chin, shuffled his feet beside the cable spool, looked out at Jason again, held the gaze for a few beats. Then he cleared his throat.

"Well, don't know if I should tell, Ray, no offense. I got sort of invited to start in on this moneyline thing by another man at Slugger. From that I kind of figured you had to be asked. It ain't for everybody, see. Besides, I would've guessed you'd have known the man. But that's all I'm gonna say. Maybe said too much already. I got the feelin' this outfit don't mess around. Maybe we just oughta drop it."

"Okay, but one more thing I'd like to know, George—what outfit?"

"Don't know. Don't want to know. I just get a bad feelin' about it, that's all. Look, I got a visit from that blond guy, Haskell, works for that detective agency that Worthington hired to investigate the Gorham thing. Spooked the hell out of me. I figured he was gonna ask about Gorham maybe snitching on the union, bein' as how that's the rumor, right? Well, yeah, he mentions that, but that ain't what he burrows in on—no, it's mostly about this betting stuff. Hell, he knew I was in on it right from the get-go. Scared me shitless! So please don't ask me no more questions, Ray. You want some more coffee?"

"I gotta ask, now you brought it up, George—what'd you tell the man?"

"Not a damn thing, Ray. I told him I didn't know what he was talking about. Just shut up. He got kind of nasty too. Kept mentioning how it was a shame about my mother-in-law's sickness and medical bills and how it'd be a shame if I lost my job. I just plain lost it, I sure did. Told him to get the hell out. The wife got so sore at me over that she didn't speak to me for a week, near 'bout. Now that's all I'm gonna say, Ray. You sure you don't want more coffee?"

I was thunderstruck. Blondie was running interference for the betting line? Or was there a link between whoever was running the moneyline and Slugger? He had information about Slugger workers who were on the betting slips? But it was clear that George was clamming up. No point in getting him angry at me. I needed to be on his side.

I pointed to my cup that Ellie had just filled up. "Reckon not, George. I'm sorry that Blondie, that's my name for that Haskell fella, tried to push you around like that. The thugs from outfits like the Pinkertons and the Burns goons and these H & R guys, that's what they always do. I seen it over and over in the eastern mountains where I come from. But you done right good by throwin' the sorry bastard out. He ain't got no right to threaten your family like that."

"Thanks, Ray. Don't reckon I did myself no good in the long run, though."

"I disagree, George. By my lights you never lose in the long run by standing up for yourself and your rights. If you get any hint of a job action at Slugger behind this you just file on it and let me know. We guys on the line can make sure WIA national hears about it even if Billy Jenkins is too weak to take action to defend you."

"Hey, that Jenkins is tight with Haskell too, Ray. I seen them head-to-head at the Sunrise coffee shop last week afore the first shift, just the two of 'em. I was goin' by on the bus, there's a stop right across the street from the Sunrise, and right there is a big fat window. I'm half-ass looking and all the sudden I seen Billy's white topknot—you can't miss that hair of his—bobbing up and down and I looked harder on account of that, and bang! There's your Blondie, sure as I'm settin' here now, right in the booth with Billy."

I was dismayed, but not quite so shocked at this news. It figured. Billy was a sweetheart union boss trying to kiss rather than kick butt with Worthington. I'd seen that already. So he'd naturally want to get in with Worthington's allies, the boss-man's muscle, H & R. Still, it stank, no way around it. This visit was paying off in a big way. Yet it was time for me to go, I could see that George was really nervous now. Time to lower the tension level.

"That boy of yours, he's a damn good shot, I'll give him that," I said, "wish I had a son like him."

After a little more chit-chat I made my thank you's and goodbyes and left.

Chapter Twelve: Radio three

Mel Allen: Mel Allen back live here at Wrigley Field, Chicago, folks. Say that Lucky Strike jingle you heard about during the break ain't lying one bit, LS does for sure mean FT—fine tobacco. I bet 'ol Red Barber here smokes 'em, too, don't ya Red?

Red Barber: Well, yeah, when I smoke the stuff, that is. You know me, Mel, sometimes in this July weather I'd rather have a little..."

MA: ...snort! Once a radio man, always a radio man, I guess. Back to the game. It's two away here in the top of the ninth and the Cubs are knocking on victory's door again, leading by a run. What's the prognosis this time, Doctor Barber?

RB: The Cubs have a one run lead over Cincinnati, who have Harper on second on a walk followed by a sacrifice fly by Coleman, but the fans in Chicago haven't popped the cap on the Falstaff yet, Mel. They've learned the hard way. But judging from their stance, Kingman at second base, Larry Bruce at shortstop, and Findlay at third base, they know they've got to stop the run, so they're playing it deep.

MA: True, Red, which is on the money since the bases are loaded and Jersey Jack, the clean-up hitter for the Redlegs is up.

RB: Yep, and if Jack ends up anywhere short of safe on base, the game's over, Mel, and the Cubs end the first half of the season in second place, not the basement.

MA: Well here's the pitch to Jersey Jack. Fastball high outside. Swings and a crack of the bat! It's just a pop fly just over second base. Harry Kingman's dropping back off the bag for it, he's got his glove up…

RB: Jeez! the sun's in Kingman's eyes, he's wandering, he's lost the ball, Mel…

Here comes Jackson, the right fielder, on a hard charge…Ball's dropping now…Now Bruce at shortstop's going back for it…

MA: Oh no! I don't believe it! It's a pileup just back of the dirt — three men in a heap! There he goes! Harper rounds the bag at third, Red, charging for home like a wild bull!

RB: But the ball's still loose, bouncing towards third base. Findlay's coming over from third to field it on the bounce…Harper is in for the tying run …

MA: Now here comes Jersey Jack around second heading to third for a go at it, but I gotta say he's moving none too fast. Kingman scoops the ball up, cocks his arm for the throw to third…

Help! Findlay's still off the bag at third…Kingman can't throw…

RB: Jersey Jack rounds third…How could this happen, for God's sake!

MA: Kingman throws to home…Jersey Jack is moving like he's got lead in his feet, Red, what's going on…

RB: Jersey Jack is out at home…tagged standing up! You don't see that every day, Mel!

MA: Look! Jersey Jack's gone over to the batter's box…He's picking up something…

RB: Well, will ya look at that, Mel? It's his bat, only it's busted!

MA: Whoa, fans, it's even more fantastic than you thought! This whole thing started with a pop-up due to a busted bat!

RB: Jeez, Mel, d'ya think Louisville Slugger can make up a new jingle on that one?

MA: I dunno about that, Red, but Jersey Jack's back in the dugout on his knees, thanking the Man upstairs.

RB: …maybe he's thanking somebody in them new Sky Boxes instead, Mel, one of the Fat Cats, you know, the inheritors of the late Alphonse…uh, one of the more colorful characters known to inhabit this town…

MA:…we better stick to the Lord, Red, He's a whole lot safer for your skin, and from the look of it, Jersey's plenty grateful for something out there…

RB: Now I gotta wonder about that, Mel. What's he got to thank the Lord for – Jersey Jack was out standing up!

MA: Do ya think the Big Fan in the Sky is a Cubbies fan too, Red?…

RB: Nah, Mel, look at the track record…Lord's gotta have more clout than that!

Chapter Thirteen: Ray

"Man you can't make it on this shit they're payin' in here, you know you can't."

Jack Duvall was holding forth, the auto-lathe worker who'd led his fellows to confront Worthington early on when the company had shut down the lathe room. He had a nose like a knife blade, black hair slicked straight back, and a voice rumbling like a boxcar on a rough patch of the line. The boys in the lathe room were lined up on the smoke break bench. The company was still not letting us work on Durkin's or Gorham's old lathes, so that meant that there were only two auto-lathes of the four running for the day. I was sitting down at one end, trying to jot down some notes on the case but listening all the same.

"Look Jack, I was reading in the paper the other day about the medium family income, ya'll, and we're makin' less than the average, and I ain't lying." That was Will Davison, who had a hog-jawed and tobacco-jammed mouth, tiny ears and a nose the shape and color of a Roma tomato. He'd fought for the union, so I heard, and demanded that blacks be allowed in it, a fight he'd eventually won because he'd caught the leader of the whites-only faction stealing from the union's petty cash, discredited him just before the vote.

"How you figure that?" said Duvall.

Davison had done his homework. "If you're in your first year in here, you make a buck sixty-five, am I right? And maybe you'll make some piece rate, put that up close to two dollars, so Okay, say two dollars. Working the regular week, that's $4,160 a year. They say the average family income is $4,500. That's how I figure that!"

"All's I know is I can't make ends meet," said Henry Stover, thin as a pencil with a flat nose and a flat head sporting a one-inch flattop. "Milk is 99 cent, gas is 32 cent, costs me six-forty to fill'er up. I gotta burn two gallons a day just to get back and forth to this job. That's nearly a full tank a week. Rent's one-fifty a month. Time I pay for gas, rent, mebbe sixty or seventy for food, school books and shoes for four growin' brats, and what I still owe on that hunk a junk I drive, I'm 'bout broke by the end of every month."

The boys on the bench were in full cry talking like they do every day during smoke breaks, only this was an all-day smoke break for Duvall and Davison, and for the second day in a row, because the lathes were still behind police tape. I guessed that Worthington hadn't figured out what else for them to do.

Then, sitting two guys down from me, a guy named Al Burleson broke into my thoughts. "Damn nigs, they just set on their asses and collect damn near as much as a working white man."

I turned to look at Burleson. Another skinny guy, Burleson had a left leg shorter than his right, swayed side-to-side when he walked, but strange enough, it helped him do the lathe job, his left hand being the one that took the bats out at the bottom, was always lower down when he leaned that way. Rumor was he was in the KKK. Danny B had told me Burleson was trying to turn the union back into white only.

I just looked at him and shook my head. Guys in the hills and guys in the mills all over the South will work and vote against their own self-interest if some silk-stocking lawyer type, some banker, some Governor-appointed member of the White Citizen's Council plays the race card. They'll start a rumor that so-and-so Black man is after so-and-so white man's wife, sister, daughter or what have you. Or they'll let it be known that workers can expect a cut in the piece-rate if they form an integrated union or let blacks into the whites-only union the company just barely tolerates. Most northern liberals look at that and think we're just a bunch of dumb peckerwoods down here. And maybe we are, or leastways a bunch of us are, but the Yankees ain't under the gun like we are. They ain't starving or slaving to keep from starving in a company, a town, a state controlled by pin-striped country-club racists that don't mind using the state police, the local sheriff, the sheriff's posse or even the Ku Klux Klan to do their dirty work.

And those northerners don't know the other side of the story, neither. The Southern Tenant Farmers' Union, for example. They fought — black and white, men and women, side by side, all during the '30s and right up to this day to break the hold of the sharecrop system on poor farmers. They won some victories, created integrated coop farms, lost some battles, suffered deaths, beatings, and imprisonments. And there is no way to just let it go. You have to fight that snake every time it raises its poisonous head. I figured I'd try and talk to Burleson in private sometime and tell him what his real inheritance is as a white workingman. But for now, he had to be checked. So, against my better judgment, I piped up.

"Hey, Al," I said, "why doncha take a good look at the foot that's standin' on your neck? The foot that's holdin' you and your family down. The one that's set up this here wages and piece-rate system for you to take or leave it. While you're at it, tell me what color it is, man."

Burleson braced me at the lunch break. I figured it was coming, so I just stood up when the buzzer rang and waited for him. He stuck his face up next to mine, chewing on the butt of an unlit cigarette he'd stuck in his mouth at the buzzer.

"They say you're some kind of hot-shot organizer from back in the hills," he growled like a hoarse tomcat.

"Maybe," I said. "Been around enough to know it ain't black folks we're fighting if'n we want to get a fair shake for us an' our families. If that makes me a hot-shot, they's a helluva lot of us white men what's learned that lesson these last few years."

"Fuck that fairness, shit, man. That's liberal talk. I just want to keep my family fed and don't want to mix with no coloreds or mongrels."

By then we weren't alone. Duvall, Billy Jenkins and Davison had come up to listen. "I ain't talkin' mixin' here," I said. "Some white guys don't mind, some even enjoy a black man's company, some don't care for it a'tall. Some black folks don't care to spend their time with white folks either, got better things to do and better people to do it with, way they look at it. That don't make no never-mind to me. What I'm talkin' about is fightin' for our rights, our incomes, and bottom line, our lives. I'm talkin' about a man havin' enough sense to pick the right tool out the toolbox for the job he's gotta do. You wouldn't pick a thin-bladed scroll saw out the box to cut a steel chain, would you?

"Well, boys," I said, stepping back to make it a circle that included Jenkins, Davison and Duvall, "we got chains around our bodies and minds in this here plant. They keep us thinking we ain't worth much. They think we're a bunch of lower-class workin' stiffs, bunch of peckerwoods and shiftless coloreds. Just take your measly paycheck and be damn glad of it." I could see Duvall and Davison nodding their heads. Burleson's face got stiffer and stiffer with every word. I wasn't out to convince him, though. But I was out to contain his influence. I marched on.

"So we need bolt cutters," I said. "And union unity is the only tool strong enough to cut them chains. It ain't a matter of like or dislike, socially mixing or not. It's a job of work. You gotta have the right tool. Maybe this will just come down to a simple vote and that'll be it. But maybe not. Maybe we'll have to strike. Maybe we'll have to take this plant over and sit down like the brothers of the UAW did at the Cadillac plant in '35, black and white. Maybe we'll have to block entrances and roads and push the scabs back and go to jail. Gimme the right tool and we'll get the job done. Gimme some real union unity and we'll get free."

By that time another half-dozen boys had come up to hear it. A few clapped, a couple said their yeses and one, the young guy Ted Sadderly, said "right on!"

I turned to Burleson. "You're a good worker, Al. I seen you churn out more bats than anybody in this plant. I seen your wife come pick you up after closing. I seen the way you hug your kids. I seen the way you've helped some of your brothers in here deal with the foremen when they tried to cheat us. We need you in this fight. So like the song says, stick with the union — the whole union of all the workingmen. And quiet as it's kept, the women too. I'd appreciate it and so would every man here."

I stuck out my hand.

Burleson stood there with his fists clenched. He started to reply, then he started to turn his shoulder away.

"He's right, Al," said Davison, putting his hand on Burleson's shoulder. "You *are* a good man. We need you. And he's right about the race stuff, too. This is about winning our rights. It ain't about popularity contests. It's basic, we gotta join with our fellow black workers, see their side of it. They get the worst end of it, damn it, and you know it just as well as I do. We gotta stick together. You can do that, man, 'cause I know you. We been goin' back more'n ten years here. We're fishin' buddies, you know? We keep each other's pickups running. Way things are goin,' kids growin' up an' all, hell, looks like my daughter's like to start dating that boy of yours."

Burleson's face loosened up. He stretched a sardonic grin across his face. Fake-punched Davison on the shoulder.

"Besides," Davison added, "we can't afford to go down losing like we done last time. Worthington split us up. Remember? They said they upped the day rate on account of that black guy that supposedly cut double the day rate of billets for three weeks in a row? So a bunch of the boys turned against having blacks in the union. They sat out the vote. That cut our numbers down and we lost. But it turned out the whole thing was a lie. They fired that man the day after the vote. Seems he couldn't even make the day rate, let alone double it. Suckered us good though, didn't it?"

"Not so fast with that shit," came a voice from the back of the group. Everybody looked at where it come from, kind of parted away from the sound, and as they did, I could see Billy Jenkins of all people, the union chief, now standing all by himself. "Well, I ain't necessarily against anybody, colored or white, but if you're honest about it, and if you look at the production sheets, you have to admit that it's the white workers that carry the load around here for the most part. Now there may be some good coloreds. But some of them drag us down. Don't produce as much, give the bosses the idea they can take advantage. And they don't show up to the union meetings, most of 'em, neither. Now that's a fact." With that he looked around the group. There were maybe three or four heads nodding in agreement.

"And why do you think a black man might not want to show up at union meetings run by a man with attitudes like that, white boy?" came the voice of Harvey Sampson as he strode into the center of the group, right up to Billy Jenkins.

Billy immediately backed away, looking like he'd like to shrink to half his size.

"I dunno, you tell me, you so goddamn smart," he snarled out of the side of his mouth.

"Because we ain't got time to waste on getting insulted and disrespected by lies like you just told or by the likes of you either. Because we never get any union jobs like shop steward. Because our grievances don't get backed up and pushed like the white brothers' grievances do. But any man that says we ain't loyal to the union is a liar. We're right there when there's a union action and we vote straight down the line to support the local's leadership every time. Even you,

Jenkins, since you're the only name on the ballot. How's that for a start?"

"I think Harvey deserves an answer," said Davison. "He's damn right about them sticking with us when we take action on the shop floor. I can vouch for that. Like them or not, facts are facts."

There was general head nodding all around. I kept my mouth shut. I'd won, whether Burleson came around or not.

"I don't need an answer. What I do want is that you white brothers talk less *about* black men and talk more *to* black men. When you got a problem with one of us, or hey, all of us, then come take it to the one you got a problem with. Or if it's all of us in general, you come to me. That's the basics of respect, right? That's manhood. And that's what a labor union's supposed to be about too. Am I right?"

There was a long silence. Billy Jenkins shuffled his feet and stared daggers, first at Harvey, then at me.

"Yeah, well, maybe so, far as the union goes," Burleson finally spoke up in a grudging voice. "But somebody's got to stick up for the white man, way this country's goin'."

Billy clapped Burleson on the back and bumped his shoulder with a fist.

The group started to break up. We'd just killed fifteen minutes of our valuable lunch break. Everybody drifted away. They left Burleson standing alone. He started to sway off towards the john, but he paused and turned his head back to look at me. His eyes were black and hard as anthracite. A thin white streak showed on his lower lip. He curled the upper one into a sneer. Pointed his index finger at me and dropped the thumb down, hammer on the pistol.

"Durkin," he said.

Just the one word. Didn't say more. Didn't have to. The threat was real. But my question was about tense — was it present or did it also include the past? I recalled what Irma Durkin had said about Billy Jenkins being like a mean cowardly cur dog that slunk around and attacked silently from behind. Burleson had a bark, though—was he Billy's bark? Did they work in tandem? Bark and bite? Or was I mentally hooking Burleson into the Durkin case just on account of his racism and the union issue with no real evidence of connection to the murder at all?

The rest of the shift went quietly into the past. The set-to with Burleson still rankled, but I had to let it go. I'd be extra careful from now on, that was all. It's always downright depressing when one of us gets suckered by the race trap, and make no mistake, Burleson was from the hills, he was one of us. I kept sitting on the bench going over the incident in my mind. I decided I'd sounded too damn high-and-mighty, too self-righteous. That was one of my flaws, for damn sure. But it had happened, I had said what I'd said, no going back. That's the damnedest thing about time, it always marches forward, never back. Always away from birth and towards death.

I got up a couple of times to shake the tension out and walked around the plant. Went into the P.R.O. section where Danny B was laying in a new bat for Hank Aaron, he said. "Got a lot of weight just behind the label," Danny said. "Not so much at the tip end." We jawed about the pros and their bats for a few minutes, then I popped the question.

"Say Danny, you know anything about a 'spose to be betting man comes around Slugger to take bets against the money-line?"

Danny suddenly shifted his back to me and hunched over the lathe. "Hold it, Ray," he said, "gotta check the taper on this section with the calipers." With that he grabbed a pair of calipers off the hook on the cement wall beside his lathe. Keeping his back to me, he said, "now what was that...oh yeah, some type of betting scheme. Naw, man, don't know nothing about that."

Just then Bob Stills, the shift foreman in the P.R.O. section came by. "Okay Ray, knock it off now, this ain't no social hall.

Let the man do his J.O.B. We got a back order situation on the Braves here."

I clapped Danny on the shoulder. "Later alligator," I said, putting a hard edge on 'later,' but Danny didn't look around or speak, just raised the back of his sawdust covered hand in dismissal.

Now I had another thing to brood about on the lathe room bench.

The shift finally crawled to a close. I got up with the other guys and filed out by the punch card rack in the main entrance/exit. I lifted mine from my slot and was about to put it into the punch clock when I noticed some words printed in red block letters down the side.

"S T O P   O R   Y O U   A   D E A D   B E T"

Rather than make a fuss or call attention to myself I just stuck the card in the slot and let the clock punch it, then dropped it back in the rack and went on through the warehouse towards the rear exit. That's where I saw a curious thing: Billy Jenkins carving on an old reject bat with a serrated knife. Not just any old serrated kitchen knife. A serrated switchblade knife. *You don't see many of those around*, I thought. *Never seen one used for wood carving neither.*

Oh well, there's worse hobbies I guess, so I shrugged and walked on down the wide warehouse style ramp and out into the sunshine and clear air.

Chapter Fourteen: Margaret

Ray was carrying a whole bunch of tension when he walked through the back door as he came home from work. Margaret gave him an extra-long hug and suggested he get a shower and wash the sawdust and some of the tightness out of himself, which for once he did without having to first give her the Cecil B. DeMille review of his day. After he showered she just walked up to him, took his big callused hand in hers, steered him out the back door and down the porch steps and led him on a nice long walk around the neighborhood. Nothing like a little easy motion to drain the tension out of a body.

"It was a helluva day, dear heart," he started in.

"Shush," she said, "that's off limits till after supper, then we'll give it a good going over. This here's a happy hour walk. Now just take a look at them nashturshalums climbing the fence we're coming up on here."

"Nashturshalums? Ain't never heard of that."

"You have, actually. They're nasturtiums, the flowers Winnie-the-Pooh talks about, remember? We read that together just before lights out when we were first courting. Only in his goofy way he called them 'nashturshalums.' And that bunch growing over there are just gorgeous, the blue ones, you don't see them much this far north."

"I get the point. Take time to look at the flowers, get my head out of my rear end."

"You said that, I didn't," Margaret whispered at him, with an open grin.

So it became a flower walk, not much of a talking walk, which was just what they both needed, far as Margaret was concerned. She was always amazed at how folks in Little Appalachia, poor as they were, took pride in their tiny yards, planting them with flowers, mostly annuals and a few perennials, not so many shrubs, which were more expensive. You saw lots of flowers that a person could get cheap at the farmers' markets and discount store parking lots. The folks kept them in front stoop pots and well-tended little beds along the back alleys and fences in the neighborhood.

After the walk Ray made notes of some of the things he'd witnessed at Slugger then called his AA sponsor to talk over his tensions and review how he'd handled himself in the set-to with Burleson. Of course Margaret didn't listen in on the conversation, but when he came into the kitchen she could tell by his smile and the loosened shoulders that it had gone well. Funny how that happened almost every time. They say that's what makes AA work—one alcoholic talking to another about what keeps them sober and focusing on that instead of what they think are their insurmountable problems.

Margaret fixed one of Ray's favorite suppers: navy beans, onions, cracklins and skillet cornbread with some greens. She threw in the cracklins on account of it had been a really tough day even though she knew they weren't on the top of the government's healthy food pyramid, but what the heck, Margaret thought, a body has to live a little and Ray's four food groups included at least two from the pork family. Then, after some molasses over the last of the corn bread for dessert, they settled back in the office over coffee and got down to business, which was reviewing the day and planning for tomorrow.

Ray told Margaret about the run-ins with Worthington, Burleson and Billy Jenkins, as well as the funny way Danny B had acted when Ray had brought up the moneyline issue. Like Ray, Margaret wasn't surprised about Billy taking a racist line on blacks in the union, not after what Irma Durkin had told her about the role he and his family had played in the aftermath of the dynamiting of the Wade family home out in Shively, and then in the Braden case, trying to foreclose on Fred and Irma and lying under oath about the Wades.

They hadn't had much of a chance to analyze Margaret's interview with Irma Durkin until then, so she went into details about that, especially connecting the dots with the wild nighttime visit from one James Haskell, a.k.a. Blondie.

"What I don't get about Blondie," Ray said, thinking out loud, "is that he keeps turning up in conflicts with all kinds of folks on all kinds of shit that don't have much if anything to do with the murders down at Slugger. I'm talking moneyline with George Salvatore, off the premises meetings with Billy Jenkins, and now this threat agin' Fred Durkin and his wife out to their home. And another thing — he threatened me later on that same day him and Blackie tried to roust me at our door, like I told you, saying he'd drawn a bead on me back at the showdown at Breathitt. Bein' as he's a known liar, maybe he ain't from the mountains a'tall — maybe he's from around here an' has a history with these folks an' that's why he turns up all the time when there's muscle work to be done."

"You know, Ray," Margaret said, "it might do us a lot of good to see if we can find out just how far this vendetta has gone into Slugger and into the union, and also where Haskell fits into the local picture. Maybe he does, maybe he's just a thug for all seasons and all reasons, kind of free-lance. But be that as it may, where there's the smoke of a threat from a company thug, there may be the fire of rough-stuff." She poured them both another cup of coffee, then went on with her thoughts.

"But we need to focus on the murders too. Tie into that. It could well be that Billy and Durkin tangled over the same race issue in the union and that Billy got threatened over it enough to want to do Durkin some serious harm — even murder. And from what you've said about this incident and about things in general over there at Slugger, there's one guy you might be able to get next to and find out a little more about it."

"I know where you're goin'," Ray said, "and you're right on the money, like always—Harvey Sampson. But I got a better idea. Harvey's a very proud man and, well, I shouldn't be saying this, it's kind of against the rules, but he's in my AA group, and it might be sort of out of line for me to get real pushy with him on stuff like this. So maybe you could figure out a way to call on his wife. He's married, I know, and I bet he tells her all about what goes on at Slugger. At least it wouldn't hurt to try that. And if that don't work, then sure, I could give it a go as a last resort. What do you think?"

Margaret took a deep breath and sat still to ponder for a few minutes. Ray knew better than to interfere when she got like that, so he kept quiet. Then it came to her.

"I think it's time the women folk of the local formed a women's organizing unit in preparation for the negotiations, in case there's a need to strike, and to push for women being hired at Slugger. I mean, it's a disgrace that in this day and age there isn't one woman working on the production line at that plant! More than that, if it comes to a strike, you men don't have diddly-squat ready—no community support, no food committee, no picket line reserves, no press corps, nothin' a'tall. And it'd be a good thing to start the women's organizing unit out with one white and one black. You talk to Harvey and let him know I'll be calling on his wife so it won't be a complete cold call, right? And I'll call on her day after tomorrow."

"I think that's a damn fine idea, Sampson's wife or not! Like I always say, you're the brains in this outfit!"

"Oh, not really now, Ray, you're just as…"

"Don't shrug it off, hear!"

And so she didn't, and they spent the rest of the evening going over details and getting an early start to bedtime and love.

Chapter Fifteen: Ray

Next morning I beat it down two blocks to take the Fourth Street bus past the Oak Street L&N switching yards to treat myself to a late breakfast at the Lazy Susan Diner in Southside Louisville. I sat in a booth across a narrow table from Alice Gorham, Frank's sister and nearest relative, who worked the counter at the Lazy Susan. She'd been given a few minutes for a coffee break after the morning rush of railroad yard workers and workers at the factories and warehouses along Industrial Avenue had ended.

The Lazy Susan featured exactly that, a lazy susan at the center of each Formica table topped booth, three rows of them, one on each side of the room and one row down the middle. The counter ran across one end of the room opposite the entrance, and it had a lazy susan for every three stools. There were four other booths containing customers and three men eating at the counter. One of the booths looked to be occupied by a party of three business guys in jackets, ties and slacks, but the rest of the customers had either jeans or denim overalls and work shirts and were railroad yard workers for sure. About half the men and the one woman besides Alice were smoking. The wall opposite our side of the room featured big posters of famous locomotives alternating with railroad timetables from around the country. Picture windows ran beside the booths on our side of the room. You could just see the classification yard tower from our window, and the rumble of the diesel switchers provided a background bass to our conversation.

A short, thin, curly haired red-head, Alice fidgeted with her coffee cup, rattling it around the ring on the cheap saucer, then looked up at me out of deep gray eyes circled with pleasing crinkles made by frequent grins. She wasn't shy.

"Maybe you're surprised I'm willing to talk with a detective like you, Mr. Odle," she said, right off the bat, "but I want to set the record straight about one thing, and I know one thing about you that makes me think you'll be the right man to help me do it."

"And what'd that be?" I said, keeping it even, giving no promises I might not be able to keep.

Alice pulled a thin metallic coin out of the side pocket of her waitress uniform and slid it across the blue Formica table to me. I picked it up and looked it over, thumbing the medallion's central triangle as I'd done with my own chips in the past, the 30-day, the 90-day, the six month, the one year, and the multiples of years, each one a miracle, no one less a miracle than any other. This was a 30-day chip from Alcoholics Anonymous.

"You can tell them boys at Slugger and the cops, too, that Frank didn't die a drunk. He died sober, and I got the chip from AA to prove it."

"How and when did you get this, Alice?"

"Frank came over to my place after the meeting when he got it. The night before he was murdered."

"And why are you trusting me with it?" I was still playing it cautious, steady.

"Because Frank said he knew you were in the program, that somebody at Slugger had told him so, and he said he admired you. So when I heard you was investigating on who killed him and Fred, well, I figured you'd want to know he died sober, and I figured Frank would have trusted you with it. See, he didn't go to no meetings where them other boys at Slugger would have seen him. He won't ready for them to know he was trying to kick the booze. He'd been a bad drunk, Mr. Odle..."

120

"Just call me Ray," I put in.

"...Ray, and he'd done lots of things he was ashamed of, some of them against the boys at Slugger, against the union, and he won't ready to deal with that yet, like his sponsor told him, so he went to meetings way over town on the east side. I mean, there was years of waste. Him coming home drunk when Momma was still alive, stumbling into the house at all hours, cursing, breaking up the furniture, calling her and me names, blaming everyone but himself for losing job after job. The phone calls from jails and hospitals to come get him. Finally, when Momma died and I put my foot down and made him get out, he actually laid his fist up side of my head and it was me had to go to the hospital. At that point I liked to killed that man and done my time. And then, like all the other times, the next day here comes the crying and the sorrow and the remorse. Happened a hundred times if it was once."

She shifted in her seat, uncomfortable with the memories.

"Most of us have stories like that," I said. "Oh, the details is different, but they tell us to look for the similarities, not the differences." Alice nodded and went on.

"But then, for the last month of his life, it all changed," she said. "He came by the old place almost every evening after work just to say hello and bring me a little extra money he earned on the piece rate down at Slugger. He'd bring me some extra groceries, even some flowers a couple of times. Didn't ask for me to forgive him, nothing like that. Just come up on the porch when I was there and talked a bit, you know, passed the time of day like a regular human being. Like a regular brother. Can you understand that?"

I watched her as she talked, trying hard to make sense of the life of a drunk who'd tried to turn it around at the end. She was like so many other relatives—mothers, sisters, brothers, aunts and cousins, whatever kind you want to name—that had seen the miracle and yet, in its early days, weren't sure they could trust it. Would it last? Was it real?

And they were right to wait, twenty years of drinking would make a skeptic of anyone. We were like tornados that blew through the lives of those around us wreaking havoc and leaving behind wreckage. It took a lot more than 30 days to change all that. Yet Frank had turned the corner, it seemed, and that was nothing to sneer at.

Alice was holding on to the slim reed of hope that she could rest her brother's image in her own mind in peace. That she could let him have a little bit of dignity in the end. That he could, in death, stand up straight. I had no quarrel with that, even though as an investigator there was much more to know, much more to discover, and some of it, I could well imagine, might tear away Alice Gorham's fragile picture of dignity for her brother Frank. I would hate to be the one to do that. But nobody ever said murder was a clean business, nor that detective work was a Hallmark *Have a nice day!* card.

Alice was asking about AA, early sobriety, and if I could understand Frank Gorham's avoiding the AA meetings where he might meet up with those of us at Slugger where he'd been accused of being a company snitch, and she deserved an answer.

"Yeah. I can understand it," I said. "And I would have told him the same thing if I was sponsoring him. You don't do amends right away. That's the ninth step and usually a guy with only 30 days ain't ready for the ninth step. But getting 30 days is a miracle, sure is. I'm right glad for Frank that he done that before he died. And I'm glad you told me about Frank. What's more, it sounds like he was turning some of his other bad habits around too — not just the drinking."

Assuaging Alice's doubts was not my only business at the diner that morning. And so I asked her, "Did Frank have any visitors that he talked about, any particular fears he mentioned to you near the end?"

"You must be reading my mind," she replied. "I was going to ask you about it. Well, that is, if I decided to trust you with it. And so, here goes. Yeah, he did. There was two that stands out in my mind." She squirmed in her seat again.

"One was that man Mr. Benson from the Slugger plant," she continued. "He'd come by asking all kinds of questions about Frank and his drinking. I told the guy it wasn't none of his business and to get off my porch. He said I'd better cooperate if I knew what was good for Frank and I shut the door in his face then went inside and immediately called my brother. This was in the evening after working hours, and tell the truth, Ray, that man Benson had himself quite a snoot full of booze, you ask me. Well anyway, Frank came right over and by that time Benson had gone, or so I thought, but Frank caught him across the street hanging around beside the old abandoned garage, and I heard words but no fighting, then Frank ran that man off.

"Frank came back and told me that he was ashamed of it, but he'd been feeding inside information to the company about union matters—plans for the negotiations, possible strike plans, stuff like that—stuff he'd got from Billy Jenkins because Billy owed him. Frank had found some betting slips, some kind of organized betting on Major League baseball, and Billy's name was on them. There was a bunch of them, I guess, and it showed Billy was deeply involved in illegal gambling. So Frank used that to make Billy cough up information on what the union was up to. What they was planning, the grievances on the shop floor, stuff like that.

"Also Frank could tell from the slips that Billy was in the hole, he was in debt to the betting ring. So Frank told Billy he'd turn Billy's debts over to the enforcers instead of collecting them himself unless Billy gave him the inside dope on the union's plans. Then he basically sold that to Benson and the company for favors on the job, he said—but not for money. He drew the line on that, but he was terribly ashamed about it, and so, truth to tell, am I."

Her face, a deep rose emerging all over it, showed that she was indeed.

"Anyway, thank God, he quit. He told Benson he was through, that he'd had a change of heart and he was now for the union. He told me Benson threatened him and asked him if he wanted to end up like Durkin."

I don't mind telling you that one made me jump! Durkin? Fred Durkin was no company snitch. Almost the opposite. He'd been quiet about it, for sure, but he'd been a union man all along. And his main enemy at Slugger had been Billy Jenkins, if anybody, not Benson or the company itself.

"Why Durkin?" I asked, putting my thoughts out loud. "Fred was a union man so he wouldn't have been seen as turning on the company like Frank, at least the way you just told me."

"That's what I wondered," Alice replied, "and Frank told me he bucked on it too. But Benson just laughed and said Frank was a naïve baby if he didn't think the company didn't have a weakling like Billy Jenkins in their pocket, and everybody knew about Billy's grudge against Fred Durkin and his kind — you know I don't like to use the words."

"Yep, 'fraid I do. One that begins with an 'N' and adds, "lover," to it." I didn't see no reason to offend her reluctance at this point.

"Yes. Frank said Benson allowed as how the company liked it just fine if men like Billy Jenkins, with his attitudes against the coloreds, ran the union and kept white men like Fred Durkin in their place, not to mention the coloreds themselves. Well, I told Frank it didn't make no sense to me, but I could tell it did to him and that he was scared right enough."

But it made all too much sense to me. And it explained why the local at Slugger had made such little progress in recent years. The company was very slick about it, but they were playing the race card pure and simple — playing it through the backstory of old history and past events, among other ways, between Fred and Billy. And if they were doing that, they were probably using other events in the racial history of Louisville that had touched the lives of men and women connected to Slugger workers and their families too. They were weaving the history of racism into the shop floor of Slugger to keep little rips, little gaps of mistrust and anger, little tears here and there, that would prevent men from coming together in the tight kind of unity it takes to fight and win a bold new contract that really made a change in their lives for the better.

"But that wasn't the worst," Alice went on. "See, Frank came by one night in terrible shape, cheeks bruised yellow and purple, left sleeve ripped off his shirt, one knee bleeding through torn pants, and shaking like he'd gone back on the bottle. Oh, Ray, he was a sight! It was awful! In fact it took me a little while of sitting on the porch with him and not smelling that awful whisky to realize he was still sober, he was shaking so bad. He told me he'd been roughed up, just a warning, they'd told him to keep his mouth shut about the moneyline and to turn over the betting slips."

I tried to look surprised. Of course Margaret and I knew Frank had the slips, we'd found them in his lathe. But surprise or not, I needed to know more.

"Did he identify the men?"

"No. And I believed him when he said he didn't know them. He said they were strangers to him."

"Did he give you any description of either of them—size? hair color? anything?"

"Well, he said one of them was blond, I think. And they had crew cuts, or at least short hair. He didn't actually say that, he said their hair was kind of like G-men but they sounded like thugs in the Cagney movies."

"Did they threaten to hurt him again?"

"More or less. They just told him he'd better come up with the betting slips or else. Frank told me that he said he didn't care what happened to him, that he'd had enough, and that he couldn't stay sober if he kept quiet about this and kept breaking the law, 'cause silence was breaking the law. But he was in a terrible dilemma, he said, because it was worse than what would happen to him. He said he ought to go to the cops, but he couldn't. At least not yet. Others were involved."

Tears formed in her eyes and I knew then where this was going. I asked the question anyway.

"What others, Alice?" I said, softly.

"Me. They told him they'd cut my face if he went to the police."

"When was that night, when he got roughed up and came to see you afterward?"

"A week before he died."

That would have been the week after the week on the recorded slip we found. So it looked like Frank had not gone to the police. He'd followed the spirit of the ninth step—to make amends except when to do so would harm the person you're making amends to, or others. In this case, going to the police would have harmed others, namely Alice, if the threat was to be believed. So Frank had gone as far as he could, and taken the consequences onto himself.

But was one of those consequences his own murder?

"There is this one other thing, Ray," she broke into my head game.

"What's that?"

"This. Frank gave it to me and told me to hide it somewhere safe, so I kept it in the little jewel box I keep in the small drawer of my bureau."

I looked and Alice was handing me a torn slip of paper about the size of a business card. I took it out of her trembling hand. It had a number on it and a name. "Jeff." The number looked like a phone number, no area code.

"I worried over that slip of paper for days after Frank was killed. Worried and worried until I couldn't stand it. It looked like a phone number to me, so I called it, just yesterday in fact. They answered "Courier Journal," and I just hung up. I didn't ask for Jeff, whoever he is."

The proverbial dime dropped—in my mind and maybe as it had in Frank Gorham's plans. He might not have been ready to go to the cops, but he might have been ready to take it to the press. Or maybe that was just a plan B—or maybe a plan P, for protection. If so, he'd not had time to execute it. He'd not gotten to the press before his killer had gotten to him or there would have been a headline about it, him, and the moneyline.

"Is that why he was killed, Ray?" came the plaintive voice of Alice Gorham, as I knew it would as soon as she'd told me her brother had refused to carry the slips for the moneyline any longer. And she expected an honest answer.

"I don't rightly know, Alice. It could be, all right, but it ain't clear. I wish I knew. But I will eventually, and when I do, so will you."

"I want you to get the man who killed my brother, Mr. Odle," she said, her voice getting stronger, emphasizing my last name. "I want him caught and I don't trust the cops to do it."

"I'll do my right smart best, Miss Gorham," I said, and reached across the table and pressed the 30-day AA chip into her hand. "You hold onto this," I said, "and remember him that way."

As I rode the bus back north, up Fourth Street headed for Broadway and then toward Slugger to put in an appearance for the afternoon half of my shift, I had to wonder about my promise to Alice Gorham. I wondered who'd given Frank the warning. I also had to wonder if the mob somehow found out about the man called, "Jeff," at the Louisville Courier-Journal. And what made whoever it was decide that the warning hadn't been enough.

On the other hand, maybe it was closer to home than that. Maybe the boys at Slugger management didn't want to lose their snitch. Or maybe they just wanted to keep him quiet about what he knew. Maybe the boys at Slugger had used a

certain tag team of muscle to intimidate Frank. And maybe
the muscle had gone too far.

Maybe…maybe…maybe.

Chapter Sixteen: Radio four

Mel Allen: It's Red Barber and yours truly, Mel Allen, back live at the Braves' new digs in Atlanta, folks. And say, Schlitz sure is Milwaukee's finest beer, even if the folks up there are a mite put out with the Braves for leavin' 'em high and dry without their beloved baseball nine, Red.

Red Barber: The good fans of Milwaukee may be high but likely they ain't dry, Mel. I'da had a few nice cold cans of Schlitz myself, I was them.

MA: Yeah, Red, there's always a reason for Schlitz — in your case, pard, it's havin' a Major League team right up the road from your place in Florida, right?

RB: You bet, Mel. Well, here comes Jersey Jack to the plate, one away here in the top of the ninth, Tommy Helms on first, looking to Jersey Jack for a hit to drive him around.   It's 3 to zip, Braves, thanks to that two-on homer by Alou in the fifth.   Cloninger's pitching is driving the Redlegs nuts. Whoops, Cloninger steps off the mound for the Braves, pause that refreshes, I guess.

MA: Clemente's hotter than an Atlanta chili dog right now, Red, leading the National League in fielding, RBIs, extra-base hits, just about everything but batting average.

RB: Right, Mel. That distinction goes to Roberto's teammate, Matty Alou…

MA:…Who's only just ahead of brother Felipe, number two in the league…What a line-up! Clemente, Alou and Alou…fire-power…

RB: The National's answer to Robinson, Robinson and Powell with the Orioles in the American League, Mel.

MA: Right, Red. Say, I bet Cincinnati's owner Bill DeWitt's kickin' his own hind end over trading Robinson this year.

RB: He doesn't have to worry, Mel, there's about 30,000 fans in Cincy that'll be glad to do it for 'im, he don't watch out!

MA: Okay, Red, Cloninger's back, he's into the wind-up…here's the pitch…high and just a wee bit outside, but Jersey Jacko's not liking it. Ball one.

RB: Cloninger's either just on or just outside the plate on every pitch, Mel. Here's the one-oh pitch…fastball…crack! It's a one-bouncer right up the alley to the shortstop, he snags it, over to second, got him! Over to first, just in time!

MA: Double play! Well, will ya look at that, Red, Jersey Jack's grabbed his bat off the dirt and he's lookin it over like a meat inspector on the line. Yep, he's pointing at the bat about a foot up from the knob at the end. Looks like a perfect oval crack. Jacko's not a happy man right now.

RB: Not at all, Mel. He's stompin' into the dugout, shakin' that bat like he's gonna walk all the way to Louisville to give the boys at the Slugger plant a piece of his mind along with a piece of the bat!

MA: Ya know, Red, I been readin' up on this broke bat thing, an' what I found out is that an oval break is a sign that the wood they picked wasn't too darn good in the first place – somethin' about the angle on the grain.

RB: I wouldn't go hollerin' about that too loud, Mel, and like Satchel says, don't look back, neither, somethin' might be gainin' on ya!"

MA: Awww, come on, Red, you ain't paranoid, is ya?"

RB: Who me? Movin' right along, Mel. The Redlegs end it on a broken bat, but the fans here at Atlanta Stadium are goin' home happy. They sure beat the odds on this one.

MA: Odds is right, Red, about fifteen minutes ago I'd of given you odds the other way! Goes to show some days a man just cain't make a nickel.

Chapter Seventeen: Margaret

"Mrs. Sampson? Mrs. Louella Sampson?" Margaret said to the tall, athletic looking black woman who'd pulled the door of the two-flat wide-open at her second knock. She was wearing dungarees rolled halfway up her calf with a yellow rag stuffed in one rear pocket, her top was a bright red Tee-shirt, and her hair ran back from her forehead in corn rows. Louella Sampson also had a turf-stained gardening trowel in one hand.

"That'd be me," the woman said with a frown, "so who wants to know all dressed up like Sunday-go-to-meetin'?"

"Well, you got me there," Margaret laughed. "I'm Margaret Odle, and I believe your husband Harvey might've told you to expect me to call on you today?" Margaret put a question mark behind it, especially seeing how Louella Sampson was dressed, as if Margaret had for sure caught her in a surprise, which was not exactly how she'd wanted this to go.

They were standing on either side of the doorway of an asphalt shingle two-flat in Louisville's black West End, right in the shadow of a big oil refinery, smelling the fumes and hearing the constant low volume roar of the flare burning off the excess gas from the process. The building was neat and tidy, on a corner, and when Margaret had walked up from the bus stop two blocks away she'd seen a bountiful looking vegetable garden filling the corner lot.

"Oh lord, that man and his memory be like tellin' a mule, he hear an' he don't hear," she said. "Leastways he don't remember half of what I tell him. Now I ain't saying he wasn't told about you callin' on me, but as you can see, I won't prepared. If I'd a known you was comin' I might not'a baked a cake, but I might sure enough been made myself a little more presentable. Now I don't want to be rude, uh, I guess it's Missus Odle? Missus, right?"

Margaret nodded.

"But you might want to tell me who you are and what you want, anyway, you don't mind my axing?"

"Not at all. I'm Margaret Odle, from the Odle Detective Agency. My husband, Ray, works down at the Slugger plant, and I wonder if I could have just a few minutes of your time just to talk?"

She looked Margaret up and down. "Like I said, you dress like you an uptown woman. You for the company or the union? I don't have time 'just to talk' to nobody, as you can see, I'm about some business, and I damn sure don't have time to talk to one of them two choices I axed you about."

"Well, Ray and I are working on a contract with the national office of the WIA, the Woodworkers International of America, which is a national union that Harvey's local is affiliated with. The national office hired us to investigate the murders of Fred Durkin and Frank Gorham, to find out what really happened, and in the process, make sure that the union doesn't get blamed unless it was the union, or some member, that actually did it. We won't lie for the union, but we won't let the company get away with lying about the union, either. So that's who I am and what my work is. But that's not why I'm calling on you."

Mrs. Sampson cocked her head and put her free hand on her hip. "Well now, I think it's high time you got off the merry-go-round an' got down on it, ma'am, and give it up!"

Sock. Right up side of the head, so to speak. Margaret had underestimated the woman and had come close to insulting her. She could tell Margaret had an agenda and was selling something and was the kind of woman who didn't care to hear a lot of preamble and beating around the bush, especially from a white woman on her doorstep unannounced, all dressed up like a church lady trying to push some agenda or other. The best thing was to be humble and honest and go straight at it and let the chips fall where they might.

"Okay, I deserved that," Margaret said. Then she started firing words at Louella like a repeating rifle.

"What I want to talk to you about is forming a women's organizing unit for the local chapter of the union to help the men have a backup ability to make a believable threat to strike, and to back them up in action in case of an actual strike. Right now, between you and me, those men don't have diddly-squat worked out as far as the community goes. No alternate pickets in case they get put in jail, no food committee, no press committee, no organizers in the community for the churches and other community groups. In fact, Mrs. Sampson, near about nothing.

"Now I've been in labor fights before in the eastern mountains, I've been up against the Pinkerton gun thugs, and I'll tell you the cousins of those bastards are here right now at Slugger, calling themselves the H & R Security Agency, and I've seen what happens when the men aren't prepared and the women aren't organized to back them up. So Ray and I figured one thing we could do to help, even though we haven't been in Louisville all that long, is share what we've been through and help that way. And something we've seen work right well in labor history is a women's organizing unit — part of the union local. Now in this town the company will no doubt try to break the men up by playing the race card right off the bat, so I figured the woman's unit needed to start off on the right foot by having a black woman and a white woman be the two local leaders. Now, who you think the white woman ought to be?"

Louella Sampson just threw her head back and laughed all the way down to her knees, a warm laugh that included Margaret in it, not as the object of it, so she broke up too. Soon they both were coughing and laughing hard. Then, after a few lower level chuckles and a few deep breaths, Louella pulled Margaret inside and marched her through the flat, past a couple of easy chairs and a settee, a kitchen with an old oak tiger claw table, and out onto a back door stoop.

"You look about the size of my sister-in-law, an' if you'd be willin' to trade them uptown threads for some pants and a Tee for a little while and help me pull some of the damn weeds in this garden that I just got to get at today, I'll be glad to play some eenie-meenie-honkie-moe with you and help out all I can. I been ragging on Harvey exactly the same about them men not being ready to take on the Slugger bosses, an' that's a fact! But girl, I got to get the weeds today behind the rain we had last night. The ground's soft and they'll come up by the root. It's like a one-day sale at the supermarket—today only. After today the Kentucky sun will bake them sorry-ass weeds into the ground so hard they'll near hit back when you go after them, they be in there so strong."

Margaret could hardly contain her delight. "Just show me the way, Mizz Sampson," she said, and was about to continue when Louella cut her off.

"Forget the 'Mizz Sampson' boogie-joogie, Margaret, we on first names or no names from now on. Just call me Louella, all right?"

"Louella it is, and I'd much rather pull weeds in your excellent garden than sit around drinking tea or whatever. I don't have any ground at my place, but I've got five good-sized pots with some damn fine tomatoes, onions, one cucumber vine, two field pea vines, three snap bean vines and some poke sallet—that last just to remind me of home."

"Now I wanna hear 'bout that home place of yours just as soon as we get to working them weeds, cain't waste no time on them suckers, right?" said Louella. Not ten minutes later Margaret was changed and the two women were out in the garden. Louella laid out some thick cardboard strips for Margaret to use as knee pads, and trowel in hand, Margaret went down the first row of onions while Louella went parallel to her on a row of salad greens. Margaret dug around each invading weed, most were about four inches high, and tried to get the root, although in a lot of cases it wasn't easy since the stems were delicate and broke off at ground level. Then she'd have to dig around with her fingers and find the root in the dirt. But Margaret knew without having to be told that in most cases the weed would be back in a day or two if she didn't get the root.

After about fifteen minutes of weeding, Louella piped up.

"Now, about that home place," she said, "where is it?"

"Well, being as you asked," Margaret said with a laugh, "I'm talking midland South Carolina. Cotton country. I grew up watching migrants and sharecroppers chop, pick and bale cotton. My Daddy was an eastern county employment commission middle manager whose job was to make sure the local cotton farmers had labor—and we're mostly talking black folks here—and that the labor didn't complain so loud that it got the attention of the higher ups in the state or federal labor departments. That last part wasn't in the job description, of course, but his boss, the South Carolina Employment Commission Station Manager had left him in no doubt as to what his mission was—keep the growers happy and the colored folks, the sharecroppers and the migrants, quiet."

"We good at that, sorry to say," Louella stuck in, "way *too* good at that."

"But it didn't work. The 1920s and '30s were a disaster for cotton in South Carolina. Cotton prices fell from 38 cents a pound in 1919 to 5 cents in 1932. My Daddy told how white bankers and silk stocking planters threw the poor white farmers out of their homes and off their land, telling them that the coloreds wanted the land and if they beefed about it, then they were no good white trash. Naturally this just inflamed their already racist hatreds and kept the blame off the planters and their northern cotton industry partners. What Daddy didn't tell me was about the screams of black sharecrop farmers being lynched. That wasn't for the ears of little white girls. He said there wasn't nothing he could do for most of the colored folks, that the only welfare relief was, by the state constitution, given to Confederate army veterans, their widows and their faithful slaves."

"Now ain't that a trip? Confederate veterans an' they faithful slaves? Now how many 'faithful slaves' there gonna be after all the whippings an' lynchings gone down in South Carolina, now tell me that?" Louella was standing up straight with her hoe jammed into the earth at her side and her arm straight out full length holding its handle top.

"Exactly," Margaret said. "Well, hell, even young as I was, I wasn't stupid, and none of it made any sense to me, so I became a rebellious teenager who smoked cigarettes behind the choir loft at the Gilead Baptist Church, sneaked beer behind the stands at the R.E. Lee High School football games, made out with numerous boys of whatever denomination or none, had a crush on a so-called colored kid down at the migrant camp who picked cotton and played a mean blues on a steel slide guitar. I went to Meredith College, a Baptist girl's school, but ran off after two years, then lied about my age on the application and joined the WPA, where I ended up in the hills of Eastern Kentucky as a WPA worker."

"Hey, that took some serious guts, right there!" Louella grinned at me.

"Or a serious lack of brains," Margaret replied. "But whichever, I then did the damndest thing — I became a librarian on horseback. I was a worker in the Packhorse Library Program, begun in 1935, and ran a library in Breathitt County out of a one-room schoolhouse on Troublesome Creek. I got some 120 books and left in the shrouding mists, rains, sometime snows or whatever conditions nature held in store for me in the dawn every day on mule back. I took books, magazines — oh how the ladies and the kids loved the magazines! and old newspapers up the creeks and hollers to folks who had no other contact with the outside world. I got

136

to know every woman and a great many of the men folk in that section of the county, and truth to tell, all over the whole county. My satchels carried practical books and magazines but my head carried the good stuff: gossip and news about goings-on that never made it into print—the kind of news that people most depended on day-to-day.

"Most folks came to greet me with big hellos and open arms, but there were a few that took against me, and one man who ran me off with a pitchfork yelling, 'you're a daughter of the devil 'cause my son ain't do a lick of work, him all the time a-moonin' over them magazines! Git on outta heah!'"

Louella laughed hard and loud at that. "We got them folks' cousins right here in the neighborhood, Margaret. Churchy types always tryin' to spoil a poor person's little bit of fun!"

"Yep, they're all over, all right," Margaret said, then went on. "And when the Roosevelt administration, the war, the Great Depression and the WPA were all history, I'd found a people and a home, way up a holler in Breathitt County, where I lived and worked with the folks there. I also came out of it with a limp that sometimes kept me from walking, the result of a mule slipping down the talus slope in a sleet storm and falling over on me one night as I was making my way back down towards Troublesome Creek.

"I spent that night with a busted patella, and would have died from exposure except that a drunk from up the next holler had missed his creek and came stumbling up the Troublesome, lost, and found me. He had just enough consciousness and just enough conscience to help me get back on that old mule, and that brave mule had just enough strength to get the two of us back down the Creek to the cabin of Lillian Tharpe, the nearest, and fortunately for us, one of the best women in all of Breathitt County. She packed us in blankets and stoked the pot-belly stove with the culls of Consolidation Coal and threw something down my throat that put fire all over my insides while she prayed over my outsides."

"Limp or not, you be doin' all right with that trowel, girl," said Louella. And she was right. Despite her storytelling Margaret had done two rows of highly weed-infested garden to Louella's two and a half.

"But you ain't said how you ended up in the organizing bizness, Margaret. If we gonna get out front on this union stuff together, I gotta know what you bring to help back me up."

"Well, having been a Packhorse Librarian with all those contacts, I was a natural for an organizer, simple as that, so I joined up with various campaigns, the welfare rights work, and especially the Black Lung Campaign of Doc Don Rasmussen. He went around teaching folks about black lung and urging them to fight the coal barons for protection against the dust. As organizers we went ahead of him and got folks to come out to meetings in the schoolhouses and once in a while even in the churches. See, the churches were mostly white so they didn't support the movement like the black churches supported y'all's movement—too tied into big coal or too tied into pie-in-the-sky-by-and-by. On top of that, everybody knew our movement was integrated and most of those churches were lily white. But we'd get the folks ready and then Doc would come in and fire the folks up, then we'd come behind and get them to push for change inside the union or in their community organizations.

"Anyway, like I said, I did that and other kinds of organizing too. It's just a matter of showing folks some respect, their propers, as you might say, and then backing them up when the bosses try and divide the people by playing the race card or some other shitty little game."

"Hell, woman, you sound like somebody that'd take my back in this women's unit we talkin' about if it comes down to a fight," said Louella. "An' I'm somebody that can appreciate that, bein' as how I got throw'd out of the Colonnade Hotel dining room in 1955. Said I wasn't dressed right 'cause I wore an Afro. Well, I grew up in this town, had two good, hard-working parents who taught me right from wrong and how to act, so won't no hoity-toity white folks hotel gonna tell me how to dress my hair or keep me out, neither. So I joined up with Georgia Davis Powers and the Allied Organization for Civil Rights, fightin' for public accommodations rights for black folk. She led us on that march two years back where we went all the way from here to Frankfort and up the capitol steps, raising hell about segregation years after that had been outlawed by the Supreme Court. So yeah, all the while I raised my four kids, I learned a thing or two about sticking together."

She could say that again. Margaret's admiration for her was growing by the minute. Margaret told her about Ray, too, as they kept on digging weeds out of the various beds of onions, lettuce, collards, kale, spinach, potatoes, tomatoes, squash, zucchini, corn, radishes, carrots, garlic, green and red peppers and assorted herbs.

The two laid plans for the women's organizing unit, the committees they'd need, pretty much the ones Margaret had laid out in her opening salvo, plus some ideas about names of women to recruit. Louella was for Maryann Bow among the black ladies as another leader who could persuade the rank and file to come with them. She said she didn't know much about the white ladies, but had talked with Sally Campsten, Andy's wife, who had made it a point to spend time with the black women and families at the Slugger employee picnic the previous summer, and who also seemed to be pretty popular with the rest of the white ladies too.

As they talked about the committees and women for the unit, Louella suddenly stood up from her row of radishes and brandished her garden trowel.

"Now listen up, Margaret. I'm down with the women's unit, yeah, okay. But what we really gotta fight for is having that damn Slugger set up a quota to hire women workers— that be the bottom line for me! We ain't just no women's extra unit, we the main event too! An' that goes double for the union. It gotta be one of the main contract demands!"

Margaret was not surprised, though. Just like that, Louella's insights as a black woman had gone straight to it.

"You got it, Louella!" she said. "We'll put that front and center. The boys will have to adopt that demand or we'll fold the women's unit altogether. No women worker demand, no women's committees — no extra strike support."

They went on from there with the plans for the wording, but the deal had been struck. Ray would go for it, as Margaret knew. And he'd use every ounce of his considerable weight with the other men to get it on the agenda.

But important as the women's unit and the women worker demand was, it was secondary to Margaret's investigative purpose in being there, so as they were cleaning their trowels at the faucet at the bottom of the back porch steps, she brought up topic number one.

"Ray tells me there's quite a bit of tension sometimes between some of the white workers, especially Billy Jenkins, a man named Burleson, and some others, and your husband and some other black workers, and I was wondering if Harvey had talked to you about that, and if so, if you would be willing to share it with me. I'll be honest, Louella, I'm trying to get background information that might help Ray and me solve these murders, and there seems to have been some tension between Fred Durkin and Jenkins and maybe some of the others about black workers and their roles at Slugger and even with the union. And before you ask, the reason I'm asking you instead of Ray asking Harvey, which he will do soon, is because sometimes husbands will tell their wives things they won't tell other men, and, well, Ray says Harvey keeps things zipped pretty tight to his chest. There, now, if I've gone and done what some folks call 'signifying,' then so be it. I respect you, and if you tell me to shut up and butt out, I'll close my trap and that'll be the end of it."

Louella stood up from the faucet where she'd been bent down washing her trowel, stretched, then pulled the rag from her back jeans pocket and wiped her forehead. She was stalling for time, and Margaret was fine with that. Whatever she needed. She was just glad Louella hadn't knocked her question down right off the bat. Louella gave her a long look, then started up the porch steps.

"Let's you and me go inside and get us some tea, or hell, a cold brew if you'd rather, which is what I'm having."

So they did. Louella chose Falls City beer and Margaret took a glass of iced tea already made and cold in the icebox. They sat at an old oak table and after a few good slugs Louella opened up.

"You the radar woman, I guess," Louella said with a crooked grin on her somewhat lopsided face, nose kind of bent to the side. "See, Harvey been woofin' about something goin' down at Slugger he don't like between Billy Jenkins, that Burleson guy, and several others he ain't named. Something about them saying the black workers is cheatin' the white ones, doctoring the piece rate sheets and white guys gettin' cheated. Said he and Mike the Bow was looking into it. I axed him what he meant but he clammed up tight as hell. Wouldn't tell me jack. But he did say one of the white guys had stood up to Jenkins, and the man already paid the price for it and the less I knew about it the better."

Then she turned to Margaret and looked her in the eye.

"Now do I look like a woman that scares easy to you, Margaret?"

"Hardly," Margaret said, returning her look.

"Well, I got to tell you, I'm scared behind this here. I ain't seen Harvey acting like this ever in life before. He's scared of something. It's more than what he was talking about with this piece rate boogie-joogie, something maybe connecting with that, but bigger too. He just said there was some bad muscle, some outside ju-ju behind it and leave it be. But he won't talk and he gets all shaky and nervous as hell around here if I

141

bring it up. The other night he had to grab one hand with the other to keep from slapping me when I kept at him about it, like slow motion in tension, one hand fighting the other. Then he just turned on his heel and walked right on outta here. Didn't come back for three hours."

"Do you know where he went?" Margaret was worried because of the AA connection.

"Well, I might as well tell you, though I ain't suppose to, but Harvey, he's in AA, and he's doin' real good, okay, he don't drink no more, but he had me worrying something awful that night, at least for a while."

Margaret reached across the table and laid her small hand on Louella's large hand as it sat balled up on the tabletop.

"My Ray's a recovering alcoholic too, Louella, and he goes to some of the same meetings as Harvey. I know he wasn't supposed to tell, but he did, when we decided that I should come here, in case it came up." Margaret was afraid that she'd take offense, but once again honesty paid off.

"Don't worry about that anonymous shit, Okay? Harvey don't give a damn who knows he in AA. And damn, girl, no wonder we hit it off. We got to stick together now — keep them men out of trouble and fight by they side at the same time!"

"Amen to that!" Margaret agreed. And she sang the "Amen" song all the way home on the two busses she had to ride to get there. The women's organizing unit was on its way. She'd made an ally and confirmed some of Ray's suspicions about the double-dealing bastard named Billy Jenkins.

Chapter Eighteen: Ray

The afternoon at Slugger passed uneventfully once I arrived after my breakfast with Alice Gorham. By five-thirty that evening I was sitting in a metal folding chair in "the happy hour" Friday night AA meeting. The idea was to get the weekend started sober on the very night many of us used to start our binges. Most of the regulars must've had other plans, there were only twelve people in the room. "Must've been a sale at the Liquor Barn," we always said when attendance was low. But there were a couple of newcomers I hadn't seen before. You could usually spot them hiding behind the metal poles that held up the ceiling just in front of the back row of chairs. Kind of dumb looking, you know, what with the poles only being eight inches thick. The 'ol boys hiding behind it looked kind of split up, half and half, which I always figured was about right, half wanting to get sober and half wanting a drink so bad they could taste it.

Danny B sat in his usual chair along the left-hand wall, facing the room from the side, along with the rest of the old timers and gurus of the group—kind of like the army brass on review. That wasn't for me. My sponsor, Jimmy G, and I sat in the middle of the pack with the rest of the ordinary drunks. There were three other guys I knew from Slugger scattered around the room: Andy Campsten from the cutting room, Nick Silvia from lacquer, and Bob Stills, who worked pro-section with Danny.

Then my fellow Sluggerite, Harvey Sampson, came in during the preliminary readings. He sat right next to me so I leaned over and shook his hand without saying anything.

Something was wrong with Harvey. His handshake was wobbly, not like his usual solid grip. Little beads of sweat glistened under the flickering fluorescent lights, his shoulders were caved in and he almost cringed in his seat as he stared at the cracked gray linoleum tile floor. I put my hand on his upper back, gave it a pat, and let go. He nodded right quick then stared back at the floor.

The meeting ran short due to the poor attendance as everybody spoke their fill and the allotted time hadn't been used up for the meeting. One of the newcomers brought up the topic of procrastination, talking about putting off working his fourth step. He'd done that several times before and then gone back to the bottle, he said. It didn't take the regulars long to tell him his real topic was fear. As always, I needed to hear what was being said, and I put in my two cents also, saying that fear got a whole lot stronger when it was self-centered fear—fear of looking bad, losing something you had, or not getting something you figured was owing to you. When they got to Harvey, he just said he reckoned he'd pass. His voice was shaky, almost a whisper.

When I raised my head and opened my eyes after the Lord's Prayer, Harvey had done a bunk. I yakked a little bit with the newcomers and gave them my phone number. While I was doing that I noticed Danny B, Bob and Andy in a heated discussion over in the corner by the Coke machine. Not much serenity there from the look of things. No ride tonight, I guessed, with Danny so intent on whatever was going on between him, Andy and Bob.

I did a quick checkin-in with Jimmy G, letting him know how I was doing on the case, what the gist of the conversation had been with the newcomers, and my general spiritual condition, then headed up the street and around the corner to the bus stop.

When I got there Harvey came out from the dark doorway of a building next to it. Once again I was impressed with how different he seemed to be from the big solid guy I knew at the plant. His shoulders were still bunched in, he walked stiff with a slight stoop. "I wanna thank you for trying to buck me up in there," he said, voice still shaky.

"Won't nothin'," I said. I figured he must be here to talk with me. The buses on this route didn't go anywhere near where Harvey lived, somewhere over on the west end, whereas this line went east and north. But I didn't want to look like I was eager or pressing him.

"You can tell me what's on your mind," I said. "Don't want to butt in, but be glad to listen if'n it'd do you some good."

"Yeah, I need to talk, man. Shit be fuckin' with my mind something bad. Don't make no habit of dealing with white folks, no disrespect, but the word on the street is you okay. Street says you took a bullet for a black woman back in the coal wars. That right?"

I nodded. Didn't want to interrupt the flow, but it damn sure felt good that Harvey had acknowledged the old incident. Yes, I'd jumped into the line of fire back there in Breathitt County when the gun thugs had opened up on the black lung meeting. Grabbed a woman, hardly knew if she were black or white, didn't make no never mind to me. She was trying to fold her baby into her chest and shuffle her toddler behind her at the same time and wasn't hitting the deck like she needed to. I took her down and covered the kid. Took a shot in my shoulder in the process. That shot paid off big time with Margaret nursing me, which started our eventual love and marriage. Harvey took a big breath and went on.

"Besides, Louella says your wife Margaret and her is getting up a ladies organizing unit to back the men of the union in case of a strike, came to her as the first woman she called on. She figures y'all to be one of the few white folks around here got their eyes on the prize and not on skin color. So I guess you all right."

145

"Thanks for the vote of confidence, Harvey," I said, "but it ain't necessary. So what's on your mind?"

"Be that damn betting line, you know, the moneyline, the odds, whatever. Thing is, I in trouble with the Man behind it. Owe 'im big time. They don't play. You know what I'm talking 'bout?"

"Yep. Reckon I do at that," I said. "The mob, or some type of Outfit. What makes you think they're after you? They do anything? Threats? Anything physical?"

"Yeah. Message on my time card. Say 'pay for your play or this you last day'."

"I figger you didn't take it to Benson, right?"

A couple of love-birds walked by just then and interrupted the flow. Man wasn't much to look at, but the woman, she was something else. Dark willowy brunette with a walk that flowed more than she stepped. They were giggling as they went by, the man's arm around her waist, tight, hips swaying side to side in unison. No crime to look, I guessed. But Harvey wasn't interested in romance.

"Naw. No way. The bosses' stooge? Don't deal with him no matter what. See, I played against the moneyline. Maybe you don't know about this, but it be goin' on at the plant for some nine-ten months now. Well, I seen how I could maybe make some extra, bein' as how my lady is always hurtin' for food money. Way it works with Louella and me, I take care of the rent, the car—gas and repairs an' all—she take care of the food and clothes for the four kids from what she get takin' in laundry. Gets most of the clothes we need from the white folks she washin' for, you know, but yet and she still have to pay out cash for the food. Never be quite enough. So I figure I help by gettin' some change through the baseball bets. Did okay for a while, you know. But four weeks back I upped my bet, blew it big time. Then again two weeks ago. Owes 'em two-fifty now. Ain't no way I can pay that much. Dumb-ass that I am, I axed 'em if I could go on time payments. Now I get this rap on my time card."

Just then a bus pulled up, spat out the air brakes, rocked up and down on its suspension while an older white guy got out followed by a teenage boy. They went opposite directions down the sidewalk, the man passing us, the kid going the other way. I nodded at the man, he looked at me then at Harvey, scowled and walked away shaking his head.

"Damn redneck!" said Harvey, then jerked his head back, looked at me. "Sorry, it's just…"

"You're right, damn redneck," I said, chuckling. "They's good recknecks and bad 'uns, just like any other type of folks."

"Then you a good 'un," laughed Harvey.

That took a little of the edge off. The bus had been my route, so, given it was after seven, I was stuck for a long time. The buses ran less often after seven, and I wasn't sure of the schedule. Harvey wasn't done, either.

"Thing is, reason I'm runnin' this down to you, man, it ain't the money. I ain't asking for no money, nossir. Never would do that to you, Ray. But I been watchin' you and I think you're more than you seem to be on the surface. No problem, Ray. But Louella says Margaret told her you here from the national WIA on account of them murders, that and to buck up Jenkins and turn this union fight around. Am I right? Well don't answer if you don't wanna. But if either of them things is true, you need to know something."

"Since we're being straight up, Harvey, yeah," I said. "I'm working kind of halfway undercover with the national WIA, trying to find out about the murders and keep the blame from being put on the union if the union ain't done it. But I ain't here to cover up nothin' neither. But, listen, if what you got for me is gonna get you hurt, man, I can get it another way."

"Naw, ain't like that, Ray. And don't you worry none about your secret. It's safe with me. Be anything I hate worse than a racist, it's a snitch."

"Okay, what you got?"

147

Harvey took a deep breath. "It's Danny B. I seen him after hours, when I was pullin' the floor clean-up in the cutting room. He won't on the detail, but he was in the plant, long about ten at night. He was havin' it out with Gorham. Over in the warehouse section, up on the scaffold where they keep the pro bat models, right? the ones they keep for each batter as a pattern? They be in each other's face. Hissin' and spittin' like a couple of ringtail cats on a fence. Well, next day Gorham turned up dead in the lathe." Harvey shut up. Just looked at me with an open question on his face.

I nodded. Gave Harvey a beat or two, then when he didn't say more, I replied.

"Okay. This investigation is confidential," I said. "I cain't tell you what it means on account of that, and, truth be told, I cain't anyway 'cause I just don't know. It's early days yet. But I gotta tell you, Harvey, that I really 'preciate you tellin' me. Yeah, the info might help, but mainly, I like it that you could cross a whole lotta lines that might divide us and tell me about it." I was done talking about the investigation, but I wasn't done with Harvey's troubles.

"So, if you don't mind a question back, I'd like to know who the 'bettin' man' is at the plant. Fact is, somebody else told me a little about the scheme, but wouldn't tell who the runner was."

Harvey looked at me like I was a man from Mars. Dumbfounded.

"Well, if you gotta ask. Sure. Why, we was just talkin' about him—Danny B. But hey, I figured you might know that, him being your friend in the program. I mean, I know he ain't your sponsor, but you guys is close, right?"

It took all I had to keep a poker face. I was outraged! Confused! Shit—fucking flabbergasted! My good pal in AA? No wonder Harvey looked at me like I was crazy.

"Well, looks like you didn't know that," Harvey said, sounding more than a little fearful at my reaction. "Sorry— guess that's bad news hittin' you all of a sudden."

"Yeah, damn straight, kinda took me by surprise," I said. Had to admit at least that much. Harvey just stood around and shuffled his feet. It was clear to me that he'd felt like he'd stepped in something, and he damn sure had. But I had to keep the damage down so I asked him some more about the money he owed, if he had any plans to pay it, and so forth and so on. He told me that in addition to Slugger, he'd been working a third shift over at GE's huge Appliance Park in the punch press units, where they start a lot of guys out. Pay was lousy, he said, but if he could keep himself in one piece by jiving the moneyline muscle, he could pay off his debt in three weeks. I said that was good, maybe if they knew they'd get their money they'd back off, but in my mind I wasn't so sure.

Harvey asked me when my bus was due. When I told him I didn't know for sure, he offered a ride, which I took. We shook hands in the car before I got out at my place. His grip was solid again.

Chapter Nineteen: Ray

Margaret leaned back from the daisy-design of the cloth covered table, set her fork in a plate now empty of the cornbread and white beans, rice, collards, and carrots we'd had for a late supper.

I'd just finished blowing off steam about Danny being the runner for the moneyline all this time and keeping his good AA buddy in the dark. Margaret responded, all business, since I was reporting on the day's business. She wasn't going to let me wallow in my misery, at least not yet.

"That's tough, Ray, I know. We'll come back to that. Now what about the other business of the day?"

I told her all about my talk with Alice Gorham, including Frank dying sober, Benson's threat to Frank and his bragging about controlling Billy Jenkins. I explained about Frank's role with the moneyline slips, before Danny B as it now appeared, his roughing up and the threats to Alice and himself, not leaving out the partial description of the attackers, with the implication of our two H & R pals.

Then I went on to tell her about my conversation with Harvey and his troubles, and the bit about Danny B at the plant the night before Gorham got it. Somehow I'd managed to give her the gist of the set-to on the smoke bench too, and of course, I told her about the warning on my time card.

I didn't go into what happened at the meeting itself but I covered the talk I had with my sponsor afterwards.

"Well, that's a crop of corn and a half," she said, trying to calm me down. Even though we'd had a great supper, I was still half-shaky with a fiery combination of anger, hurt, and bewilderment.

I was done reporting, so it was time to focus on the key elements, not to mention my feelings. She knew it, so she started in on the Danny B thing first.

"Could be Danny just got trapped into being a runner, Ray. Maybe he'd made a bet or two that went sour, just like Harvey, and the muscle came down on Danny to force him into the scheme. Or maybe he's just so downright ashamed of himself he's scared to tell you, so damn afraid it'd lower his image in your mind. Maybe he thinks you'll get drunk if he tells you something like that."

"You think he put the message on my card?" I said. "I mean, what else is goin' on behind my back?"

"No evidence for that, dear heart," she said, raising her hand in a stop sign. "Now don't let your head go runnin' down the road too far and too fast. You could blind yourself to all the other ways it could be happening."

"Well maybe," I said. "Could've been Burleson put the warning on the card. Seen him popping up off that bench and running out elsewhere in the plant two or three times this afternoon."

Margaret nodded, the curls in her auburn hair flashing in and out of the shaft of warm last-of-evening sunlight coming into the kitchen from the west window. It lit the left side of Margaret's head then slanted on down to touch the petals of the daffodils she'd cut that day.

"Him, or it could be you stepped in something you don't even know about," she said, "and that broke the boar out of hiding—the killer himself. You don't know right as of now whether the betting ring is tied to the murder itself or if somebody in that outfit is just trying to steer you away from that angle to protect himself."

"Yeah, it's just too damn soon to know much," I said. "Being as tomorrow's Saturday, and we only work a half-day, I can call on one of the boys in the afternoon and try and find out about the betting stuff. Think I'll see that kid, Sadderly, maybe I can sneak up on him by talking about the union, giving some old labor warrior advice, you know. Kind of elder him a bit, then hit him smack up front with the betting ring, see what he's willing to say about it.

"Then maybe I'll have time to see Mike the Bow too, ask him about the Benson and Billy Jenkins angle. That man's got more sense than half these jokers, and for some reason, even the most prejudiced of 'em talks to him all the time. Man knows a helluva lot about what goes on at Slugger, that's for sure."

"Sounds good," Margaret said. "I sure wish we could help Harvey, though."

"He's a proud man, that one," I said, "won't accept no charity or nothin' that even comes close to it."

"I know," said Margaret, then she scrunched her eyes closed, something Margaret did when she poured all her considerably strong thinking ability into one tiny point. I picked at my plate, wiped out the last of the rice, sopped up the rest of the gravy with the last of Margaret's iron-skillet cornbread.

"You know, Ray," she said, not just opening but flashing her eyes at me. Uh-oh, here it comes, I knew, another brainstorm likely to get me into some sticky wicket or other.

 "What if we asked Harvey to work with us on the investigation? Now that he knows what we're about, he could maybe use the payment of his debt as a lever to find out more about who's behind the betting ring. Nothing too risky, don't want him hurt, just maybe he could ask to give his payment to somebody higher up, somebody over Danny B, tell them he wants to make sure his debt is cancelled, that type of thing."

I gave it a once-over while looking out the kitchen window, now dark. No moon to speak of, I noticed. No stars either, not like back home in Lawrence County where the stars at night looked like millions of clear quartz crystals embedded in black granite.

"Sure," I said, feeling a surge coming on, "we can just get him a check for services rendered to the national union. Put him on our account. That way it's all on the up-and-up, no charity, no messy expense vouchers. He can just write up a bill to the Odle Agency for investigating services."

"Perfect!" Margaret said snapping her fingers. "I'll go write up a request to the union to add him to our account, then in the morning I can call the union HQ and get it put through quick fast and in a hurry."

We just sat and grinned at each other. We were damn near insufferable when we figured we'd come up with a smart way out of a jam. Maybe we were just a mite too cute, but we loved that about ourselves. The hell with anybody that didn't like it.

I got up and did the dishes while Margaret went into the front room to write up the request. When I'd started workin' on the pots I saw she'd started working the jack loom I'd built for her some years back. Made out of mountain cherry, it glowed a mellow reddish brown in the photographer's lamplight I'd set beside it. Margaret did placemats, curtains, pillows and even clothes from time-to-time, keeping the old patterns of the Scots-Irish hill people alive and in use. Every once in a while she'd send some to a folk gallery they had over to Berea College. Used to be I'd go to Berea too, visiting my old buddy Joseph Dillworth, a professor of religion and the editor of the magazine of the Committee of Southern Churchmen. The Committee was a rag-tag outfit, or non-outfit, because it sure wasn't organized. Just a loose conglomeration of activists like me, poets, writers and preachers that loved the South and fought like hell to see justice come to pass. There was no particular theology to it, just the rock-bottom idea that what we were supposed to be doing was the work of bringing folks together to do right by one another. Bible calls it reconciliation. That was the name of the magazine, "Katellagete" or "Be Reconciled" in Bible Greek.

Reason I was involved was that the Committee had sponsored me to help bring white and black workers together just for conversation in a cotton plant down in South Carolina when I was a young man what didn't know his ass from a hole in the ground but had more guts than brains. Me and my Black partner got run out by the Klan, but I'd made my soul journey once or twice a year to see Joseph at Berea ever since. Since I'd been with Margaret, she'd joined me on the trips and taken a few of her weavings to sell in the folk art gallery. She made a little extra out of it, and what's more, usually got letters or cards from people that bought one of her creations, and that made her feel good, more connected to the larger world. Joseph and I used to sip a little whiskey, well, Okay, sometimes a lot, back before I got sober, and we'd talk. Beatenest talk you ever heard.

Memories of Joseph, the Committee, and Berea took me right through doing the dishes and rounding up the garbage and trash, which I then took out into the alley and stuffed in the big stoved-in galvanized can that leaned up against the backyard fence.

And that's when they came for me.

One stepped out from behind the telephone pole next to the garbage can. It was pitch black, there being no money wasted on streetlamps in the Little Appalachian ghetto. Couldn't see a face, then realized he had a stocking over it. He was a big 'un, though. Six feet or better, two-twenty or so. The bat in his right hand looked not even half the thickness of his arm. He raised the bat to swing and I grabbed the garbage can lid by the handle, holding it like a shield. I heard the sharp click of hobnails from behind me and felt rather than heard the swoosh just before the lights exploded in my head. I staggered, reeling around towards the blow from behind, the man who'd swung rippling in a visual strobe effect, face also invisible, his hair a shock of white in the black and white shimmer. Then the first guy's bat slammed into my shield, then bounced onto my head from the front. The world went glaring white then folded into a brilliant yellow circle surrounded by the black of space. The circle quickly receded, smaller and smaller, and the inky black got bigger and bigger till it ate my universe.

There was a faint hum. A dim pale blue bar slid from left to right. Then it got bigger, turned into an oval and moved almost out of sight, then came back and expanded some more. I looked into it as it became a tunnel. At the end of it I saw a face. What a lovely face. Brown eyes set fairly close, a smallish nose, lips that pursed slightly, like somebody humming. That's what it was — humming. An old mountain lullaby. "What'll I do With My Baby-O."

I was on my side. A cool wet feeling seemed to come over the back of my head and across my cheek.

Then pain. Throbbing was too simple to describe this pain. It had parts. Like a machine. No, more like a jarring bad symphony of pains. Head section was the percussion, blaring brass section on the shoulder, a few screaming saxophones down in my knee.

I didn't want to face the music and it went away, leaving black behind. Quiet black.

When I came to again I snapped to awareness fairly quickly. Margaret was still humming, this time "Red Wing." I guess it was mostly habit, but I heard my own rumbling voice, reduced to a near-whisper, just barely audible, try and mumble the chorus line in the old Wobbly version of the song: "Oh you cain't scare me, I'm sticking to the union." She had an ice pack on the back of my head and a cool wet washcloth on my temple and cheek. There was a knotted rag with ice tied to my left knee. I tried to sit up.

"Whoa there, cowboy," she said in a voice that was honey and cool water all at once. "You've had quite a few knocks. The doc has come and gone. You'll live, he says. A concussion and some right bad bruises, it seems."

155

All I wanted right then was a little nip of the old John Barleycorn. Damn! The sumbitch hits you when you're down. The craving, the cells screaming out for relief. I tried to struggle up. First a bottle then the goddamned bastard that did this. I tried to shout "Get the hell back, I'm coming up!" But I just rasped something. Tongue felt like number 40 grit sandpaper scraping on a rough-sawn plank. "Gotta fight. Cain't let no shithead take ME!" I was yelling at the redheaded kid that used to beat me up once a week in grammar school. Waited up the creek near my house every Friday. This time he had a stocking mask over his head. Carried a bat. Had a shock of white hair—or was that the strobe effect of my brain? I started up again, tried to slam him with my fist. Collapsed back down on something soft. One more time I shouted. But it still come out like rasp and scrape. No real words. Just noise.

I didn't go all the way down and out this time. Light and shadow swam in and around me. Finally the room settled down and it was just me and Margaret. And I was going to be all right. I breathed a deep one. Pain didn't go away, but I knew it wasn't all there was anymore.

Margaret was here, she'd take care of me. Hell, more than that, I would take care of me. I would accept Margaret's help. Oh I would fight back, no question on that. But I'd use the tools I'd learned to use in the last four years. I wasn't going back to the hell of drink. I would get over this. It would pass.

"Thanks, love one," I managed to croak. "I'm okay now. Just think I'll rest awhile. Figger this out tomorrow."

"Sounds good, dear heart," I heard her say kind of far off. "I'll be right here when you wake."

Chapter Twenty: Margaret

Some eighty hours after the attack on Ray Margaret took the Sixth Street bus across Broadway down towards the Ohio River to the West Jefferson Street Metropolitan Center, where the County Clerk's office and the Recorder's Office Deed Room were located. It was in a huge concrete building with a granite facade and faded institutional green halls. Margaret had decided that if you were a mope and walked with your head and eyes down all the time, the endless alternating brown and burgundy linoleum tiles would make you dizzy from watching them flash by. Her eyes were certainly about to cross before she got to where she was going.

Margaret found the right room after a few trials and errors, took a number and waited. Finally she got her chance to search for the Recorder's records of ownership of the development known as Rone Court in Shively. Ray and Margaret had decided they needed to get the lay of the land, literally, about the ownership and possible debts and financing that had put the pressure on Fred and Irma Durkin, not to mention on how Billy Jenkins was tied into it.

Ray was a huge sight better but still taking one more day off before going back to work at Slugger. She'd left him content to sleep and hold his hurts into himself, which was his way, a pitcher of lemonade and some aspirins waiting beside the bed. He wouldn't be up and around until the afternoon, so Margaret had arrived at the eight a.m. opening of the Recorder's office to follow her itch, which had grown pretty powerful by this time, a good four full days after her talk with Irma.

Margaret first looked up the property by its address in a standing card file stretched across the front wall of the large room. The card file had three-by-five cards permanently attached through a center hole at the bottom to a rod on which they slid so that you could thumb through them and read them but not remove them. Once she found the right one, it told her nothing except the file code letter and number where the record was kept in the deed book, and its location in the County Recorder's file system. Margaret copied that information down on a slip of paper she tore off the pads that the County provided, along with stubby little yellow number two pencils, and then went up to a high counter that ran halfway across the middle of the room where she again waited until a very harried lady clerk took the code down and went in search of the file. It took five minutes or so for her to come back to Margaret with the file, a grumpy frown on her face, so Margaret gave her as big a smile as she could, thinking she would be way past the frowning stage and into snarling if she had that job. The lady directed Margaret to the reading room off to the right where Margaret sat among other Deed Room detectives at a long table and read through the pages of filings about the Rone Court development: the Titles, the Deeds and the Loans and Refinance transactions recorded by Jefferson County.

The search took her all of an hour and a half. That was because the Rone Court might have been a solid construction project as far as the houses went, but following the money trail led Margaret to a house of cards. The financial backers had several layers of loans to them, debt being used to finance debt, shakier and shakier with each layer going back. Margaret was sure as hell no banker, but it looked to her like somewhere between a Ponzi scheme, a shell game, and a pea-and-thimble con, so it took her a while to figure out which set of investors had control of the actual property. But finally there was a bottom line, and it read: "Jason A. Albright and Company, Incorporated."

158

To find out about the Albright Company, Inc., Margaret had to go to the Corporation Commission, which had its Records Office in the same massive building, but about a half a block on the other side, which involved walking the tiles once again. Margaret almost started counting them this time, but decided that might be suicidal. She waited a while longer in another dreary office and then got her chance to go digging through corporate records, same card room to file clerk to reading room process, until she was given access to the incorporation papers, which were public records that listed the agent, officers and directors of the corporation. Two things struck Margaret. One, the money — forty percent of the money for the corporation came from investments funneled to it from a consortium of three whiskey companies: Four Roses, Seagram's Kentucky, and Stitzel-Weller. The rest came from individual investors. Two, the connection — the agent for the Albright Company was one Harrison Jenkins. And its Chief Executive Officer and Chairman? One Alan Sims Worthington.

But there was one more thing. Curioser than all the rest. An add-on, ten years later, dated June of 1964. A refinance note of purchase of the mortgage of Rone Court properties. The debt was sold to another company in one lump sum and paid off, cleared from the books of the Albright Company. Boom! Just like that. And there was a copy of the new deed of trust in the name of the new owner of the property: The Pension Fund of the International Brotherhood of Teamsters! The kingdom of the notorious Dave Beck and his titular heir, one James R. Hoffa.

Margaret copied all of that down in her trusty notebook and skedaddled. She and Ray would have a strategy session just as soon as his head was up to paying attention to anything more than aches and pains. Margaret imagined herself playing Florence Nightingale for the better part of the day, chicken soup, lemonade, hot tea and maybe a gentle massage, and then sitting down with him after supper for a short talk before he took a very early bedtime.

Naturally when she got back to the Jacob Street apartment Ray was sitting up on the back porch and acting antsy as all get-out. She figured if she'd had been another half hour later getting home he'd have been pacing the floor, injuries and all. The man is the beatenst thing she'd ever seen when it came to taking care of himself. Didn't know the meaning of the idea, hadn't made its acquaintance at all.

Margaret got Ray settled in a folding chair with a glass of milk in his hand and some of the peanut butter cookies she'd made for him, then quickly filled him in, figuring to get his mind on something outside himself would be the best medicine, and he calmed right straight down, sure enough. Folks laugh at the idea of a grown man getting happy on peanut butter cookies and milk, but Ray does, especially when he's hurting. Beats the hell out of his hitting the bottle, which Margaret had never seen him do, and God willing, never would.

"Knew it," Ray said through still half-swollen lips, keeping the words to as few as possible. "Worfington ain't so proper as he look."

"No, he isn't," Margaret said. "The record shows that he's mixed-up financially with Billy Jenkins, either directly or through Billy's daddy. They sure put the screws to Fred and Irma Durkin on the Wade issue. It was only when the Braden's lawyer filed a contempt of court case that they backed off."

"Racist bast'ds!" gruffed Ray. At that he looked down the alley at the scene of his beating and took a deep sigh, or started to, then hissed in pain, choking off the breath. His ribs still hurt something awful. Margaret fought the urge to rush over to him and put her hands on him, knowing it wouldn't do the slightest medical good and that he wasn't emotionally suited to it either. She and Ray had worked out their cues on these things over the last three years and the previous cases they'd worked together. He was working on being open to her help, even asking for it more and more, and she was working on respecting his boundaries. That was their deal. But Margaret couldn't help but shake her head and she could feel the wet coming into her eyes, try as she might to stop it.

"Somp'n else," Ray managed to say. "Been 'memberin' that night, some of what I seen. Like I tol' you, was flashin' black an' white afer th' firs' hit. Well, seen th' one what done it, face black, but like a fishn' net, but hair white, solid white."

"You think it was Billy Jenkins?" Margaret asked, immediately recognizing that the hair fit Ray's description of Billy.

"Ain't sure," he replied. "Coulda been the flash, strobe effect...but yeah, think so. Be like him."

"Yes, like Irma Durkin said, like a cur dog to attack you from behind in the dark," Margaret said.

They both spent some time digesting this along with the implications.

"Worfinton coulda sicc'd 'em on me, 'im an Blackie," Ray said, then eased out a painful cough.

"For sure," Margaret managed to say after a minute. "And Worthington is hiding behind his antique desk, flintlock musket and false claim to Kentucky aristocracy. But let's not let our hatred of him blind us to the other issues here, all right."

"Wha that?"

"Well, like I said, the financing of Rone Court was a house of cards. Whiskey money, sure, but that wasn't but forty percent of the whole. The rest came from individual investors—hot money men trying to make a fast buck. Now, since racism would indeed work in such a way in this place and time, selling that place out in Shively to a black family, when most of the houses in Rone Court were newly built and up for sale, would in fact have hurt the sales value of the unsold properties quite a bit. Am I right?"

"Yep. No doubt."

"So Worthington, through the Jenkinses, dad and son, could have been trying to limit the damage when, before the dynamite, he was leaning on the Durkins to sign the petition and push the Wades to leave, thereby trying to appease his bigoted investors. He might have been sitting on some financial dynamite of his own that was about to blow."

"I get it," said Ray.

Margaret looked out from the porch across the side street at the houses facing the empty lot next to their corner. The windows were opaque in the cloudy early afternoon light so that they mirrored their building, sending Margaret's thoughts back to her.

"You know, Ray, I can see Irma Durkin as she was when I ended my visit, my feeling that she'd been grateful that someone had understood, that someone, especially someone white, and more especially a woman, a Southern woman, had not only understood, but had wanted to be with her, and had honored her for her courage, which I'd done before I left. And I wondered all the way home on the bus what had gone on in the years since the Wades had finally been forced out. What had forged that courage. Had she taken heart in the midst of the kind of daily petty cruelty she no doubt faced every day from her neighbors? And had Rone Court festered in its disease of racism? Or had some degree of healing come?"

They both sat still on that for a little while. Then Margaret picked up the thread.

"I didn't ask her about the current situation on Rone Court — and I should have. Was it still something that would push Fred Durkin to antagonize Billy Jenkins? Harrison Jenkins? And now that I know what I do about Worthington's role, being behind things back in the shadows, what about pressures on him? Would he still hold a grudge — after all, his investment went sour too."

"That man? Oh yeah, my dear, you bet. He ain't let go of nothin'."

"But that was then, Ray. Twelve years before Fred was killed and stuck in the lathe at Slugger. It's hard to believe Worthington carried a grudge strong enough to kill for that long, isn't it? People do that sort of thing, I know. But does Worthington strike you as that kind of man?"

Ray was sure. Margaret wasn't. They discussed that possibility for a while. Or more like it, Margaret ruminated out loud and Ray either confirmed or negated with short responses, given his condition. And Margaret analyzed other ideas, such as whether or not Billy Jenkins could be that kind of man, or whether any of the others on the racist rump committee at Rone Court could somehow have used the site at Slugger for the murder just to throw suspicion in the wrong direction when the murder had nothing to do with Slugger or anybody associated with it and everything to do with the events of 1954 in Rone Court. But in the end, although they didn't entirely rule those choices out, they downgraded them pretty much.

"It just keeps coming back to that damn baseball bat factory," Margaret summed up, "the union, racism on the shop floor and in the management office, and the moneyline. That's way more than enough, and now we've got this financial stuff going back to Rone Court for an extra motivating factor in the Worthington-Jenkins-Durkin mix.

"Now that reminds me, to bring it up to the present. The Recorder's files showed that eventually, in fact just last year, the construction loans for Rone Court were paid off, basically all in one lump sum. And would you like to know who paid them off? And who now owns Rone Court properties?"

"I have a feelin' you're a-gonna tell me…an' I ain't gonna like it."

"The Pension Fund of the International Brotherhood of Teamsters, that's who."

"Shit. Worse'n I thought. How much?"

"One and a half million dollars."

163

Ray made a major effort to speak. "Wish I could whistle! Now I ain't one to go agin' my brother workers," he said, haltingly. "There's a lot of good Teamster locals and brothers…tryin' to clean up the worst of that bunch of bums at the top…but let's call a spade a spade…that loan was paid off by the mob."

Margaret picked up where he left off to save Ray the pain of talking. "That means Worthington is deep inside their pockets. Now we know a whole lot more than we did about this moneyline stuff. There is no doubt in my mind how the mob put the moneyline into Slugger. They don't have their hands dirty running Danny B or some other worker on the shop floor. Worthington's the one standing there at Slugger making sure it works out to the benefit of the mob."

"Which makes it Benson too," put in Ray.

And that put one James Haskell's allegiances in a new light. What if he was in Louisville before the murders? What if his connections with Jenkins, as shown by his threats to the Durkin family, preceded the deal with Worthington to investigate the murders? What if there was a convenient connection between Worthington, the mob, and H & R? Or what if the connection of convenience was just Haskell/Blondie—or Blondie and his pal Blackie working free-lance and it involved thuggery and intimidation before the murders? What if the fox was guarding the hen house? What if the fox had killed the hen? What if Haskell was acting solo as a Worthington-mob hit man? And as they now suspected, what if Blackie had teamed up with Jenkins to assault Ray in an act of physical reprisal and intimidation?

They decided that there was enough of a difference between the Durkin and Gorham cases to pursue different theories on them—but it looked awfully much like the Gorham case might involve a mob hit. Still, Margaret and Ray decided they had to keep their minds open. It was too early and they had jack-all for evidence yet.

So they decided to put the Rone Court-Worthington connection on the back burner for now and go with Ray's gut feeling that they needed to dig deeper on the goings-on with the piece rate sheets, Durkin, Jenkins and the racist dust Burleson and crew were throwing into the eyes of a lot of the white workers as the contract talks were heating up. Was the company behind that? And what did Durkin, or Gorham, for that matter, have to do with it?

"Way I look at it," Ray said working up to a major speech. "Jenkins and Worthington don't just stop with Rone Court…stuff don't happen that way. It spills over into Slugger. Billy's too cozy with Benson. He fakes like he's a whipped dog anytime he gets near Worthington or Benson."

"Right," Margaret said. "So we need to see how they're doing it. If they're doctoring the piece rate sheets to lower the white boys' pay and blame it on the blacks, then we need to bring that out into the light and bust that scam up."

"Okay, but how you get into their offices? Them piece rate sheets is in there. Each of them has a set, Benson for the company, Jenkins for the union."

"Right. But I've been thinking on that and it so happens I have a nifty little plan. Now here it is."

Margaret laid out the basics. Then Ray made some good changes. And together they came up with a plan of action for the next day that was dangerous, to be sure, but had a fair-to-middling chance of breaking open at least one of the knots in the case.

Chapter Twenty-One: Radio five

Mel Allen: *All I gotta say is that Jim Maloney has sure earned his keep today, Red. He's workin' a shutout here at Crosley field in Cincinnati and it's two away in the top of the ninth with the Redlegs up by 7.*

Red Barber: *Yep, Mel, Jimbo won't have to back up to the pay window this time, he's been tearin' up the pea patch with an even dozen strikeouts so far and he's still in the game after nearly nine full innings of defense.*

MA: *All right, Red, now he's just got to deal with the Mets catcher Greg Goossen, a man who'd like to show the fans back home in New York at least a little of that Big Apple razzle-dazzle right about now...*

RB: *Well, here's his chance 'cause Maloney's into his windup, here's the pitch...low and outside for ball one, Mel, and Goossen steps back for a little confab with his inner angels.*

MA: *Okay, but he better have some pull with the powers that be 'cause Maloney's got some juice of his own upstairs, he's working on another 20 game season like he had last year, Red.*

RB: *Goosen's back in the batters' box and here's the next pitch...swing and a miss to a fast ball down and inside — just nicked the plate, Mel!*

MA: *Make it one-and-one to Goossen, who steps back from the box for another celestial consult and a knock of the bat on his heel.*

RB: *He can knock away with that bat but he can't knock Maloney's .254 earned run average for the '65 season, Mel, one of the best east or west of the Mississippi.*

MA: *Goossen's got the goods himself, Red, batting .290 in his rookie year last season and coming in with a handsome .979 fielding percentage.*

RB: That's some mighty tall cotton he's standing in, I'd say…

MA: Tall indeed, Red, but now he's got himself back in the box and Maloney's winding up…fast ball…scorcher! Blew it right past Goossen for strike two! That's one and two now, Red, Jimbo's got Goossen where he wants him for the next pitch.

RB: Righto – he can throw any old kind of junk at Goossen and the batter will have to give it some respect on account of it might, just might, nick the plate for a called strike three, Mel.

MA: And natch, Greg's backing out of the box…he's got to make this swing count, got to look it over real close…

RB: Well, close or not, he's gonna want a real hard knock if it's going to do any good at this stage, Mel.

MA: That's for sure, but it's the age-old contest between pitcher and hitter, Red, the final pitch for the final out or the start of a rally, one-on-one and may the best man win…

RB: …and here we go, Goossen's back in the box…and Maloney's wasting no time, here's the windup…the pitch…

MA: What a swing, Red!…Goossen swung like he'd have hit the ball all the way to the Merchant's Paper sign on top of the building sticking up a half mile back of center field!

RB: But all he got was air, Mel! Strike three, the game is over!

MA: That's all she wrote, Red – except another shutout for the record books to the account of one James Maloney!

Chapter Twenty-Two: Margaret

Ray created a diversion for Billy Jenkins upstairs in the burn room while Margaret snuck into his office disguised as a cleaning lady. She was all decked out in a drab gray dress, an apron, and a galvanized bucket on little rollers she'd gotten at a cleaning supply store just a block down Broadway from the Odle Agency home and office. She'd stuffed a mop, a broom, and a dustpan into it, not to mention assorted dust rags and a can of Spic 'N Span.

The cleaning lady routine fit into Slugger's monthly cleaning day where they forced the men to take a half-shift off on a Saturday so that the plant could be cleaned of the huge accumulation of sawdust—more to keep it from gumming up the machinery than out of any consideration for the health of the worker. They hired a contract cleaning outfit to do the job and Margaret was dressed to look like one of the contract cleaning ladies.

Margaret had given Ray forty minutes to get Jenkins diverted upstairs to the burn room, then sidled in the back entrance and, quickly as she could, shuffled down the side hall, dragging her bucket full of cleaning junk, and sidled into the unlocked door of Jenkins office. Ray had loosened some screws at the back of the burn machines the night before, those flame tempering machines that burned and brought out the relief on the grain of some models of bats.

The first thing Margaret did once inside the office was to lock the door. She could always explain that she'd mistakenly locked it if Jenkins showed up but she couldn't move fast enough if he suddenly came through the door and she had files or other incriminating stuff in her hands. Then Margaret leaned against the door and just took it all in—and there was a lot to take in even though the space itself was small, just a cubbyhole, really. But where Worthington was putting on airs of a Kentucky Colonel with old-timey antiques and aristocracy, Jenkins was a gadget hound. Two walls were lined with files, to be expected, a third wall took Jenkins' modern blond Swedish desk, polished to a high gloss, office chair, and personal file, but the fourth wall in the windowless room was full of electrical stuff all set up on a counter than ran down the length of it—a big T.V., a video camera, a Xerox machine, a Xerox Corporation Magnafax Telecopier with a phone hooked up to it, and an IBM electric typewriter. As that ole Southern gentleman radio ham Red Barber would say, Jenkins was standin' in tall cotton. And again, it made Margaret wonder about what he'd given up to Slugger in exchange—you don't get those perks for nothing. But Margaret wasn't there to admire the latest expensive gadgets or play twenty questions about Jenkins and Slugger management, she had some work to do.

And she got down to it, first turning on the Xerox machine—because if she found anything good, she would want a copy, and the good luck of finding a copy machine wouldn't be worth diddly if it wasn't warmed up by the time she needed it, and that took a while. Next Margaret started going through the file cabinets, all except one, which was locked. It looked like Jenkins kept duplicates of all kinds of Slugger records. There were safety records in files marked for each area of the plant—cutting room, sanding, lacquer and burn rooms, warehouse, receiving, shipping, P.R.O., and so forth. Then there were other drawers with files for P.R.O. bat specifications, files headed by players names and date ranges. Margaret wanted to stop and go through those, it would have been fascinating reading, some of the names alone jumped out at her—all the way back to Ty Cobb! But she had to push on.

Then Margaret hit the jack-pot! Production records—by year, week, month, section and employee. There was a summary sheet for each month with columns with the employee's name down the left side, divided into sections— sanding, cutting, lacquer, and so forth, with columns across the top labeled by "RATE" " + " " – " "DIFF" " %". Numbers filled the columns. Margaret grabbed the monthly summaries for the past six months and put each one through the Xerox machine, at an agonizingly slow one-at-a-time. She could have whistled Dixie all right, only Margaret didn't whistle that hateful song anymore, and couldn't stand it when she heard it played or sung, which was still all too often. It was a song of blind loyalty to a regime of oppression, mass murder and slavery, and despite the obvious, the oppression wasn't just against black folks. It had twisted the souls of her kin too.

Good as Margaret felt about the production sheets with the piece rate records on them, she knew she wasn't done. These looked like the real deal—square as a picture frame. They wouldn't prove anything had been going on that shouldn't have been. They'd come in handy if she and Ray found something that didn't line up with them, but by themselves, they weren't much. She had to keep looking.

Well, there was that one locked drawer in Jenkins' desk. Margaret had jimmied file drawer locks before with paper clips, hat pins, all sorts of stuff, but this one was different—it had a regular padlock on the handle of the file door. Nothing doing. Any monkey wrenching would give the whole thing away, so that was out. Jenkins' secret was safe in that drawer, whatever it was.

So Margaret kept looking elsewhere. He had some plaques and photographs on the wall over his desk, the kind of stuff you'd expect. Baseball teams thanking Louisville Slugger, signed pro player photos with Jenkins, a plaque given by the Louisville Little League for donated bats. Margaret turned to the opposite wall where Jenkins had a scoreboard depicting the score for a Louisville Colonels game—Louisville 5, Visitors

3, with the various innings and runs per inning below the final score. The sign was about two feet high by three feet wide. And thick. It stood out from the wall by a good four inches. What a strange thing to have on the office wall, she thought.

Being the mischievous soul that she was, Margaret reached up to the little white plastic knob beside the Visitors score number and turned it, changing it to six. Then she reached up to the Colonels' knob and turned, or rather, *tried* to turn it — but it wouldn't budge. Strange, she thought. Was it stuck? She tried again. Nothing doing. Well, actually, it moved just a bit. And Margaret heard a scraping noise, kind of like the number panel was scraping paper or something. Something that was jammed behind it. Curiouser and curiouser, like in the child's book about the monkey.

Unless? What was making the noise that sounded like something scraping paper? Margaret wouldn't know unless she climbed over the filing cabinets below the sign and satisfied her intense curiosity and looked at the back of that sign! Oh, this was going to be hard — and painful. Margaret looked around and found a huge book, a baseball almanac, and placed that on the floor. Then she put one foot on it and managed to get one hand on the scoreboard and lifted. She was in luck! It was suspended from the wall just like a picture — by a wire hanging from a nail. Margaret lifted it a little higher and the wire came up over the nail and the whole thing toppled over onto the tops of the filing cabinets! Margaret almost fell off the book perch with it, but managed to stop her fall by shoving her foot against the desk — thank God it was so close! She stood there for a moment, catching her breath and terrified that someone had heard the crack of the wooden scoreboard against the steel of the filing cabinets. But nobody came to the door.

Her hunch, a hundred to one shot, proved out. There was a rectangular doorway on the back of the scoreboard, like in a mantle clock, which she opened — and there they were! Papers!

171

Margaret pulled them out. Production sheets. She wasted no time in sorting through and copying the same months as she'd copied before, not needing to look, knowing in her mind and heart that they were different, not needing to know how they were different. That could wait.

Margaret got the last sheet out of the machine, cut the power to it and watched the little green light fade out as she put the originals back in the little compartment in the back of the scoreboard. Then she scrambled up again. This time Margaret stood the scoreboard on top of the file cabinets and put one hand under it, lifting the board herself, while she used the handle of the mop to lift the wire over the nail.

Somehow she managed it without falling. Once Margaret was back down she straightened the scoreboard using the mop handle. She even dusted a little on top of the filing cabinets right behind the scoreboard, wiping off any prints she might have left there.

That's when she saw a little plastic baseball bat on a key fob with the logo of the Louisville Cardinals. She turned it over and saw the initials F. D. and quickly stuffed it into her maid's apron. No time to think, but F. D. could stand for Fred Durkin, and that was all the time she had for deductions at the moment.

It took Margaret about ten seconds to admire her handiwork and to stuff the newly Xeroxed sheets into her apron. She went around the office and dusted a few things, emptied the office trash into a plastic bag she'd brought, and put a couple splashes of Spic 'n Span and water on the floor and wiped them just enough to leave a noticeable film to make it look like the maid had been a little sloppy — but she'd been there.

Then Margaret cautiously opened Jenkins' door, looked left and right like she'd been taught to do when crossing the street as a child, and seeing no oncoming traffic, slipped out and down the hallway. She hadn't gone ten feet when the booming voice of Billy Jenkins bounced off the hallway wall and he popped out from an archway as he rounded into the hall and charged right past her, nearly knocking her over.

"Sorry ma'am," he threw his tinny voice over his shoulder as he barreled on down the hall. Margaret didn't say a word, just kept her head down and eyes averted and kept putting one shaky foot in front of the other till she was out the back of the plant and into the alley, then the two blocks down Jacob Street and home. But in her apron pocket Margaret had a mother load of gold. Or so she hoped.

Back in the office Ray and Margaret cleared everything off the old oak desk and laid out the two sets of production sheets side by side, one month at a time. Just by chance they took April's regular sheet, the one from Benson's file drawer, out of the stacks first and went down the left hand columns till they got to the sanding room stats.

MANIT/2100	PROD	+	--	%	PAY DIFF
Burleson	2856	456		16%	1.81
Duvall	2568	168		7%	1.72
Wilson	2782	382		14%	1.79
Odle	2655	255		10%	1.75
McGeorge	2245		-155	-7%	1.58
Davison	2334		-64	-3%	1.62
Handy	2476	76		3%	1.68

"Well, that Odle fella is right about in the middle, not at the top," Margaret said with a grin and a chuckle, "despite his having a swell head half the time."

"Yeah well, he helps pay the grocery bill, I reckon," said Ray with an equally big grin, "besides other services for which he don't get paid."

"Perhaps not in cash, but I'd hate to think he feels unrewarded," Margaret said, arching her right eyebrow.

And they turned back to the sheets she'd just thieved at great risk.

The layout was plain enough. Ray explained that Burleson, Davison and Duvall were white workers, McGeorge, Wilson and Handy were black. Burleson, racism and all, was fast as all get-out, and was into the company the most at 16% piece rate bonus, making $1.81 per hour instead of the standard $1.65. The others were scattered up and down the scale, and poor McGeorge, who hadn't averaged the Manuit, or day rate, for the month, had made less than the standard wage, at $1.58 an hour.

"That's a sad case, Margaret," Ray explained, "Elvis McGeorge is a good guy, but his wife has cancer and he's taking care to get them three boys of theirs off to school in the mornings in April, get her situated, then get to Slugger by seven for the shift. Plus the ole boy just worries his head all day, lost in his miseries, an' don't put his mind on the sander and so he don't turn out the work. Then that's a double boomerang on him, comes back to haunt him when his pay's low, cain't pay her medical bills, which is now gone through the roof an' the doctors is threatening to cut his wife off."

Margaret just shook her head. How could a doctor cut off a woman fighting for her life against cancer? Their oath bound them first of all to do no harm. Wasn't refusing treatment doing harm? The old Woody Guthrie song had it right, "some will rob you with a fountain pen." But they had to push on, so Margaret pulled the April sheet from the stack she'd gotten from behind the scoreboard plaque and laid it beside the official one.

MANIT/2100	PROD	+	--	%	PAY DIFF
Burleson	2245		-155	-7%	1.58
Duvall	2476	76		3%	1.68
Wilson	2782	382		14%	1.79
Odle	2655	255		10%	1.75
McGeorge	2856	456		16%	1.81
Davison	2334		-64	-3%	1.62
Handy	2568	168		7%	1.72

"Well I'll be damned!" Ray and Margaret both chorused at once. It smacked them right in the eyes — the best and worst of the blacks and whites had been reversed. Burleson's production had gone to McGeorge and Duvall's had gone to Handy, and vice versa! But the big question was..

"Why'd somebody go and do that?" blurted Ray.

"It's what Irma Durkin hinted at and what Harvey Sampson might as well have said point blank," Margaret replied. "The racists in the plant are going to throw this out there and bust up the union solidarity at some crucial moment. My guess is it will come when the contract talks are at a high point of tension, when you need everybody to be together. Jenkins has this little bomb in safekeeping, but it won't come from him, it will come from Burleson or one of his kind, and Jenkins will act shocked as hell about it, of course, and wring his hands as Burleson or Duvall or someone like them leads the white Blockheads to walk out."

"You're damn right, and the crackers will figure the blacks were cheating on them, and the blacks will feel it was a frame-up, and then they'll split the union, and the union will lose it's power and have to take whatever deal is on the table from Slugger, and Billy will sign it, and the boys will hold their noses and vote for it, and Billy will get some big thank you gift under the table — probably a new car or some shit like that, something shiny, you can bet on that."

"And the working folks will be sold out again," Margaret said, "all due to the account of race."

"But not if we can head 'em off," Ray shot back, jumping up from the desk.

"You got that right!" Margaret said, raising her hand to his, which he grabbed. "We'll be like badgers layin' in the cut!"

Later, deep into the night as Margaret lay awake, unable to sleep, she realized that for all the progress they had made on possibly stopping the sabotage of the union and the contract negotiations, she and Ray weren't all that much closer to the primary mission of the Odle Agency in Louisville.

She had nothing to report to Irma Durkin about the brutal murder of her husband.

Chapter Twenty-Three: Ray

I woke up to darkness and rain. Looked out the bedroom window and couldn't see anything but gray. It was early, about five, but I should've seen some sunlight creeping under the shade on our east-facing window. Instead, it looked like the clouds had come in overnight and blanketed Louisville down to the height of a tall man's hat. I eased my still achy body out of the bed so as not to wake Margaret, pulled my old green khakis off the nearby cane-bottom chair and put them on, then crept barefoot out of the room and down the hall to the kitchen to put the coffee on. Somewhere between the bedroom and the kitchen I realized that the rain and gloom were inside as well as out. In fact, the tide of darkness had been rising all through the early morning hours when I'd tossed and turned and tried to shut down the squirrels running on the wheel in my head.

It didn't seem to matter whether the work was going good or bad, there were just some days I woke up in darkness. My soul had aged overnight. I'd become old. Old and very, very tired. I'd seen too much, been in too many fights with forces that bore down on me like a huge load of coal, like in the old days where you had to bust it out of the seam face a mile under ground, throw it in a sack and carry it out to the coal cars on your back. A bent back it was, too, because the close, tight cavern at the seam wasn't tall enough for a guy like me to stand straight up.

I could feel the dark tide rising, my strength draining away. My vision was narrowing down, seeing nothing but gray. My skin felt the cold rain even though I was indoors. Somewhere way off some piece of my brain knew this would pass, knew I had to do something, take some action to get rid of the darkness, but the main part of me just wanted to slump down on the cracked linoleum floor right there in the kitchen. To give up. Let the world go wherever it was going, fall under the blows of the rain coming down, let the tiredness in. Let the tiredness win. I started to give way. My back slowly bent at the waist, my legs began to cave. I put my hands on the kitchen counter to keep from going down. I lowered my head. Listened to the rain thrumming on the back door stoop.

I wanted to cry, but too much had happened that I could cry about, so I didn't know where to begin. But my brain did. It didn't have any hesitation, knew how to select from the dark side of me, the deeds I'd had to put down on my AA fourth step inventory, the ones that hurt even now.

I moved down the counter and over to the back door, took my old railroad hat off the peg, opened the door and stepped out onto the stoop and into the rain. I took a deep breath. Just stood there. In my mind I stood on the porch waiting to be let in to the family home by an angry brother. My mother was laid out inside. He'd called over to the fishing camp where I'd said I was going that morning. But that had been a lie. I'd been going from Lawrence County, which was dry, where a man couldn't get a legal drink, over into Ashland, where you could—if you knew where to go, and I damn sure did. A friend at the fishing camp had taken the call. My mother had suffered a massive heart attack and didn't have long to live. She called for me, Ray, her favorite son, her oldest, the one she hoped would someday change and live up to her hopes for him. My friend came to the bar where he knew he'd find me and we drove like thunder over thunder road, like in the song, on roads where angels feared to tread, to get back up the holler to the family home in time. But I hadn't made it. She was laid out on the old cherry wood bed when my fighting brother and his curses against me had been pulled off of me by the other men in the greater family.

There she lay, dressed all in white, the white coverlet up to her ribs. Her gnarled hands folded on her breast held a single white gardenia. There was nothing to say, nothing to do. I'd let her down the final time. My head fell to my chest. My eyes closed on the finality of it. A roughened hand took my upper arm and led me out of the room.

Back in Louisville on another porch, I let the rain stand-in for my tears.

After a while I mumbled the Serenity Prayer a few times. Even though a lot of folks would say different, I knew that these dark tides that came over me were things that fit in the prayer as "things I cannot change." I asked the rain for the serenity to accept this one. Seemed like the rain would do for a Higher Power, at least for now.

Then I turned and went into the kitchen. Margaret was pouring us each a cup of coffee into the dark blue mugs we'd carried with us from Lawrence County. She'd known what was going on with me the whole while, I reckoned. Knew it, and knew she couldn't do a thing about it, so she didn't try. She looked at me then, smiled, and opened her arms up to me. I bent down and gave her a neck hug, then a kiss on the cheek.

"Looks like rain," she said when we broke the hug, a tight little grin on her face at the sheer idiocy of saying that. It was something she did when I was drowning in my own gloom-bath. I came back up one level, almost automatically.

"I reckon so," I said, "be good for the crops."

Margaret shuffled over to the oven and shoved in the tin tray of biscuits she'd been making while I'd stood on the porch.

"Hat's dripping on the floor, sweetheart," she said.

I pulled it off and stuck it back on the peg by the door.

Harvey had told me where Sadderly lived, over on the west side in the black neighborhoods, naturally. He being a lefty, that would be the case. Had to live among the oppressed. I felt like I knew this guy inside and out because from what I'd been told, he was just as hot-shot as I was at his age. My bus chugged along slow as molasses, slowing for potholes big enough to swallow a good-sized cat, the bus throwing black diesel smoke that was so heavy it came down and back alongside the windows in the lashing headwind. The rain had come and gone, but the air was thick with humidity and the clouds were still hanging gray and low over everything.

Looking through the grime out my window I could see the boarded up buildings along Broadway as we got west of 22nd street. Harvey Sampson had told me that as late as the 1950s this area, both south of Broadway for several blocks and north of Broadway up to Walnut Street, had been a thriving business and social section for black folks. There had been all kinds of retail stores, theatres, even a giant concert hall. But the main thing the old timers remembered was that it had been a place where black folks could feel equal and powerful among their own kind. Racism had excluded them from any kind of respect and dignity in the larger society, defined by the powerful as white. Integration hadn't come yet back then, and a lot of black folks doubted it would be worth it when it did. What they wanted was respect and resources, not necessarily joining up with white society. So more recently, when the talk came down about rebuilding the Walnut Street black commercial district, they'd gotten their hopes up for a while.

The city was still making noises about renovation, but they'd kept the black community out of the planning a good deal of the time, and almost entirely out of the funding. But times were tight, the War on Poverty funds had gone to the war in Vietnam, and the project to rebuild the old Walnut Street area had gone into deep freeze.

So the folks were talking about doing something similar, using their own resources, along Greenwood Avenue and 28th Street. Danny B had told me that Ted wanted to be where the action was, so he'd moved just south of Broadway at 26th and

Maple, had himself a little apartment in the attic of a house owned by a black widow there that needed the extra cash. Ted had met the lady at the Walnut Street Baptist Church's mission, where he'd hung out just hoping to get to know a black family well enough to ask where he might rent in their community.

Of course he'd made sure he wasn't too far away from Broadway, maybe saw it as some kind of link to the whites, the middle class, the land of his anonymity, where he could just walk the streets and nobody would think a thing about it, nobody would wonder who the hell he was and what the hell he was doing there, I thought, not being very kind to the kid.

I guess I had a thing about my people always being invaded by do-gooders from outside the hill country. I mean there was a damn army of them — social workers, kids called "Appalachian Volunteers," research students, even professional recreation experts sizing up our hollers and creeks and mountain tops for putting in some kind of resort. And not a one of them had much to give us — now we'd welcome an army of doctors, for instance, who could go up the hollers or even set up some clinics so's we didn't have to travel four or five hours or more to get to a doc. Or people's lawyers so's we could sue the hell out of the coal interests that was polluting and destroying our soil and water. But these folks, like Ted here, were mostly college kids and professors and folks with degrees in subjects where all you had to do was talk and write up stuff — not *do* anything, and for sure not do anything that would actually change the sorry conditions we had to endure. But in the end, I had to admit, only we could do that job — we had to organize.

I got off the bus at the corner and walked a half block east on Maple. The rain had mostly quit, just a little mist and the steady drip you could hear coming off the eaves of houses and leaves of the trees. The house was covered in that fake brick asphalt siding and had a tin roof. There was a large maple tree right beside the front porch, which sagged to the right a little. The paint on the porch pillars and railings was peeling, but I could see where somebody had chipped off the loosest stuff and slapped some primer on it to keep out the rot. I stepped up on the porch, gave a three-rap knock to the door, then stepped back. I'd learned to step straight back about three or four feet when I'd been organizing back in Chicago. Makes a man seem less threatening, especially if a woman opens the door, more especially if there wasn't any screen, as was the case at this place. I always made sure I was straight back from the doorway so I could be seen right off. Makes folks nervous to open to a knock and not see anybody right away. I pulled off my railroad hat and waited.

It took a while, but finally the door creaked part way open and an elderly black woman stuck her head out. "Yes," she said, voice strong but high-pitched. Her hair was uniformly gray, pulled back and tied off with yarn. Her nose was long and skinny, as was her whole light brown face. She wore rimless glasses and had a small pink splotch just back of her left temple. The hand that gripped the door above the knob was kind of arthritic at the knuckles.

"How do you do, ma'am," I said, holding the hat in both hands at my waist. "I hope I'm not intruding at a bad time for y'all. My name is Odle, and I've come to visit with Ted Sadderly, an' I understand he rents here. He told me he was goin' to tell y'all to be expecting me. Hope he did that an' I hope it's all right."

The woman cocked her head and looked kind of sideways at me as I talked. At first I figured her hearing was better on the right side instead of the left. Then I realized that she was just sizing me up, trying to decide whether I represented some kind of threat, although being as how it was the south and I was a white man, there was threat enough with me just standing there. I didn't say anything, just waited her out, a slight smile on my face.

"He ain't here, Mistuh," she said, her voice getting stronger on the 'mistuh.' She opened the door enough to stand in it

182

and face me full-on. "You sound like a man from the eastern part of the state. That right?"

"Yes, ma'am," I said, surprised. "Blaine, in Lawrence County, if'n you want to know."

"Been here to Louisville very long?" she said.

"Not long a'tall, just been workin' at the Slugger plant near 'bout six weeks."

"Thought it might be thataway," she said. Then she grinned and pulled the door wide open. "Whyn't you come on in and tell me all the news from Lawrence County. Me an' my kin's from a holler near Adams, you want to know."

"Well I'll be tied," I said, "Adams is just over a few ridge tops from Blaine."

"What I know." she said. "Why I'm askin' you in. Name's Missus Nancy Whitfield, pleased to meet you," she said, and walked back down the little hallway into her front room.

We got to talking over coffee and biscuits with honey. She sat on an oak rocker with a velvet pad in the seat while I sat in an old upholstered armchair slightly frayed on the arms on which Mrs. Whitfield had put some hand-embroidered doilies. There was a little round table between us, a coffee table. A settee that matched the armchair was situated directly opposite across the room. She had a small, nickel trimmed, coal-burning parlor stove in the corner. The windows had curtains, not drapes, and it was clear to me she'd embroidered those too. A worn oval hook rug tied the armchair, rocker and settee together.

After about a half hour of naming folks we knew and what I could tell her about them lately, we hit on the subject of the fight in the UMW between Jock Yablonski and Tony Boyle. Boyle was president of the union and a lot of the fighting miners I knew had him pegged for a combination crook and secret scab. Seemed like the union grievances against the coal companies for violating the contracts were delayed months and even years, something that had gotten a whole lot worse under Boyle. So was he doin' sweetheart business with the bosses behind our backs? Plus he rammed through a change to the union constitution that reworked the selection of district leaders from election by the members to appointment by him. He'd used that new power to kick ol' Jock out of running District 5. The boys had gone out on a one-day wildcat strike the day after. Jock had filed a lawsuit against Boyle over that, and things had gotten heated up in the weeks that followed. Good thing we weren't one of those unions with 'brotherhood' in the name because they wasn't any brotherhood to be had.

"Ain't that a shame," said Mrs. Whitfield at one point.

"Yep. And it got so bad I nearly got shot over it!" I said.

"Do tell," she said, and meant it, so I did.

"Seemed I pulled up at a little gas station in Pike County one afternoon while workin' on the Black Lung Association campaign. Right smack across the road was a general store about half stove in. Well, no sooner than I stepped out of the car this craggy-faced ol' boy come out of the gas station with a pistol an' pointed it my way and said 'You workin' for Boyle or Yablonski?' I was about to say Jock Yablonski by God when I noticed somebody come around from the back of the general store on the other side of the road. I gave it a quick glance and saw the man had a white beard an' a shotgun, butt-to-shoulder, the barrel pointing over to my direction.

"Boys," I said right loud so's nobody could mistake my words, "I ain't against nary a thing except black lung an' I ain't for nobody except Doc Don Rasmussen. Just tryin' to get a little gas to make it to the schoolhouse up the way here so's we can talk with the folks about fightin' the coal industry on black lung what's killin' our brothers down in the pits."

Mrs. Whitfield was chuckling to herself by this point, holding her hand over her mouth in the way of being polite and not wanting to make me feel like she was having too much fun at my expense.

"Well I see you here in front of me," she said between giggles, "so I suppose neither of them guns went off right then."

"That's right. We could agree on black lung an' most everbody in the hills of Appalachia likes and admires Doc Rasmussen, so they let me fill up that ol' Chevy and drive on out of there in one piece. Anyway, I didn't hang around." I stopped. Mrs. Whitfield had got real solemn in the face, frowning, and looked down at her feet in the high-snap black leather shoes. I figured it was best to wait her out. After a good two full minutes of silence except for the old Sessions mantle clock ticking away, she spoke.

"My Willifred wasn't so lucky. Back in '38 we lived over to Letcher county, just over the line from Pike, and he didn't have a car but he did pull the mule-wagon up in front of one of those general stores. He was carrying a load of dry corn feed to sell to the white folks that ran the store. But he was also carrying a petition for John L. Lewis and the union. The six white men at the store got into him and roughed him up just because he didn't call them 'sir.' When they did that, they found the petition. Those men were all Elkhorn Coal company thugs. They took him out back of the store and made him disappear.

"We'd only been married six months but I was carrying his child. Finally it was a white woman that told me.

"I come into the store after I'd been missing him a good two days an' done been all over asking about him and I asked the man behind the counter if he'd ever seen Mr. Willifred Whitfield. I was good an' big in the belly with the child by then. He mumbled something like he didn't know no nigger by that name, but a white woman who was shopping came up to me outside as I was leaving. She lived near the store, she said, and asked if I could come up the path behind the store a little way. I did, and she told me the story. She said those men were clannish, they were the bad 'un Harrises and Rogerses, that they had taken my Willifred to a cabin they kept back up behind that store in the holler. Said they called it the Adams Mountain Hunt Club and what they hunted was colored folk and union organizers."

I shook my head at this, knowing all too well the kind of gang she was talking about. There were a few, just a few, but that was all it took to terrorize a huge swath of territory for black people, not to mention union men or anybody who stood up to the coal barons and their scab Sheriffs and goons. Nancy Whitfield went on.

"I said I knew where it was, that I'd been past it when I had gone hunting raccoons in the area a time or two. She said I ought never be seen anywhere around there ever in life again, that they would kill me too. She said I'd better get on back to where I come from right quick and never to say where I got the information." Mizz Whitfield looked up at me with wet eyes yet a firm line of determination in her lips and on her face.

"I'm truly sorry to hear that, Mrs. Whitfield," I said. "My people have a powerful lot of death and heartache to account for."

"Yes, they do," she said, nodding her head. Then after a silence, I asked her if anyone was ever prosecuted for her husband's murder. She said no. The worst of it was that she'd see one or two of those men from the Harris and Rogers clan around the area from time to time and never knew if they'd been the ones to kill her husband. There was no way to investigate it. Even to ask the slightest question was to risk her life and that of her child.

"Then what about your child?" I asked.

"He grew up strong and handsome, if I do say so," she replied. "He left the hills and ended up in Pittsburgh working in the mills. Now he's with the United Steelworkers, assistant manager of his local."

"You must be right proud of…"

Just then the front door opened and heavy footfalls started going up the staircase.

186

"Oh Mr. Sadderly!" said Mrs. Whitfield in a lilting high voice. The footfalls stopped. "There's a man here to see you, from the factory where you work."

Ted Sadderly came down the steps and turned into the front room. He didn't see me over in the corner at first, so I took a few seconds to study him. I guessed him to be about six feet, medium build, a face with high cheekbones and a big nose, brown hair tousled and long with a natural wave in the back, sideburns halfway down to his jaw, black-framed glasses. Maybe about 25 years old. This day he was wearing green khakis, a Tee-shirt with a picture of Martin Luther King on it, and an old denim-striped railroader's cap.

"Who's looking for..." he said, then he saw me. "Son-of-a-gun! It's Ray! I mean it's good to meet you, Mr. Odle. I've heard a lot about you."

"Shouldn't believe everything you hear, Ted, might get a wrong impression," I said with a chuckle. "But whatever that might be, pleased to meet you too. Just call me Ray, even the Pinkerton goons do that, at least when they've got a gun to their heads." I stood and stuck out my hand. He took it and smiled.

"Oh no...Ray. What I've heard, it's all good. 'Bout you organizing in the black lung campaign over in Breathitt and Pike and Harlan. Real serious work, what I heard."

"Serious enough, mebbe, but not necessarily successful. I ain't no hero, so don't you go-on about it like that, you want to get along with me." I wanted this guy to be honest with me and give me the straight stuff, not tell me what he thought a rough-tough union man wanted to hear.

I figured I'd taken advantage of Mrs. Whitfield's mountain hospitality long enough so I suggested Sadderly and I go for a walk and see the neighborhood. She laughed and said she understood, after all we had business to discuss. "Just go over about six blocks to Greenwood so's you can see what we fightin' about around here, that is, if you're interested a'tall," she said, eyebrows raised in a challenge.

"Sure will," I said. "We all need to learn what other folks is up against these days. Gotta stick together."

Chapter Twenty-Four: Ray

On the way over to Greenwood, Sadderly chattered constantly as we passed by boarded up two-flats, corner stores with old men hanging out front passing the paper bag wrapped bottle, and here and there a poster with a black fist and the words "JOIN TO WIN" over the logo of the Greenwood Improvement Association. Seeing that took me back to a summer I spent in Chicago as a trainee in an inner city Appalachian community organization by the same letters: Jobs Or Income Now — JOIN, where I learned about the plight of my mountain brothers and sisters who'd left the hills for the lure of the factories only to find the same oppression and tough times there. Seeing the sign also made me realize that a good slogan has no racial ownership. Sadderly was nervous as a squirrel in fall, going on about the bad conditions in the black community and how the folks were fighting back by organizing. I noticed he seemed to go out of his way to avoid talking about Slugger or the union.

We came to a nearly deserted street-corner park full of weeds that someone had cut with a raggedy mower or maybe a hand sickle, and sat on a wrought iron and oak slat bench. The sun had finally put in an appearance and was slanting in low behind us. The few Queen Anne's lace whose heads had survived the sickle floated before us in the mild breeze, ringed with liquid gold halos in the sunbeams — a weed, so they say, that always seems to grow in the rough, rocky spots.

I looked around the park, halfway thinking the H & R might have followed me, then shook my head at my paranoia. I looked at Sadderly.

"Why don't you tell me about the betting ring," I said, not taking my eyes off his face. Boom. Point blank. I wasn't sure he was in it, but I figured if he was the question was worth a shot. Sure enough I saw his face go blank, his eyes go wide, even as his head recoiled like he'd been slapped. He looked at the weeds growing around the bench for a long minute. I just sat there.

"Got me," he finally replied. "Guess there's no use in trying to lie to you, Ray. You ain't nobody's fool."

"Good you know that," I said. I was coming down harder. The money-line scam was complicating my investigation into the murders. Too many people had been acting funny around Slugger and nobody was opening up on account of the scam. They figured I might have to blow the whistle on that, which I wouldn't do unless it had to do with the murders, but I'd only been at Slugger a short while, not enough time to get inside the trusting zone of most folks. I had to find out how deep Danny was in on this, whether he was over his head. Just because Danny was sober didn't mean his thinking was always straight or that he'd overcome an alcoholic's natural tendency to be impulsive as hell and do stupid things. I had to apply pressure somewhere and with Sadderly looking up to me the way he seemed to be doing, with him being young and probably scared, I decided he was my leverage on the other men in the situation and I wasn't going to mess around. Either he'd cough it up or he'd clam up. He coughed.

"I…I don't know what you know, so let me lay it out for you. I guess I got no choice but to trust you with this stuff—not that I wouldn't anyway, you bein' who you are and all." He looked at me with uncertain eyes.

But lay it out he did. It went pretty much like I'd expected and confirmed what Harvey had told me. Danny B was the bet-taker, the bets ran against the moneyline, and thcy used the little forms I'd found in Gorham's lathe. Most guys lost money in the end. It was like betting against the house in a blackjack game in Vegas, you're going to lose over the long haul. Ted was getting into it, rambling on about the odds and his schemes on how to beat them, never mind he didn't gamble, when I let him have it.

"So how come you been talkin' up this loony idea of a wildcat strike with the likes of Campbell, Duvall and them other malcontents, Sadderly?"

Ted's face went paler than I thought possible for a man still conscious. I grabbed his upper arm thinking he was going down, then he jerked it away. But he wasn't ready to talk yet. He looked out across the Queen Anne's lace, and he was in a rough rocky spot all right.

"What are you, some kind of seer or something?" Sadderly shot me a hard look out of the corner of his eye. He still wasn't ready to take me full on. I didn't reply, best to let him stew. He gave me another of his best hard looks. This time I grinned back. Then he broke eye contact. "Yeah. I guess you oughta know. I wasn't supposed to talk about this, but some of the boys and I are looking at a strike over this bullshit contract Worthington is trying to foist off on us." Sadderly stood up, paced over a few feet and returned. Stood over me. Mr. Powerful. Whatever, I thought, let him roll on. He started talking again, chopping the air with the blade of his palm.

"It sucks! For one thing they say the Manuit rate is going up across all the jobs in the plant. For another, the bastards want us to drop the demand we put in for a COLA. We'll be working harder than before for the same pay and with inflation running at three percent we'll actually be losing ground. Meanwhile there's never been more demand for Slugger bats and those management shits are raising prices. They've got the dough to make a better deal for us but they won't!"

I could actually see Sadderly's chest expanding. Now I had a braggart in front of me. But I sat there like it was all just fine and all I had to worry about was the sunshine in the park. Pride goeth before a fall, they say, and I had Sadderly's right ready for him. I suddenly reared up from the bench and grabbed Sadderly by the open neck of his Tee and twisted it tight up to his throat.

"Now listen to me, Sadderly. I'ma tell you this but once. You so green at this stuff you act like you're dumb as a post. First, you fucked up by joining a rump group of malcontents with Sam Campbell leadin' it. He's a racist coward who works best in the dark. If anybody's a snitch along with Gorham, it's him. Unions is about unity — all the workers, solidarity — ever hear the song? It ain't about a bunch of egotistical assholes meeting behind the bat bins plotting some wildcat bullshit. Wildcats almost never work. Guys got to prepare, got to settle their finances best they can so they can take the hardship of a strike. That means they gotta help each other. Ones that have should be ready to help the ones that have not. Shit! If I didn't know you better I'd break your simple-ass head thinkin' you was a provocateur. And yeah, us hillbillies know words like that, least we do if'n we been around working men's fights long enough."

Sadderly had practically gone limp now, all the puffery gone out of him like air from a balloon. I let him go and he dropped down onto the bench, put his head in his hands, stared at the ground. He would not soon forget this lesson.

On the bus back home I didn't bother to look out of the grimy window. I closed my eyes and tried to let go of the anger. Don't do nobody no good. Sadderly had broken down and named all the men in the rump group. No surprises, really. He was right scared and I wanted him to be.

I guess I got lost in reviewing all that Sadderly had said — and all that it might mean, because the next thing I knew I was jolted awake by the screech of the bus's brakes. I looked out the window. I was two stops past my own. My knees creaked as I stumbled groggily down the steps. The sun hid behind the clouds. There was a little light from it, but not much. That about fits, I thought.

Chapter Twenty-Five: Margaret

Harvey Sampson, Ray and Margaret were seated in the office with coffee and some little corn cakes Margaret had made for the occasion. Ray had just returned from his morning with Ted Sadderly. Margaret explained to Harvey that the Odle Agency was interested in working with him on the Durkin and Gorham cases and that they wanted to get to know him a bit better outside of the facts of his work at Slugger. Harvey's face had a pinched look and his voice was tight too. Not to mention he'd been calling Margaret, "Mrs. Odle."

"What say we drop the Mrs. Odle and Mr. Sampson stuff," Margaret said with a smile, "and just go with Margaret and Harvey and Ray. This is an informal interview, so I think we'll get along just fine with first names anyhow, don't you?"

"That'd suit me fine, Mrs.—I mean, Margaret," he said, easing back in his chair and shaking his head with a rueful chuckle. "Ain't too many times I been invited into white folks homes on a first name basis in this town, you understand. But Louella said you was all right folks so I ain't surprised. Besides, Ray wouldn't be married to no Mizz Ann no kind of way."

"Now that's a term I haven't heard in quite a while, Harvey. I grew up in South Carolina, a rebellious teenager with a black boyfriend, so I learned some Black English, not all of it complementary, like 'Mizz Ann.' Some of it thrown at me, and some of it deserved—and whether deserved or not, all of it understandable. You might say I got more than one black-on-white haircut in my day" Margaret said, starting to chuckle.

Harvey reared back in his office chair and let loose with a big belly laugh at that. "I guess you must've been to the barber a whole bunch of times, Margaret, you went with a black kid when you lived in South Carolina. It's a damn miracle that you still alive. And what about him? He still alive and do he still have his…"

"Yes to both questions," Margaret I said, her laughter dying out. "He's a college professor in California, sociology, and he's the father of two sons, so no worries there."

"That's good to hear, Margaret. See, I come up from Georgia myself. Little area around Gainesville. Ain't always been here in Kentucky. My Daddy was a sharecropper, we lived in a clapboard shack what used to be a slave quarters. I could wake up at night and tell the direction of the wind from the sound it made whistling through the cracks and holes. Made different notes on each side of that shack.

"Daddy fell deep into debt farming those shares. The crops was bad several years in a row an' he got cheated at the grading station. He owed the plantation store for the rent on the shack, and the food we had to buy there 'cause it was too far to town and the white plantation boss wouldn't let us plant nothin' for ourselves to eat. Then there was the so-called taxes, the water bill from the plantation well, and the 'lectric bill from the one bulb outlet we had, not to mention the farming tools. The Sheriff come and told Daddy since his debts couldn't be paid on time, he was too far behind, he had to either sign a work detail contract or be put out off the plantation.

"Well, Daddy signed the contract, but he didn't see that if he didn't pay his debts after 30 days he would be fined, so when the 30 days was up and Daddy had only earned enough to pay some of his debts, that cracker took my Daddy to court, the judge gave him 30 days for non payment of fines. They put my Daddy on the County prison farm, work him like a slave for another big white landowner just like the Civil War never happened. But the trick-bag was they charged Daddy room and board for his time in these stick camps where the men slept while out on the work details for the white landowners. So that added to Daddy's debts, and that add to his jail time. Bottom line? Daddy, and men like him, they never, hardly never, got they original debts paid off. They was slaves, sure as shit."

"Damn right he was a slave," Ray interjected. "Just like miners are slaves to the company store in the hills of eastern Kentucky, West Virginia, Tennessee, Virginia, Pennsylvania, and Georgia too, come to that."

Harvey nodded. "We all know what that's like. But for a black man in the south, he ain't got no place to hide, no other job to go to. He got the shotgun man settin' up there on his horse watchin' him all the time while he work. Only time he ain't under the gun is when he sleep.

"So my Daddy, he done what slaves always done in them situations. He run. He got the word to Momma, me and my baby sister one day and the next night he come by on the run, said he couldn't take us with him, but he'd send for us some day. Well he done what he said — three and a half years later. Momma got thrown out of our house the day after he run. We begged on the street for about a month before she got taken in by a white family. We lived in a shack out back of they house and she slaved for them, did all the housework and nursed they old grandma too. I worked they garden and did handyman jobs."

"And how many white ladies have maids with hidden slave stories like this and never know it," Margaret said, shaking her head.

"And never want to know it," Harvey replied, then went on with his story.

"Sis, she didn't never go to school 'cause they didn't have no bus routes for black kids in that neighborhood, so she stayed home and helped Momma what little she could. Then one day a man showed up and brought a letter from my Daddy. I was fifteen years old at that time. The letter had some Western Union money in it and told us where he was, here in Louisville. It was enough money for bus tickets. We left the next morning before sunup, walked all the way to the downtown of Gainesville, Georgia, caught the first thing smokin' for the north towards Nashville.

"Once we got to Nashville, Momma and Sis hung around the Trailways station, waitin' for the bus for Louisville, but I was so mad at the world I stayed outside on the street while they was in the waitin' room. While I was out there I met this blind dude played a slide steel guitar. That man's music shook me to the roots, that's all they was to it. I was big for my age an' the liquor store was next door an' I had some cash left over from the bus tickets I'd bought for Momma, so when the dude axed me I copped my first store-bought booze and give it to him. I ran an' told Momma I won't goin' with them just as she was gettin' on that bus for Louisville. God, it broke her heart, but she wasn't gonna miss her bus to Daddy after all he went through and that was that. Sis had her head and arms out the window all the way out of sight as that bus pulled out, last I looked. All I had eyes for was the blind blues man 'cause he heard all the ruckus and struck up the Tin Cup Blues right loud an' that's all it took to snatch my attention back to him."

Margaret felt the lump in her throat grow bigger, looked over at Ray and watched him choke one down too. But Harvey was deep into his story and just kept on rolling.

"That man was the spiritual son of Blind Lemon Jefferson all right an' he taught me slide guitar too, so I guess I'm the grandson of sorts, although I can't claim no kind of level like his. They called him Blind Roosevelt Graves. He and I hung out begging and playing the backroom hooch joints around Nashville and up to Memphis for about eighteen months, then one day he disappeared on me. I found out a couple of years later, this was early 1963, that he'd gone back to Mississippi

196

and died on the last day of 1962. By then I was a full-blown alcoholic, petty thief, grifter, hustler and general no 'count jackass. I come north to Louisville just to break my Momma's heart all over again in 1964 with my behavior. But then the miracle happened and I hit bottom, literally lying on a graveyard slab with the po-lice standing over me and a man in white pulling the body bag zipper up. They'd pronounced me d.o.a. only I ain't arrived nowhere yet. I shook my head and said "Hey, fuck this shit!" an' scared the hell outta the E.M.T.s and the po-lices too. After two days in the hospital they tossed me back to the street, but that po-lice was a friend of Bill's, as we say in the Program, an' he gave me an AA meeting schedule. So I showed up one night over to the Walnut Street meeting. And it was Danny B telling his story that night. Seemed he was just as crazy and insane as I'd been. Figured that if he could do it, well, so could I. And here I am. But maybe you understand, Margaret, bein' as how you're hitched to one of us."

"Indeed I do understand, " Margaret said with a smile, "and I'm honored that you told us your story — or part of it. It's not easy to do and I hope you know it wasn't required — not that part of it. Since I play dulcimer and Ray does a mean washtub bass and jug, we'll have to try jamming together sometime and see if we can cross some Delta blues with down-home mountain blues. Can't have all murder and no music or it'll warp your soul, seems to me."

"Amen to that," put in Ray. "You ain't heard nothin' till you heard my Delta jug doin' 'Sun Gone Shine on My Back Door Some Day,' not to mention the low down gravelly on the 'K. C. Moan.'"

"I'm down with that," said Harvey.

Then Margaret paused and pulled her hair back behind her ears. She was a mite nervous. Nothing for it but to plow ahead, though.

"Okay, let's get down to business," Margaret said after her pause, glancing at Ray, then focusing on Harvey. "Here's

197

what we have in mind." And she laid out the job of Odle Agency Case Investigator on the Slugger murder investigations to Harvey, the way she and Ray wanted him to work as a full member of their team under their direction, but independently too, having his own leads to follow up and go where they took him, how to report in to Margaret as communications hub, and what Odle Agency was able to pay, the funds coming from WIA, and how the pay system would work.

They spent some time going over Harvey's background at Slugger and the people he knew, the ones he felt trusted him and the ones he felt he could communicate with, which included Mike the Bow, Andy Campsten, Bob Stills (a nice surprise), and really surprising to Margaret, given what Ray had told her earlier, George Salvatore! Ray asked about that one, showing the surprise he also felt.

"Yeah, I can see you kind of blown away behind that, Ray," he said. "But the deal is, George and I talk about our kids, who are near 'bout the same age. He's a worried daddy and I am too. His kid ain't exactly on the straight and narrow and mine is also deviating from the path I've laid down for him. So yeah, we talk sometimes after the shift. See, he's just up the line from me, sorting and stacking the rounds for the billet lathes, so I get my rounds for P.R.O. from him. So we snatch a few words several times a day an' I can tell when something's up with him and him with me. Besides, quiet as it's kept, George may not look it, but he's solid for the union. So we cool on that front too."

That explanation made sense and it made Harvey an even stronger asset for the team. And it cleared up something that had worried Ray about George Salvatore. They could cross him off as a trouble spot in the planning from here on out.

"The thing is, Harvey," Margaret said in wrapping it up, "from what you say and what I've seen, we've got a tiger by the tail here and it's too much for just the two of us. We've got a racist issue going with Jenkins. We've got Worthington

198

and his family in the background of that. Then we've got whatever is going on with the production piece rate manipulation, which of course ties into the racism back-story through Durkin and the Wade case. Next, we've got this moneyline thing and some type of blowback on Gorham from that, involving we're not quite sure who. Well, I should say, involving Danny B, and we don't know *who else* inside Slugger, with threats, bribery or blackmail. Then there's the possible direct mob involvement with debts, blackmail and God knows what all.

"We need your experience, your level head, and besides, you've got a lot of truck with the boys down at Slugger, both black and some of the whites too, which we need right bad about now. But this isn't a lightweight situation here, Harvey, and you should consider all the angles, including your family, before you decide on it. There's danger on this job. Ray's been attacked once already. We need you, that's for sure, but it's your call."

Then Ray piped up, "And whatever you decide on this, you have Margaret's respect and mine."

Harvey sat silently for quite a few minutes. He nodded his head every once in a while, pulling at his chin with his left hand in between nods. Then he spoke.

"Yeah, that respect thing, you know?" he said. "That's the reason I'ma say yes to this thing. Sure, I need the money. Y'all know that. I laid that out to you the other night, Ray. But I don't scrape an' bow to no man, woman neither. Black or white. But respect go a long way with Harvey Sampson. So yeah, I'm in. An' the respect go both ways, Margaret. Ray knows I respect him all the way, an' I'm learning to feel the same way 'bout you, too. You got a helluva mind on you, girl, don't mind me sayin' it like I would to a sister!" And with this he grinned from ear to ear.

Margaret laughed with him and got out the contract she'd drawn up for independent contractors, went over it with

Harvey, and he signed it, bearing down hard so the carbons would make two copies.

Chapter Twenty-Six: Radio six

Mel Allen: *Marichal is back on the mound warming up for his fifth inning for the Giants here against the Redlegs and he's smokin' hotter than a steam locomotive today folks. The man is the class act of the National League this year, wouldn't you say Red?*

Red Barber: *That's right Mel, he's got the Cy Young award hands down by my vote. He's won 14 games and it's still three days before the All-Star game. His winning percentage is bumping up against the 800 mark, just incredible! The Giants are trailing the Dodgers by two games right now, but if this keeps up the L.A. squad is going to have to dig deep to stay on top and get to the Series against the Orioles.*

MA: *Yeah, Red, a win for the Giants today would sweep the three-game series with Cincinnati and put them ahead of L.A. They're on a roll – six-one in the first game, four-two last night in the second. But there's no doubt about who's on top in the American League, it's Baltimore all the way. What a line-up! Robinson-Robinson-Powell, wham, slam, that's it, ka-bam! Jackie, Frank and Boog. Near 'bout unstoppable this season.*

RB: *Well, it's batter up here in the top of the fifth Mel, Giants up 2-1 on the Redlegs. Marichal's got Jersey Jack at the plate, so let's see if Marichal's still got his stuff. He struck him out last time up on four pitches.*

MA: *Here's the windup – now the pitch – high and fast – Stee-rike one! Just nicked the outside corner. Geez, Red, that ball sounded like it hit the catcher's mitt before it left the hand of Marichal.*

RB: *Broke the sound barrier all right, Mel, or at least the hand-eye barrier 'cause Jack just stood there. Must've blinked.*

MA: *Second pitch a-coming – same pitch, fast on the outside – swing and a miss! Strike two! Jersey looks frustrated, folks, that* *swing was for the fences, not his usual style. Juan's scuffing at the pitcher's mound now, probably thinking up his next pitch.*

RB: He doesn't need to do that, Mel, all he's gotta do is shoot the next one just as hot but a little low and inside, mark my words.

MA: Well here's the windup. It's fast, low, Jersey Jack swings — dribbler down the third baseline, Jack's hauling it for first, Hart's charging the ball, scoops it, throws — out! It was close, folks. Too close for Jack! He's got his face up at the first base umpire's nose. This ain't looking good. Nope! No sale. Ump's motioning Jersey Jack to the dugout. Jack kicks the first base lime line. Stomps off towards the dugout.

RB: Whoa, Mel. Here comes the batboy — well for the love a Mike, will ya look at that! Boy's got Jersey's bat — in two pieces! No wonder it was a dribbler. Another broken bat.

MA: Say Red, isn't this getting to the epidemic stage with Louisville Slugger? I haven't counted 'em up, but seems to me like it's been a half-dozen or so in the last month.

RB: That's right, Mel. I'll have the boys in the studio check on it for us, and fans, we'll let you know next game or two.

MA: Okay, Red. Shoot, this might sound crazy, but in a race as tight as this a bunch of broken bats might even affect the pennant!

Chapter Twenty-Seven: Margaret

"You've got to keep your eyes on the prize, Ray, that's all there is to it!" Margaret's voice cut through the air hard as flint. "There is absolutely no use in your going on with that 'solidarity requires you to captain this wildcat strike' stuff. If those boys are going to go off half-cocked and screw up, then you will just have to let them go on and do it. They aren't babies, after all, they're men. You have to respect their rights even when you think they're heading for disaster."

"I'm not talkin' captain of nothing, Margaret. I'm just talkin' a little coaching here and there. Besides, it ties right straight into the case because that Kluxer Sam Campbell is involved and I think he ain't just a bigot, he might very well be a snitch for H & R. After all, he's their kind of asshole."

They'd been at it for an hour, ever since Harvey left after Ray had reported on his talk with Sadderly and about the rump group that was talking wildcat strike. The argument had started in the kitchen over post-supper coffee.

Margaret had heard Ray out then whirled around and moved very deliberately, not fast, just set her jaw, and walked on over to the old roll-top desk and pulled the WIA contract for their current job out of the bottom drawer. "Read this," she said, "and show me where it says you have to deliver a strike or even to talk some undisciplined hotheads into or out of a strike. Just show me!"

Ray had no comeback for that and said something about life isn't just a contract on a piece of paper, then Margaret had come back with the eyes on the prize thing. She knew he'd hear it as a reference to discipline in the struggle for justice since it was the title of a Civil Rights freedom song. She was right, of course. And she knew exactly what he was thinking. He would say that there was too much on the line to let some piece of paper tell them what to do. And movement discipline had to be balanced with movement initiative and boldness. No workingman ever beat the bosses by holding back when some action would change things. These particular idiots at Slugger were fixing to get themselves, and by extension, the whole union local, sandbagged by H & R and Worthington. Margaret could read him like a book as Ray pushed off from leaning against the mantle-piece and started pacing back and forth in front of the desk.

"I know what you're talkin' about with that eyes on the prize," he started in again. "Okay as to the union. But what I'm afraid of, dammit, is that Sadderly and the others in that bunch are gonna give H & R a shot at taking Danny down for the murder. It's like dominoes," he said, and started ticking off the falling dominos one by one as his voice got hotter and his pacing feet hit the deck harder.

"One, Danny threatened Gorham and sure as shootin' he was overheard. I got to stop those knuckleheads. Two, an off-the-wall stunt like a wildcat and H & R will take the threat evidence they already got and cook up some more, or hell, maybe even find some more, and stick it to Danny. Three, then he's on trial for murder, locked up at the Jefferson County jail, the strike's busted, the press is all over the union for the strike, never mind it won't authorized. Four, with all that hullaballoo there's no chance we'll get a shred of information out of anybody. We'll never find out who killed Gorham and, five, we won't fulfill the terms of that piece of paper you just whipped out on me."

It was time for the counter-move. Margaret raised her left hand and index finger and punched the palm of her right hand with it. "You wanna play counting games, Ray, then fine, try these numbers. One, you step out on that wildcat picket line to talk with Sadderly or anybody else and make

Blackie and Blondie's day. The cops are itching to bust somebody but they've been ordered to take their cues from H & R. Blackie and Blondie are just waiting for you to show up on the line. It's you they want more than anybody. They get the cops to bust you right then and there." Punch.

"Two, while you're down in court on a violation of injunction charge, Blackie and Blondie tell the court you're the ring leader, so they hook you up on an added conspiracy count, and bang! You're out of commission for 90 days." Punch.

"Three, that's when they take Danny, frame him up, and whether he's actually involved in the murder or not, they intimidate every other man in the plant from talking to you when you finally get out of the jailhouse. You're toxic from that point on. So that's the end of the investigation, just like you said. But precisely because you got involved in the strike, not because you didn't."

"Come on now, Margaret, I can control those guys," Ray whined. "They all think I'm some labor hero out of the past coal fights. They respect me."

"Yes, certainly, of course you can, like that racist Sam? Like Sadderly, who didn't come to you about this idea in the first place?" Punch. "You're his hero, yet he doesn't even give you your propers? Right—total control."

With that he stomped into the kitchen and came back with a dinette chair and thrust it down on the floor, sitting straight in front of her, the chair facing backwards. This was standard Ray Odle procedure for this stage of the argument. He sat with his arms draped over the chair back.

"I gotta do what I gotta do!" he said, glaring at Margaret.

Margaret glared straight back, never wavering. "I know that," she said. "Just do this: think about it real good one more time before you say yes to any of those hotheads."

Ray stared some more, then nodded. "Okay," he said.

"Okay," said Margaret.

The Odle bed was decidedly chilly but they both managed to mumble the nightly, "I love you," before dropping off to fitful sleep.

They always did.

Chapter Twenty-Eight: Ray

The next morning I hit the back gate at Slugger determined to find out more about the betting line scam that had now overlapped with the rump group in that some of the same workers were involved in both. That had to get teased out. I couldn't know which motive might be the right one for Gorham's murder—a double cross of the mob bosses over the betting line or some type of snitching for the company against the rump group and their strike plans.

But when I started down the yellow brick road to the auto-sanding room Arthur Benson, the security man for Worthington, blocked my path and held up his hand like a crossing guard at a grammar school.

"You been transferred, bub," he growled. "You gotta report to Bob Stills in P.R.O. You ain't gonna be sneakin' around them sanders and lathes no more. Gonna work in there where I can keep a better eye on your goings and comings. You gonna take the knob cut-off job."

The knob cut-off job meant that you used a special saw to cut the end knobs off the bats after they'd been shaped and worked up through the final sanding. After that, the bat went to the lacquer room to be sealed and coated with hard-finish lacquer. I couldn't believe my ears. Worthington was transferring me into the P.R.O. section—right into the hub of the betting line activity. That would make my job a helluva lot easier—wouldn't have to sneak around on smoke breaks and lunch breaks to talk to the guys who'd probably know the most about the betting line deal. Of course I couldn't let

Benson, or through him, Worthington, know how happy I'd be. Right at home in the briar patch.

"Ain't no way I'm goin' in there with those uppity snots, Benson," I said, putting both hands on my hips in a defiant stance. "I'm stickin' with the sanders."

"Go tell it to Worthington, then, Odle. I ain't gonna tell you again. My orders are to transfer you to the cutoff job in P.R.O., simple as that."

"Well, now you've invited me, I do believe I'll just step around to the boss's office and do just that!"

I stomped away from the yellow brick road and down the hallway that ran down the side of the building to Worthington's office, Benson following behind telling me I was asking for a demotion, which of course was dumb since I was at the bottom of the pay scale anyway. When I got to his office I went right past his secretary without so much as a by your leave. Worthington was hunched over his desk, red in the face, speaking almost secretively on the phone.

"Yes, I know it's intolerable," he said. "We're doing everything we can, of course, but it's just as likely due to lousy hitting. I mean, really, it's much more likely, statistically, to be the batsman and not the bat."

Just like Worthington to use an English-sounding word like "batsman" to impress whoever was on the other end of the line.

"All right, I'll have a meeting with them and go over it. Maybe they aren't looking at the grain as well as they should. You can rest assured that Louisville Slugger is now and will continue to produce the best bats the world has ever known. Good day, Mr. Bristol."

Bristol—had to be Dave Bristol, the new manager of the Cincinnati Redlegs, and it had to be a complaint about the bats. The rumor was that there had been a lot more broken bats than usual lately.

"And what the hell do you want, Odle? I've got enough troubles without you screwing up the works!" He was dumping his frustration from the phone call with Bristol on me. I filed that one away for future use and replied.

"Just a clarification, yer honor," I said in my most hillbilly twang. "Wanted to make sure you didn't want me to keep on the job in the sanding room seein' as how that's next door to where the murders occurred."

"Look Odle," he said, standing up and shaking his right index finger at me, "when I send Benson to pass on an order, you can take it as gospel. Now quit bucking me on every little thing around here and get on with the job. Both jobs, as a matter of fact. I haven't heard a word from you about solving this mess."

I just stood there in front of his desk for a long minute. Then I turned to the doorway and started out of the office. "I send my reports to the WIA, Worthington. When and if they decide to share information with you, then you'll hear from them."

"Don't play some phony tough guy with me, Odle. I can make it easy or hard or impossible for you to do that job, and you know it. We agreed to cooperate within limits, don't forget. I've stuck to that deal so far. What about you?"

"The deal holds. Because of that I'm assuming this new assignment will be better than the sanding room—am I right?"

"Yes. I suspect there may be something a little out of the normal going on in there."

"I suspect that too. But we may not define 'out of the normal' the same way. There's always that line, boss man. Workers versus management. Labor versus capital. It's rare that those opposing interests run together, but they do every great once in a while. That's the basis of our deal—and it don't go no further."

"Understood. Now get out of here and let me deal with keeping this business afloat."

"You just do that," I said. "Sounds like you might have you a little quality control problem in billets or maybe in P.R.O.."

"That'll be my business, Odle."

"Let's hope so," I said and sauntered on out the door.

When I stepped through the archway from the main line into P.R.O. I stepped into a meeting in progress. First I noticed that the whole P.R.O. crew was lined up, including Harvey Sampson, my newly appointed undercover Odle Agency teammate, who was also their billet selection man. Harvey stood against the entry to the unit along with two other men from the billet crew. Then going around the room, machine by machine I checked out the four lathe workers, the three hand sanders, and finally the two drying control men. They all stood in a row looking at Bob Stills, the P.R.O. foreman and quality control man, who had the floor.

"The boss has passed on complaints from four teams in the majors. It's mainly the Redlegs, but also the Braves, the Yankees and the Orioles. Now you know and I know that a lot of the cracked bat problems come from those so-called sluggers insisting on using these damn new-fangled maple bats. But the record speaks for itself—there's been too many of 'em even with the ash bats, even for rookies, let alone some of the best hitters in the league. I'm even talking about Jersey Jack of the Redlegs. He's been raising some kind of hell. So we gotta double down, boys. We gotta make these bats crack-proof."

This was greeted with a general shuffle of feet, a couple of shrugs, and one mumbled, "bullshit," from an unknown quarter.

"Now you boys in the billet crew, you gotta remember to do them billets on the square, split the ash right smack down the grain, and saw the damn maples off the grain, like we taught you.

"Now here in the P.R.O., Harvey, that starts with you and selecting the billets on the basis of grain. I know you're kind of new to the P.R.O. section, but we gotta depend on you, man. If the grain ain't right, Danny B and Bugsy here can't do a thing about it, and they been a little worried lately, so they tell me. They say maybe you need some more trainin' on that job. Whaddya think?"

Harvey moved out from the corner of the lathe room where he'd been standing and walked up right close to Stills. "I think it's kinda funny that the first man you look at behind what's goin' down just happens to be black, that's what."

"Okay, let's not get into a racial thing here," countered Stills. "I just heard from the lathe men here that some of the billets looked like there might have been a twist in the grain. That's all. It's an easy mistake to make on the ash bat, seein' as how the grain is tight and hard to see all the way down the length of the billet."

Harvey nodded. "Okay, I'm glad it ain't racial," he said. "Specially when workin' in a shop all white other than me. Yeah, I'll do that trainin'. Sure. And as to the grain on the ash bat, you got to check the slope of grain. See, that's the angle, the number of degrees, that the grain slopes away from a straight line down the centerline of the bat. You look at them vee's that form where the grain comes together at the center, then measure the degrees of separation from the center line four inches up and that's your slope of grain. It don't take much to make a difference. For example, you get just 10 degrees of slope, you bat is 30% weaker at the sweet spot where it connects with the ball. Hell, man, even 5 degrees be enough to crack a bat if it hit just off the sweet spot."

With that Harvey whipped out a clear plastic protractor. " Yeah, I watches 'em real good, man."

"Shit, Harvey," replied Stills, "you might as well be teaching that training course I was talking about."

"Thanks, Bob," Harvey went on, "but you best look to the sanding boys too, behind a flat spot in the wrong place, the porous cells on the ash be too open, be just as likely to smush a bat. An' while you at it, better make sure them lathe boys got they calipers on the handle right, too, 'cause everbody know that you take too much off there, you get her less than 15/16ths they be too much of a whip effect on up the bat."

"Now wait just a goddamn minute, Sampson," Danny burst out, shoving himself off the lathe machine he'd been leaning on, stepping into Harvey's face, "these men here have been doing their jobs for a long, long time, and ain't no black son of a buck gonna put 'em in a bad light just to throw the shit somewhere else!"

Harvey stood completely still, arms folded, a picture of confidence without a hint of aggression.

"You sayin' that 'cause they experienced they can't make no mistake, Danny, or is it behind they white, same as you?" Harvey didn't back off an inch.

"All right, knock it off!" said Stills. "I'm the foreman and quality control man here and I'll decide who's responsible for what. But Harvey has a point, Danny. If we're going to be thorough here and find out what problems might be due to our work, we've got to regroup across the board. I'm saying every man in this section is just as responsible as any other man. We all have to look out for each other. The big boss is gettin' calls from the managers in the leagues and he's plenty pissed about it. If the shit comes down from Worthington, no tellin' who it's going to hit. So between y'all and me, I'd rather we settle it among ourselves and keep the boss out of it. We can stick together and get this operation in ship shape. Whaddya say?'

That struck a chord of pride in every man, so they all muttered or spoke a solid "okay by me," or words to that effect.

"Good, so that bein' the case, I'm going to spend a few hours with each man here going over his job and looking at his work. If anybody's gotten into some bad habits, we'll just straighten it out on the Q.T. and that will be that. But before I do that, this here is Ray Odle, and I guess most of you know him one way or the other, but he's now going to be our knob cutoff man. And Odle, this little talk by Harvey on bat science goes for you too. You're the last man besides me that looks over these bats before they go to the lacquer section, so you're the last one that can see the grain at all. So keep a sharp eye."

A sharp eye indeed, I thought. And not just for the slope of grain. Knowing Harvey's desperate debt to the moneyline racket and Danny B's role in it, the reaction I'd just witnessed may have had a lot more to do with that than with race. Although from now on I wasn't going to cut Danny any slack.

Chapter Twenty-Nine: Ray

The smoke was thick as a coal-fired smelter under low hanging clouds in the back room of the Starlight Bar and Grill when I knocked the secret knock the boys had given me and was admitted. Stupid kid stuff as far as I was concerned — secret knocks, back-room meetings — no way to run a labor action. But Sadderly had asked me to meet with them and had gotten the okay from the group.

The atmosphere had been decidedly cool for a few days around the Odle household due to our disagreement about my "bullheaded consarned idea" of getting involved with the rump group in general and this particular meeting in particular.

What finally convinced Margaret that I should go — and she should back me up by sneaking in through the back alley door — was that she'd done some research and suspected at least one sinister figure from the eastern coal wars was in Louisville. More than that, she suspected the guy had infiltrated Slugger and was among the rump group of hotheads from the way I'd described the men in the group.

So based on my solemn word to four-square refuse and block any wildcat strike tomfoolery, she figured we might, just might, come out ahead by exposing this joker if he showed his face.

Margaret had had dealings with the family in question back in the day in Logan County, West Virginia, and Breathitt County, Kentucky, and could identify the bastard. I'd agreed to come and get her if there was to be any kind of rump meeting. I hated that part of the idea on account of there might be some rough stuff if we was to expose a skunk in the woodpile. But sure enough, when Sadderly told me they were going to meet at the Starlight after work, I eased down to the apartment as soon as the whistle sounded, got Margaret, and when I went around to the Starlight's front entrance, she positioned herself at the back door on the alley.

Inside the smoky cavern I stood right still until my eyes got used to the dark, then I began to call the visual roll: in addition to Sadderly, who'd opened the door, Mike the Bow was over in the corner, elbows resting on a shelf jutting out from the wall. I'd asked Sadderly to get Mike and Harvey into the meeting so I'd have some backup. When I saw them I was pleasantly surprised that he'd been able to pull it off. Nick Silvia from the cutting room stood beside Mike puffing on a cheap cigar like he always did when not at his job. Andy Campsten, one of the lacquer room guys was there too, sitting to my right just inside the door. But what really shocked me was the grim long-nosed face of George Salvatore, who was leaning against the back door like he was standing guard. I'd have thought he'd a had more sense than to be hooked up with this knuckle-headed outfit, but more than that I never figured him for a lefty type, which clearly was what this bunch was dominated by. That made me wonder if he was here on his own or for somebody else.

One thing though, I was glad not to see Danny B. I wouldn't have figured him for this, so if he'd have been here, it would've been a phony deal, a company plant. Which would've meant that in addition to being hooked into the betting line scam, he was also betraying his brothers as a worker, and I couldn't have taken that on top of all the other let-downs he'd dealt me lately.

There were five other guys in the room, four of whom I'd seen before, but didn't know, and one other man, a stranger whom I only vaguely recognized, which made a total of eleven. The stranger had a hawk nose, close-set eyes, and nearly all gray hair, no spring chicken, for sure. But the more I looked at him, the more I got a crawly feeling up my spine.

Then a skinny shave-headed figure emerged from the deepest shadow of the back of the room, making it an even dozen — Sam Campbell, the right-wing racist I'd butted heads with a few days back in the auto-lathe room. He stepped into the weak light shed by the overhead fixture, took a last draw on his cigarette, pulling the air through the tip until it glowed like a furnace, then flipped the butt onto the floor where he ground it out with the heel of his work boot. He nodded at me. I was shocked as the proverbial shit but tried not to let it register on my face.

"Ray," he said.

"Sam," I replied.

"Sometimes appearances can be deceiving," he said with a phony sardonic smile.

"Sometimes," I said.

"Before I go any further, I need a pledge of secrecy from you — that you'll let what you hear and who you see remain in this room and not disclose anything at all to anyone outside."

"Ain't no way I'll be able to do that, Sam. You oughta know that."

"Then you're out!" With that Campbell turned his back on me and pointed to the rear door of the room like a king pointing his scepter. "Andy," he motioned to Campsten, "you put Mr. So-Called Tough-Guy out the door, will ya? We ain't got no room for scabs in here!"

Andy didn't move. "Why don't you ask him why he said that, Sam. You afraid of him or something?" he said.

"Yeah, let's don't jump the gun," said Joe Dillingham, stepping up to Sam, his deep voice modulated. "After all, we've all agreed not to do anything violent or illegal, but Ray doesn't know that. Maybe there's things like that he needs to know before he can make a decision."

"Right on!" said Ted Sadderly, "this ain't no Star Chamber of the left."

"Okay, I see my comrades have corrected me, and correction is part of my party's system, so I stand corrected, comrades. Let Ray have his say." Sam turned to me, gave a little nod.

"Let's start over," Sam continued. "Ray, as you probably can understand, we are planning some…ahh…industrial action, as the Brits say, and need secrecy at this stage. So I'm asking, are you willing to keep what you experience here a secret?"

"Long as it don't violate the law, play into the hands of Slugger or break up the unity of this union, local or national." As I said this I slowly revolved about my two feet to look at the face of every man in the room, making sure they could see that I meant business. "Otherwise I'll keep your secrets. I've kept many a secret from the bosses about many a labor action in my day. And I'll add one more thing—ain't a man or woman alive who can fairly call me a scab. Not a one!"

Mike the Bow's deep rumble of bass jumped in. "I'm sure Sam didn't really mean…"

"I apologize," Sam cut him off. "It was uncalled for," he said in a smooth oily voice. All I could see was a snake's head rearing up in front of me. "Now I hope we can move on." He looked around the room and saw that most of the men nodded, a couple mumbled their assent, so he continued.

"What I meant earlier about appearances being deceiving is that my bigotry has been an act. I'm an organizer, Ray, for the Progressive Labor Party, the PLP, which I'm sure you've heard of." He thumped his chest, then resumed chopping the air with his left hand as he spoke.

"My comrades in the PLP and I decided that since most of the workers at Slugger are white, low-income, and many from Appalachia to boot, they were likely to be prejudiced against black people. That being the case, having an organizer who could act like he could relate to their prejudice was a good plan." Sam paused a minute to light another cigarette.

"Of course I plan to lead them out of that and show that black men are workers too and are actually the vanguard of the revolutionary working class, them being the most oppressed. So now you know it's okay for me to be in this group. We are the vanguard of the working class at Slugger and we're planning a wildcat strike to rock the foundations of the bosses, not only at Slugger, but also across the class structure of Louisville."

During this horse crap I noticed the reaction I'd pretty much expected from the other men. Instead of drawing closer and becoming more intense as they surrounded Sam, the other eleven men seemed to kind of step back. Mike the Bow fiddled with something he pulled out of his pants pocket—a broken watch, I decided. Harvey Sampson stiffened, his lips turned down, his cheeks tight as he too turned away, giving Sam a quarter of his back. Andy Campsten shuffled his feet as if he had an itch in his socks, pushing first one leather shoe toe against the other ankle, then reversing the scratch. Each man displayed some kind of nervous or downright negative reaction.

Goes to show you can usually trust working folks to know bullshit when they hear it. The PLP was notorious for pointy-headed ideological crap driven by rich kids feeling guilty about where their money came from. Either that, or malcontents from legitimate unions who'd failed to gain any allegiance from the rank and file and split off, joined the PLP and had tried to out-radicalize, or out-tough, their former brothers or sisters. And they would use the hell out of real workers and real workers' fights just to build their local chapters or get headlines for themselves—usually with disastrous results. And when the deal went down they'd end up slinking away while the rest of us got our heads busted, or worse, and ended up in jail. I hated the PLP and there was no way I was going to let them get anywhere at Slugger.

The only man who pushed forward was the guy I was trying to remember and hadn't ever seen before at the Slugger plant. Then, as Sam paused in his tirade, that man jumped in, and just as he started talking, it clicked.

"Right on, Comrade!" he practically bellowed. "I'm Fred Barnes, Sam's comrade from the PLP regional office in Cincinnati. I ain't got no more money than any of you. I come in on the Trailways just to be in solidarity with you boys. We're behind you men here at the Slugger plant one hundred percent. You've got a real chance to start it, and it's up to you, right here and now at Slugger. I say we call a strike in a week's time!"

I looked around to see how many of the men noticed the switch from 'you' to 'we.' There were several frowns and only a couple of nods of agreement. But "Fred" went on like he had everybody on his side.

"Let's draw up the grievance list: first it's workers taking over seats on the Slugger board of directors so we have a voice in corporate decisions governing our fate; second, Worthington has to go; third we have our own security force designed to make sure everybody follows union rules; next we double the base wage; then we want a solid union shop, no wishy-washy elections crap!" By this point the man's voice was nearly shouting, his face red as a beet.

"And brothers, we put it on the line—literally! We show up on strike day, throw up our picket line, and meet any fuckin' scab that tries to cross with an axe handle up the side of his head. And that goes double for the fuckin' pigs! 'Cause sure as shit them pigs are going to come try and break us up— Worthington will go for an injunction and the judge will declare the strike illegal and then we'll have to fight the pigs! And the only way to fight the pig is with the gun. We have to be armed so they won't fuck with us. They see a few pistols, a few rifles, they won't dare cross our line. They'll know they're dealing with real men! So what say, comrades, are you ready to be a fighting vanguard union or not?"

That did it for me. I knew the whole deal right then and there. This man had quite a family tree—and I knew what it was. This was the guy Margaret had feared was in town—had to be. Margaret had warned me that this guy was the newest generation from the tree of the poisoned fruit, the anti-miner Sheriff of Logan County, West Virginia. That ground and its forests were sacred to fighting mountain folks for having been watered with the blood of our forefathers and foremothers two generations back in the 1920s at the battle of Blair Mountain and at the Battle of Matewan. But this man, this so-called Fred Barnes, wasn't in fact no "Barnes" of any stripe.

Margaret, bless her heart and, more to the point, bless her sharp eye and keen mind, had gone through the files of the Louisville Courier-Journal down at the library the same day Blackie and Blondie had braced me. She'd been looking for background on labor unrest in Louisville and she'd come across a little item about labor unrest out at the massive GE plant and over the Ohio River at the Olin Mathieson ammunition plant, and how an interstate team of state police agents had been commissioned to seek out so-called "outside" agitators. The group photo had included one "Payne Chaplin, Jr." I'd heard Margaret's whoop all the way out in the back yard and come running to see what was going on only to find her waving a photocopy of a newspaper photo.

"This sharp-nosed son-of-a-bad-buck," she'd pointed to a man in the photo, "is the grandson of Ron Chaplin, the dirty Sheriff that set up Sid Hatfield—hero of the battle of Matewan, as you know—for murder, and ran the army that fought our grand-brothers and grand-sisters at the battle of Blair Mountain. And he's right here in Louisville getting set to provoke and then betray this so-called labor unrest!"

"Now I get what happened at GE, Margaret," I replied. "Remember that newspaper story you dug up about how a bunch of crazies over there went out on a wildcat strike a couple months back, before we got to town? The story told that the punch press boys shut down the presses and ran through two of the six buildings trying to get the rest of the workers to go out with 'em, started a bunch of fights on the factory floor. Got the cops called in and a bunch of boys locked up in jail. And all that goin' down right before the contract was up for re-negotiation? The company got an injunction against the union in court, the union got a big fine, used up the strike fund when they paid it, so there was no funds to support the strikers if they had to go out. Then the company threw down a hard-nosed bad deal on the table at the contract negotiations, take it or leave it. The union was screwed on account of they had no funds to strike with, they'd paid it all out to the court. Typical case of provocation by an undercover copper working for the bosses — and now that you show me that picture, I bet it was that sonofabitch Chaplin!"

"You're probably right, Ray. I doubt the Staties got any interest in the Louisville Slugger, but if this case goes deep enough, you never know, and if so, this Chaplin slug might just turn up in it — so keep them hazel eyes of your'n on the lookout!"

I'd done just that — and my baby blues didn't have to look far now. He was right in front of me and running his evil line like there was no tomorrow.

"All right, I need a solid fighting union comrade to step up and volunteer for this fight," Chaplin hit the top of his pitch, "to work with me and Sam on organizing the first picket line — who's it gonna be? Step up, damn it! Don't hang back!"

I stepped up. One, two, three steps into the center of the room where he stood until my nose was just inches from that Chaplin hawk-nose. Far from being happy to see me, Chaplin, Jr., shrank away, rocked back on one foot. As he did so I motioned for Mike the Bow to come to my side, the same to Ted Sadderly.

"Ray?" he said, a huge question mark in his voice.

"Didn't expect me, ehh — Payne?"

"I don't know no Payne!" Chaplin blurted out, face instantly bright red.

"You don't? Well, let me introduce you to him," I said, whipping out my pocket watch and turning the shiny silvered back towards his face, making it into a miniature mirror. "Meet Mr. Payne Chaplin, Junior," I said, drawing out the 'junior' with a mountain drawl and thumping my forefinger into his sternum. "Son of Payne Chaplin, Senior, who is the son of Mr. Ron Chaplin, deceased Sheriff of Logan County, West Virginia and enemy of the miner's army at Blair Mountain, not to mention the man who ordered the murder of Sid Hatfield."

I put my watch back in my pocket, no use in breaking up my grandfather's pride and joy over a lousy scabbing bastard like Chaplin, if he was to fight. I could hear the snorts and shuffles from the other men in the shadowed edges of the room. I looked around to make sure Sam wasn't about to jump me and there were no other allies about to jump to Chaplin's aid. But what shuffling there was seemed to be away from Chaplin, not towards him.

"Well, well, so we meet again, Payne Chaplin, you sorry son of a buck," said Margaret as she stepped into the room from the back storage area where she'd been hiding all the while. "Remember me? The Library Rider your Daddy tried to run out of Breathitt County in the 30s? You were just a little pup back then, weren't you? But you was mean as a pit bull puppy even then, and just as dumb, Payne. Looks like you ain't changed a bit."

"I ain't ever seen this bitch before in my life," Payne said, turning to the other men in the room. "She's crazy as hell. And so is this asshole," he said, stepping up and thumping me in the chest. "They ain't got no proof. They must be on Worthington's payroll, boys! That's what's going down here!"

I went back at the sorry son of a bitch.

"Family tree aside, Chaplin, you're here to snitch for the Staties!" I growled, taking his finger off my chest. "You ain't no friend of the working man! You're the fruit what ain't fell far from the tree—you're just like your old man and your grandpa, you're here to provoke these men into a fight they're gonna lose, maybe get killed, you talking guns and shit, and for sure get their union busted up!"

"That's right!" said Margaret. "He's here to break up ya'll's union just like he did over at GE!" Margaret then ran the whole story down to them.

"Well boys," Margaret wound it up, "GE knew the union couldn't strike company-wide, and they drove a hard bargain. The union got next to nothing. The local had no bargaining power—no chips. The workingman's power comes from his labor—he can give it or he can take it away. This man is an agent for the bosses, I'm telling you—and always has been. It runs in his family!" Margaret had been stepping closer and closer to Chaplin with each statement, getting louder and louder too. At the last she was right up in his face.

Chaplin suddenly pulled back his right fist and cocked his arm half-assed like he was going to take a swing at her. I just stepped in, eased Margaret back, then stood between him and Margaret, put up my dukes and stood there. Everybody leaned into the center of the room where we stood, waiting for the action. It never came.

"Go ahead Chaplin, take a swipe. But either before or after, I'ma gonna have a look in your pockets, see what you're carrying. You've got the morals of a snake and a pig in one body but you ain't got the brains of either, you're dumb as a box of rocks. So you just might have something on you that'll prove what I'm saying."

Chaplin's arm swung but in a fake round-house as he tried to wheel around and run for the back door but Mike the Bow and Sadderly grabbed him and held him firm, elbows practically touching behind his back like chicken wings, immobilizing his upper body.

"Believe we gonna check you out, white boy," Mike said. I went through Chaplin's pockets and pulled out $240 in crisp twenty-dollar bills to the amazement of everyone in the room, then a switchblade knife, then—a set of car keys to a Lincoln!

"Well, well, well, come in on the Trailways did you? got no more money than us boys? This here's more money than any of us makes in two weeks plus a set a keys to a Lincoln! And what you got all tucked away in this little hidey hole here?"

I pulled a business-sized card out of a little compartment in his wallet. It had nothing on it but a printed phone number. Handing the card to George Salvatore, I said, "George, why dontcha give this number a ring on the pay phone in the barroom and then come back and tell us who answers it."

George took the card and left the back room. Chaplin struggled even harder but Mike and Ted held him hard and fast. I kept pouring it on.

"Like Margaret, my wife, just said, that business with GE where the wildcat went down and a judge called the whole thing illegal? Union got fined thousands of dollars? That was the work of Mr. Chaplin here, all right—but he had a partner, a big one. None other than the Kentucky Bureau of Investigation, boys—the Staties. You can read all about it in the Courier-Journal. If'n you don't believe me I'll get the back copies for you."

Just then George came back from the barroom. His face was dark as a thundercloud.

"What'd they say when they answered the phone, George?" I asked.

"KBI," he said.

It was all I could do to save Payne Chaplin from a major beating right then and there. It wouldn't do to get the KBI on our asses for no real result except the satisfaction of my personal feelings or those of the boys in the room. As it was he took a few hard knocks to the gut and shoulders as Mike and Ted frog-marched him out the back door of the Starlight and booted him down the alley, whereupon he bounced off a couple of trash cans then ran like the demons of hell were after him. And I guess in *his* mind, they were.

When I got back into the room I also noticed that Sam Campbell had done a bunk too. I asked Harvey to check around the outside and in the closets just to make sure, but that racist bastard had evidently followed his leader.

Chapter Thirty: Margaret

Now that Ray and Margaret had taken care of the government agent, Margaret filed away the question of why there was one at all in a piss-ant union dispute with a company that wasn't the worst outfit in town and the dispute itself was still less an event on the big labor stage. Right then they had to cool this bunch of hotheads down and get them some help. Because sure as shootin' they'd be looking to Ray next to fill the shoes of the late and not lamented fink they'd just thrown out the door. It didn't take them long.

"Hey Ray, whyn't you lead the strike action, man?" It was Sadderly, of course, who looked up to Ray, but had no experience and not a whole lot more sense.

"Yeah, you've been in the fight for a lot of years, Ray," George Salvatore surprised Margaret by saying, as, despite Harvey's medium-strong endorsement, she hadn't figured him to take much of a role in this action at all. "We need a man with that kind of experience, seeing as how we almost got snookered by this Chaplin guy, you know?"

"And we need a white guy who's got the respect of the black men in this outfit," added Mike the Bow, "and let's face it, the only one really like that is you."

Ray put his hands up to stop it right there.

"Whoa boys," he said, shaking his head. "Now I ain't wanna seem an ingrate. But I got a job to do, and y'all boys might as well know that I'm here working for the national office of the WIA to keep your local union from getting framed on these murders, and to do that I gotta find out the truth about who killed Durkin and Gorham and why.

Especially why. So I gotta kind of walk a tight rope here. I cain't go out organizing no union action or lead no picket lines with you boys, even if I thought it was a good idea and you was ready—which at the moment, I don't and you ain't."

This of course brought a whole bunch of back-wash and whining, but when it had died down Margaret stepped up, made them all take seats on some unused bar stools that the Starlight had for overflow in the back room, and took over the discussion.

"Gentlemen, I know I don't look like the hard fighting, oh-so-experienced union *man* that my husband is, the man you wanted to lead you just a minute ago. But the deal is, I've been in just as many fights as Ray, maybe more, and I'm telling the truth as I see it. So let me make my point, okay? And if I'm wrong, well, you can kick me out of here like you did Chaplin. I'll ask Mike here to give me one word answers to some questions, just one word, mind, and then we'll see—agreed? That okay with you boys?"

They agreed, and Mike stepped up next to Margaret.

"You boys have a strike fund worth at least $20,000?"

"No."

"You boys have strike support committees organized in the churches, synagogues, civic clubs and such-like all over town?"

"No."

"You boys have the wives and women-folk organized to spell you on the picket lines?"

"No."

"You boys have an internal committee set up to resolve disputes between the brothers when the going gets hot and you get at each other's throats?"

"No."

"You boys have a publicity committee that has met with the editorial boards of the newspapers and radio and TV here in town and over to Jefferson County too?"

"No."

"You boys have…"

"Okay, we get it, we get it," jumped in Andy Campsten.

"I guess we ain't ready after all," said Mike the Bow. "Maybe you could help us get organized and get all this stuff you talking about, you know, get it put in place. We just need to get some popularity, then we could go on strike."

"Are you kidding me? Popularity?" Margaret said, half laughing at him. "You boys strike the Louisville Slugger plant long enough to really hurt production and inventory? We're talking about a bat shortage for the Little Leagues and sandlot leagues and high schools and colleges? Then the day comes when the Single A and Double A and Triple A and finally, the Negro Leagues and Major Leagues of U.S. baseball start running out of bats? Popularity? You'll have boys and girls and Moms and Dads and baseball fans from every corner of the USA heading for Louisville in everything from mule carts to Cadillacs and they'll be gunning for you boys. You'd be the biggest traitors this country's seen since Benedict Arnold!"

"Well, you got a point," Mike said sheepishly. "But what I said about you—and that includes Ray—helping us get ourselves together on this stuff still stands. We got contract negotiations coming up and I don't trust that damn racist Billy Jenkins, 'scuse my French, no farther than I could throw 'im."

There was a general muttering of assent to this statement about Billy. Then an endorsement again came from that previously unexpected quarter, George Salvatore.

"You're right, Mike. He's a snake. I seen Jenkins runnin' out of Benson's office with some production sheets in his sweaty little hand the other day, so I just eased myself along behind his sorry ass. He run into his office for a little minute then ran out again, left the door ajar, so I jumped in for a peek at them sheets. Well boys, they was skewed all to hell. Showed my production down from what I'd actually got paid, showed a lot of colored workers up! I bet it'd be the same for a lot of white workers. Looks to me like 'ol Billy boy's tryin' to stir the pot and get colored and white workin' against one

228

another. Now why would the union chief be doin' that just before the contract negotiations?"

Why indeed? But Ray and I had nailed the low-down on the production sheets in the office the other day after the raid, so we knew, and what George said next just confirmed it.

"But that ain't all. I had just ducked out that door and down the hall not more'n ten feet when here come Jenkins with Burleson and Duvall hot footin' it right into his office. I hung around for about five minutes then heard some more fast slapping footsteps so I started moving again only to see Benson coming down the hall from the head office and go right into that same door. So there they was, Jenkins, Burleson, Duvall and Benson in that office with them jimmied production sheets."

A low whistle sounded from the corner where Ted Sadderly was sitting.

"You got that right," said Andy Campsten, jumping off his stool and smacking his fist into the palm of his hand. "We got to take action on Billy Jenkins."

Sadderly jumped up so hard he kicked his stool back into the corner. "I say we drag that son of a bitch out of his office first thing tomorrow and call a workers' meeting and confront him with the production sheet issue. Demand he turn 'em over and then vote to fire his ass as union president right there on the spot!"

"Right on!" said Mike the Bow. "Enough's enough!"

Then Harvey stepped into the middle of the room. The light from the one high window slanted off the side of his face as he paced back and forth, speaking in a deep steady voice. "I'm just as mad as anybody in here," he started off. "Fact is, I could break Billy Jenkins' kneecap and shed no tears, believe you me. And I ain't never had no use for Burleson or Duvall. But we dealin' with Benson here, and we dealin' with the Slugger company too. Whether Worthington is behind this or not, we dealin' with a plot to break up this union just before, or even right during, the contract negotiations. So we talkin' high stakes here, brothers, high stakes."

With that he slowly turned through the semi-circle with his right hand out level with his waist, including each of them.

"Am I right?" he said. Then, not waiting for answers, he went on.

"So we got to be careful and take maximum use of all the weapons we got. And this be a weapon, this production sheet thing. We caught them out, so that make it a weapon of theirs we can turn to a weapon of ours. Am I right?"

This time Harvey stepped back to the semi-circle next to his stool and waited for the rest of the men and myself to respond. He'd given them something to think about, and they did, so it was a little while before he got a response.

"You've got a point," Ted Sadderly broke into the silence. "And what's more, you've made me realize we need to think this thing through from the angle of timing, too. It's a weapon, all right, but we need to figure out when to use it. Like you said, they may be planning to spring it on us to divide black from white either before or during the negotiations—but it matters whether it is in fact before or during, right? So we need to figure that one out as to when we fire our weapon, so to speak. But what I'd like to say, really, is to ask a question to Mrs. Odle here, and Ray. And that is, what about you all helping us, like Mike said, with the strategy on this? I haven't heard an answer on that yet."

The ball was back in the Odle Agency court. Margaret looked over at Ray, who was sitting on a stool literally twiddling his thumbs and looking at the floor. But his radar was working just fine, so he looked up at Margaret and grinned. She nodded at him but he shook his head side to side so slightly you almost couldn't see it, like a baseball pitcher shaking off his catcher's signal. Then Margaret just sighed, took one more deep breath, and laid it out.

"All right, we'll do that, at least some of it," she said. "But you men have to do the work. It's not our local, it's yours.

And it isn't our fight, it's yours. Once this case is solved we're moving on. Our pay and working conditions for the rest of our next four years, never mind the rest of our working lives, won't be affected by the outcome of this contract. But yours will, one way or the other. And another thing. About this so-called weapon. You might want to think about it real hard. How strong is it? What does it consist of? You've got George's word about what he saw in Jenkins' office. When Billy produces the production sheets, who is to say they've been jimmied? Can you prove that? And can you show racist intent? You've got a weapon of sorts, George's statement of what he saw, but have you got the old smoking gun?"

You've never seen a bunch of faces fall so fast in your life. The beaming glow of triumph in the eye that had accompanied Mike and Ted's proclamations of action against Jenkins went out like stadium lights when the night game is over.

"Them bastards will just say George is lying," said Mike the Bow. "That he made it up. An' they'll demand proof that the production sheets is jimmied. All's we've got is paystubs."

"Which don't show production numbers, just piece rate pay totals," said George Salvatore. "We'd have to go back into each pay period and figure out the piece rate and divide the day rate and the hourly and…"

"And it would take a math professor to do that," said Andy Campsten, "which none of us is qualified for, not to mention a year and a day to compute it all. Besides, even if we did, most guys don't keep them stubs for long, and the few that do, Benson would just argue it was an honest mistake and we'd lose our point about race and the union. Our weapon would be a squirt gun. It would just fizzle."

It was time for Harvey to make another move. He'd been clued in about the production sheets, of course, as a member of the Agency team, so he knew exactly where to find the smoking gun the men were needing. He was looking a question at Margaret as Andy was finishing up, so she gave him the nod.

"Well, I think I know where to find the smoking gun," he said quiet and deep again. "Thanks to Ray and Margaret here, the smoking gun exists, and we have it. Let's just say that this is the kind of thing that can get a man in a whole lot of trouble, so I'm going to tell the rest of you generally that there is a hidden set of double production sheets. One set, normally kept by Benson, is the regular set and it shows one thing. The other set, kept in Jenkins' office in a totally off-the-wall secret hiding place, is the jimmied set he's going to spring on us at some point."

The faces that had fallen a minute ago rose in hope and anticipation. Margaret heard a few muttered, "all right!"s here and there, and several men even stepped closer to where Harvey stood.

"Now it so happens that, uh, there's a copied duplicate of these sets somewhere—don't ask where—that proves the whole scam," he went on. "We could pull a xerox out at any time. But the best and strongest weapon would be to accuse Billy of trying to split the union and of jimmying the sheets and cheating workers, then force him to produce the original jimmied set from their hiding place at the moment he springs the accusation on the black workers, right? So I'm going to ask two of you, one white and one black, to come with me, break into Jenkins' office and make a "discovery" of the jimmied set tonight. That way we'll know where it is and can force Jenkins to cough it up when he tries to pull his scam later on. I just want two of you because there's no need for more and it's best to keep the risk to a minimum. But be that as it may, I need all of you to support the plan. Are you with me on this?"

"Doesn't it kind of depend on who is going in with you?" asked Ted Sadderly.

"No. Either you trust me and trust my judgment, and you trust each of your brothers in this circle to carry out the mission, or you don't. In or out, that's the deal."

There was a long moment of verbal silence punctuated by heels rubbing the rungs of stools as well as a couple of coughs.

"I'm in," said Andy Campsten.

"Me too," said Mike the Bow.

And then the rest joined in, followed at the end by Ray and Margaret.

Chapter Thirty-one: Radio seven

Mel Allen: Here we are back for the bottom of the fifth, ball fans. Say Red, take a look at those flags out past the center field scoreboard, willya? Man o Manischewitz, the wind's shifted 180 degrees around!

Red Barber: That's right Mel, she's a blowin' to the infield now, just the opposite the way it blew at the start of the game, and opposite of the prevailing winds out here at Wrigley Field too. It's a pitcher's ballpark now.

MA: That'll be good news for Dick Ellsworth. He's not having his best day today, Red.

RB: Yep, but he seems to have the number on Gordy Coleman, the first baseman for the Redlegs. Whiffed him twice in two trips to the plate.

MA: Right, the pitchers have the advantage now, and just in time for the face-off between Ellsworth and Jersey Jack, now tapping his shoe with the end of the bat. Stalling around outside the batter's circle. What's he up to I wonder?

RB: Maybe he's waitin' for the wind to change again, Mel. After all, it's Chicago. The cabbies tell me if ya don't like the weather, just wait a minute, it'll change for sure.

MA: Okay, Jersey Jack is in the batter's box now. Ellsworth's into his windup…here's the pitch…low and outside, ball one.

RB: That's another thing goin' on with the wind, Mel. It's gettin' downright furious out there, not only blowin' into home plate but it's kind of a crosswind too.

MA: You said it, Red. It's pushing the pitches towards the outside for right-hand batters like Jersey Jack. Ellsworth's winding up, the pitch...high and outside, ball two.

RB: Ellsworth is struggling with this wind. It'll help him if a batter gets a piece of the ball but it's hurtin' him now on his control. He's normally one of the best, Mel. Twenty game winner last season.

MA: Okay, Red. Let's see if he can get it down and a little more inside on this one. Here it comes…swing…it's a bouncing grounder just left of the mound…the short-stop Kessinger has it, flips it to Glenn Beckert on second ahead of a charging Coleman…Beckert to Ernie Banks on first…OUCH! Jersey Jack is out – he's hit into a double play!

RB: Mark your score sheet folks, that's a GDP for Jersey Jack.

MA: And should we score one for the wind here in Wrigley Field, Red?

RB: Dunno, Mel. But Jersey Jack is looking like a lost soul trotting back to the dugout.

MA: Boy is he down and out, fists clenched, head shaking back and forth.

RB: Wait a minute, Mel, Jack is turning back towards home plate. He's stopped the bat boy. Wants to look at his bat.

MA: Uh oh, Red, now he's shaking that Blond Louisville Slugger S2 back and forth like he's conducting the Chicago Symphony. Yep, just as I thought, he's running a finger up and down the backside of the bat…

RB: Opposite the label, Mel. It's gotta be a crack. Bat didn't break, but Jack has gone so red in the face he's matching his socks!

MA: He's not walking back to the dugout, Red, he's stomping.

RB: I guess that answers your question about the wind effect, Mel. Chalk it up to the bat.

MA: Right. Say Red, this is getting to be a habit, this business of cracked and busted bats. Haven't you noticed a lot more of that than usual?

RB: Sure have, Mel. Somebody ought to pay a visit to Mr. Worthington down in Louisville and check it out.

MA: Knowing our Commissioner, General Eckert, it might just happen – NOT!

RB: I didn't say that, folks. It was Mel Allen…

MA: Who you say who when I say who…say who?

Chapter Thirty-Two: Ray

Margaret and I were relaxing in our box seats just behind the home team dugout in the Louisville Bats Triple-A ballpark on an unusually mild August afternoon watching Jersey Jack Danielson of the Cincinnati Redlegs conduct a batting clinic for the city-wide Little League. We were sipping Coca-Colas from bottles and crunching down on peanuts, and of course Margaret shelled a half-dozen every few sips of Coke and stuffed them down the bottle neck, a habit she'd brought up to Kentucky from South Carolina, and one I confess I'd picked up too. It was damn good, a great mix of the salty and the sweet.

"This is kind of fun," said Margaret through a mouthful of peanuts. "I'm glad you suggested I come with you, dear heart. Couldn't be a better day for it, either."

"Yep," I said. "Although you'd a thought Mr. Danny B was bein' asked to do a dance with the devil when he found out Jersey Jack would be the one to give the batting clinic. Griped all day at Slugger yesterday."

"Whatever happened to that AA serenity and "absolutely insist on being happy," if I got the quote right?" Margaret said.

"That's the quote, all right," I replied. "I dunno, I guess none of us is perfect. But Danny, he's been off his serenity for some time now, and we both know at least one reason that might account for it."

"You mean the moneyline?"

"Yep, I do indeed."

The P.R.O. section had been ordered to bring a supply of foot-long souvenir bats to the event, and as the newest man in P.R.O., Bob Stills had given me the nod to do the honors along with Danny B, who had started the afternoon off by giving a short explanation of how the professional bats were made while I passed the souvenir bats out to the kiddies. It had gone well. Danny B had the gift of the gab, all right, and his talk about sizing the bats, turning them on the lathe and how each pro player had his own "recipe," was peppered with examples of pro bats he'd brought to the ballpark.

While Danny had been charming the kids I'd passed out the mini-bats with the Slugger logo and one or another pro players' signatures on them. Most kids were grateful to get the little bats, but every once in a while one would want a different signature, and I'd tell them that's what trading was for, just like with baseball cards, so to get to work swapping bats. That satisfied all but the grumpiest whiners and this one kid named Billy, who was a wiseacre, who challenged me on the grounds of the size of the bat.

"Hey mister, why'nt ya give us a real bat," he said in a sassy tone of voice. "I bet the great Louisville Slugger company makes a zillion bucks off of these pro players' signatures, so you could afford to give us kids real bats."

I was about to do a W. C. Fields imitation and tell him what he could do with the bat I'd just given him, he had that kind of grating voice and attitude, but I stuffed it back down and smiled, and gave him a charitable reply.

"Well, I'm sure they could if it was just a matter of money, young man," I said. "But you see, that way you wouldn't have nothin' to work for in your development as a pro ball player. And I'll just bet that some day you're gonna get one of those bats for free on account of playing major league ball. So we'll all just hang on till then." And before he could reply I moved right on down the line to the next bunch of kids. After I finished up the mini-bat distribution I went back to the stands and took up my position as a spectator with Margaret.

Jersey Jack started off the clinic wowing the Little Leaguers by swatting pitches from Cliff Brown, a pitcher on the Bats first string, knocking them over the home run fence and as far as I could tell, halfway to China.

Then Jersey Jack started giving the little shavers the basics of how to hold the bat and how to give it a smooth even swing and meet the ball just right to get good wood on it. Things went right along, each kid taking Jersey's advice and giving it his best shot. Some hit the ball right solid and knocked it into the outfield, some not so well, popping it up or hitting little dribblers into the infield. And then there were the inevitable strikeouts, who got a second chance, after which they got a hearty, "better luck next time."

The ballpark grounds crew had been hired at overtime pay to field baseballs and give them back to Cliff on the mound, keeping the process going. Most kids took their results in stride, thanking Jack when their turn was over, and grinning from ear to ear when he gave them an autographed baseball card, poster and Cincinnati Reds baseball cap.

I hadn't paid too much attention to the individual Little League batters, but then I noticed that Jack had his six foot three frame hunched over that same kid that had whined and sassed at me earlier. I could see and hear Jack and the kid perfectly.

"Now Billy, you get a good grip on that Louisville Slugger Little Leaguer bat," said Jack, "it's the right size for you, so no need to choke up the handle quite so far. That's right, put your hands there, and there. Okay, good. Now remember what I said about where the label should be—nope, not thataway, that's too far around towards the pitcher. If you have it that far around you'll likely crack the bat. You need to turn it away more. Like this, see, and…"

"Is that how you've been breaking so many bats this season, Jersey Jack?" said Billy, using that same grating, sassy-ass voice he'd used on me, turning a fake innocent face up into

Jack's, which suddenly turned bright red as Jack grabbed the bat from the kid's hands and slammed it to the dirt.

"Shut up, kid! You don't know what the hell you're talking about!" he yelled, stepping back from the batter's box in a stagger. Then Jersey Jack looked around wildly at the ballpark, shook his head, and yelled, "we're taking a ten minute break!" as he stalked off into the dugout and disappeared from sight.

Billy's face crumpled, his fists balled up and his eyes filled with tears. Never mind the kid had it coming, this was customer relations and bad for business, I was out of my seat in a flash and over the dugout roof, jumping down to the turf behind home plate. I ran over and put my arm around the kid.

"He didn't mean it, Billy," I said. "Jersey Jack's had a rough time lately. But he didn't intend to be mean to you and I'm really sure you didn't do nothing wrong." At that point one of the Little League coaches arrived and took over the comforting duties.

I went through the door behind the dugout and started down the dank cement hall towards the home team locker room. I hadn't gotten very far when I heard voices—and they weren't happy ones, either. As I got a little closer I recognized them both. Jersey Jack's from his yelling at the kid just now, and the other one from great familiarity—it was the voice of my AA pal, Danny B.

"The hell with that!" said Jersey Jack. "You can't back out now, you weasel. Sure, you got your deal fixed, but what about me? I ain't got mine paid off yet. Them bastards'll break my goddamn legs if I don't keep payin' 'em off, Danny, an' you goddamn well know it."

"But it's killing me, man. All the lying, the sneaking around. I tell you, that Ray is a dangerous son of a bitch an' he's watching every move I make. Shit! I thought cozying up I could throw him off but he's gotten tight with Sampson and others that know I'm runnin' the moneyline, Jack. If he gets his wind up he might just figure out the rest of it too!"

"Then you better make damn sure he don't, that's all I got to say. And I better not see no slackin' on my special bats neither! A deal is a deal. You're in till I say it's over — got it? And don't get no crazy ideas about running to the Man, hear?"

"Hey, you quit fucking with me — I ain't no Gorham, you know. I ain't turned on you or the moneyline, so don't put me in that bag."

"No, you ain't, you miserable shit. You ain't got the balls he did." The room echoed with wild laughter. "One look at Haskell and Rogers and you'd pee your pants!"

"Aww fuck you, Jack, just go to hell."

The mad laughter broke out again, only this time it was headed my way.

I beat it, taking care to move quiet as possible while gaining speed as I zipped back up the concrete hallway, out through the dugout, up the VIP steps and into the box seats to Margaret.

I'd barely reached the box, still crossing the aisle to my seat when Jersey Jack emerged from the dugout. The general manager of the Louisville Little League was waiting for him. After a short conference Jersey Jack went over to Billy and apologized, saying that he'd had a rough week at bat that had included two cracked bats, but that was no excuse for doing what he did. He told the kid he'd get him a real Jersey Jack pro bat, they shook hands, and that was that.

Jersey Jack went back to coaching the next kids in line on batting basics, and after five more had taken their turns, a pale and slinking Danny B emerged from the dugout, crossed to the exit ramp, and disappeared from the ballpark.

Margaret looked a question at me, I nodded, and I eased myself out of the box seats and followed Danny.

Exiting the park I was just in time to see him duck into a shabby corner bar at the end of the block on the opposite side of the street from Bats Stadium. It was 2:35 in the afternoon.

Chapter Thirty-Three: Ray

I didn't know what kind of drunk Danny B was going to be when I eased up onto the bar stool next to him after he'd been in there just over two hours. I'd been waiting outside on the corner hoping he'd just popped in for a quick one, but it had been in vain. The shift had let out at the Oak Street yards and assorted odd-job manufacturing plants near by and the joint had filled up an hour ago, so when I went in the bartender had fallen behind in clearing the glass from in front of the drinkers, and judging from the collection in front of Danny, he was drinking shots with beers back, a dangerous combination.

The flush on his face and the width of his pupils told the same story. So did his words when I spoke to him.

"Why don't you let me drive you home, Danny? Don't look like you're in any shape to drive, old buddy. Besides, prob'ly ought to put the plug in the jug right about now, okay?"

"Shee-it, ish fucken Ray, my man. Wha' you doin' in a bar, Ray? Thas' what I'ma ashin' you."

I got stern right then and just picked Danny's arm up at the shoulder and pulled him off the stool into a standing position.

"I ain't messin' with you, Danny. Let's go." And with that I got my hand under his armpit and escorted him out of the bar. Thank God he didn't resist, just shuffled along beside me mumbling a bunch of crap about, "jus a little slip," and, "firs' one in more'n 25 yersh."

We managed to get to the parking lot beside the baseball field and I got Danny's keys out of his pocket without a fight and drove him home. I had to keep punching him back to focus on how to get to his apartment. Although we were friends in AA, we didn't socialize outside of meetings and the suppers we shared with other guys at Brown's Hotel, so I hadn't known it but he lived just a dozen blocks from my place up Floyd Street. It was a little first-floor two-room apartment with a tiny kitchenette. The place was neat as a pin, not a thing out of place, which surprised me for some reason.

I put Danny on the slightly worn couch and put the coffee on the two-burner range. He quickly slumped into the corner pillows of the couch and dozed off. That gave me a chance to look around.

Danny had furnished the tiny place in used mahogany. The sofa and easy chair as well as one chaise that filled the small sitting room were mahogany, as was the coffee table and one chair-side lamp table. He had what looked like an unused old coal fireplace whose short oak mantelpiece had an old oil lamp sitting on it.

But it was what he'd hung over the mantle that got to me. It was a framed mat board with all 25 of his AA annual birthday sobriety chips stuck on it—the coins, like the one Sally Gorham had shown me. They went ten across, five down, so there was room for twenty-five more of them across the bottom. I reckon Danny was planning on getting fifty years before he died. And now he wouldn't make it. Because if he was honest at the next meeting, when they called for newcomers to identify themselves he would have to put his hand up and give his name. He'd wiped out 25 years, just like that!

Putting up that hand would be the hardest thing he'd ever done—harder than the first time. Much harder. I'd seen a couple of alcoholics with considerable time sober do that in my day, but none with 25 years. I wondered if Danny had it in him. I could see him sitting as he always did on the side row of the Friday night meeting—the guru's row, where the guys with great sobriety and experience sit and survey the rest of us from the side angle. I could hear the stories my sponsor, Jimmy G., had told me about this guy and that guy who had built up some time in sobriety but then had let ego or resentment or some other foible build up to the point where they quit going to meetings, slacked off on working the steps, then how it brought them down and they took a drink. How devastating it had been for them to lose that status, that dignity, that pride of accomplishment.

I also recalled him telling me about Harry S., a man who'd had a slip and kept it under wraps so well that nobody figured it out until he'd been caught by a fellow from his home group who'd seen him at a bar in another town quite by accident. How Harry had been so high and prideful he'd threatened bodily harm to the man who'd caught him out if he were to tell the others back in the home group.

While I was meditating on all this Danny came to with a snort.

He jerked upright from his slump on the couch, looked wild-eyed around the room, shook his head—and saw me standing by the mantle.

"What the hell!" he roared. "How'd you get…" Then the memory hit him like a huge pressure wave. It pushed him back into the sofa, like a man in a rocket ship taking several Gs of force. His body vibrated with it, his jaw ground side to side.

"I got some coffee on the stove, Danny," I said, gentle as I knew how. "Why don't we have a cup and talk about it. Ain't the first time an alcoholic had a slip."

"Goddamn," he muttered, his head down, staring at the floor now. "Goddamn." But he took the coffee I brought to him. Good and strong it was, too. I sat in the chair across from him.

We drank in silence for a few minutes. I could see the wheels rolling in his head. He stood at the turning point. What to do? Fight it? Be defiant? Be slick and fob it off? Or break down and accept it, be honest and take the painful road back to recovery? The one thing I couldn't do was tell him anything or make a suggestion. It was totally up to him. He knew the score. I could only be there to listen.

"Guess you caught me red-handed, Ray," he said with a sickly grin on his face.

He was being slick. I felt sick inside.

"Guess I know what I gotta do though," he went on with a phony grimace.

"What's that, Danny?" I said.

"Gotta be honest. Gotta put my hand up as a newcomer, that's what," he said. "Who'd a thought it. Danny B, guru extraordinaire, twenty-five years and counting. Takes a fall over some bullshit."

"Want to talk about the bullshit, whatever that is, Danny?" I said, leaning over just slightly.

"Naw, Ray. Ain't nothing you'd be able to help me with. Just that same old debt mess I told you about before. But I'll get out of it. I don't know why I picked up that drink this time. Shee-it, man, I had plenty of reasons to do it before and ain't never done it till now. Just have to pick myself up like old Frank sings about, right? Dust myself off, start all over again."

"Whatever you say, Danny." I was flat disgusted by now, listening to this jive performance. I stood up to go. "Think I'll head home, Danny, seein' as you think you've got it all under control again." He didn't hear the sarcasm even though I laid it on right smart thick.

But Danny's eyes went wide again and he knocked his coffee cup over as he dashed around the coffee table to grab me by the shoulders as I got to the door.

"Damn you, Ray. You think you so fucking hot shit. Well, fuck that! But I'll tell you one thing. You better keep your mouth shut about this, hear? I'll tell it when I'm good and ready — me! Not you! No fucking ignorant half-ass with as little time as you is going to take down a man like me. Got that, hillbilly?"

I looked him in the eye, clamped my hand around each of Danny's hands one at a time and deliberately lifted them off of my shoulders.

"Sure, Danny," I said, even toned. "Whatever you say."

I opened the door and walked into the night. Now I'd been "hillbillied" by my closest friend in AA outside of my sponsor.

Chapter Thirty-Four: Margaret

Ray and Margaret were back on Jacob Street, this time sipping coffee instead of coca-cola, munching on some oatmeal cookies instead of peanuts, sitting on the Salvation Army issue oak swivel chairs in the office instead of the box seats at Bats Stadium. Margaret was staring down at the pattern on the linoleum floor tiles, not seeing them, but fixating on them nonetheless. She was vaguely aware of pale blue and soft red hatching against a sage green background. They were snacking on some of their favorite stuff because they needed all the "feel goodies" they could get after the impact of Danny's fall from grace.

"Well, Margaret, to sum it all up," Ray had said after they'd gone over it for quite a while, "I'm angry and I'm hurt, I'm disillusioned yet I ain't surprised one bit. Bottom line? It's what we alkies do. We drink. It's a disease of the mind and body and spirit. Danny's sick. And the fact that he won't deal with it is part of the sickness."

"Right. I see that," Margaret said. "But what else do you see, Ray, from what he did tonight that might have a bearing on this case?"

"I'm not sure I get what you're a-drivin' at, sweetheart."

"His remarks about not letting some ignorant hillbilly take him down. He's got a lot of pride and a lot invested in his status, maybe way more than anybody might have realized. He threatened you, right? That wasn't just him being slick at that point, was it, Ray?"

"Nope, you're right. He was for real right then."

"So if he was that way with you about something like telling on his drinking slip—what would happen if the stakes were higher?"

It didn't take Ray another split second to see where Margaret was going and to gallop on ahead of her.

"Like Gorham and Jersey Jack threatening to rat Danny out behind his debts, or worse, blackmail to the mob!"

"Bingo!" Margaret said. "Of course we're just speculating here, but it's got to move way up the list of the possible scenarios, seems to me."

"True," Ray came back. "But I'm not sure the mob would've cared all that much about Danny's debts—and Danny would've known or figured that, so the question is why would he use an extreme measure to shut Gorham up when in his own mind it may not have been absolutely necessary? I mean, figure the risk. It's huge. An' our boy Danny ain't too big on risk, seems to me."

"Those are good points, dear heart," Margaret said. "So if Danny is going to be It with a capital 'I', then there's got to be more involved, some additional motivating factor."

They kicked that around for a while but got nowhere. Then they discussed the case more broadly. Margaret kept coming back to staring at the linoleum floor and its cross hatching. Something important about the case was at the edge of her awareness but it wasn't coming through.

"Baseball!" she finally snapped out. "It all comes down to baseball. We're such dolts, sometimes, Ray. Well, speaking for myself. I'm a dolt sometimes."

He started to protest, but it was no use. Margaret held her hand up in the universal sign to shush.

"We've got to figure this baseball angle out. All there is to it. The Slugger is about baseball. The moneyline is about baseball. Danny B makes pro *baseball* bats. Jersey Jack plays pro *baseball*. The union is made of workers that make *baseball* bats. Slugger is trying to suppress a union to exploit the labor of workers who make *baseball* bats. Jersey Jack is griped off because he's had a run of cracked *baseball* bats.

Ray jumped on the bandwagon. "Danny B is a runner for the *baseball* moneyline. Durkin was a sawyer of *baseball* bats who stuck up for the black workers who make *baseball* bats — not to mention for blacks at home against Jenkins' old man and Worthington's finance company."

"We've taken our eyes off the ball, no pun intended. We're just not digging into the baseball angle enough here. That's what I'm getting out of this."

"Okay, let's just do that for a minute. Why is Jersey Jack threatening Danny B?" Ray put the question.

"Because Danny B seems to want out of something they've got going between them," Margaret answered.

"Which is what?" The big question, and he knew it.

"Something to do with the moneyline." Margaret came back.

"Something dangerous, something that might have involved Gorham and got him killed, since Jack threw that at Danny B," he said.

"Right. But there's something else. Something about paying "them," whoever that is, paying them off. And the paying off seems to involve both Jack and Danny B."

"Yeah, Jack said his wasn't paid off yet but seemed to think Danny B's was." Ray was up and pacing now.

"It's obvious, isn't it?" Margaret said.

"The moneyline?"

"Yep. They both owed the moneyline, and Jack still does."

"And he and Danny are into something that will help Jack pay it off, something that helped Danny pay his off already, something they can't quit because, as Jack said, these guys will break legs!"

"That's got to be the mob, simple as that," Margaret said.

"So what are they doing that's connected to the moneyline that may have involved Gorham and got him killed? That they can't quit doing yet but is dangerous? Yet helps them, or at least Jack, pay off a mob debt?" Ray said, then he went on.

"If you'd a heard them two, you'd have to wonder if the scheme they're tied together on has got something to do with *skewing* the moneyline."

Margaret had it in a flash and laid it out.

"Baseball," she said. "Back to that. And if it's that, then somebody knows about it. It's awful hard to jimmy baseball games without somebody knowing it or at least suspecting it. The thing is, we don't know enough about baseball to even start looking."

"I know where we can do the digging, Margaret," Ray said, coming to a stop in front of my chair. "There's a guy in my home group, I shouldn't tell you his name, but hell, this is a murder investigation, so yeah, he's called Radio Ralph. The man is a walking, talking encyclopedia of baseball. He's got the best baseball card collection in the damn USA, I'll bet, right here in Louisville! Keeps 'em catalogued six ways from Sunday down in his basement. And there ain't a crummy, measly half-fact or even rumor about baseball this guy don't know."

"Well, jump on the phone and see if you can go see him, Ray, no time like the present!" Margaret said, pushing for action.

"He ain't got no phone, sorry to say. He's kind of like a cave man, and Danny says he's a crank, so maybe he won't give me the time of day, still less anything we can use, but I'm on it," Ray came back.

With that he lost no time, picked his old railroad hat off the hook on the office wall and gave Margaret a quick hug, then beat it out the front door to go see Radio Ralph.

Chapter Thirty-Five: Ray

I needn't have worried. Ralph couldn't have been nicer. We went down into that gloomy basement that Danny B had described, sure enough crammed with old wooden file cabinets, piles of bound register books rising from tables and even off the floor, and yep, Ralph's high antique desk sat under a green shaded lamp hanging from the ceiling. He seated me on a wicker easy chair next to a lamp table with eight inches of register books stacked on it, went upstairs to get us some coffee, instant, while I looked through one of the books, which happened to be records of the 1954 Dodgers' season, a year in which they finished second in the National League.

"You know, I used to sit here on this stool like a steely-eyed shithouse rat," Ralph said when he got back downstairs, "me against the world, hating anyone who knocked on that door up there on the main floor of this house. It was just me and baseball and the rest of the world be damned. Didn't have a wife, kids, anyone to care about. Well, that was when I was a dry drunk. Wasn't pouring the shit down my gullet but I wasn't happy either. I might as well of had the jitters for all the serenity I had. It took working the steps before my world started opening up. Six months ago I'd have run you off!"

He laughed and I laughed with him, but I was also thinking that the cranky reception Danny B got might have had more to do with personalities than the state of Ralph's sobriety.

I got down to business and told Ralph in a general sort of way what I was looking for—a connection between Jersey Jack Danielson and anything that would affect the normal working out of the averages that the statisticians based the moneyline on. That's when his face shut down tighter than a teller's window after bank closing, just slammed shut. I thought I was going to get the Danny B treatment after all. It was like night and day, or day and night to get the sequence right. His voice got real steely just like that rat he talked about.

"Who wants to know, Ray? The only reason I'm still talking with you is out of respect from what I've seen of you in the meetings and what others say about you. So be real careful with your answer, hear. Make sure it's rock solid truth. No bullshit."

"I want to know, Ralph—me. I'm investigating the murders of Frank Gorham and Fred Durkin down at Slugger. You know that from things I've said before. Like I said a minute ago, I've got reason to believe it might tie in with the moneyline, that Gorham may have found out something and tried to use it in a way that got him killed. One type of thing he could have found out was that somebody involved in baseball was doing something to the game that affected the game outcomes. I have my reasons to think it might have involved Jersey Jack. That's it, that's why I'm here, because you know more about the game than anybody short of an official statistician—and maybe more than them."

"There's something you aren't saying, Ray. Point blank. And if you don't come across with it, I'm afraid you'll have to leave," said Ralph in a low, nearly growling voice. "I may not have a family, but I'm kind of fond of my skin, especially now that I'm sober and have a life again."

"Yeah, Ralph, there's one other aspect to it and I'll tell you what I know. But you've got to come clean too. So my question to you is: how deep are you into the moneyline?"

That question was like a palm to the face, shoving Ralph back about two inches, he was so taken aback.

"Man, you don't jive around, do you?"

"Not hardly," I said, but kept an even smile on my face.

"Okay," he said. "I admit it. I'm down about eight hundred dollars to them and I'm struggling to pay it off. I've quit betting on it and I'm paying fifty dollars a week, but that's hard on my wages at the radio station since my work is only part time. I do a little work on the extra board down at the Oak Street yards of the L & N when I can, but it's still hard. Now, your turn. Give."

And I did. I told him about the argument between Jersey Jack and Danny B and that I knew Danny B was the runner for the moneyline. Ralph confirmed it, at least as of the time he quit playing it. And I made sure Ralph knew I wasn't hooked in with Danny B in any way, shape, or fashion—not as a co-conspirator on the moneyline. I also made it clear that Danny B was no longer my best friend in the program, not as far as I was concerned.

We sat there for a long minute after that, Radio Ralph looking up at the uncovered steel beams that ran across the basement ceiling, me looking at him, hoping for some insight now that he had the crop. A squirrel jumped down into the window well outside the wall above Ralph's desk, rattled around in some dead leaves, came up with an acorn and skittered back out. Then Ralph's face slowly began to stretch into a full-on wide-mouthed grin as something dawned on his mind.

"It's gotta be the bats," he said, shaking his head slightly in bemusement. "The cracked bats. Jersey Jack has had a run of cracked bats so bad over the last few weeks that everybody on the inside in baseball's been talking about it. Hell, a few of his buds on the team think he's jinxed. The rumor is that one or two of them asked Don Heffner, the Redleg manager, to move him out of fourth spot in the batting rotation so somebody else can bat cleanup. All on the Q.T. of course, 'cause everybody knows about Jersey Jack's volcanic temper. You get on the wrong side of that man? You're dead meat."

An unfortunate choice of words, I thought. Or was it? "But I thought he'd gone to Heffner and demanded he complain to

Slugger—leastways that's what we got down at the plant," I said.

"Oh yeah, he did that, and more. He stormed all over the place. Threw a few busted bats, charged the front office, made quite a scene. Some of it got reported on TV and radio. Yeah, got it right here on my tapes. But the other rumor is that he went so far as to demand that Heffner not only complain, but cancel his Louisville Slugger contract and go with Adirondack Company for his bats—if not the bats of the whole Redlegs team. How's that grab you?"

But I barely heard the last half of that. I jumped up from my seat. "What did you say?"

"I said 'the other rumor is that…'"

"No, before that, something about a tape."

"Oh, that. Yeah, you see I tape the radio broadcasts of all the Redlegs home games off 84WHAS, my station, and the Mutual Game of the Week, whoever is playing. So I've heard a bunch of the cracked bat incidents on radio. You know, Mel Allen and Red Barber yukking it up over Jersey Jack's misfortune, at least at first, then trying to describe his anger without making baseball look too bad later on."

"Bingo!" I yelled. "Then we've got a smoking gun if there is one to be had! We just have to find out if the times Jersey Jack had his cracked bats were important to the game. If they affected the outcome that was predicted by the moneyline."

"I get it!" said Ralph, slapping his fist into his palm. "The issue isn't any one or two games. It's if enough games were affected so as to skew the averages. And since Jersey Jack knew it, and if he is betting against the moneyline on those games, he can win every time—and believe you me, that's huge! We can review the tapes and find out if the broken bats affect key games. That's a start. But the real question is how would Jersey Jack know? Wouldn't he have to bet ahead of the game? How would he know the bat would crack? And on which play? The critical play to affect the whole game?"

254

"I can't really say," I said, half lie, half truth. Because I knew. Oh yes, at that point I knew. It all fell into place. There was only one answer to Ralph's last set of questions. And it was back at Slugger. Or actually, at that moment, it was probably hung-over back at a certain apartment in Little Appalachia. But for my purposes I needed the smoking gun and didn't want to distract Ralph, so I kept my mouth shut.

Then Ralph threw in the clincher.

"But Ray, this is bigger than Jersey Jack," he said, jumping out of his seat again. "There's been a rash of busted bats in a few other teams in the National League. Most of it's gone below the radar, though, 'cause it ain't been on national radio or TV. But it's there."

"So it's big enough to really get the Outfit's attention," I said. So how big was it, I wondered? The thing about the moneyline is consistency for the mob because they make the odds—and a raft of busted bats would mess that up for the mob. But if you know which batters are going to be off on a given day…then you, the bettor, can beat the odds.

"Them guys don't miss much—and this is a real chunk of change, all right," Ralph said.

No, they don't miss much at all, I thought. And they don't tolerate much either. Especially quitting. That put the plight of Frank Gorham and now Jersey Jack and even Danny B in a new frame.

Ralph then went over to the back of his basement hideaway and opened a pad-locked steel file cabinet. Inside he'd inserted hard plastic dividers labeled by season going back at least fifteen years. Amazing work considering that for all but two of those years he'd been doing it drunk. But he didn't have to look very far. Ralph just pulled the dividers out for the current 1966 season. He took a set of plastic boxes out, each holding reel-to-reel tapes, and went over to a tape player and recorder system set up on the side wall opposite his desk, inserted one of the reels, lined it up, started the tape leader, and pushed the button.

I got out my notebook, then we just sat back and listened. By the time I left Ralph's basement and took the first bus for home I was in the dark outside — but I was in the know inside. All the way home I felt like the case was nearly solved. Ray Odle, master detective. The Sherlock Holmes of the eastern mountains.

Then after I puffed out my chest and told Margaret all about it and she congratulated me on my brilliant success, she merely pointed out that the smoking gun I'd found was aimed at the moneyline scam, which was important, but it didn't aim at the murder itself.

We still didn't know who'd killed either Durkin or Gorham.

Or why. But we were getting close to why.

Chapter Thirty-Six: Margaret

The Rone Court block and the modest one-storey blue-gray painted German siding ranch house were just the same as last time Margaret visited there. The grass had been trimmed, though, so it looked like Irma had found some kid from the neighborhood to take Fred's place behind the mower. The '62 Chevy four-door was there so Margaret knew Irma hadn't run out on her since she'd called on the phone to request another visit. In fact Irma opened the glass storm door as Margaret approached and welcomed her in with a smile and the greeting, "coffee's on, come on in."

They took their respective places around the dinette counter in her kitchen as before, but didn't indulge in chit-chat, they didn't have that kind of relationship and both knew it. They were friendly, but not friends in a serious way, the relationship had a purpose. So Margaret brought her up to date on the investigation, especially the part about the production sheets and how it confirmed what Fred had suspected.

Then, waiting for Irma to put her coffee cup down after a sip, Margaret pulled the plastic key fob she'd found in Billy Jenkins' office out of her pocket and laid it on the dinette counter.

"Oh! Where did you get this?" Irma exclaimed, putting her hand up to her lips as if in fright.

Margaret told her vaguely that she'd found it at Slugger, concluding that, "I would guess from your reaction that it belonged to Fred?" making it a question.

"Yes, it was something he treasured, actually, tawdry as it may seem. Sammy James, the Kentucky Colonels catcher back in the 50s gave it to him when Fred played Little League ball one year. I remember he turned this house and the carport and the car upside down looking for it about a week before he was killed. He was fit to be tied, he was. I'd almost never seen him so messed up." Irma grabbed her two hands together and squeezed, pushing them against the counter top, her voice wavering. "One minute he was raging, the next he was crying, then he'd get white as a sheet with fear. I thought he'd gone mental on me."

Margaret reached across the table and put her hand over Irma's. Irma took a deep breath, then calmed down a bit and gave Margaret a weak smile.

"Don't you think it might have been fear?" Margaret said. "That maybe he found those phony production sheets?"

"Yes I do, Margaret. And I know where you're going with this, and I believe you are right. I believe my Fred confronted Billy Jenkins with his prejudice and lying and manipulation of the union in the form of those production sheets. And what's more, I believe my Fred made the stupid mistake of threatening Billy to go to Mr. Worthington with them unless Billy paid him off."

"Was Fred hard up for money?" Margaret asked, keeping the focus on Fred, not the family as a whole.

"Well, you might as well have it all, Margaret. I didn't tell you last time you were out here, but…yes. Fred was involved in some gambling scheme they had out at the plant. Something to do with betting on the outcome of the major league games. He did pretty well for a few months, or so he said, then he got behind. I kept getting short-changed on the grocery money and then one day about a month before he was killed, he had to go out to the shopping center on some errands and left the bank statement out on the desk he uses to do his accounts, so I looked at it, I admit, and I was shocked to see how low it had gone. We're savers, Margaret, always have been, yet our savings was gone! Flat gone!"

The agitation had come back into her hands and she wrung them in and out on the counter, not waving them about as some women and men might do, just keeping them in front of her, planted on the counter, but wringing them for all she was worth.

"So I knew he was in trouble with some gang or the mob or whatever criminal group is behind that awful scheme at Slugger. And that's why he might have tried to demand money from Billy Jenkins. And that's…that's…"

Finally the hands came off the table and went to her head, covering her ears as if she was warding off a terrible noise, then flew away from her as she spoke…

"…that's why he was killed! It was the foolish, foolish gambling that made him go too far with Billy! Not just the fight for his fellow workers!"

She balled her hands into fists, brought them down onto the counter with a bang, and planted them in front of her again as she broke into sobs.

But not for long. Margaret didn't touch her, she could tell Irma wanted to get a grip on her own. She was nothing if not proud. Finally she heaved a deep sigh.

"I know it's hard," Margaret said. "You think you've lost your hero."

"I want to believe he died for something good. Not for something grubby and stupid."

Irma had been looking straight down at the counter, now she looked up at Margaret. She was looking for answers, for something hopeful.

Margaret gave it to her. It was the least she could do.

"He did. None of us is perfect. Name a hero or heroine and I will show you a human being with faults. Your Fred was a brave man who, with you, took a stand, did the right thing, and stood up to an awful attack from your friends and neighbors out here, and did so for years, and I have no doubt you still suffer from that. And Fred stood up to a bunch of racists at Slugger too. In fact he took action to investigate their evil doing. And he confronted it too. The fact that he had a weakness should never take away from that. You should remember him for his good heart and his brave stand for justice and let the rest go."

Irma Durkin's body eased onto the back of her stool for the first time since they'd sat down. "You think so? You really think so?" she said.

"I do. I'd be proud to stand with him anywhere," Margaret said.

And meant it.

On the way home Margaret tried to figure how it had been done. She knew one thing. Billy Jenkins was a weak union chief, Ray told her that. Weak, and a sneak. And judging from other things Ray had said, and what Irma Durkin had said during her first visit, he was at least one other thing too—he was a coward.

But cowards can also be killers. The question was, did Billy do his own dirty work or hire it out? Did the cur dog do the biting itself or incite another more vicious dog to do it?

Chapter Thirty-Seven: Ray

Jefferson County Medical Examiner James Bronson bent his massive head to study the third of six autopsy photographs spread out along the conference table in his office. They were close ups at different angles of the neck area of the body of Fred Durkin. He'd done the same with each of the preceding two — slide his roller chair in front of the photo, bend his head, study with the naked eye, then with the magnifying glass. I held my breath each time. Nobody in the room said a word, coughed, even breathed loud enough to be heard above the slight sigh of the slowly turning overhead fan in the high-ceilinged oak-paneled room.

Margaret sat on the opposite side of the table, while Jefferson County Police Homicide Captain Arnold Schmidt leaned against the wall behind her. I stood behind the M.E. Harvey was behind me, also leaning against the wall.

After reviewing the autopsy shots of Durkin, Bronson moved on to the three photographs of Durkin's neck area on the auto-lathe where he'd been found dead, mangled, neck and face almost beyond recognition. I didn't know whether Margaret and I were lucky or unlucky not to have seen it, of course, as we'd been called in by the WIA after the fact. It would have been a terrible and gut-wrenching sight. But seeing it might have, just might have, led us part way to where we were now.

Bronson finished studying the sixth photo, put his magnifying glass down, cleared his throat and looked at the Captain, who'd been the one, of course, who'd called him in. It had been quite a performance on our part — me, Margaret and Harvey — to get Schmidt to make the call, but he finally quit stonewalling and listened to all the information Margaret had pulled together about Rone Court, the financial shenanigans by Billy's family, Billy's jimmying of the Manuit sheets, which we produced for him, and the racism ploy to gut the union campaign and win himself a sweet deal. All of that, plus my recollection of Billy carving with a serrated switchblade led Schmidt to admit that, though circumstantial, we had at least the outlines of a case. Enough to call the M.E. and take a second look at these photos.

"It's entirely possible," Bronson rasped out. "In fact, it's probable that the transverse cut across the throat was done by a hand-held knife and not by the lathe. I can't say that's what killed him," he shrugged. "The lathe did too much damage to be sure if the transverse cut was pre or post mortem. But it could have gone that way. Somebody could have cut this guy's throat and then run the lathe over him a couple-three times as he was bleeding out."

Bronson sighed. "However, these photos show a transverse cut that I now see has a slightly different serration than the rest of them. It also has what appears to be a curve, continuous, at one end. That could be a hand-held knife — and although most of the middle flesh of the neck is mangled, there's enough indication of starting point and ending point for me to say that it could have been a curved jugular cut. The knife on a lathe doesn't curve — the bat turns, the lathe cuts an even pattern, but it doesn't make transverse curves, at least not the auto-lathes at Louisville Slugger. I'm sorry that I missed it."

Bronson straightened his back, stood full upright beside the conference table and stuck his hands in his Navy blue suit pants pockets, rocking back on his heels.

"That, gentlemen and lady, is all I can say."

Of course there were more questions. Lots of them. What type of knife could produce those serrations? Would Durkin have been dead when he went into the auto-lathe? Was he approached from front or behind? And so forth.

But true to his science and his reputation as a gruff no-nonsense man in his sixties who didn't suffer fools or amateurs lightly, Bronson clammed. He'd said what he said and that was that.

But it was enough. Less than an hour later two uniformed officers frog-walked Billy Jenkins into an interrogation room at Jefferson County Jail. They cuffed Billy's hands to a short chain fastened to a ring on the steel table top and his ankles to the table legs, left, and let Billy sit.

For another two hours.

In the heat.

Margaret, Harvey and I were watching through a one-way mirror on the wall opposite Billy.

Then Schmidt walked in, parked his beefy hip on the table and put the knife on the table. Said nothing for a good ten minutes. Billy stared at the knife like it was a cobra raising its head.

"Ya know Mr. Bronson, the County Medical Examiner, Billy?" Schmidt asked, then went on without waiting for a response. "He just told me something right interesting about this knife I found under the rug under your bed. Said—by the way, how come you got a switchblade knife under your bed, Billy? Funny place for an item like that?"

Billy looked sideways, his white hair flopping over his eyes, and stammered around a bit. "I...I...well, it's to keep...you know...kids...from..."

"Bullshit. Sign of criminal intent, Billy, but anyway Mr. Bronson told me that the cut that must have killed Fred Durkin came from a blade just like the one on this knife." Schmidt didn't mind a little exaggeration now and then. "Whaddaya think about that, Billy?"

"Well...I...I...don't know...I..."

"Say, Billy, you don't mind if we record this little talk, do ya?" Schmidt broke into Billy's yammering.

"I…well…no, that's okay…I ain't done nothin'…"

This was about two weeks before the famous *Miranda v. Arizona* case filtered down to the local level so Schmidt could get away without giving Billy the warning that we all came to know by heart later on.

"But you cheated Durkin out of his pay upgrade, right Billy boy?" barked Schmidt, raising the volume and the ante.

"Why…no…no, I didn't do nothin' like that…"

"And you faked the Manuit sheets to stir up the whites against the blacks, right Jenkins?"

"No!" Billy raised his arms as if to ward off a blow but the short chains jerked them back. "That's a lie, a d…d…damn lie!" he coughed out.

"And you're a damn scabbin' liar," I shouted as I busted into the room by pre-arrangement with Schmidt. "You've cheated black workers and white workers and blamed the one on the other, damn your eyes, Billy!"

"What's this hillbilly doin' in here?" Billy said, getting some backbone up.

"He's a special deputy Sheriff on this case, Jenkins," said Schmidt, cool as ice, "and you'll respect him or you'll go to jail for interference with an investigation if nothing else."

"Well, he's lying, an' he ain't got nothin' to back it up, neither."

"Oh yes he does, Mr. Jenkins," Margaret said, as she walked in with Harvey right behind her. "And we've got the proof right here," whereby she placed the faked Manuit sheets on the table just out of Billy's reach.

"Come right out of your office, Mastah Jenkins," drawled Harvey in a fake accent. "Right where you was keepin' score, you might say."

"Well, that don't prove nothin' about Fred," said Billy, pushing his back against the seatback as far as it would go as if somehow he could put some distance between himself and the barrage of truth hitting him from the front. Then he paused, gathered himself, and went on the offensive.

"So what?" Billy snarled, slamming the chains on the steel tabletop. "Yeah, I did that. Damn proud of it, too. Keepin' the nigs in their place. But you can't jail a man for cheatin' on production sheets."

"Actually, you can," said Captain Schmidt. "It's a violation of wage-hour laws and if it's intentional, it's a criminal offense." He leaned over the table to put his face into Billy's. "Now that we've got that on tape, Billy, you're going to jail."

"And then there's fraud," Margaret said, coming around to stand right beside Billy. "Misleading the union rank and file on the contract, which grows out of the Manuit sheet issue, is a fraud. That's a civil offense for which you will be sued by the WIA and not only lose your job but damages will run up into the hundreds of thousands. You're now broke, Billy, and deeply in debt."

"Yeah, but that ain't the worst of your troubles, Billy," Harvey chimed in, putting his hands on the table and his hip on the corner opposite the one occupied by Schmidt. "You see, we're onto the moneyline scheme too. And we figure you're behind that at Slugger, and, well, if it got around that you ratted out the next man above you in the structure…"

Sheer terror constricted Jenkins' face in an instant at the mention of the moneyline and ratting out anyone. Billy reared back against the chair, raising his hips he pushed so hard. Then he found his voice and it shook almost as much as the chains rattled against the table top.

"No! No, no, you can't do that. Look, okay, I'll admit it. I did those other things, the Manuit scheme, the white against black, lining my pockets, yeah, okay…I ain't killed nobody though…but if you go throwing my name around saying I ratted on the moneyline, I'm a dead man. And I ain't did that. It won't me that brought the moneyline into Slugger. I ain't lying."

At this Schmidt leaned over the table back into Billy's face.

"Okay, Billy. You've got one chance. One chance only. Who's behind the moneyline?"

"I can't, I just…"

"Have it your way, then Billy. Harvey, get the word out on the street, you know what to do." Then turning to the door he shouted down the hallway. "Come and get him, boys."

"Okay, okay. Wait. Just wait," Billy said, his voice shaking.

"One word, Billy. A name," said Schmidt.

"W…W…Worthington."

"Now admit the other thing, you cur dog," I said with a low growl, "you snuck up behind Fred after hours when he'd gone to Worthington about the Manuit sheets and the union and the Rone Court mess and slashed that line across his throat—didn't you, Billy—it's your way, ain't it!"

Billy had broken, but he tried one more way.

"It won't me. Worthington said Durkin had to go, that he was threatening the moneyline. It won't the Manuit sheets, it was that damn moneyline. So he told Benson to get Haskell and Rogers to do it."

"No sale, Billy," I said, my voice going deeper and deeper as I spoke. "Blackie don't work that way. It was you. Your knife. Your way—up from behind. Like the cur dog you are. Dogs like that get eaten up by the mob every day. They'll love to feast on your sorry meat."

"Don't…d…don't. I was in a bind. Worthington had me in a dead man's bind. Either way. Just like you do."

Tears rolled down Billy's face. His hands shook, his arms trembled. His body was racked with fear. I had not a whit of sympathy. He'd killed as a coward and betrayed his brothers in a devil's bargain.

"I had no choice. I just…I had no…choice," Billy whimpered.

"Throw the dog a bone," I snarled and walked out of the room.

Chapter Thirty-Eight: Margaret

Attorney Clive Simpson pulled his '65 Bel Air into the driveway of the Jenkins house on Rone Court in Shively and came to a stop behind the '62 Plymouth sedan in the carport. Clive Simpson had been appointed by the Jefferson County District Court to represent Billy Jenkins in his murder case and had arranged the visit on the theory that the Odles were willing to testify in mitigation at Billy's sentencing if for no other reason than they opposed the death penalty and the County Attorney was considering asking the Court for it. He thought that if the prosecutor knew that the Odles, or at least one of them, would testify for Jenkins, it might discourage him from a death penalty prosecution in the first place. But in order for that to work the Odles needed some sympathetic information to go on—something in Billy's background or family history that might help explain his character or actions. Simpson thought they might do better at trying to get it from Mrs. Jenkins than from Billy, who was still acting sullen and uncooperative around the Odles.

Ray and Margaret had accompanied Clive Simpson on the stuffy drive out to Shively and they were glad to get out of the car. They were about to step over to the walkway leading to the front door when it opened and Elizabeth, "Betty," Jenkins came out.

She took two staggered steps off the front porch, barked, "Don'ch'all nigger lovers come no further!," then whipped out a pistol she'd been holding behind her back and fired. Margaret felt a burning singe at her hip just as Ray grabbed her and pulled her back around the front of Simpson's car.

Simpson dove for the ground and crawled behind his car at the rear.

Betty Jenkins fired again, this time at the ground under the car but didn't hit anybody.

Ray hissed at Margaret, "Gimme your purse, dammit, before this lunatic hits somebody!"

Margaret said, "No, Ray, guns ain't the answer."

"It is for starters," Ray hissed and grabbed her purse, ripped it open and pulled out Margaret's .44 revolver, which he immediately fired up into the air.

"Throw that gun down, Mrs. Jenkins, or the next shot's gonna hit you and do some serious damage!" he yelled.

"Do your worst, Odle," she shouted back in a quavering voice. "I'm gonna shoot myshelf anyway after I kill y'all race traitors!"

Margaret heard the slight slur of the "s" indicating that Betty had been drinking. She risked a peek over the hood of the car and saw Betty's face streaked with tears. She was crying hard but silently.

"We want to help Billy now," said Margaret.

"Help? Lyin' bisch!" sobbed Betty. "You tryin' to kill my Billy, the only thing I got left in thish world."

At that point Simpson spoke up from behind the Chevy. "Mrs. Jenkins, I'm his lawyer. The Court appointed me to keep the State from killing Billy — that's why we're here, like I told you on the phone."

"Hah! A lyin' woman an' a lyin' lawyer. All you gonna do is sell my man down the river then step up to the pay window."

Betty Simpson broke down into deep wracking sobs. She choked out a few words between them. "All'sh…I…got…is…my…Billy!…Ain't…nobody ever…ever…tried…to understan…that man."

Margaret spoke just loud enough for her voice to carry the ten feet or so over the hood of the car to where Betty Jenkins was slowly sinking to her knees in her despair.

"What is Billy like around you, Mrs. Jenkins?" she asked, trying to get the talk away from death and killing.

"Whadda you care?" came the reply. But then Betty went on. "He ain't what you hoity-toity folks would call a good man, but he'sh my man. Don't nobody know what that man been through." The sobs broke through again, drowning the words. After a while she went on.

"My Billy, he was beat every night by his drunken Daddy till Billy was ten year old an that sorry man ran out on him and hish Mom. Said Billy was a basht'id on account of his white hair. Won't no son of hish, he had black hair. Alwaysh sayin' hish wife must've shacked up with Santa Claush. Used to take a set of grash clippers to Billy's head and cut all hish hair off then beat Billy unconshesh. But y'all don't give a damn about that."

More sobs. Margaret waited. Waited some more as the upheaval began to subside. "What about you, Mrs. Jenkins?"

"What the hell you think, *lady*?" She said with a drawled sarcasm dragging out "lady." "Hish old man beat on Billy's Mom when he won't beatin' on Billy." Then Betty fired the pistol again, this time at the Chevy Bel Air, hitting the driver's side window, shattering it.

"That ish, he beat on her till one night Billy jumped on hish back with a knife and tried to cut his throat. The son of a bisch barely threw Billy off in time, but he slipped and fell and knocked hishelf out on the kitchen table. When he woke she were gone and he left an' never come back. Billy saved his Mom's life, that's who Billy is."

"I see that, and that's a good thing that the Court will want to know about. It will go a good piece towards saving him," Margaret said, raising her head above the hood of the car to look into Betty's eyes. "But what about you, how does he treat you?"

Betty, still on her knees, began to sway from side to side and shake her head. "Nooooo, no, no, no. No you don't, *Miss Lady-girl*," she said in a sing-song voice. Then she growled.

269

"Thish dumb cracker gal ain't fallin' for that trick. I ain't gonna talk agin' my Billy. I take my licks but you don't need to know nothin' 'bout nothin'." But the tears rolled and the sobs came back and Betty doubled over with her head sinking down near the ground, one hand out clawing the grass to support herself and the other waving the pistol around above it.

"Noooooo. No. No. No!" she said, this time with no sing-song. This time Margaret could hear the flat tones of despair. "Ish over with me," she said.

Margaret was around the car and limping towards her, Ray a blur as he ran past.

"It ain't no good," Betty wailed. "No good a'tall."

With that Betty Jenkins put the pistol to her head and fired.

Ray's leaping body landed just short as Betty slumped to the ground, his left arm outstretched, hand extended, fingers open toward the gun.

The weather of the heart driving back from Shively to downtown Louisville was deep in black cloud, threatening a rain of reproach and recrimination. But silence prevailed as each one, Margaret, Ray and Simpson, replayed the death scene and the aftermath in their minds. The cops had been called by Rone Court residents who'd no doubt witnessed the horror from behind partly drawn picture window shades. The police crime unit had come, done its time consuming meticulous duty, called the Medical Examiner who'd come, examined Betty's body where she lay, declared the obvious, and with his assistants, had gathered up the body and departed. Like Kipling's hymn about the captains and the kings, the officialdom had come, seen the wreckage left by the tumult and shouting, and departed, leaving at least these three humble and contrite hearts.

But during the long homeward drive Margaret and Ray also kept seeing the wreckage of the Jenkins house. The overturned dinette chairs, the cigarette butts all over the floors, the leftover food rotting on countertops and living room chair and sofa.

And the empties. The cheap vodka bottles. Enough to fuel what had no doubt been a three-day binge. Betty's binge in answer to the one phone call Billy Jenkins had made from the Jefferson County jail. They didn't know what he'd said—not exactly—but they knew enough. He'd told her the worst— probably what the prosecutor had told him trying to scare him into a detailed written statement implicating as many individuals as could be named in the moneyline fraud. He'd threatened Billy with death, no doubt.

And Billy had passed it on.

It was clear enough from the liquor boxes piled by the garbage cans Margaret saw out back that this binge wasn't Betty's first. Call it what you will, thought Margaret. Heavy drinker, binge drinker—alcoholic. And what does an alcoholic do with terrible news like Billy delivered to his wife in that phone call? Sometimes they go to extremes of all-or-nothing emotions. Margaret had heard Ray say many times that when he was in his alcoholic head he was behind enemy lines.

"But we didn't know she was an alcoholic," she heard herself say. "How could we?"

"You could have asked Billy," her conscience replied. "You could have spent time with him at the jail getting to know him as a man you'd been responsible for bringing down."

But they'd been in a hurry. Sure, it had been three days since they'd cornered Billy in the interrogation room. They hadn't spent it trying to understand Billy Jenkins the human being. Instead they'd been out collecting corroborating evidence of his guilt and trying to get more evidence on Worthington's role in the moneyline scam. Why was that? Expedience? Press of business?

Or was it that they found Billy's racism so repugnant that they lost sight of his humanity underneath it?

271

Margaret had no answers, only questions. She knew Ray had a sponsor and a step in AA to work through to see if he owed Billy an amend for his part in the whole tragedy.

But for Margaret there was a scar on her heart. Like the old blues song lamented, "nothing to say, nothing to do, what's done is done and I'm gonna be blue."

Chapter Thirty-Nine: Margaret

It had been a week since the tragedy in Shively. Margaret had felt blue, spending a lot of time trying to understand where they'd gone wrong, where her side of the street of responsibility stopped and where Ray, Betty and Billy's began. Finally Harvey and Louella had taken her by the emotional scruff of the neck and given her a good shake.

"This shit happens, y'all," Louella said. "You did your job, and at the end of that, they's a line, and on the other side of that line, what happens is God's business. You don't need to be messin' in His business, for real."

Harvey put in his two cents backing up Louella and reminded Margaret, and Ray too for that matter, that they were in danger of losing the momentum they'd all built up if they didn't get to Worthington soon and use the Jenkins arrest and the manuit sheet discoveries to pry him loose.

Margaret came to her senses and dragged Ray to his, then all four of them planned their next move. It took just a day to set up. They knew that Worthington would have fear of two things: the mob behind the moneyline and, even though he'd descended into the slime of conspiracy to murder with the likes of Jenkins and probably Haskell and Rogers, he still craved respect for the Louisville Slugger brand. His pride in that, along with the fear, would be used as leverage to get him, and to get his help to get to the others.

Ray had called Worthington and told him if he wanted to save Slugger and didn't want scandal running across the front page of the *Courier-Journal* he'd better meet them at his office in one hour even though it was a Sunday afternoon. Worthington squawked for a few minutes but finally agreed.

The tableau in Worthington's office was arranged around the blue-blood trappings of his power. Harvey stood by the back office door comfortably leaning against the jamb, his arms folded loosely across his middle, one foot forward of the other. Ray and Margaret sat in the leather swivel chairs in front of the desk.

At the meeting-before-the-meeting the Odle Agency team had brought each other up to date on their respective investigations, Ray on the contents of Radio Ralph's statistics and radio tapes, while Margaret reported on her most recent interview with Irma Durkin, and Harvey on his interviews with Danny Bunce. The team had decided that, given Ray's history with Danny, it was better for Harvey to try and push Danny into a mistake, or even an admission about the bad bats, but it had been no-go. Despite Harvey's best efforts, and even though he had shown a lot of fear, especially when threatened with being ratted out to Haskell and Rogers, Danny had kept mumbling that he had nothing to say.

Their problem with Worthington was that Billy's confession would be challenged and Worthington's lawyer would discredit the source. They needed more. The Odle Agency team had concocted a very loose script for the confrontation with Worthington that Margaret hoped would get him to either confess his part in the murders or at least play along with them to the extent that they could use him as leverage on the Gorham case. The Odles had decided that in order to make it work they all had to bear down on Worthington, give no quarter, and run a hell of a good bluff.

Harvey went first as lead-off man. "Boss, we've got you cold. Billy Jenkins has confessed to the whole thing. We had it pretty well figured out, but he's in jail and he's finked on you. He flat accuses you of ordering him to kill Fred Durkin.

So this ain't a discussion about who, or even why, 'cause we know that too, it's a discussion of whether you have the brains of a half-smart alley cat and want to keep your sorry ass from the death house by cooperating with us."

Worthington's face went white at the mention of Jenkins but he flattened himself against his seatback and came out snarling.

"If you think I'm going to fall for some stunt from you three low-lifes, why you've…"

"Yeah," broke in Ray, "got another think coming — and going, big boss. In fact we've been thinking for a long time and we've been digging too. What's known as investigating. So shut up and listen and we'll lay it out for you. Not that you don't already know it all — since you're in the thick of it. But so you'll know how deep we've dug the hole we've put you in."

Then Margaret laid it out.

"First, you pulled the moneyline scheme into Slugger because the Teamster's Pension Fund owns your underwater debt on Rone Court and made that the price of keeping your knees intact.

"Second, Billy Jenkins is your flunky and has been running the moneyline along with Frank Gorham. In addition, Jenkins runs the union along company lines and fiddles the manuit sheets so that come contract negotiation time he can slip a false sheet here and there to the racists and arouse them against the blacks and break the union solidarity.

"Third, Rogers has been your muscle on the moneyline, threatening and beating Durkin and Gorham and others who got behind or who looked like they might talk about the scheme out of school.

"Fourth, Fred Durkin found out about the fake manuit sheets and came to you through Benson and you let Jenkins, Haskell and Rogers know it would be fine and dandy if Durkin met with a fatal accident.

275

"Fifth, you've gotten a lot of calls from Major League managers, especially Davis at Cincinnati, because of a whole lot of bats strangely cracking at the worst times and throwing the game. And you doubtless have heard a much more serious squawk from Mr. James Riddle Hoffa of the Teamsters—or maybe somebody higher up in the Mob. It seems that not only have the bats cracked at suspicious times for the game—they've screwed up the odds on the moneyline too."

Worthington's look-down-the-long-nose expression changed at that remark—his eyes got narrow and his face flushed. He took the bait.

"I don't concern myself with mere recreational gambling," he said in a disdainful huff.

"No, you're way above that game," Margaret agreed. "You just gamble with people's lives—like with their homes and life's savings balanced on the thin edge of racial rumors and redlining. More comfortable in the rarified precincts of the boardroom or the investment broker's club lunch room. Bourbon and branch water and carefully drawn maps in black and white and red lines. Isn't that more your style, *Mister Chairman* Worthington?"

He half rose out of his seat at that, then shook his head like he was clearing his vision from a boozy hangover, sat back down and said, "I won't respond to rabble rousing or ancient history."

"Yeah, but that ain't the funniest part," Harvey jumped in. "When I was checking for witnesses on the Gorham case, Bob Stills told me Frank Gorham had asked why someone would designate a billet with an over-wide slope of the grain for a P.R.O. bat. Stills told him nobody would, and Gorham just gave him a funny grin like the proverbial Cheshire cat."

"There's no evidential basis for any of this," Worthington replied, flipping his wrists as if to shake off some dust.

"Just bear with us, Worthington," said Margaret. "Ray, what about the news on the radio?"

"I've been listening to taped radio broadcasts," Ray chimed in, "games where there's been a series of cracked bats. The gist is that Jersey Jack Danielson has been having a run of cracked bats at the wrong time and losing games for the Redlegs — and just coincidentally throwing off the moneyline for those games too."

Margaret put up her hand to stop Ray and threw the next punch herself. "We also have the betting slips that Frank Gorham hid in his lathe that show a match up with the game broadcast tapes — that show Danny B. and Jersey Jack hitting it big at the expense of the moneyline, that is, of the mob. We've got a witness, too, who can identify a man at Slugger who picked bad wood, made and marked the bad bat with the crummy slope of grain…"

"And one crooked ball player who'd pick up that bat when the right situation came up on the field and take it to the batter's box!" said Ray.

"Frank Gorham. Jack Danielson. Having got hold of the betting slips and wondered about the payoffs, Gorham figured it out and got it confirmed by catching Danny Bunce in the act of stamping the bad bats for Jersey Jack. Now you're going to tell me you didn't have even a hint about all of this?"

Worthington sat like a stone statue. Finally he opened his slash-thin line of a mouth and said, "I have nothing to say to you."

Ray slapped the desk. "Well, hang on to your silk stockings for just a little while longer, Bud — you're gonna talk in the end. The best is yet to come."

"Then Frank turned to blackmail," Margaret said. "He used his possession of the slips to threaten to snitch Bunce and Danielson out to the mob. Now why would the mob care? Because they don't want any bozo batsman or bat maker causing even the slightest deviation from the law of averages they've worked out as the baseline for the betting odds, that's why. So what Jersey Jack and Danny did would be intolerable to the mob. Jack and Danny knew it, so Gorham and his threat had to go. The next question is, of course, who did the actual murder?"

Worthington's forehead had begun to glisten under the overhead lamp.

"Well, we eliminated Jersey Jack on the grounds that the murder was done after hours at the plant," said Harvey. "It would just be too risky for him to be here during those hours. He'd have no legitimate explanation at all. Danny Bunce, on the other hand, could say he was checking on this or that or come up with some other half-ass but fairly believable reason for being at the plant."

"So does that mean Mr. Bunce did it?" Worthington quavered, eager to blame somebody else.

"I doubt it," said Ray. "He's too weak and he's gone back on the booze."

Worthington's slash got tighter at this as he realized another decoy was being eliminated. His chair was inching back, too, as if it had a will of its own and wanted to get distance from the onslaught of facts. He reached into his suit coat, pulled out a monogrammed handkerchief and mopped his shiny forehead.

Ray was relentless, now standing right beside the desk chair as Worthington abandoned his rigid posture to adopt an angle of slope tilted away from Ray. "Neither Jersey Jack or Danny Bunce would mash a man's head in the auto lathe. Too honest and too bloody. But they'd drop a dime and get somebody else to do it, and they'd know who to call, right Worthington? You know people like that yourself. You get a call from Jersey Jack or Danny Bunce by any chance?"

Wham! A shot to the gut. Worthington uncoiled from his seat and practically leaped at Ray. "You take that back you sorry ignorant piece of shit!" he shouted. "You have no right to accuse me — a man of my standing — of facilitating a murder! And don't deny it, that's what your remarks amount to! By God that's actionable and I'll call my attorney if you repeat that scurrilous tripe one more time here or anywhere else!"

"Well, well, without being a skeeter I seem to have gotten under the good gentleman's skin," chuckled Ray.

"Cut the jokes, Ray," said Margaret, voice level but hard.

"What Margaret wants me to get to, Worthington, is that Danny B would just have called in the thugs he knows because they've been all over this plant, hired by and reporting directly to you."

Worthington's eyes got big as saucers. "You mean…"

"H & R," said Ray.

"Specifically, one James Haskell and one Simon Rogers," Margaret said, "gun thugs with no telling how much workingman's blood they've got on their hands from the coal fights back in the eastern mountains."

"You heard it, boss-man," said Harvey, "them goons of yours most likely are killers."

"The logic is solid as a rock," Margaret said. "It bears up."

"So what you gonna do about it, Worthington?" Ray said, leaning over the executive in his executive chair. "You gonna hide behind your prissy social standing and let Frank Gorham's blood stain your hands or are you gonna work with us to see that justice is done?"

To give him more credit than Margaret could imagine that he would earn, Worthington didn't try to flat-out deny that H & R could have killed Gorham, and he didn't just try to throw the Odle Agancy out of his office, fat chance he would have had of that. But he did try evasion, the lesser of the evils and the slicker response, the path more suitable to a man like him.

"I'll need evidence, not just supposition," he said.

"Evidence?" Margaret said, "Let me repeat it for you," and ticked it off with her fingers. " One, we've got betting slips involving the moneyline and Slugger employees. Two, we have testimony of participants that first Frank Gorham and now Danny Bunce were the runners, thus evidence that your plant is involved in a corrupt scheme. Three, we've got, or

279

can get, eyewitness evidence of doctoring professional baseball bats being sent to Jersey Jack and others. Four, we have taped and statistical evidence of cracked bats influencing game outcomes, and five, circumstantial evidence of corruption stemming from this plant against the moneyline, with a strong deduction of blackmail."

"But that last part isn't evidence. And none of it is evidence against H & R."

Ray was champing at the bit. "Them sumabitches never leave evidence except bullets in the…"

"Okay, Ray, it's okay," Margaret, standing next to him and putting her hand on his shoulder until he eased off the chair. "We'll get back to H&R in a little while. Let's go back to Durkin."

Margaret took Worthington through the background of the Durkin family's involvement in the Wade and Braden housing and racism case, their stand for the Wades and Bradens and against the racist neighborhood committee and their refusal to testify against the Wades and Bradens. She recounted the attempts by the financiers of the Rone Court developers to have them suddenly foreclosed and evicted, the witness intimidation case brought against the financiers by Braden's lawyers, and the way the financiers had to back down and leave the Durkins alone.

"Then there's the fact that the agent for the financiers had been Billy Jenkins' father, right Worthington?" Margaret moved to the front of his desk. "And the fact that one of the directors of the holding company for the developers, with a percent interest in the development, had been none other than one James T. Worthington himself. Not to mention the fact that Jenkins — with your consent, right Worthington? — had seen to it that Fred Durkin had been harassed, underpaid, cheated out of piece-rate pay, and kept out of the P.R.O. section for years after the Wade incident and its aftermath had ended!

"So when Fred Durkin found the scam piece-rate sheets in Jenkins' office, what did he do?" she continued. "He too had fallen victim to the moneyline scam going on under your supposedly unknowing nose right here at Slugger. He too, like others, was under financial stress from the debts he'd piled up. An otherwise honest man, he had fallen down and into the temptation of blackmail. He went to Billy Jenkins and threatened to expose him and his scheme and demanded a payoff so he could get out of debt to the moneyline.

"Durkin came to you over it, Worthington, and Jenkins thought he had to take action. He'd know your blue-blooded high-toned behind wouldn't stand for it, and Jenkins is nothing that you haven't made him."

"Damn right," volleyed Ray. "He owes everything to you—his job at this sweetheart local of the union, his payoffs in the way of cars…

Worthington slapped the desk at this and yelled, "That's a lie!"

"… and God knows what other goodies he gets from you," Margaret said, "but his family goes way back doing deals with you, Worthington.

"I can see you sitting right here, your hands forming that tent of yours, your chin tucked into it, calmly saying something like, 'it would greatly benefit this company, not to mention the course of the contract negotiations under a weakened union, if that man met with an unfortunate but timely accident,' or some such. Kind of like old King Henry with his meddlesome priest."

"Don't forget Mr. Billy Jenkins has called you out," said Harvey, "point blank."

"On top of that, you're guilty of other criminal offenses," Margaret jumped in before Worthington could recover his wits. "One, you're guilty of criminal obstruction of justice, withholding of evidence, and possible aiding and abetting after the fact. Two, you knew about the production sheet jimmying from Jenkins. Three, you knew, also from Jenkins, that Durkin had found out about it and had threatened Jenkins with exposure. Four, you knew from Durkin himself that he was calling Jenkins on it, demanding action from you when Jenkins didn't pay off. Whatever the case on that, you've clearly been covering up these basic facts about the murder for weeks."

Margaret stepped back from the desk like a lawyer in court before the witness stand and pointed the accusing finger at Worthington.

"The sum of all of this is also *evidential*, counselor, is it not?" she said in a matter of fact voice that was at the same time hard as nails. "Murder, accessory to murder, obstruction of justice, racketeering, conspiracy to racketeering? Would you like to accompany me to the Jefferson County Sheriff's Office and explain that to Captain Aaron Schmidt, the officer in charge of the Durkin investigation, just for starters? Come on, let's go!"

Worthington sat still, visibly shaken, his face paler, sweatier and shakier than even Margaret thought possible. He hunched his shoulders and rested his elbows on the desk for support as if he couldn't sit up without it. Then he wiped his increasingly wet forehead with the now-also-wet handkerchief.

"You know I cannot do that," he said in a weak wobbly voice after some minutes. "I admit nothing, but I am vulnerable. I hate the position you have put me in, but I suppose I must face my vulnerability."

Ray jumped all over that. "We didn't put you nowhere, Worthington—you did. You put yourself there and the sooner you see it and admit it the better off you'll be. Billy Jenkins has been singing like Hank Williams, so ain't no use in duckin' and weavin' no more on Durkin."

Worthington slumped over his desk and put his head between his folded arms like a grammar school kid during a rest period back in the old days. Ray didn't let up.

"Look, big boss, you deserve a life sentence, but we're lettin' the jury stay out on that till we see how you work with us on gettin' Blackie and Blondie for Gorham."

"Better known to you as Haskell and Rogers," Margaret chimed in.

Worthington folded. He let out a huge sigh, raised his ashen face and lifted his hands in surrender. "What do you want me to do?"

"Get them here," Margaret said. "Now."

Chapter Forty: Ray

Margaret and Harvey were in opposite sides of the door when Blackie and Blondie came rushing into Worthington's office where he sat like a cherub beaming at them in false normalcy behind his desk. Captain Schmidt and his crew were standing by, hidden in Billy Jenkins' office down the hall. Harvey had wired his desk for sound using gear snatched from Jenkins' high tech office. There were microphones hidden in the top drawer on each side connected to a tape system that sat on the narrow shelf that usually held the center drawer.

Despite what Margaret had said about what we had being "evidential," that was mostly bluff. We had jack crap for physical evidence. We had Jenkins' confession, but that could and would be challenged as being coerced, obtained without presence of counsel, by the high-priced type of lawyer that Worthington would get for himself. It was fifty-fifty whether it would hold up if Billy took it back.

We knew pretty much what had happened with Gorham now, but as for having a case that would stand the burden of proof in court, we not only didn't have one, we were damn sure that one couldn't be had—ever, not by us and not by the police. The police and their methods had failed after nearly nine weeks of investigation—in fact as far as anyone knew they didn't even have a clue as to who had done the Gorham murder and why.

So we had to trap Blackie and Blondie—to use their own egotism, racism and high and mightyness into getting them to sneer at us and give us the evidence we needed out of their own mouths, to snitch on themselves as well as Billy Jenkins, which would give us some insurance on Billy. I'd learned some time back that what we private operators lack in authority and power we can sometimes make up for in cunning, treachery and deceit. This was one of those times.

When the two H & R agents surged through the door, I closed it behind them and said, "Welcome to the party, boys, nice of you to drop in."

They both whirled around mechanically, arms snapped out from their sides for balance like mechanical dancers on a metal windup musical toy.

"What the hell—how'd you get here?" barked Blondie.

"Invited myself," I said. "In fact, you might say it was me what done all the invitations. See, it ain't Worthington's party. It's an Odle Agency party and you boys are the guests of dishonor. Some law enforcement officials are on the way, but we thought it'd be right smart nice to have a little private celebration with you boys first. Kinda get in the party mood."

"You just gonna sit there and listen to this shit, Worthington?" said Blackie.

"I'm afraid so," Worthington replied. "They've got me in a vulnerable position, and that's all I'm going to say."

"I told you he'd be worthless in a fight," said Blondie. "Them stuffed shirts always are."

"Now that's one thing we can all agree on," I said, stepping up to the two men as Harvey moved to cover the door. "But we ain't here to discuss the aristocracy. We're here to discuss murder. The murder of Frank Gorham, a murder you two scumbags committed."

"We ain't staying for no so-called party, asshole," growled Blondie, and started to shove past me for the door.

"Wait a minute, Simon," said Blackie, a.k.a. Haskell, "let's see what this dumb hillbilly has to say. Could be a laugh a minute. If he's crazy enough to run it to the cops, then we might ought to know what he's going to say. He ain't so smart, but that woman of his might just have enough brains to weave together some lies we'd have to explain our way out of."

Margaret, who'd been quietly standing by the coat rack in the corner, came to the middle of the room at that point.

"What this mentally challenged old woman knows," said Margaret in her best high-falutin Meredith College voice, "is that the Odle Agency has you clowns by the growth issuing from the scrotal follicles, otherwise known as the short and curlies."

"Bullshit. You can't prove dick," said Blondie, meanwhile crossing his arms across his chest as if to defend himself from body blows. But Margaret moved in closer to him and punched out the words in the air with her fist in short jabs like she was methodically working the heavy bag at the boxing gym, sharp and bitter.

"We know you killed Frank Gorham, and you'll answer for that. We know all about the moneyline and how Gorham got on to the little scam that Danny Bunce and Jersey Jack Danielson and a few other ballplayers were running against the line and the mob. Danny made the bad bats and we have witnesses and a few of the actual reject bats to prove it. Jersey Jack and the others flubbed the hand hold on the bad bat just when the team needed the cleanup hit the most, cracked the bat, hit into a disaster, and it skewed the moneyline for the day. Those guys had bet against the line aforehand, of course, and made a cartload of cash. But Frank found some of Danny Bunce's betting slips, figured it out, and came to Danny and laid a little blackmail on him."

Then Margaret inched closer and closer to Blondie, her voice rising. "Cost him his life when Danny, a coward at bottom, called his crime pard Jersey, who then called in a fixer from the Big Leagues, who knew there were reliable thugs right here at Slugger who could make the whole problem go away — both for himself and Danny and for the Big Leagues too."

Now Margaret was in Blondie's face, punching her index finger into his chest. I was afraid he'd slap her, but he didn't. He was fixated on little Margaret like she was a coiled rattlesnake. His upper body even tilted back away from her as she went on, louder and louder.

"And that was you two gunsels. A little more working man's blood on your hands would hardly cost y'all any sleep now would it? Not after your agency's history at Matewan, Blair Mountain, Breathitt and Lawrence and the other killings large and small. Why a little hit like this hardly even counts, a little snipe like Frank Gorham, right boys?"

Then Blackie broke the spell with a loud laugh. Blondie stepped back at first then pushed Margaret away. She staggered then righted herself. I started to jump to her defense then pulled up short. No, she could handle herself. It won't my place. Not yet.

"Yeah, you got it about half right, mountain mamma," Blackie said between laughs. "So what if you're right about Gorham? Trouble for you is, you can't prove none of it. You're just whistling Dixie. But, what the hell, you want to nail old stuffed-shirt here, it's the Durkin hit you need to be goin' after. On that one, old Worthy-ton here, he didn't just go along with seeing Durkin 'go away' as he likes to put it. Hell, he damn-all ordered Billy to get rid of that man. Said it was part of our job to see that the union got busted up and this Durkin man was a threat, a big threat, to the success of the contract negotiations. Now when your boss tells you that, you don't need no Ps and Qs to know what to do, way Billy looked at it. The thing was clear, ain't I right, Jim."

"I said no such thing!" roared Worthington, face flushed, eyes wild with fear. "Mr. Jenkins totally misunderstood me!"

Now we were getting somewhere. But then Blondie jumped in.

"Shut up, Simon, for Chrisssakes," he barked. "Can't you see they're just trying to get us to talk?"

287

"Awww, hell, Jim. Gimme a break. It's just two dumbass hillbillies and a nigger. What harm can they do? Ain't nobody gonna believe them. Who? The cops? They're just bluffin' on that score anyway. You see any cops? We been here a good ten, fifteen minutes and they ain't showed up. It's a lot of bullshit."

Blackie looked at all of us, sweeping the room with his eyes. Then he shook his head and got a wicked grin on his face. "That's just the kind of attitude that gets us in trouble, Jim. Like with Gorham. You couldn't just plug the guy down by the river, no, you had to get all cute and do him like Billy did Durkin."

"Shut up, goddamnit," yelled Blondie. "Time to get outta here and have a little talk with Billy," his eyes whipping back and forth like a cat ready to pounce on a mouse.

With that Blondie and Blackie headed for the door.

Which opened just then and was filled by the bodies of Captain Aaron Schmidt, Jefferson County Homicide, and his Lieutenant, Caleb Bailey, backed up by four other County officers.

"You called for us, Mr. Worthington?" said Schmidt, acting innocent of what was going on as he and his crew came into the room.

"Well, now that I've heard these gentlemen out, I'm afraid it's all been a sort of misunderstanding," said Worthington in a slight quaver as he stood from behind his desk.

"Yes, sir, we were just sorting it all out here," said Blackie as he and Blondie sidestepped towards the door.

"Don't let them get out of here!" I barked to Schmidt. "They've named the murderer of Durkin and confessed to the murder of Gorham!"

Harvey jumped back towards the partially open door to block it, but just as he did, Danny Bunce came rushing through and got to the middle of the room, blurting as he charged in:

"Hey Simon, I got here as soon as…"

He never finished because Blackie grabbed him from behind and slapped his hand over Danny's mouth. Just as quick Blondie pulled his .45 automatic and put it to Danny's temple.

"Nobody moves or he's dead!" he barked.

Chapter Forty-One: Ray

Everybody froze.

Then, after what seemed like a helluva long time, I saw Schmidt start to ease his right hand back inside his jacket.

Blackie whipped out his gun and rotated it across the arc of everyone in the room as he backed towards the door to get better coverage. "Hands up! Don't nobody make a move for his gun or he's a dead man—or woman—too," he said, tossing a sneer at Margaret.

All hands went up except Worthington's. Mr. Exception, I laughed to myself, always had to be treated special.

"You too Worthington, we're done with this job," Blackie growled. "You might say the contract's expired."

Danny B was shaking like a leaf in an October wind and I didn't exactly blame him. His face was chalk white. I was afraid he would faint and get shot on account of it. Then Blackie stepped over to Blondie and whispered in his ear, but I was close enough to hear it.

"Let's back out real slow, you first, then me. I'll get the car. You take him to the open gate in back and I'll pick you up there. That way they can't trap us in the hallways. Got it?"

Blondie nodded.

And with that Blondie started backing out of the room, Blackie covering him with the pistol. Schmidt tensed and inched forward, as did Harvey, but I motioned them back. No use in taking stupid risks with Danny B's life—or anybody else's. Following my lead, none of our side moved until Blackie eased himself out of the door and we heard footsteps receding down the hall.

Once they were gone for about ten seconds I said, "let's move real quiet and slow out of here and into the yellow line down the main hallway. Blackie's supposedly going for their car and gonna pick him up back in the open area where they bring in the logs. Captain Schmidt, Margaret, Harvey and I will head back there. You boys in the uniforms head real careful-like out the front and see if you can see Blackie and his car.

"Captain, if'n you catch sight of Blondie, then stop. He looked kinda rattled. I don't think he trusts Blackie all the way, which means he's got at least a lick of sense, 'cause I don't give even odds that Blackie will show up."

We moved. Schmidt, Harvey and I headed down the yellow brick road. I assumed Margret was hanging back for safety because I didn't see her when we turned out of the administrative section but I was so focused on watching ahead for Blondie I didn't think about it at the time. We passed the sanding rooms off to the side with no sight of Blondie and Danny B. About a minute later I heard the squeal of tires and then what sounded like pistol shots. I tensed, looked at Schmidt, who started to run back towards the front end of the plant, punching his walkie-talkie, and put the speaker up to his ear. All I could make out was static and garbled voices. It didn't last more than twenty seconds.

"Blackie got away," Schmidt said, coming back to us as we kept moving up the hallway. "The uniforms saw him get into the car, ordered him to halt. Blackie laid rubber, so they fired at the car to disable it but missed. There's an APB on him now. He won't get far. He was not coming for Blondie."

"So much for honor among crooks," said Harvey.

"Figured as much," I said. "Blackie's headed for the home of Billy Jenkins out in Shively — that's where your men should be headed, no time to waste!"

Schmidt spoke some commands into his cop radio.

Meanwhile we crept on forward down the yellow line, finally reaching the big archway into the huge yard in back where the logs were brought into the plant and stacked. We lined up, Harvey and me on one side of the arch, which had a protruding buttress sticking out into the opening from the hallway on each side, and Schmidt on the other. Schmidt cautiously stuck his head around the corner of the buttress.

A shot cracked the air and a bullet smacked against the buttress a few feet above and to the right of Schmidt's head.

"That's as far as you assholes go!" yelled Blondie. The voice sounded pretty far off.

"I can't even see that sonofabitch!" said Schmidt. "Where the hell could he be?"

"Come with me," said Harvey, and led us behind the archway into the adjacent room on the right, which was the room where he worked sorting rounds. We stepped up to one of the two exhaust fans and looked between the now motionless blades.

At first I couldn't see him, then as I scanned the far end of the stacked logs I spotted Blondie and Danny high up on top of the stacks, backed up to the ten foot high steel fence, about twenty feet to the right of the closed gates. Blondie had gone for the gates, seen them closed, then taken his only option — to climb the stacks and use Danny for cover while he jumped from them onto the fence, then lower himself down the other side. I'd known the gates wouldn't be open. It was Sunday and they were locked. I figured the distance from us to Blondie to be about fifty yards, give or take a few. Way too far for Schmidt's service pistol to hit anything from the vantage point of the narrow exhaust fan opening.

Blondie was standing and Danny was kneeling at his feet, facing forward. Blondie had the gun aimed at Danny's head. Danny B looked shaky, his hands in front of him in an attitude of prayer.

"I'm gonna try and talk to him," I whispered. "I don't like it that he's so nervous. He's gotta know Blackie done him wrong now that he's back there and sees the locked gate. His back's right up agin the wall. Lemme see if I can at least calm him down some."

"I don't know, Odle," said Schmidt. "You could drive him over the edge. You and he have a history, from what I understand. Not a good one, either."

"Right, but we're from the same mountains and that might help."

Without further palaver I stepped around to the buttress and stepped out into the open with my arms and hands raised.

Blondie fired again but missed by a country mile, the bullet chipping off the buttress high again and wide.

"Listen, Jim, let's talk some sense," I said. "I ain't got no weapon and I ain't trying to do you no harm. No tricks. You know me. You know my word is good. You may not like me, but you know if I say no tricks, then that's the gospel."

"Yeah, but ain't no good can come of this, hillbilly. We're enemies, always have been. Either I kill you or you kill me. If you had the gun you'd have shot me and you know it."

"Depends. Not if I could help it. If you put me in a corner, then yes. But right now that's just talk. We got us a situation here that's real. You and I both know that Simon is gone. He took off. The cops tried to stop him but he got away. There's a dragnet out for him and they'll get him. You know that. And when they've got him, what do you think he's gonna do? You think he's gonna stick by you? You seen what he done just now. Look over there at them gates. He knew it was Sunday, Jim. He knew you'd get back here into a box canyon of logs and closed doors ten feet high. He set you up, brother. Now you think on that."

Blondie fired again, this time obviously for the scare value, a shot out of frustration.

"Shut up, Odle! I say shut the fuck up! You're lying! You're always lying. You goddamn hillbilly. You always lie. You people lie every time you move your lips! Hah! How do you know a hillbilly's lying? 'Cause his lips are moving! Hah!"

Even though he was at a distance I could see Blondie's knees starting to tremble.

"Simon's gonna rat you out when they catch him, Jim. He's gonna fit you up in a frame. What's the odds on that, man?" I kept boring in on him. It was risky, I knew, but if I could get him to see the end game he might just crumble and give up.

But it went the other way.

"The odds on that are bad, you're right. Same as the odds on this shitbird getting out of here alive. He's a weakass yellow fuckup, this guy here. He got me and Simon into this and now he's gonna pay. He ain't gonna live to rat me out. He's the man behind the whole thing, him and that slimy Jersey Jack. Well I can't get to that baseball bastard, too much protection, but I can get to this coward, so say goodbye to your bat makin' buddy here. I only wish he could fry like the murdering fraud that he is!"

With that Blondie pulled back slightly on his pistol, taking aim.

I saw the bright splotch of red suddenly bloom on Blondie's forehead before I heard the sharp report of the gun! Freed from Blondie's tight grip, Danny slumped.

But then I realized that the sound had come from behind me, along with the smell of gunpowder. I wheeled around to the sight of black smoke! I looked back at Blondie, but he'd fallen flat on his face. Then I jerked my head around to the rear again and saw a long dark rifle barrel sticking out from the opening between the exhaust fan blades.

I ran back there only to see Margaret pulling back the antique Kentucky Long Rifle that had graced the wall in Worthington's office ever since I'd started working at Slugger. She was pale in the face. I had no idea how she'd managed to make the shot. I stepped over and grabbed her shoulders just as she started to sag.

"All those years shooting targets and varmints back in Breathitt," she said, her voice in a quaver, "never thought I'd have to use one of these on a human being. It was all I could do to hold the damn thing still, Ray. My eyes were twitchy too, I was so scared of what I was about to do. I hated to pull that trigger. It went against every cell in my body."

I pulled her tight to my chest and Margaret's body shook as she let the tension, the fear and confusion out. This was the act of a kind, moral being. It saved a life as it took a life. My wife made a judgment that no human should ever have to make. A judgment of God. And it was tearing her up inside. Danny B for James Haskell. Who was to say? But it had to be said. And she'd been the only one with the power to make the call. A terrible power. A terrible call.

Captain Schmidt didn't see it that way, of course. It was easier for him. She'd done the right thing. He now had an arrest to make, a live defendant if he could get hold of Danny B.

There was no time for talk so Schmidt and his men took off running for Danny B. I held on to Margaret and watched. When the police got about a hundred feet from him I saw the most miraculous recovery you could imagine. Danny stood up and ran over the tops of the log stacks, right up to within a few feet of the top of the steel gates. Then he took a flyer and jumped up on edge of the gate, lowered himself to a hand-hold, and the last thing I saw was his hands first holding on, then letting go as he must have dropped to the sidewalk on the other side of the gates.

Later, back in Worthington's office, I was surprised to see that the Slugger manager hadn't tried to go on the lam himself. Either he'd developed a little sense or he was counting on his high-priced lawyers to get him out of the mess he was in. Maybe he figured the loan of his firearm would count for something.

As the uniformed officers cuffed Worthington and led him out of his office his step was reduced to a shuffle. It did my heart right good to see that man humbled.

At any rate we all convened a little rump debriefing for Captain Schmidt. Schmidt led it off with a comment about Margaret's shot. "If I hadn't seen it with my own eyes I wouldn't have believed it. That was the only way. No Police Special could have hit him with any degree of accuracy at that range. We didn't even try, too much chance of hitting Mr. Bunce."

He turned to Margaret. "You, lady, are amazing. I thought those guns went out with the Civil War. Damn good thing Worthington kept his powder and kept it dry, too," he said.

Margaret had pulled herself together by then, so she, Harvey and I filled him in on more of the details we had on both murders and offered to turn over the various pieces of circumstantial evidence we had — the betting slips, the research we'd done on the back story of the Wade case and resulting hostile relations between the Jenkins family and the Durkins, the production sheet scams and the use to which we figured it was yet to be put (with the agreement to keep that under wraps for now), and the moneyline information. I agreed to give a statement under oath about the conversation I overheard between Jersey Jack and Danny B as well as the tapes I'd listened to with Radio Ralph. And of course Schmidt could always subpoena the tapes if it came to that to prove Jersey Jack's involvement.

At any rate the session with Schmidt and his boys took a lot of time. We had to go over everything twice — once for Schmidt and again with the District Attorney, focusing on things that could be questioned if they were put into evidence in a trial. And lawyers being lawyers are finicky so we had to justify everything six ways from Sunday. It was getting late and I was getting mighty damn antsy.

Sometime in the middle of all this Schmidt got a squawk on his radio. He'd ordered a crew of uniforms to go as fast as they could to Billy Jenkins' house, knowing Blackie was headed there to exact his revenge. Of course Blackie didn't know we'd already arrested Jenkins. The officers reported that Blackie had shot the door lock off and charged into Billy's house in Shively like a bull in the china shop, breaking a coffee table and a lamp in the process. But by the time the cops had arrived Blackie was gone. They had no idea which way he'd gone from there.

Shively was south of town. Yet I had no doubt that Blackie had since turned east, heading for U.S 60/460, running for the hills of eastern Kentucky. I couldn't be rock solid sure, but I'd bet a dollar to a donut I knew where he was going to end up. I had to deal with Danny B first, and it would be better for Blackie to think he'd made a clean getaway. Then, I'd be on his trail.

All I needed was a photo of the man. It didn't take much convincing under the circumstances for Worthington to cough up the one he'd been sent for the files from the H & R H.Q.

All during the skull session I'd also been thinking about where Danny B probably went — the cops had tried his apartment to no avail — and along about the time we wrapped it up with Schmidt the dime dropped and the music began to play.

I knew where Danny had gone.

When I got outside it was just beginning to get dark. I told Margaret where I was going and to tell Schmidt about it after a couple of hours or so. I needed time for some personal business before the end.

Chapter Forty-Two: Ray

The fog lay low on the dull lines of steel that ran parallel away from me, narrower as the distance grew, merging into a single thick black line at the horizon. I walked down the main track of the Oak Street L&N classification yard where they made up trains for all parts of the country. Misted pools of weak, blotted light marked my way every fifty yards or so. I peered at the edges of the circles of light, looking into the darkened rims of the circles they formed, staring at lumps of coal, lumps of switch boxes, lumps of discarded oil drums—looking for a lump of discarded man.

Switch engines rumbled, pushed lines of freight cars up the main incline to the "hump," then let them loose. The cars rolled down the other side where switchmen had set the tracks to guide them into different sets of rail lines. Tankers with oil. Box cars with furniture. Grain cars with corn and wheat. Gondolas with coal. Slat cars with cows. And long lines of flat-cars with big-rig trailers. Each siding held train sections bound for somewhere else. Nashville, Chattanooga, Chicago, Gary, New Orleans, Albuquerque, Vera Cruz, Des Moines, San Diego, Seattle, San Francisco, Culiacán, Pittsburgh, Wilmington, Mexico City, New York, Savannah, Miami.

I'd worked those lines a few weeks myself some years back. Back then those towns were the names of promise, place-names calling out to commerce or travelers like magnets, pulling with the power of hope for better prices, better jobs, better times, even something like better weather, maybe not so cold, maybe just…better.

But not tonight. Not for me. I had a different job to do. The cars rumbling by spelled out dark shapes of nothing but fear that they might crush a certain man, a man impaired, a man seeking them for an end to things. I crossed a lot of rails, dodged in and out of the weak light, looking.

Finally I saw a gray heap on the rails, a soggy cocoon way down at the end of the yard, a good half mile from the hump, maybe a mile or more from the yard entrance. It was Danny and he wasn't going anywhere. He was in the bag, drunk. The evidence hadn't run off and left him. It was right there. One pint bottle lay beside him, cracked across the Four Roses label, the other stood at attention on the track, a soldier dead but still standing. Which was more than Danny had managed. I nudged him with the toe of my work boot. The cold would make it easier for him to react. I'd been there before, so I knew.

He grunted, rolled over, left hand over his face. The hand was blue from the cold and from the fact that his blood basically wasn't circulating there. A newly emptied pint of alcohol on top of who knew how much more had put his brain on emergency power, shut down everything but the head and heart. Danny pulled the hand down, exposed one eye, then the other. "Got something…for you," he said, hoarse, barely audible above the rumble of switch engine diesels in the distance, the clanging of bells, the banging of boxcars as they rolled down off the hump and slammed into their train mates.

I squatted down, hunkered in the old Appalachian way, weight balanced between shoulders and butt, heels flat on the soot-black gravel beside the rail. Danny rolled halfway over, up on one elbow. He tugged at something in his pants pocket. The stain on the crotch of his pants fabric was still wet enough to cling to his thigh. "It's right here." He struggled some more, finally got the whole pocket lining out. Something flat and shiny in the half light flipped out and clinked against the rail. Danny flopped back down on the gravel. "Shit, don't lose it. I gotta…" He retched. It was dry. Nothing left in his gut.

He flopped back to face me. I waited. I knew he had to do it, make the gesture of congratulation to me, and as sick and hurt-to-the-bone as I felt, I couldn't bring myself to take that away from him.

Shit, I still cared for him. He'd shared his gift of solidarity in sobriety with me even if he couldn't keep it himself. He hadn't been my sponsor but we'd hung out together—I'd followed him around when I was new in the program in Louisville. I'd gone where he'd gone and done what he'd done and it had helped to keep me sober.

"Happy birthday, Ray," his voice was gruff. "Congratulations. Keep coming…" his voice broke, "…back." Danny cried. Something like hoarse hacks at first, then the voice got into it, and he sobbed.

My tears made no noise. But when Danny looked up, he could see them. We were together, AA brothers, one last time. I'd passed another year of sobriety the day before. Of course I'd marked it on my calendar—it was a huge day for me. Five years. I'd gone to supper with my sponsor, Jimmy G. We'd talked about the fact that now that I was getting better acquainted with Louisville AA, it was time for me to start working the 12th step a little harder, looking for opportunities to sponsor newcomers in the program.

It took a few minutes, then Danny quit crying. "You know the whole story," he said, half whispering. "That's why you're here."

I waited while a line of four tankers rolled by several sidings over. They slammed and cracked, loud and sharp against the cars already standing on the same track. Like rifles blasting and echoing in a military funeral.

"Yeah, I know, and yes, it *is* why I'm here," I said, a little vibration creeping in on the 'here.' I looked across the yard, saw the fog was lifting. I looked at my watch. Seven o'clock. Danny noticed.

"Bout that time?" he asked.

"Yeah. They're on the way by now."

300

"How'd...?" He stopped. Shook his head, clearing a little of the fog in the weather in there. "Oh, right. Margaret."

"I told her to give me some time to find you," I said, nodding. Danny took it in, then pulled himself up to a full sit, leaned back on both arms. His eyes opened wider, uncrossed.

"How'd you get to looking at me?" he said, voice stronger now.

"It was a whole lotta stuff, Danny. The moneyline, of course. Won't like you, it won't honest. Then I overheard you arguing with Jersey Jack after the Little League batting clinic, didn't hear all of it, but it must've hit you hard 'cause I seen you ducking into that bar afterwards. So I had to wonder what you had going with Jersey Jack. But the big tipoff was that reject stamp, man," I said, letting the anger rise in my voice.

"So when I saw you stick that Jersey Jack bat with the reject stamp and take it home under your jacket that night, it hit me. It was so out of character. I'd been falling for it, right hard, too. So I did some research with Radio Ralph.

"But it was always about the bat — and about the batter, I come to figure. But that's not it either, is it? It's always been about character, about fear. You lost out on the moneyline, got sucked into debt, and the fear took over. So you relied on your wits and tried to beat the system on your own power, you and Jersey Jack, and you started living a lie with one person after another. You grew in contempt for the union, for your brothers in the program, for everbody that called you friend, Danny."

I paused. But time didn't. The trains kept rolling by. And I had a job to do. So I went on.

"Including me. But mostly, including yourself. And one day I saw that, and I knew it was you. And when I knew it was you it hit me right in the gut."

"What? Couldn't take the double-cross, hillbilly?" Danny B, my supposed brother, snarled, his voice now coming out of the bottle he'd just drunk.

He'd just made my job easier. I wasn't about to choke up anymore. My voice got hard. He'd caused a lot of death. Hurt wives, ruined families. Damn the sympathy. I had a job to do.

"Nope, Danny. Don't have nothing to do with that, not no more. Has to do with Frank Gorham, a human being. Mixed up, maybe a little sick in some ways, but a man to be respected, Danny. A man with a good wife, children and a future in which he could have done his own kind of moral recovery—just like you and I did. But in your fear and obsession you threw him away, you treated his body like that of a alley dog and his soul like pig's offal. You'll have to answer for that."

I put one hand over Danny's neck and passed my arm under his chest to grab his other shoulder and grip him in a quarter-Nelson, then lifted the killer onto his feet and marched him to the east edge of the Oak Street yard. The police sirens got louder and louder with each step we took.

Chapter Forty-Three: Margaret

It was three days after Margaret shot Blondie and Blackie was still on the lam. Ray was fixing to go after him the next day. But today was union business day. The Slugger contract negotiations committee had been smoking like a bunch of steam engines in the roundhouse such that the breakout room at the Brown Hotel nearly made Margaret choke when Harvey finally called her to step through the door. She and Louella had been parking their rear ends on folding chairs right outside the partition for the last two and a half hours. When they went in Margaret saw a dozen Slugger workers sitting around a long folding table strewn with papers, cardboard coffee cups and four empty Krispy Kreme donut boxes with the lids half up. More than one of them had turned his seat around to sit reversed on it, hunched over the seat back with arms and elbows resting on the table. Ray was one of those, sitting about two-thirds of the way down on the opposite side of the table from the side where Harvey showed Margaret to an empty chair. Mike the Bow wasn't seated at all but was pacing back and forth across the rear of the small room.

George Salvatore sat at the head of the table. He'd been elected as chairman of the Slugger workers' contract preparations committee, a committee charged with putting together the union local's strategy for the contract negotiations that were to start in two weeks. Margaret recognized Campsten, Sadderly, Burleson, Davison and Bob Stills among the others. There was one black worker she didn't recognize, and two others she didn't know who were white.

While Margaret had been cooling her heels and warming her can on the outside of the paper thin partition she'd heard the boys wrangling over the wage demands. Some wanted to go for a full 50 cent raise across the board, some for a progressive wage spread across the hierarchy of skilled positions, the higher skilled jobs getting more than the less skilled workers. Some argued for an inflation index. They were all over the place. Unity was in extremely short supply—almost as short as civility. Then Margaret got a surprise in the form of the voice of Bob Stills, the P.R.O. supervisor.

"You boys are all fighting each other, and it seems to me it's out of ignorance of tactics, of what's possible. Most of us have never been outside of the nest of this union local. We're a bunch of homebodies here. We ain't never been in a fight like this, let alone in a lot of fights beyond this one-factory industry, let alone outside of Louisville. Now there's one guy in here who has, and he's asked us to listen to him and his wife. Yep, I'm talking about Ray and Margaret Odle. I took the liberty of asking Mrs. Odle to come down here, and she's waiting outside this room right now. What say, brothers, to getting a little expert advice at this point? Seems we ain't gettin' all that far down the road on our own."

That sparked an uproar, of course, especially from Duvall and Burleson, yelling about pinko this and commie that and challenging the Odle's "credibility." What surprised Margaret about that was that Duvall knew the meaning of the word. But Stills had a reply for Duvall, and gave it.

"Credibility? Mrs. Odle has my vote. Though I don't know her, I know Ray. And he's solid. Not my cup of tea in terms of politics, maybe. But nobody in this plant has his brother workers' interests more at heart—and nobody here has more experience and accumulated wisdom in fighting with management for a contract. So let's not be idiots. Let's take what's in front of us. I move we ask the Odles to consult as advisors to this committee and furthermore ask Mrs. Odle to come in and start right now."

George called for a second to the motion and got one from Harvey. There was no debate and it was approved 10-2.

Ray came out and got Margaret and Louella and as soon as they took a seat Duvall and Burleson started up again. "See, they're bringing in the coloreds, next thing you know they'll be takin' over this damn outfit!" Burleson snarled. But he forcefully was gaveled down.

George turned to her and said, "Mrs. Odle, you and Ray have been fighting alongside working folks in unions for thirty-some years from what I hear tell. So, way I look at it, we'd be fools to let y'all go without asking for what you think we ought to put on our list of demands. I'm sure you brought Mrs. Sampson here for a reason too, so I'll just get to it. What do y'all think we should ask for in these negotiations? Fifty cent across the board?"

Well, George was wasting no time asking straight up and down like that, so Margaret decided to give it to him and the other men just as straight. She stood up to speak, making sure each man around the table could see her face and gestures.

"We'll get to Mrs. Sampson and our joint issue in a minute, but as to wage demands, you should begin to demand two things: a degree of power over the means of production and at least a part of the worth you create," she said. Then Margaret paused to see if anybody was on to her meaning. It didn't look like it, so she ploughed ahead.

"What happens here is that Slugger's owners bought a bunch of equipment and leased the buildings for the plant, right?" People nodded their heads. "So that's their major investment—their capital assets. And those are durable goods. They last. They go on and on and so the cost of using them, attached to the product, the bats, goes down and down. Sure, they repair the machines. They upgrade some from time to time. But that's not a huge cost in any one year. After that, they put out money for two things—logs and you guys, your work time. Now the logs don't cost them all that much in relation to the price of the finished product, the bats, right? I mean, how many bats do they get out of a log? I don't have the number, but it's a lot, I'm sure."

"It's 60-70 pro-sized bats," said Bob Stills, "maybe 100 or more scholastic or Little League bats."

"Right, that's a lot." Margaret said. "So the cost of that wood is small, a few bucks a log, and the money coming in is great—except you have the cost of the work time—that's you men. So what's that time worth? How much time do you actually spend on a single bat? Not the P.R.O. bats, I'm talking about the ones that make the company the big bucks—the ones that go out all over the land with the Major League signatures burned on the bat but are mass produced. It's seconds here, seconds there, right?"

There was a general nodding of heads and murmurs of "right." So Margaret continued.

"In other words, a few seconds at each stage of the process by maybe ten different workers—say two minutes. Two-three minutes worth of a worker's time who gets paid a buck-sixty-five an hour, right? That's less than ten cents a bat! Ray tells me you guys ship sixteen thousand bats a day! Okay so add in a penny or two for that reducing the initial cost of that capital I talked about—but that was paid off years ago. So you see what's goin' on here. You boys are creating a hell of a lot of surplus worth for Louisville Slugger. And all you get is a lousy buck-sixty-five an hour!"

Margaret shut up at that point. She looked at Ray. He gave her a big grin and a thumbs up. Then he continued the analysis.

"And you need to have a say-so about the means of production," he said, "the speed of the line, the lay-offs, the quality control, the management of suppliers, the investment in tools and machines. After all, some of the newer machines will take some of your jobs. So you need to have a seat at the table where those decisions are made. If they want efficiency by replacing grunt work on the line with machines, you need to make sure each and every worker is trained for a new job — one having to do with managing the machines or how they are used."

There was a long, stunned silence.

Finally Bob Stills spoke up. "I never heard it put like that before. But it sounds fair to me."

"Ain't that some type of Communism?" said Duvall, looking to Burleson for support.

But his day was done. "Shut up, Jack!" said Mike the Bow. "Yeah," said Will Davison, "we're talkin' about puttin' food on the table here, maybe getting what's due for once in a damn while. But my question is, how do we do that?"

"The way to do that is through a worker shop management committee that meets with management on those issues, and also by profit-sharing," Ray replied.

"How does that work?" asked Bob Stills.

Well, the committee is like a glorified grievance committee, y'all already have those, but it looks ahead instead of after the fact, and at the big issues instead of at the little ones. And it has a set number of votes on the Slugger company board — that'd be Hillerich and Bradsby's board of directors. That's where the big decisions get made.

"Okay, that'll take some doing. How about the money part?"

Ray answered. "Well, each worker gets a certain percentage of the profits of the company in addition to his wages. Profit percentage paid out as reported over a certain period of time — say each quarter or half of the year. So in the contract negotiations you first demand that a profit-sharing plan be put in place, then you as a union hire an expert to negotiate the percentage and other details for you."

The discussion went on from there, excitement growing by the minute as the idea of surplus value and the right of the men who made the value to have a piece of it began to catch on. After about an a half hour of questions and discussion, Margaret called a halt.

"We can go into this more at a later time, but right now we're only talking about half the demands for this committee, it seems to me. Louella, why don't you talk about the other half?"

Louella stood up and went to the head of the table next to George Salvatore.

"We talking about women—w.o.m.e.n. The other half of the human race. The half you guys ain't got in your factory or in your union—and the main reason y'all is weak. You need us 'cause y'all is in a whole world of hurt if these fat cats decide to stonewall you on the contract and you have to strike. We all know what's gonna happen. We been over it, quiet as it's kept, an' every one of us that is a wife or girl friend of y'all knows all about it behind y'all be cryin' on our shoulders for weeks about it. No strike committee, no community committee, no substitute pickets, no press committee, no food committee, you know I could go on with it. Bottom line? Y'all need us. Good news is we want to help. Other good news is the price of our help is a place in the production line at Slugger and a seat at the bargaining table in the union. So what y'all got to say about that? We serious about solidarity or we just jeffin' and jivin'?"

Margaret and Ray truly enjoyed the way Louella and Harvey, with their help, handled the wrangle that ensued from Louella's opening salvo. In the end she carried the day and the motion that the Slugger local of the WIA admit a 33% quota for women members for itself immediately and make that a demand for the coming contract.

They held hands on the bus all the way down Broadway from Brown's Hotel and never stopped grinning.

Chapter Forty-Four: Ray

I moved slowly, carefully, stiff in the cold fog that rolled off the side of the mountain as Harvey and I descended through giant fifty-foot pines, slipping quietly from one to the other as we came down the hillside. An old song with many versions ran through my head, "in the pines, in the pines, where the sun never shines, I shivered the whole night through." Lead Belly and Bill Monroe and many others had sung about the black girl, the coal train of convicts, the sorrow and death that plagued the mountains and the people it mourned. I was hoping not to add to that history, but I had a murderer to bring to justice all the same.

Harvey and I were trying to get down to the cabin Nancy Whitfield had told me about, where I had every reason to believe that Simon Rogers, a.k.a. Blackie, was holed up. Thanks to that one little conversation with Mrs. Whitfield, I'd put two and two together and figured the Rogers she'd mentioned when she talked about the gang that killed her husband included the family of our man Blackie. She'd said they had a gang hideout, a cabin up behind the general store at the intersection in Blaine. We hadn't seen it yet but had reached the top of the ridge we figured was just above it and had begun our descent, and it was after a couple hundred yards down that we'd hit the fog. It was a fluke, a chilly Labor Day. We'd waited a week after the confrontation at Slugger, time for Blackie to feel that he'd gotten away with things.

Captain Schmidt had been deputized by the State Police, obtained directions from the store owner, near about at the

309

point of a gun, and led a mixed contingent of sixteen of his County men plus ten Staties who were approaching the cabin from below. Fortunately there was no phone in the cabin, so the store owner hadn't been able to tip off the men inside it. He'd clammed up when Schmidt had asked about the number of men staying up there, or whether Simon Rogers was one of them.

Harvey descended a good thirty feet apart from me so as not to present the gang defending the cabin with an easy shot at the two of us. The trees stood six feet or more apart, spaced almost as if they'd been planted by a landscape architect, spaced not by the hand of man but by the dictates of sunlight. Good for nature, good for the gang in the cabin, bad for us trying to approach them in secret. We'd agreed beforehand that when we got within sight of the cabin the State Police would fan out and form a large circle so that we'd all be in visual contact. Then it would be up to me to make the next move.

The Staties had shotguns, rifles, and sidearm .45s. I had my .45 Colt revolver, Harvey had a 12 gauge shotgun and a pistol. Schmidt and the Staties had agreed to hold their fire so long as they were out in the circle where they'd be behind cover. But if they had to go in and they were fired upon, they'd return fire—and shoot to kill. I hoped like hell it wouldn't come to that, but hope and reality didn't necessarily come together in my past. Not where H & R was concerned, not where gangs like the one Nancy Whitfield had described were concerned either. That gang had killed a man because he was union and black. Now those boys or their kin were hiding out a killer— committing a felony for which they could go to prison for several years themselves. And I had no idea how many of them there were.

What I did know was that one man in that cabin had nothing to lose.

I was about to step out from behind a pine trunk when I heard a low whistle from Harvey's direction and looked over to see him point to his left and down the hill. Following his signal I could see a low one-room log structure with a cedar flake and bough-covered roof. It had two small window rectangles covered by pine board shutters hinged at the top. The shutters had holes, one set high, one lower down. Eye holes and firing holes, I decided. One other thing stood out: the area all around the cabin out to about forty yards or so had been cleared of trees, nothing stood but stumps, making a clear field of fire from the cabin. It was more of a fortress than a hunter's cabin.

Harvey and I maneuvered to our left, keeping our same distance apart, and came down another fifty yards, took cover behind tree trunks and waited. There was no door on this side of the cabin. It must be on the other side. I would have to go around when the time came.

After about ten more minutes I saw the men from Schmidt's detail emerge from the fog, moving up on the right flank. I waved and received a return wave. Then after five minutes more Harvey signaled that he'd made contact with the Staties on our left flank. It was time for my move.

First I went away from the cabin, putting myself out of easy shotgun or pistol range. Then I started to circle, moving from tree to tree. I could feel the eyes in the eye holes of the shutters boring in on me. I decided not to run or scamper from tree to tree. I walked brisk, to be sure. Somehow the sharp aromatic aroma of the spruce and pines pierced my senses like never before. I felt the moist breeze playing on the hairs standing up on the backs of my hands. The sun split pine needles clustered in threes as it slanted down into the glade through which I walked. They say when you are in extreme danger that your senses pick up the slightest odors, sounds, touches and magnify them. I swallowed back a sour taste as I tried to wet my vocal chords for the words I would soon have to speak. Well, Ray Odle, I said to myself, you qualify on all counts, all senses.

But I kept my head up and went from tree to tree in a wide arc around to the front of the cabin. Nobody shot at me, nobody said anything. The only sound was a freshening breeze in the boughs that began to blow the fog away. That and the slight crackle of the dead brown pine needles underfoot. It took me about ten minutes to reach a tree that stood directly in front of the cabin.

I eased half my body out from the side of the tree. One more sour swallow. One more inhale of the scented breeze.

"Simon, I know you're in there and you've been following me as I've walked around here to the front of the cabin," I said in a loud voice, but not a shout. He was listening and could hear me well enough. "You know who I am. You know I don't lie."

A shot slapped the bark off the tree about a foot above my head as the rifle report rang out in a loud crack! There were no words to follow. That was one answer. But I went on as if nothing had happened. I didn't duck behind the tree.

"You know I don't lie. We got sixteen County men here led by Captain Schmidt of the Jefferson County Homicide, plus ten Staties, my Odle Agency man and myself. They's enough guns out here to take care of all of you. You've been in enough battles in the coal wars to know what that means. You cain't escape and neither can your friends inside there with you. It's over, Simon. So let's end this thing right. You and your friends come out, hands up over your heads, no guns, one at a time."

I heard a bump noise like a boot hitting wood from inside the cabin and ducked behind the tree just as a shot rang out again and a bullet thudded into the tree right at chest level. Another wordless answer.

I heard a crunch of pine needles to my rear and turned to see Schmidt ease up to another tree behind me. I faded back to him for a conference.

"It's no use, Ray. He's not giving up," he whispered. "I think we have no choice but to rush the cabin."

"Give me one more chance and some wait time," I said. "It's got to be working on him, the hopelessness of it all."

"Not a guy like that, the way I look at it, but have it your way. Won't hurt to wait him out a little longer, I guess."

"Thanks," I said, and went back to my tree.

"Listen up, Simon," I yelled. "You've got five minutes to give yourself up. After that we're coming to get you with enough firepower to do the job. Forget your hero fantasies. It will be cold-blooded efficient killing. Clock's ticking, Simon. It's your call. Think about the men with you—if nothing or nobody else. They prob'ly got families, you need to think about them, the wives, the children. This ain't just about you and me anymore."

Silence. No shots. No words. Nothing.

And then he opened the door and walked out, hands up. I heard at least a dozen clicks as guns were made ready to fire.

"Hold your fire!" I shouted at the top of my lungs.

Blackie walked ten feet out in front of the cabin and stopped.

I stepped out from the tree and moved to within a few feet of him and stopped. We stood facing each other, holding each other's gaze. His eyes blazed with hatred but his words carried a different message.

"It was the families bit that sank in, Odle," he said. "I ain't gonna have them on my conscience. Give me your word my men will be treated fair. That ain't nobody get hurt, then I'll tell them to stand down." His words were right but his tone was sly—and false. Nevertheless, it was all I had to go on.

"You have my word," I said after a deep breath.

"I need to hear it from Schmidt too," he said. "Just to be sure."

I turned around and motioned to Captain Schmidt. He stepped out from his tree cover. I waved him forward. He held his .45 in front of him, aimed at Blackie's chest, as he slowly walked up to within six feet of us.

"Mr. Rogers wants your guarantee that his men will be respected and not hurt if'n they go peaceable," I said.

"If they surrender, they'll be taken into custody unhurt and held over for the judge, my word. No tricks and no harm."

I turned back to Blackie. "That satisfy you?"

"It will have to, under the circumstances," he said, and stuck out his wrists. "Okay, I'm your prisoner, Captain Schmidt."

Schmidt quickly put the cuffs on Blackie, told him he was under arrest for the murder of Frank Gorham. Blackie couldn't help it, he smirked.

Then, true to his word, Blackie yelled out, "Stand down, boys. It's all over. No gun play. You come on out now an' nobody gets hurt."

Then Schmidt yelled out to his men. "Advance on the cabin, no firing unless fired upon!"

As Blackie and me moved to the nearest tree, the circle of men closed in, guns forward, each man aiming dead ahead. When they got to within ten feet of the cabin they stopped.

Nobody came out of the cabin. It stood silent as the grave.

Schmidt yelled out, "All right you men inside there, Mr. Rogers has surrendered and we've agreed to peaceable arrests. No funny business. You can come out now, hands over your heads, no weapons!"

"Tell 'em again, Simon," I said.

"C'mon, it's okay, boys," Blackie shouted.

Still no one moved.

Schmidt repeated his order, adding, "This is your last chance. Come out or we're coming in!"

Nothing. No response.

Schmidt's men moved in. When they got to the cabin they lined up, one man on each side of each window, two men on each side of the front door, and I figured they'd done the same for the side door. Each man had his pistol out now, held up, ready to fire into a window. The men beside the doors were ready to charge on Schmidt's command.

Schmidt stayed with me and Blackie, gun out and ready to fire. I kept my gun out but pointed it at the ground.

As the County men and Staties readied to charge the cabin I looked at Blackie for signs of betrayal. Not anything you could read clearly. Just a slight upturn at the left corner of his mouth. A little twitch. I almost called a halt. But hesitated.

Schmidt's men charged through the cabin door. I heard a lot of yelling but no shots.

Suddenly a man ran out of the cabin, Schmidt's second in command, a Lieutenant, yelling, "There's nobody in there, Captain! The damn place is deserted—but there's a tunnel entrance! The son of a bitch has been stalling us the whole fucking time while his men got away!"

This time Blackie grinned from ear to ear, but said nothing.

"Well, go up the goddamn tunnel, Lieutenant!" Schmidt barked.

"We are, we are!" replied the Lieutenant.

"And send eight men in a straight line out from where the entrance would be if it were outside, straight out in the woods. Execute a search pattern on the double!"

"I'm on it!" And with that the Lieutenant ran back to give orders to his men.

Just then Harvey came up from having come around the cabin. He'd been at one of the windows in the back and had gone inside the cabin's side door, then come back out that way.

Schmidt motioned to the remaining two Staties. "You two men go with Mr. Odle and Mr. Sampson here and escort the prisoner back to the cars. I'm going to stay here and direct the search for these thugs, at least until dark. After that, well, we'll see."

I expected Blackie to have something smart to say about then, but I was wrong. Not a peep. Just the continuing fire of pure hatred coming out of his eyes.

The five of us started down the hill. I figured it was about a quarter mile back to the road and another quarter mile down the road to the cars. We ought to get there before dark, but barely. We walked with one of the Staties in the lead, just ahead of Blackie, and with one behind. Harvey walked to Blackie's left, me to his right. Then, after we'd gotten out of sight of the cabin and Schmidt and the rest of the Staties, Harvey started over to my side. He said he wanted to tell me something about the scene in the cabin, but as Harvey crossed behind and beside him, Blackie stumbled on a raised root and bent double to catch his balance, throwing his cuffed hands down his right leg below the knee in a blur of motion.

He came up with a gun, firing on the fly, aiming for me but missing. Harvey fell, yelling and grabbing his shoulder.

I whipped my revolver from my waistband and fired, blowing Blackie's kneecap out. He went down hard. I stepped over to him and fired again, this time blowing the gun out of his hand, making a huge hole in it.

The two Staties had their guns out of their holsters but it was all over before they could get the safeties off and fire.

I wheeled back to Harvey. He had a small circle of blood oozing from his shoulder. I ripped off his windbreaker and tore his shirtsleeve and undershirt. It was a flesh wound, the bullet had seared the edge of his shoulder as it had passed by. Painful, sure, but nothing a compress and time wouldn't fix. I ripped up the rest of Harvey's shirtsleeve, folded it into a square, and made him press it hard onto the wound.

"Detective Odle's crime-stopper secret number eight, pard, check the prisoner's boots for a boot holster, okay?"

"Got it, Ray!" Harvey said through a grimace of pain.

Then I went back over to Blackie. He'd already turned pale with shock. His hand was pouring blood. I ripped his shirt too, made a tourniquet and used a stick and applied it to his shooting arm. I did the same for his leg above the wounded knee. That slowed the blood flow down quite a lot. His eyes rolled back into semi-focus. I put my jacket over him and raised his head on some fallen pine boughs.

I cursed myself for a fool not to have given Blackie a thorough search — and I included Schmidt and the Staties in my condemnation. We were all fools and damn near paid the price. Blackie had gone for a boot gun, one of the oldest tricks in the book. He'd had his right high-top hunting boot fixed up to be extra wide at the top so as to have an inside pocket into which he'd stuck the barrel of a .32 revolver, just as if it was in a short holster. It wasn't a quick draw but Blackie could get to it doubled over like he'd been when he faked the stumble and went down. His only problem was just bad luck in that Harvey had moved towards me just as he'd gone down for the gun. Once he went down Blackie was committed and couldn't stop, he just had to try and aim at me past Harvey.

I sent one of the Staties on the double back to Schmidt with the news and for him to call in an ambulance team on his walkie-talkie. I figured they could come up the road and haul the stretcher maybe what was now a good 250 yards or so up the woods. The first 200 would be rough going in the dogwoods and laurel, but the last fifty would be the more open pines. I didn't think Blackie had lost so much blood that he wouldn't make it. It might be dicey, but I thought he'd pull through.

While we waited I thought about Blackie's move. Harvey had the good sense to leave me alone. I was in no mood for conversation. Why had he come out of the cabin? He could have gone up the tunnel with the rest of the Hunt Club gang. Disappeared. We wouldn't have known it. He might have got away to live another day.

It was the hatred. Mountain men had turned it on each other and themselves for generations now — ever since the coal had started to fail them. Ever since the bosses had pitted them one against the other in order to control the natural indomitable need of men and women for dignity. Force folks to bend, to cavil to the dictates of iron necessity in the mines and competition for scarcity ruled over by bosses gouging coal from their hills and profits from their bodies and souls and you get a hatred of man for man, brother for brother, woman for woman, I finally decided. In this case we were two mountain men gone separate ways, divided by the system, turned from what should have been brothers. Men who should have been fraternal allies, solid friends, comrades in the struggle for a better life for themselves, their families and their communities—transformed into enemies. A process whipped into myths and songs and false stories like the Hatfields and the McCoys where the economic and social and political truth is buried, or worse, turned into the tinseled lies of commercial success. What Blackie was shooting at when he fired that boot gun was himself. At his own demons, not me. I was just the mirror.

It didn't take as long as I'd feared for the men with the stretcher to get up the hill to us, about forty-five minutes. I walked them down the hill, and before they put Blackie in the ambulance with the emergency worker and one of the Staties, I leaned over to him. His eyes were focusing pretty good by then, so I knew he could understand every word.

"You're going to stand trial for the murder of Frank Gorham, Rogers. A man who tried to turn his life around, a man whose turn for the good you cut short. You'll pay for that, and I'll be there to see it."

One of the emergency workers had cleaned Harvey's wound and patched him up good and proper. Harvey declined the pain relief shot on account of it having codeine in it, so we bought some extra strength aspirin in Lexington on the way home to Louisville.

Chapter Forty-Five: Ray

Two days after Blackie's capture Margaret and I were standing on the front stoop admiring the first tinges of yellow on the sugar maple across the street. We were waiting for Louella and Harvey Sampson to come over for an Odle Agency backyard shindig when a big black Caddy limo pulled alongside and idled at the Jacob Street sidewalk. The rear most door on the limo opened wide at the same time a burly no-neck guy swung himself out of the front passenger door and motioned me to get in.

"Boss wants ya," he said with enough gravel in his voice to make up a yard of cement.

"You from New Orleans or Chicago?" I said.

"Chicago," he said.

"Where we going?" I said.

The man ducked his head into the open door, whispered, then came back up.

"Nowhere special, just a rolling, ah…" and the head went back inside and back out again. Either the man had short-term memory problems from too many thumps up side of the head or his IQ was in the 70s.

"…ah, a rolling conference," he concluded. "You'll come back here."

"Yeah? Back here's good," I said. "But will I be drawing breath or laying on the sidewalk?"

"Like I said, the Boss just wants to talk. If he wanted to hurt you, you'd already be hurt. If he wanted you dead, you'd already be dead. Point blank. Now cut the bullshit."

"I think it'll be okay for me to talk with the man in the car, hon," I said to Margaret. "I'll see you and the Sampsons in a few minutes. Cain't wait to taste that barbecue from Little Jim's they're bringin'. Bet Louella's made up some of them hush puppies she's so good at too. Now just take a deep breath like you're always tellin' me and it's all gonna be fine. This here is just puttin' the final touches on things. I think you know that."

She put up a brief little fuss but in the end she knew I was right. I got in the Cadillac and moved into the jump seat facing what turned out to be two men in the back.

The man on the left was in deep shadow, but nevertheless I recognized him as the one with the initials S. G., not to mention the answer about Chicago versus New Orleans. I was right smart impressed that he was all the way up in Louisville calling on little 'ol me. Last I'd read, he'd high-tailed it to Mexico after serving a one-year bit in jail for refusing to testify to a Chicago grand jury.

The other man I recognized from pictures in the newspapers and the fancy tailored suit, silk shirt, silk tie and diamond tie pin he always wore. He was Harry Lipscomb, Attorney at Law, listed as "of Counsel" to the Major League Baseball Owners Association and a known high roller in Vegas, Chicago and elsewhere. He was also reputed to be a pal of Jimmy the Greek, and Ed DeBartolo, that shady big-time gambler who was always trying to buy a major league ball team, Chicago Mayor Richard Daley and others.

"Well boys," I said, "to what do I owe the honor of this meetin' with you gents. Seems I'm standin' in tall casino cotton."

The man on the left, no slouch in the clothes horse department himself in a fine gray pinstripe, chuckled, then spoke in a throaty near-whisper.

"Let's just say it's an off-the-record meeting of the Club Belvedere," he said, and resumed his little chuckle, which caused Lipscomb to hack out a little laugh of his own, monkey-see-monkey-do.

"Gee, I didn't know I'd been inducted. I'm mighty proud, not to mention a little puzzled, bein' as how the last I heard that club went out of business in the 40s way up in Chicago-land."

"Oh, we renew it again from time to time," said the man on the left, "in special circumstances."

Lipscomb leaned over and raised his hand as if to slap me. "You shut up, Odle. You must have a death wish. You got any idea who you're dealing with here?"

"I do indeed," I said, defiant as hell. "And in a business kind of way I got more respect for him than you," pointing to Mr. S.G. in the corner shadows. "You're just a legal hack, a mouthpiece, as the syndicates and the ball club owners call you. So I'm willing to listen to what the real man in this vehicle has to say, especially since he's come a helluva long way up from sunshine and margaritas to see me. Otherwise I'd be gone outta here."

Mr. S.G. chuckled a little bit louder at this exchange. He now leaned a little forward himself, enough for me to see his facial features. It was him all right, none other than Sam Giancana with a Mexican tan on his face.

"The respect is mutual, Mr. Odle—in a business kind of way, as you put it. You have conducted yourself well in this admittedly minor matter of these few, shall we say, miscreants? A few, especially two, who have tweaked my nose but done no real or permanent harm. And their little game is over, thanks to you. You have my appreciation. Now I know you would not accept any, ah, material form of appreciation, so I offer none. That is correct, right?"

"Yes, and no, with respect," I said, not wanting to irritate the man unnecessarily, but I had my own ideas.

"Well, let's go with the 'yes' for a minute and come back later to the 'no.' I suppose also that I am right to conclude that you have no ambition to take the matter of the moneyline, shall we say, any higher up the scale of the legal power structure? You are a persistent man, I know from the way you have pursued this case. But you are not ambitious for headlines or fame in the law enforcement field, am I right?"

"That's right, Mr. G. I came here to solve two murders on behalf of the WIA national office, showing no fear nor favor to either side at Slugger, company or union. I done that. The case is closed as far as I'm concerned. I got my own opinions about the moneyline, but I can keep them to myself provided we get back to the 'no' part of my answer to your question about appreciation."

At that point Lipscomb, who'd been squirming like a night-crawler worm over on his side of the back seat couldn't stand it any longer and erupted again.

"Now lookahere Odle, who the hell you think you are, you stinkin' hillbilly, trying to pull some lowlife two-bit extortion on Mr. G. here." With that he leaned over and rapped his knuckles on the glass divider between the front seat and the back compartment where we were sitting.

"Jason," he barked to the front seat passenger, "why don't you take that pistol and slap this asshole up side of the head and teach him some manners!"

"Shut up, Lipscomb!" hissed Sam Giancana, giving the man a deadly reptilian look. "I'll be the one to give Mr. Jason his orders." Lipscomb scuttled back, cowered into his corner and practically disappeared into the shadows.

"It seems I have made an error in judgment in bringing Mr. Lipscomb," said Giancana. "Nevertheless, he represents certain interests that for the moment run with mine. Which are that this investigation go no further into either the moneyline or major league baseball. Would you understand me if I said—capish?"

I laughed at that myself.

"I would, Mr. G. And like I said, I'm willing to close the case. But that said, on to my 'no' answer, if you're willing?"

"You have my attention."

"I want the debts of Mr. Harvey Sampson, Mr. Fred Durkin, deceased, and Mr. Danny Bunce to the moneyline cancelled and I want the moneyline ended in Louisville."

Giancana sat back and was silent for some time. The Cadillac rolled past Brown's hotel. People went in and out of its revolving door as bellhops picked up their suitcases and ladies' hat boxes. A taxi whipped out in front of the Cadillac but our driver smoothly accelerated around it. He was an excellent driver, I decided, having negotiated downtown Louisville traffic so smoothly that I hadn't even noticed we were in it—but then I guess my attention had been somewhat riveted on the interior doings.

"I'll agree to forgive the debts—you'll need to write the names down and give them to Mr. Jason. But I cannot shut down an entire city to the moneyline. There are too many lives involved—capos, street chiefs, runners. Not to mention certain other organizations that would like nothing better than to muscle in on it in a vacuum. No, Mr. Odle, that is out of the question."

"Then I could...what did you call it? Persist?"

"And you could...what did Lipscomb call it...be deceased? But let's not quarrel," he said, spreading his hands out between us in a smoothing gesture. "I'll meet you part way — the only thing I can do. I take it your worry is that men of your union are losing too much money. Perhaps they are foolish because they are feeling pressures from low wages and trying to make it up on the moneyline. All right. That is understandable. Foolish, but understandable. What I can do is downgrade the line to a nickel line. That is, the maximum bet will be five cents per point either way on the score. It will limit losses, and of course gains as well, but over time there should be very few large losses. We will still come out ahead across the mass of bettors but it will limit our profits too. That's my best and final offer of appreciation."

"Then I accept."

"You show good sense, Mr. Odle. A practical man lives long. Unfortunately I am not such a man."

Giancana must have had a button or some way of notifying his driver to head back to my apartment because we pulled up in front within about ten minutes of ending the negotiation. On the rest of the ride he talked about the Club Belvedere and how Ronald Reagan, who was now Governor of California, used to come in there and gamble at the illegal casino and rub shoulders with all kinds of "friends" of Giancana's, including Sinatra and other entertainers, politicians and actors. I never heard another peep out of Lipscomb.

I wrote out the names for debts to be cancelled on a piece of paper I had in my pocket and left them on the drink table in the middle of the space between my jump seat and Giancana's back seat. When we got back in front of the Jacob street apartment I got out, stuck my head back into the doorway of the Caddy, and said: "Thanks for the ride, Mr. G." No handshake offered by either party. It had been strictly business.

I watched the Cadillac ease out onto Jacob Street and slide like a giant black shark down the block, make the turn on Floyd and go out of sight. Then I practically skipped through the flat to the back yard, wasting no time to get to Little Jim's barbecue, Louella's hush puppies, and Margaret's black-eyed peas and greens. Not to mention the homemade peach ice cream to come at the end.

Chapter Forty-Six: Margaret

When Ray came down the back porch steps Margaret couldn't wait to hear the news. She had been wringing her hands just a bit during Ray's absence, but Ray laid all her anxiety to rest when he told the story. By the time he was through she, Harvey and Louella all had a good laugh about his put-down of Lipscomb, but the main reaction was that Louella gave Ray a great big hug and a none-too-stingy kiss on the lips, followed by Harvey's more tentative man-to-man hug, since his shoulder was still sore.

Then Louella spoke through tears and a tight throat. "I never dared hope we'd get out from under them mobsters. I thought they was gonna hurt my Harvey bad. Then y'all hired Harvey and I saw maybe we'd survive, but not without months and months of hard work and flat-out living on the edge. Now this—boom! The debt is gone. They ain't after us no more. I just don't know how to thank you. I really don't."

"That goes double for me," said Harvey, shaking his head in disbelief.

Margaret didn't know who felt more awkward, Ray or the Sampsons, but she just looked over at Ray and he piped up with the right thing.

"I did what either of y'all would have done if'n you'd a been in my shoes. No more, no less. I just had a shot at it, that's all. An' it was for the whole Slugger crew, you know. Everbody will get a break on the nickel line, them that's fool enough to keep on bettin' on it. I only wish I could stop the whole damn racket. But I gotta accept the fact that I'm powerless over that. So I just have to let it go."

Margaret reflected that letting go and accepting powerlessness were easy to say and hard to do sometimes, thinking about the death of Betty Jenkins. Despite her best intentions and their best actions, a needless death had been the response to them. Not necessarily the result, but certainly the immediate response. Dark memory refused to be "let go" at times, recrimination would not cede a space in her mind without major effort to remove it. The remedy was usually a requirement of action for others, getting out of oneself. But that sometimes took more moral fortitude or just plain energy than Margaret had to give it. So the mental space was occupied and sadness held sway. Not for too long, not for too often, but it still haunted her. So it was with an effort that Margaret turned away from that problem and into the solution of being in the present with the little gathering meant as a celebration.

She joined in as they all decided to pass on from the subject of the betting line and pass something much more immediate that demanded joyful attention—Little Jim's pulled pork barbecue! They got busy distributing the barbecue, Cole slaw, greens, black-eyed peas, and of course, the hushpuppies and iced tea all around.

It was a good thirty minutes before anybody said anything except "pass the…" Then everyone paused to let things settle before getting on to the peach ice cream. The conversation resumed at that point, and the topic was the union contract negotiations, which were still dragging on.

"You don't really think they'll win the profit sharing, do you?" Louella had thrown her long left leg and tight clam-diggers over the side of the heavy iron yard chair she'd picked to sit in. She waved her ice-tea glass back and forth as she talked, holding forth, a skeptical frown on her face. "I mean, those boys, present company excepted, they don't really know how to fight, do they? I mean is they ready to put it all on the line? You could fool me on that, from what Harvey say. Ain't that right Harv?" With that Louella pointed the tea glass and her bare foot in the direction of her husband and Odle Agency Investigator. Harvey was leaning comfortably up against the back porch steps, his second Little Jim's barbecue sandwich in his hand.

"Never underestimate the power of the black man and his hillbilly allies, once aroused, I always say," Harvey replied through the large mouthful of sandwich, at which Louella rolled her eyes.

"Well, the fact is they may or may not win it," Margaret said, a bit more seriously, "but they will fight for it. That I believe—for one thing Harvey will fight for it, and so will Mike the Bow, Andy, Ted, and believe it or not, George Salvatore and Bob Stills."

"Yeah, and the women gonna fight for jobs and membership in the union, too—best believe that," said Louella. Then, reflectively, she went on.

"You know, even though it's not on the union demands, one victory is already won, right here in this little yard," said Louella. "I'm talking about us, you know, becoming friends, Harvey working with y'all, us forming the Women's Committee, demanding women workers, wiping out that mob debt—all of that has changed my life big time to the good. It's the struggle that matters. It's the gettin' it together. Can't nobody take that away from us. That's the stuff that counts when you come right down to it, far as I'm concerned."

Ray moved over to sit down next to Louella. "You've hit it on the head, Louella, like you usually do. An' me and Margaret have decided that it's those things that have made it clear that we should make Louisville our headquarters from now on out. We won't sure when we come here if this was the place, but with what's happened here on this case, and with you two working with us and becoming good friends, well, now we know."

Margaret moved up a step and sat beside of Harvey. Over to her left the sun was going down through thinly spaced clouds over the Louisville skyline, throwing violet splashes onto the softened edges of buildings like a kindergartner had painted it in temperas. She took a sip of her Coca-Cola with peanuts, savoring the sweet and the salt. And looking over the little back yard, Margaret savored the group, the two couples here in a border state of the southland, the black and the white.

She also savored the way things had wrapped up on the Slugger case. Blackie, one Simon Rogers, had been convicted of Murder for Hire, a form of first degree murder, for the death of Frank Gorham.

Blackie had been sentenced to 20 years to life instead of death mainly because of the testimony of Ray Odle and Alice Gorham. Ray had told the jury and judge that, bad as Rogers was, there was no man beyond the redemptive power of the love of his fellow man, and that Rogers had been used by forces higher up all his life just like all working men. Alice Gorham said she had hated Simon Rogers in the abstract but that now that she'd seen him in the trial she realized that he was a child of God too. She asked the judge if he could tell her why the state used its power to kill a man to show that killing was wrong. The judge of course chose to hide behind his robes and made no reply to that one.

Then there was Danny Bunce, a.k.a. Danny B. He had pled guilty as an Accessory to Murder rather than go to trial on a Conspiracy to Murder in the First Degree charge, which would have carried either the death penalty or life in prison. Ray testified for him as well, explaining the destruction Danny went through as he crashed back into alcoholism under the pressures of his debts and the terrible fears as the moneyline scheme bore down on him. Ray was careful not to say that this justified Danny's actions one whit, but that he knew from personal experience that Danny had helped many men get sober and live changed and positive lives, and that he knew to a moral certainty that it was possible for Danny to get sober and live that way again. So a life prison sentence would do nothing but cost lots of money and destroy that outcome.

Something must have stuck because the judge gave Danny twelve years, about half of the average sentence for the crime. "He'll be eligible for parole after four years," Ray said. "If he sobers up and works hard in there, he'll likely make it." Margaret and Ray had visited Danny in the defendant bullpen right after sentencing and Ray had told Danny that he'd visit him once a month after they transferred him to the La Grange prison, which was about 35 miles from Louisville.

Billy Jenkins got his life sentence handed to him on a hot day in September and collapsed into his lawyer's arms. But it was premeditation, no question in the jury's collective mind, not after all the Rone Court evidence along with the Manuit sheet evidence and the testimony of Worthington, who turned on Billy one more time to try and save his own skin from a conspiracy charge. And though he struggled with the decision, had several sessions with Jimmy G. about the ethics and morality of it, Ray decided not to go to bat for Billy. He said it wouldn't be honest, that although he had some empathy for Billy as a workingman, Billy had turned him sour with his cowardly racism and lies.

Jersey Jack had beaten the rap as anyone might have guessed. Lipscomb farmed the case to some of the mob's best and brightest lawyers so it was no surprise that he got off. The evidence was slim even though Danny B took the stand against Jack. It was one crook ratting on the other one.

Later that night, after Harvey and Louella had gone, Ray and Margaret went back out on that porch for their "nightcap," as they sometimes called it, a soda and lime, a little hand-holding and a look at the stars on clear nights, and it was one of those nights. They could see at least some of the Milky Way diving down to the southwest, away from the downtown. There was no moon. The World Series was coming up, the Orioles against the Dodgers. Ray figured the Orioles would win it for the American League. The backyard cricket chorus was in full cry.

Ray and Margaret looked at each other and he gave her that half-crooked smile of his. They tipped their jam jar glasses over one to the other and clinked.

"We did rather well on this one, dear heart," Margaret said.

"Looks like it. An' I think we found us a right good home place in this town, too."

"And some real friends," Margaret said.

"An' a good brother worker for the Odle Agency too," Ray added.

A few sips later Ray went on.

"And how 'bout Mr. Alan Sims Worthington? Crying crocodile tears on the stand. Saying he didn't mean for Billy Jenkins to up and actually kill Fred Durkin. But Benson sold him out good and proper, didn't he." Ray and Margaret both had to chuckle at that. Benson had indeed sung like the storied canary. More like a mockingbird in full opera mode.

"Yep," Ray went on, "and then the big surprise when Duvall turned on him and told that he'd been there when Worthington had told Billy Jenkins that Durkin had to be dealt with 'by any means necessary.'"

Worthington had good lawyers, of course, a whole team of them, and they'd yelled hearsay and all kinds of objections, popping up like jack-in-the-boxes so much Margaret thought the trial would never end. So he beat the Murder for Hire charge. But the jury saw through the rest of it all and convicted him of accessory before and after the fact—after the fact on account of he didn't report what he knew to the police and then he covered up.

"I must say it warms the cockles of my heart to know that sorry son of a gun is locked up as we set here," Ray said with a grin spreading across his face.

"Even though he only got three to nine years, at least he's wearing prison made denims instead of Brooks Brothers wool and silk stockings for a while," he went on. "They'll work his sorry butt, too, out there at La Grange. Ain't nobody ride easy out at that joint. It's a workhouse. Yep, he'll do some serious

330

work for a change." And with that he broke up into chuckles, covering his mouth with his free hand, restraining himself from guffaws out of a sense of keeping with the mood of the evening. Now Ray was not normally vindictive, but with that type of boss situation he cut no slack.

Margaret felt the cool of the early fall settle down over them, then she felt Ray's arm go around her shoulders as it so often did, an almost automatic response to the change in temperature. Some women might shrink from what they might feel was an overly protective gesture, but she knew Ray wasn't being protective so much as instinctively affectionate and that was just fine by her. She reached over and put her free hand on his thigh and gave it a squeeze.

"I forgot to mention in all the hurly-burly of getting the barbecue, greens and potato salad ready, sweetpea, that we got a little envelope in the mail today that might just interest you."

"What'd that be?"

"Seems that place where you worked organizing in the cotton mill many a year ago down in South Carolina has had a murder during an organizing drive." Margaret looked at him, her eyebrows raised in a "how can you beat that?" gesture.

"You cain't mean Falls Cotton? That place where the Klan run me out when I was barely able to shave?" Ray jerked his upper body sideways to get a good look at Margaret and splashed some of his drink down the steps. His eyes were big as saucers.

"The very same," she said with a grin. "Textile Workers Organizing Committee, which as you know came out of the CIO's textile worker unions trying to organize in the South, has been trying to get some black and white worker dialog groups goin' down there as a prior step to bringing in a union sign-up drive. Well, they sent two black and white worker teams into the plant and about six weeks into the campaign one of the black workers got killed. Shot when he walked up onto the porch of his boarding house. They want us to go in and check it out, do what we do. So what do you think? You interested?" Margaret had to cover her mouth to keep her giant grin from showing.

"Does the wild bear…?"

"I think this wild bear does," Margaret laughed, then kissed him with all she had.

Afterword

Although Slugger is a work of fiction and all people, events and places are used fictitiously, there are a number of historical people, places and events referenced in the novel that readers may wish to know the bare bones facts about. A short summary of these follows.

Louisville Slugger: The famous bat was born when Bud Hillerich made a bat for a slumping hitter in Louisville (whose bat had cracked) in the early 1880s and then patented his form of bat in 1884, naming it the Louisville Slugger after the moniker of the hitter he had helped. Hillerich broke new ground in sports marketing by paying baseball great Honus Wagner to use his name on the Louisville Sluggers in 1905. Frank Bradsby joined the company as a partner in 1916 and Hillerich and Bradsby began their long history as the company that has made millions of professional and amateur baseball bats bearing the signatures of Major League stars ever since. Contrary to the picture painted in this novel, Hillerich and Bradsby's Louisville Slugger baseball factory was not a bad employer and even innovated several cooperative management/worker practices over the years. They have had several union disputes, of course, and as a Southern employer, paid lower wages than northern factory establishments often did for general production workers, but in this they were not exceptional. The author worked at Louisville Slugger at re-sand and knob cutoff jobs in 1969.

Dr. Donald Rasmussen and the Black Lung Campaign: Dr. Rasmussen came to West Virginia in 1962 and opened a clinic to treat black lung, treating some 40,000 miners during his lifetime. In addition to the clinic, Dr. Rasmussen he provided the medical gravitas in a movement to obtain compensation for workers with black lung disease and to improve mine conditions so that the illness might be prevented. He expanded diagnostic techniques, appeared before lawmakers and confronted both mine and union leaders whom he considered insufficiently attentive to their health needs. Amid internecine union warfare, Dr. Rasmussen received death threats, The Washington Post once reported, and for a period he carried a sawed-off shotgun. Dr. Rasmussen died in 2015 at the age of 87 of complications stemming from a fall.

The Wade case, SCEF, the Bradens: the events of 1954 recounted in the novel of the purchase by Carl and Anne Braden, founders of the Southern Conference Education Fund (SCEF), of a house in Shively, its subsequent resale to the African-American family of Andrew, Charlotte and two-year old Rosemary Wade, and the bombing of that home by residents of Rone Court and others are accurately described, as is the trial and sentence of Carl and Anne Braden for alleged "sedition" against the State of Kentucky, later overturned by the Circuit Court of Appeals. The characters and actions of Billy Jenkins, Fred and Irma Durkin and the supposed ownership trail uncovered by Margaret Odle are fictitious.

The Radio Runs, Mel Allen and Red Barber: The radio segments are fictitious but based on actual line-ups and plays taken from baseball almanacs and statistics, then changed to accommodate the appearance of Jersey Jack Danielson. All of the baseball facts cited by Mel Allen and Red Barber in the story are accurate. Mel Allen and Red Barber were real radio and television Major League Baseball play-by-play announcers. Red Barber had a long career that included years with the Cincinnati Redlegs and the Brooklyn Dodgers. Mel Allen became known as the voice of the Yankees when he joined up with Red Barber in the 1960s. The two partnered in calling the Yankees games from 1954 to 1964.

Organized sports gambling: Betting outside of what federal law called "social betting" was illegal in 1966 everywhere except Nevada, effectively Las Vegas. And even there a 10% federal tax had cut down on the number, type and action of betting on sports. Outside Nevada the betting was strictly in the hands of organized crime. Seeking to dismantle organized crime's grip on sports wagering, then-U.S. Attorney General Robert F. Kennedy worked with Congress to enact various pieces of legislation aimed at giving the federal government a collection of laws with some teeth. Several were passed and formed the legal backdrop for the criminal nature of the moneyline scheme in *Slugger*.

James Meredith and the March Against Fear: On June 7th, 1966, James Meredith, who had integrated the University of Mississippi in 1962, began what he called the March Against Fear, which was initially a personal attempt to walk from Memphis, Tennessee, to Jackson, Mississippi, to promote black voter registration. On the second day of his march Meredith was shot in the leg by an unknown gunman. Within hours, the nation's three leading civil rights organizations vowed to continue the march -- The Southern Christian Leadership Conference (SCLC), The Congress of Racial Equality (CORE) and the Student Nonviolent Coordinating Committee (SNCC). The ensuing three week march struggled with death threats, arrests, and tear gas, as well as internal tensions, including the slogan "Black Power." James Meredith recovered and rejoined the march at its conclusion in Jackson.

West Walnut Street African-American Business District: West Walnut Street between 6th and 13th street was once a thriving business community for African-Americans during the era of segregation and Jim Crow. The businesses that dotted old Walnut Street included those for everyday needs like restaurants, churches, banks, insurance companies, news and printing services, barber shops, salons, gas stations, independent doctors, lawyers, real estate agents, and more. However, the area was also well known for entertainment, including several theaters, nightclubs, and other gathering places. Clubs like the Top Hat drew crowds from out of town, as well as local black and white residents who came to see the top jazz musicians of the time. Derby Week was a popular time on Walnut Street! But as the novel indicates, during the 1960s urban renewal and white flight to the suburbs coupled with a lack of investment by the city and county led to its abandonment and near ruin.

Georgia Davis Powers: Ms. Powers was a civil rights leader and key figure in the Allied Organization for Civil Rights in 1960s Louisville, helping to win public accommodations anti-discrimination victories as well as initial fair housing achievements. She went on to become the first African-American woman elected to the Kentucky State Legislature, as a Senator, in 1968.

Jock Yablonski and Tony Boyle and the UMW: Jock Yablonski was a coal miner from childhood. He became active in the United Mine Workers after his father was killed in a mine explosion. He was first elected to union office in 1934. In 1940, Yablonski was elected as a representative to the international executive board, and in 1958 was appointed president of UMW District 5. Yablonski clashed with Tony Boyle, who became president of the UMW in 1963, over how the union should be run and his view that Boyle did not adequately represent the miners. In 1965, Boyle removed Yablonski as president of District 5 (under reforms enacted by Boyle, district presidents were appointed, not elected). In May 1969, Yablonski announced his candidacy for president of the union. As early as June, Boyle was discussing the need to kill him. Tony Boyle's hired assassins killed Yablonski, his wife Margaret and his adult daughter Charlotte as they slept in their home on December 31, 1969 in Clarksville, Pennsylvania.

The Brown Hotel: The Brown Hotel is a historic 16-story hotel located on the corner of Fourth and Broadway. It contains 294 rooms and over 24,000 square feet of meeting space. The hotel opened in 1923, only 10 months after construction began. The hotel cost $4 million, and was funded and owned by James Graham Brown, a local entrepreneur who wanted to compete with the Seelbach Hotel just down the street. The hotel quickly became a central part of the growing downtown Louisville economy and the social lives of the locals. In 1926 the hotel chef Fred K. Schmidt introduced the Hot Brown sandwich, consisting of an open-faced turkey sandwich with bacon with a delicate Mornay sauce. The Hot Brown became highly popular among locals and visitors alike.

About the Author

Chuck Barrett

Chuck Barrett's op-ed columns appeared regularly in the Las Cruces, New Mexico, Sun-News from 2015 to 2018 on a wide range of issues. His story, "Marching to Canaan Land," is a finalist in the 2009 *New Letters* Literary Awards short story division.

Chuck's publications include, "The Hustler," in *Rural Heritage* magazine, several nonfiction articles on criminal justice in *Cities* magazine and in the journal *Katellagete*, as did "One Meaning of Prison in America," a chapter in the book *And the Criminals With Him*. Chuck's poetry has appeared in small journals as well, and was featured in a 2016 exhibition with the artist, Melody Sears, called, "Duologue, a Conversation Between Poetry and Pastel," at the Tombaugh Gallery in Las Cruces, New Mexico.

Chuck Barrett worked at several job stations at Louisville Slugger in 1969, and assisted in the Black Lung Campaign in eastern Kentucky's coal fields that same year.

A lifelong activist, Chuck continues that work in several volunteer roles while living with his artist spouse, Melody Sears, and his Golden Retriever, Sunny, in Tucson, Arizona.

Acknowledgements

The author is deeply in the debt of two twin sisters for their help in producing this book. First is Melody Sears for her tireless and expert professional editing of the text. Any errors found by the reader are entirely due to his passing over her edits. The second is Lyric Kite for her patient and outstanding design and execution of the cover for this book.

Finally, the author acknowledges the stories, strengths an inspiration he has received from people in Appalachia and in the Appalachian Diaspora during his time in Kentucky in the late 1960s and as a worker for a few months at Louisville Slugger bat factory. He knows was standing in tall cotton.

Read Chuck's poems and articles and get advance notice of new fiction on his website at: chuck-barrett.com

He'd be pleased to get your feedback on *Slugger* at: chuck@chuck-barrett.com

Made in the USA
San Bernardino,
CA

58979952R00207